THE BAD ANGEL BROTHERS

ALSO BY PAUL THEROUX

FICTION

Waldo
Fong and the Indians
Girls at Play
Murder in Mount Holly
Jungle Lovers
Sinning with Annie
Saint Jack
The Black House
The Family Arsenal
The Consul's File
A Christmas Card
Picture Palace
London Snow
World's End
The Mosquito Coast
The London Embassy
Half Moon Street
O-Zone
My Secret History
Chicago Loop
Millroy the Magician
My Other Life
Kowloon Tong
Hotel Honolulu
The Stranger at the Palazzo d'Oro
Blinding Light
The Elephanta Suite
A Dead Hand

The Lower River
Mr. Bones
Mother Land
Under the Wave at Waimea

CRITICISM

V. S. Naipaul

NONFICTION

The Great Railway Bazaar
The Old Patagonian Express
The Kingdom by the Sea
Sailing Through China
Sunrise with Seamonsters
The Imperial Way
Riding the Iron Rooster
To the Ends of the Earth
The Happy Isles of Oceania
The Pillars of Hercules
Sir Vidia's Shadow
Fresh Air Fiend
Dark Star Safari
Ghost Train to the Eastern Star
The Tao of Travel
The Last Train to Zona Verde
Deep South
Figures in a Landscape
On the Plain of Snakes

THE
BAD ANGEL BROTHERS

A NOVEL

Paul Theroux

MARINER BOOKS
New York   Boston

This is a work of fiction. Names, characters, places, and incidents are products of the author's imagination or are used fictitiously and are not to be construed as real. Any resemblance to actual events, locales, organizations, or persons, living or dead, is entirely coincidental.

HarperCollins books may be purchased for educational, business, or sales promotional use. For information, please e-mail the Special Markets Department at SPsales@harpercollins.com.

FIRST EDITION

Designed by Emily Snyder

Library of Congress Cataloging-in-Publication Data has been applied for.

ISBN 978-0-358-71689-1

22 23 24 25 26 LSC 10 9 8 7 6 5 4 3 2 1

To Sheila

I had to admit that to me each person's worst instinct seemed the most sincere.

—ANDRÉ GIDE, *THE IMMORALIST*

A brother is as easily forgotten as an umbrella.

—JAMES JOYCE, *ULYSSES*

PART ONE
TWO LUNCHES

1

THE REJECTION RITUAL

YOU'RE SELDOM SUSPICIOUS WHEN YOU'RE HAPPY, AND so I didn't realize that the whole awful business was about to start when Vita said, "It's been ages since you had lunch with Frank. Why don't you two grab a bite?"

Whenever Frank was asked a question he hated to answer he'd say, "Look in the mirror and ask yourself that." I was tempted today, but I smiled at my lovely wife, while I contemplated my hateful brother.

As the kind of lawyer he was, Frank had a whopper license, and it helped, because he told awfully long, rather dubious stories. It was sometimes the same story, or nearly so. Now and then it was one I had told him, and he later told it back to me, inserting himself, with embellishments, not remembering it was mine. Talkers who repeat themselves pay no attention to their listeners—they're at an imaginary podium, waving their arms, broadcasting to a crowd, and are usually themselves bad listeners, if not completely deaf. Many people found Frank's stories amusing, others called him a bore, and said, "How do you stand him?"

He's a high-functioning asshole, I wanted to say, but instead, to be noncommittal, "He's my big brother." I was not a talker. I was the elusive brother, the geologist, who'd left home to be a rock hunter, and an adventurer in the extractive industries.

Yet I was often fascinated by Frank's stories. You don't have to like someone to listen. When I was in the mood, I heard him repeat them, noting how he changed them in the telling, what he left in, what he

omitted, the exaggerations, the irrelevancies, the new details, the whop-
pers.

The nun who caught him smoking. In one version she told him to
confess it as a mortal sin and lingered outside the confession box to hear
him bare his soul to the priest. In another, she forced him to kneel on
a broomstick a whole day as punishment. In the one I liked best, the
nun handed him his unsmoked half pack of cigarettes and made him
eat them. But I knew that because of wheezy lungs Frank had never
smoked.

The one about his being brutally murdered in Florida by a drug
gang, his bullet-riddled body discovered in a Miami mansion, his face
mangled beyond recognition. Our parents got the call, on a weekend
when Frank was on vacation, and they were devastated. Turned out,
the man had Frank's stolen passport on him. A great story, but untrue.

Another: his saving the life of my high school friend, Melvin Yurick,
whom he'd found bleeding at a campsite in the local woods, Yurick having gashed his hand with a hunting knife. In Frank's telling, by rescuing
Yurick he'd altered the course of history, because later Yurick became
a billionaire, as a pioneer innovator in digital media. The story was
mine—it was I, hiking with Yurick, who'd stanched the blood on his
gashed hand and helped him home. The part about Yurick becoming a
billionaire was true, though.

I listened to know Frank better, because even as a child I found him
tricky, cruel, dangerous, and unreliable, as well as (people can sometimes
be their opposites) direct, kindly, reassuring, and helpful. There was so
much of Frank, and he was so contradictory, the whole of him so over-
whelming, I had to deal with him in pieces. Although he made a convincing enough pretense of being my friend, I knew he didn't like me.

He was a local hero, Frank Belanger Esq., Injury Law, a successful
attorney in our town of Littleford. Because of our name (school kids
are such mockers of names), we Belanger brothers were known as the
Bad Angel brothers. Frank was a tough opponent but a good ally, very
wealthy from the accumulation of contingency fees from personal injury
and medical malpractice suits. *Whiplash windfalls,* he called them. He
made no secret of his ambition, crowing to me when we were kids, *I*

want to be so rich I can shit money! He defended wounded, usually poor people; so justice was money, punishment was money, reward was money, morality was money, love was money. His admiring clients quoted his well-known remark, with approval, *I bite people on the neck for a living.*

He'd plagiarized that, and other wisecracks, from a ruthless lawyer he'd worked for, named Hoyt. I was no match for Frank's sarcasm and his competitive nature, or his killer instinct. I had left home to escape his shadow. My work as a geologist kept me away, at first in the West, then in the wider world, a spell in Africa, later—my cobalt years—in the Northwest. Earlier, when I married Vita, I bought a house in town and returned more and more frequently as my mother aged and was cheered by visits. Vita, who'd grown up in the unregulated sprawl and improvisation of South Florida, found the solidity and order of New England a reassurance. And this was also a chance for our son, Gabe, to attend my old high school and be a Littleford Lion.

Usually, when he heard I was in town, Frank insisted on our meeting for lunch, always at the Littleford Diner—he'd once owned a part interest in "the spoon," as he sometimes called it, short for "the greasy spoon." If I was free I tended to agree, because seeing him, hearing his stories, I was able to gauge the temperature of our relationship. Family members have a special untranslatable language, of subtle gestures, finger play, winks and nods, little insults, odd allusions and needling words, that are devastating within the family yet mean nothing to an outsider.

But when Vita urged me to have lunch with him, I smiled—and equivocated. And a few days later I said flatly no, because of the way Frank himself asked in an e-mail, framing it as a demand, putting *Lunch* in the subject line, with the date and time, and the message, *Be there.*

I had left home to avoid orders like this. Mineral prospecting and exploration could be frustrating and expensive—I had started out with an old van and a dirt bike, taking samples of gravel from dry riverbeds in the Arizona desert, testing them for surface gold. I liked the freedom, and now and then I hit pay dirt. Early on, I was a one-man company, so I could do as I wished, and later with money acquired technology and dug deeper. In the years when I traveled internationally I specialized in industrial diamonds in Australia and emeralds in Colombia and Zambia. My contracts were sometimes with major conglomerates, which helped develop the claims, but even at my busiest I was never subjected to any rigorous oversight. My success rate spoke for itself, I was trusted by the companies that hired me, and if I happened to be given orders, they were tactfully phrased. No one in the extractive industry ever loomed over me and said, *Be there.*

As a child I was given commands by my father, and when he died, Mother was the order giver. Now that she was fading, it seemed that Frank had begun to be the dominant one in the family.

I disliked his insistence, his barking an order, so I did not reply to this lunch invitation. I was well aware that my silence would annoy him, since he was used to being listened to and, more than that, obeyed, always getting his way.

I was in my study, at my desk when Vita pushed open the door and said, "Got a minute?"

This is always for me a daunting question, but it was especially worrying that day. Vita and I had been going through a marital transition. It had begun when I formed a mining company to conduct an extensive search in Idaho for a source of cobalt—ethical cobalt as opposed to the free-for-all in the Congo, small children sitting in mud in remote Kolwezi, clawing at ore-bearing sludge. The Idaho search area was vast, the high-tech equipment others had trained on it had been expensive. This is not the place to describe nuclear magnetic resonance imagery or satellite technology in prospecting, but these had been used, without finding the coppery deposits that indicate a source of cobalt.

I knew the area, I had prospected nearby in my early dirt-bike days; the landscape had distinctive features and a morphology—a shapeliness, an attitude—I could read. More telling than that, I could sense it: some ores have a distinct taste and smell, their presence pulses in the ambient air and can be pinned down in the word geologists often use, its *facies*—the gestalt of complex rock formations. I was away for months and the result was a deposit that would lead in time to the most productive cobalt mine in the United States. Riches: cobalt is the essential element in the battery of every smartphone, every computer, every electric car, every gizmo.

My success also signaled a crisis in my marriage. In recent years, with each of my prospecting trips—trips I had taken all my married life—Vita had drawn away. Before the cobalt strike I'd been in the Zambian Copperbelt, pioneering the mining of high-quality emeralds. I was gone for months at a time and on each home leave saw a growing distance between Vita and me; with her objecting more and more to my absences, I knew I'd have to work to regain her trust. What made this hard was that, although I always returned, I made the mistake of the committed—the single-minded, the selfish—traveler, who regards travel as a mission. I stopped coming all the way back. I was distracted by a new venture. Having seen the exploitation of children mining cobalt in the Congo—a subject that Vita herself was outraged by, as a board member of the agency Rescue/Relief—I became involved in the mining of ethical cobalt in Idaho.

Then something unexpected happened. Vita did not scold me for being away. She said she happened to be preoccupied, she clucked and went about her business; and if you were outside this marriage looking in you'd feel all was more or less well, because so little was said, two busy people, life returning to normal, no raised voices, the marriage ticking away.

But that ticking, which was in fact a silence, something like acceptance, was ominous. It seemed to indicate that we were too far apart to talk—not a peaceful silence but a shadow of distrust, and now I felt our marriage was hollow and unrepairable.

I didn't have another woman. I had work and prospects. My business was booming—I was content. But I was alone.

No anger, no yelling. It was not hatred, because hatred is passion, and passion means caring. It was worse than hatred. She was indifferent and loveless. She simply didn't care.

I had returned home to find a different Vita. She reminded me that she had asked me not to take the Idaho contract, that she was (as she put it) "perimenopausal," and hadn't I been away long enough in our marriage? I told her that although I constantly referred to what I did as "my work," I did not regard it as work. I loved being active, I enjoyed the challenges of being outdoors—of bad roads and tent camps—hauling technical equipment into the wilderness, to locate a mother lode. It was treasure hunting, involving risk and expense. And my months of diligent prospecting in Idaho had paid off.

Vita was not impressed. I said, "It wasn't easy—I missed you."

"I told myself you were dead. I got on with my life."

"The strike was huge," I said. I never uttered the word *cobalt* or said that substance was in high demand as the essential metal in every serious battery on earth. I never mentioned how much money I was making. I explained that my contract included a sharing clause. It meant I had to make a personal investment on the front end, but I would profit on the back end, if we were successful.

And so it happened. It was still early but the cash flow was considerable, which was the reason I could go home more frequently. But I had stayed away too long. I came home to a different house, to a wife I scarcely recognized, and—sadly—one who scarcely recognized me. I could see the upset in Gabe, obviously torn. Vita had worked on him. He was different, too—sad, confused, watchful and, when I tried to hug him, squirming out of my grasp. The worst of it was that he had been accepted to law school, and I could not share his joy.

My great strike in Idaho, Vita now a wealthy wife, and successful in her own career, Gabe on the Dean's List—three great developments. I felt we had every reason to be happy.

That was the situation when Vita pushed the door open and said, "Got a minute?"

I happened to be busy mapping a further Idaho claim, but I put it aside because of this delicate time and said, "Sure. Have a seat."

"I'll stand." She folded her arms.

"What's on your mind?"

"Did you get a message from Frank?"

I smiled, hearing her speak his name, because whenever I heard it I was on my guard.

"Yes, a week ago, after you suggested it, he e-mailed me about lunch."

"You didn't reply."

"I'm—ah—crafting a response," I said. It was a typical Frank expression, like his others, *In this fashion* and *At this juncture* and *I'm thinking it over mentally.* Then I said, "How do you know I didn't reply?"

"He's waiting."

"Okay—I'll tell him. I'm not going. I've heard enough from him."

"You really ought to go, Cal."

I remembered his message: *Be there.* And Vita was repeating this command, punctuating it with my name.

As a geologist in seismic locations I knew that shaky ground was something actual, and undesirable, and often dangerous. I'd just had another great commercial success, but I'd returned to uncertainty in marital terms. And with Vita standing there, and my fearing a long discussion that would become a harangue possibly ending in tears, I knew what I must do. I wanted to stay happy.

"Okay, I'll go."

"You might learn something."

The lunch he'd proposed was in the week of my birthday and, as I've mentioned, the period of one of my greatest successes as a prospector—ethical cobalt. Frank was a man of insinuations, of subtle gestures and sly asides, and long ambiguous stories rather than explicit statements. But, as always in these lunches, it helped to know where I stood, and he had what Vita often called "lunchtime charm."

"Fidge," he said, rising from the booth to greet me. I was at the diner on time, but obviously he had come earlier—his coat was arranged on a hanger rather than slung on a hook.

Fidge was my childhood nickname. I'd been a restless, fidgeting youth. Apart from Frank and our widowed mother, no one else in the world used this name for me. It was like an obscure password. I was not Pascal, or Cal, to any of them: I was Fidge, with all that name implied.

Rather than a handshake, Frank gave my fingers a saucy little slap, cuffing them with the back of his hand and not a word but a snort-honk of recognition.

"Hi, Frank, how you doing?"

I sat across from him in the booth by the wall and took a menu out of the rack near the ketchup bottle and condiments. He sat with his hands folded in a prayerful posture and lowered his head. Did he remember my birthday? Did he know of my success in Idaho? And what stories was he going to tell?

He lifted his head to stare at me with his odd lopsided face. It was divided into two vertical planes, the right part, cheek, jaw, portion of forehead—enlarged by his baldness—and cold eyes, swagged downward in a frown; the left part of his face uplifted in a smile, the contradictory face you see in some Greek masks. When the facial droop on his right side was saying no, his left side—eye and crinkled forehead— was insisting yes. I imagined this complex face, with its built-in stare to register righteous surprise, very intimidating to a witness and very persuasive to a jury. His angular expression operating independently, he actually had two faces, one opposing the other. As for the set of his jaw, his bared teeth were also at odds, as though he was biting open a pistachio. He seldom smiled but when he did his mouth had, ironically, the goofy gape of a pistachio nut.

Poor guy, you think, but no. His was not an affliction, it was a boast that set him apart as someone special. What had begun in his teenage years, after a spell of mumps, as a mild form of Bell's palsy, Frank had discovered to be an asset, and he somehow contrived to remain uncured—his face fixed and asymmetric, and looking, he once told me with pride, *like a pirate*. Something else: I always felt that he was scowling at me furiously behind this face.

As his brother I often studied my face in the mirror and talked to myself, to see if my face was separated in the same lopsided way. But it wasn't, and I concluded that Frank's had become like that over decades of equivocation, the way a habitual smiler acquires laugh lines, or a doubtful one a permanent scowl.

"There's a short answer and a long answer to that," he said of my harmless greeting. "The short answer is 'I've got a ton of things on my mind.'" His eyes dismissed this as he agitated his folded hands. He said,

"The long answer is what I have on my mind, the details. I keep thinking, when Dad was my age he had a small insurance agency, and was in debt because of some bad faith policies, and two young kids. I don't know how he kept his composure . . ."

I started to say, *Dad was an optimist,* and was going to add how he was positive and spiritual, his piety giving him strength, but Frank had unfolded his hands to gesticulate and was still talking.

". . . something to do with not facing facts, being a kind of dreamer. Ask him what he did for a living and he'd say, 'Insurance, but what I've always wanted to do was some sort of forestry-related work.' He wanted to be a forest ranger! I could never live like that. What I never understood . . ."

Dad never wanted to be a forest ranger. But instead of correcting Frank, I said, "He admired you for having important friends."

This seemed not to register. Frank said, "Think of it. How he died before the reckoning came. It was Mum who had to face the music. She had her feet on the ground."

"And her parents' money."

Frank wagged his finger, using it to clear my statement away. He said, "She paid back every penny."

This was an old story I'd heard before. In an early version the debts were forgiven, Dad was absolved, but Frank had advised Mum on the procedure. Today, Mum was the heroine, having settled Dad's bad faith debt. Something was unspoken, too. I had always been Dad's favorite, and Frank's disparaging him as a deadbeat seemed a dig at me—another of those roundabout, untranslatable family slurs I referred to earlier.

"Can I get you gentlemen a drink?" It was the waitress, an older woman with a weary smile, and a pad in her hand. "And what else can I do you for?"

"Tomato juice, please," I said. "No ice."

Clasping his hands again, Frank said, "Water."

"Still or sparkling?"

"Tap water."

"Shall I tell you today's specials?"

"Pass," Frank said in a snippy voice.

Seeing the woman wince, I said, "I know what I'm going to have. A cup of clam chowder and the grilled haddock."

"Good choice. Mashed potato or salad?"

"Mashed potato."

"And you, sir?"

Frank said, "Same here."

The waitress repeated the order, reading from her pad. She then said, "I'll be right back with your drinks."

Frank leaned toward me. "Imagine, Dad an insurance stiff grandly calling himself an importer."

"It was his hobby. Some of the stuff he sold was made overseas. China, for sure. Like a lot of my drilling equipment."

Leaning closer, as though to someone on a witness stand, Frank said, "Think how hard it is to be who you say you are."

Leaving me with this enigmatic thought, he sat back, looking pleased with himself.

The waitress set down my tomato juice and Frank's glass of water and said, "Food's on the way."

Frank tapped the side of the glass with one finger, as though to test its temperature. "What was I saying?"

"Mum paid back every penny." I did not correct him. I was enjoying this skewed version of the story.

And there was more, the valiant widow repaying her late husband's debt, using her own money. And Frank taking time off from his law practice to help her. As he talked I noted the variations in the story, Dad now portrayed as selfish and neglectful, concealing his profits, squirreling money away, defaulting on his debts, undermining the family.

At a certain point in this conversation, my interest waned, I found this painful to hear, as though listening to it I was being disloyal to Dad. I said, "What about the things Dad did that had nothing to do with money? His sacrifices. His great heart. How he never complained. He loved Mum. He adored her. That counts for a lot."

Frank stared at me as I spoke, expressionless, his slanted lips narrowed, unimpressed, or else not listening. He was a relaxed and expansive talker, but he was an impatient and agitated listener, and his blank stare was an example of his impatience.

He said, "Every time I pick up a screwdriver I think of how Dad used the tip of a knife as a screwdriver. So all the knives in our cutlery drawer had a sort of twist at the tip, a weird little kink, where it was used to remove a screw."

"I do that sometimes." Frank knew that, he'd often mocked me for it. Some of those damaged knives might have been my doing.

"And not only the knives," Frank said. "What about the time he lunched the car door?"

He was disparaging Dad, yet I smiled at a Littleford word I loved, like *bollocky* for naked, *tonic* for soda, *hosey* for choose, and *What a pisser. Lunched* meant "ruined," but I hated hearing it applied to something Dad had done.

"Banged the door against a parking meter in a hurry to see a client."

"Just a ding," I said.

"Then, trying to smooth it out he pushed too hard on his electric buffer and fried the coil—lunched that, too."

"Two lunches, what's the big deal."

"One lunch too many," Frank said.

"Clam chowder," the waitress said, sliding the cups toward us. "Haddock's coming up."

"Consider being a woman that age," Frank said, as the waitress hurried away. He was nodding knowingly. "Probably fiftysomething and still hustling for tips. You know what waitresses make? Probably around a buck and change an hour."

He said this sourly, so I said, "She's about my age—and younger than you."

Frank rapped on the table and said in an insistent hiss, "Cash is king."

I was looking at his lips, how they trembled with these words, and expected him to say more. But there was no more. His statement was assertive, but his eyes looked unsure, as with the Dad story of debt, and the one about Dad using a kitchen knife as a screwdriver, and lunching the car door, and the obnoxious aside about the waitress's pay.

Dumping oyster crackers into my chowder, I began eating. Watching me with damp lips, Frank stirred his chowder, dabbing at it with his spoon, but instead of eating any, he went on fiddling with it, like a chemist with a potion. His not eating disconcerted me and made it hard for me to swallow until, self-conscious, I gave up and pushed my half-eaten cup aside.

Frank was still poking at his untasted chowder. He said, "Took Dad and Mum to the Governor's Ball. Mum just sat, dazzled. Dad goes up to Senator McBride and says, 'I remember your father.'"

"Dad was very congenial. The only people he couldn't stand were lazy aimless types. Remember his expression?"

Frank was staring at his chowder.

"He's like a fart in a mitten—nice."

But Frank said, "McBride's father was convicted of bank fraud, mail fraud, and wire fraud. He served six years in a federal lockup."

The waitress returned with two plates. "Still working on that?" she said to Frank, who'd left his spoon in his untasted chowder.

"Take it," he said and nudged it with his knuckles.

The waitress set down the plates of haddock and clearing away the chowder cups said, "Let me know if you need anything else."

"Thanks," I said and started to eat, but seeing Frank poking at his fish and not eating I was thrown, and in this delay, as though Frank was trying to find out if the fish was edible, I found it hard to swallow.

"How's your son?" I asked.

Frank said, "Look in the mirror and ask yourself that question."

He lifted and dropped the food on his plate, seeming to seek something underneath it, and he did this studiously, with a faint scowl of disgust on his lips.

I wondered whether he'd ask me about my son, Gabe. I was proud of Gabe's academic record but decided not to volunteer anything unless Frank asked. Frank's head was down. He was making a little hut of his heap of mashed potato, squaring the sides, hollowing out the middle, roofing it with flakes of his broken fish.

Just then a shadow fell over our booth, a man in a fedora, leaning toward Frank.

"Sorry to interrupt."

Frank looked up and at once his face glowed with lunchtime charm, its opposing features seeming to resolve into a smooth smiling whole of welcome. He dropped his fish knife and lifted both hands to enclose the extended hand of the man who'd happened by.

"Well-met, well-met!" Frank said, sounding warmly grateful, and he hung on, tugging the man's hand.

It was Dante Zangara, an old school friend of Frank's who'd been a politician in Littleford for years and was now the mayor. Zangara greeted me, a casual fist bump with his free hand, saying "Who's this stranger?," but Frank was still talking excitedly.

"Who said, 'The art of public life consists of knowing exactly when to stop, and then going a bit further'?" And with visible reluctance he released Zangara's hand.

"Search me," Zangara said. He had small close-set eyes over a hawk nose, and a way of licking his thin lips and spacing his words that made him seem as though he was speaking to someone taking dictation. "But, hey, I would not call that guy a chadrool. Listen, how's the family?"

"Never better," Frank said, a sweetness in his voice. "What about *la famiglia*, Zangara?"

"Connie's a wreck." Zangara raised his arms in an operatic gesture of despair. "Gina's applying to college."

"How can I help?" Frank said. He seemed to levitate in his seat, rising toward Zangara, his intense gaze fixed on the man.

"She wants to go to Willard, maybe study veterinary science. The kid's nuts about animals."

"I know a guy," Frank said. "He has the ear of the dean of admissions. I could write a reference."

"Frank, that would be fantastic."

"A distinct honor," Frank said. "Gina will make all of us proud."

They hugged, awkwardly, because Frank was still in the booth, canted forward, the table edge jammed against his thighs, Zangara toppling, and then breaking free.

"The Bad Angel brothers," Zangara said, straightening his jacket, coming to attention, with a little salute, touching his hat brim in homage. A high school nickname is forever, and it annoyingly defines you when you're still living in your hometown. "You guys are fabulous."

When this sunny visitation ended, and Zangara left the diner, Frank seemed to subside and become smaller, twisting himself back into his seat, to resume toying with his food. He'd fallen silent, but still was not eating.

I watched him resisting his food, and his stubbornness made me recall his slights and abuses when we were younger. In my angered imagination I pictured myself dragging him out of the booth and violently force-feeding him. It was the way an imprisoned hunger striker was fed, first immobilized, strapped to a six-point chair, a nasogastric feeding tube pushed into his nose and snaked into his throat, and nutritious slop hosed into him, while he gagged and struggled to breathe. Force-feeding had been used many times, by the U.S. and others on prisoners, and it was deemed torture—cruel, inhumane, and degrading, and sometimes fatal—but torture as a fine art, making it especially pleasant for me to contemplate with Frank (who once mentioned to me that he approved of it), intubated and choking to death and unable to speak, or to tell me another bullshit story.

"McBride later joined the D.C. branch of my old law firm."

I needed to remind myself that this was the father of the senator Dad had apparently insulted.

"Became a lobbyist."

Frank launched into a vaguely familiar story about lobbying, setting up businesses on Native American tribal land in Idaho, leasing agreements and financial schemes, saying, "Some of that land is fractionated," and repeating the phrase "Cash is king." But as he was still poking at his food—sculpting it, so to speak—and not eating, I could not understand his story. I knew I had heard it before, something about casinos, but this time it had a different emphasis that got my attention and seemed personal. "Mineral rights," he kept repeating, and I wondered whether he was referring in some enigmatic way to the cobalt deposit I'd discovered in that same area of the state. Yet as long as he pushed his food around his plate, and did not eat any of it, I was too distracted with my fantasy—force-feeding him to death—to follow his story.

To get him to stop, I said, "Do you want anything else?"

"Yes," he said. "I want to find the rich jerk who took a dump on me—kept me waiting in an outer office for almost an hour, seeming to take some pleasure in it, and then snubbed me when he deigned to see me. 'We'll get back to you. Have a nice day.'"

"When was this?"

"When I was nineteen, the summer I did office work for that Boston law firm." He pushed his plate aside. "I'd like to punch him in the face."

In an early, much longer version of this story the rich jerk was a young woman, and Frank had an exquisite rejoinder to *Have a nice day*. He said, *I have other plans*. In another version, it was an older woman and he demanded to see her boss. Getting even was a mission with Frank; but you never really get even, you just do more damage.

"Anyway, I heard his wife ditched him." Frank folded his arms, presiding over his strange mounded plate of uneaten food. "Turned out he wasn't doing his homework. But here's the kicker. He claimed he stumbled on some stairs and bumped his wang on the newel post. So what does he do? He sues the building's owners for loss of consortium. Because of the injuries he sustained in his stumble, his wife has been deprived of her"—Frank lifted his hands and clawed air quotes near my face—"husband's services." He twisted his swagged face into a smile. "Her comfort and happiness in his so-called society have been impaired by his damaged wang. Hey, I hated the guy but I learned something."

I wanted to ponder "loss of consortium," but I had indigestion. I was disgusted by my half-eaten meal, and I was disturbed at the sight of Frank's uneaten meal, which, scraped and combined, was lumped like garbage.

"Fidge," Frank said suddenly, shoving his cuff. "Look at the time—gotta go."

He slid out of the booth, lifted his coat from the hanger, and left in a hurry.

He had not eaten anything. He had not asked me a personal question. He had deflected my questions. To a passerby—such as the waitress

who was approaching the booth—his stories were rantings, if not bor-
derline insane. But I knew they contained a meaning.

"Someone wasn't hungry," the waitress said.

I thanked her, gave her a bigger tip than she was expecting, and
spent the rest of the day reflecting on the lunch—what Frank said, what
he didn't say, his having eaten nothing of what he'd ordered, and I grew
melancholy.

That was the first lunch. I was puzzled. *He dislikes me,* I thought, and
went no further, because who wants to enter the head of the person
who hates you? But it also occurred to me that he might have had a
stomach upset—he tended to be bilious in every sense—and maybe it
was too painful for him to talk about. Maybe he was depressed, though
apart from his divorce from his first wife long ago and a period of deep
gloom, I'd never known Frank to be depressed. He made a point of
being jaunty, especially in his cruel teasing. So I gave him the benefit
of the doubt and began to think I was reading too much into his ambiguous stories and his uneaten meal. That plate he'd left, however, the
mass of food, that slop disturbed me. He had hovered over the plate,
and lumped it and pushed it around, making it his own, then rejected
it, making a sort of statement I needed to interpret—very Frank.

Yet my birthday. He had not mentioned it, nor had he given me a
present as he often did, even a token, as in the past, like the key chain,
or baseball cap, or ballpoint pen, logo items he'd gotten free at a luxury
hotel. I knew they were cheesy mementos he'd regifted, yet they showed
he remembered.

And my cobalt strike, the Idaho mine, a big payday—he had not
said anything about that either; and speculation, mentioning me, had
been in the business news that Frank habitually read when trawling for
clients.

He had not asked about Vita, and in the past he had never failed to
do so.

You think: Odd not to mention any of this, but one of Frank's per-
versities was emphasizing the importance of something by not bringing

it up. I wondered whether that was the case at this lunch, and of course there was the sight of his mangled plate of food that he'd left looking punished, an obvious power move.

That night I told Vita about the lunch—the stories, the uneaten food, the references that seemed directed at me. As we were going through a bad patch at the time, I suppose I was looking for sympathy.

"He's a piece of work," she said, yet before I could agree she said, "But so are you."

"It's my birthday, Vee. He didn't say a word about it."

"That's the sort of thing you might do."

"Maybe by accident, but this seemed deliberate."

"You forgot my birthday one year."

"I was prospecting in Zambia, Vee!"

"Husband comes down with a severe case of amnesia in Zambia," Vita said.

One of the characteristics of a troubled marriage is that wisps of half-remembered slights from the distant past appear fully formed and offensive in the present, to be marshaled as evidence.

"A lunch, Vee. A lunch where one of the lunchers doesn't eat anything."

"Maybe he wasn't hungry."

"The way he played with his food seemed hostile."

"You play with your food sometimes," she said.

"Vee, there was something unspoken at that lunch. It wasn't just that he didn't eat anything and told those stories about Dad. It was all oblique and empty, like a ritual."

"Ritual," she said, doubtful, as if I was overdramatizing the event. "Of what?"

"Of rejection. Like the sort of thing some African tribe might do as a way of ostracizing someone in the clan. Except he was inventing the whole procedure, like creating a tradition that had never existed before. The rejection ritual of the uneaten meal."

"Oh god," Vita said.

And that was the end of the discussion, from which I emerged unconsoled.

* * *

A few days later, Vita said, "We're having a cookout on Saturday for Gabe and some of his friends. Why don't you invite Frank?"

"He doesn't like me."

"But I like him," she said, which was clearly a dig at me.

When I phoned him to invite him, Frank said he wasn't sure he could make it and that he needed some time to think about it.

"Frank, it's the day after tomorrow."

"I'll let you know," he said. This hesitation was usually Frank's way of indicating that he might get a better invitation in the meantime.

Vita said, "You're so paranoid," when I told her this.

I did not hear from Frank and assumed he was snubbing us. But on the morning of the cookout, he called and said, "See you later."

He came carrying a small brown bag, and when he doffed his baseball cap, his lopsided face became fuller and more distorted, as he said hello in a grouchy way to me with one side while offering a twinkling gaze to Vita with the other side. He went to the smoking grill and setting down the bag, he removed two hot dogs and two bottles of beer. He tossed the hot dogs on the grill and uncapped a beer, saying "Cheers," to Vita. The other side of his face still regarded me with displeasure.

Gabe and his friends waved from where they sat eating under a tree. Frank jerked his head at them, as he tonged the sweaty, split-open hot dogs onto a paper plate.

"Mustard?" I said.

"Bad for you. High fructose corn syrup," he said to me, while his eyes searched for Vita.

"I wish there was something I could do to please you."

Walking away, Frank said, "Piss in one hand, and make that wish with the other, and see which one fills up faster."

As he stood at the far end of the swimming pool, drinking his second beer, I thought: *He is here, but he is not here.* And that was when Vita went over to him. They were too far away from me to hear anything they said, though once or twice Vita glanced at me, then looked back at Frank. And the way they stood, laughing, poking each other, they looked like husband and wife, or lovers.

Frank left, taking his brown bag and his two empty beer bottles with him, facing me and wordlessly winking, and raising one eyebrow—the eyebrow flash he knew infuriated me.

"He hates me," I said.

Vita said, "Ever think, maybe it's you?"

That was the second lunch.

Not long after, Vita said, "I need to tell you something."

By then, I wasn't happy anymore, so I knew exactly what she was going to say.

I start this way, with these long-ago lunches, when Frank and I were in our late fifties, because it was a turning point, deliquescing into something I never expected. And to give a glimpse of how odd, oblique, and unreadable Frank was, I guessed there was much more to know and wondered whether I'd find out what it was. And why, in the end, I wanted him dead.

But I have to go back to the beginning, in Littleford, when it was just the two of us.

PART TWO

BROTHERHOOD

2

PARALLEL LIVES

THERE IS ONE TRUE KIND OF LOVING—HEARTFELT, UN-selfish, pure in heart, life-affirming; but there are many vivid versions of hatred. The hatred that makes your enemy abandon you is nothing compared to the hatred that impels this monster never to leave you alone, infecting you like a virus, sickening you and seeming to gloat.

My brother, Frank, resented my long absences from town, because it was harder then for him to provoke me. I knew this, but for my own mental health I avoided pondering what was in his head. And as a prospector, in the business of searching wild places for minerals and metals, I'd dealt with some rough individuals. They were ornery or contrary, but I could handle them; they were difficult, but like me they were looking for profit and were willing to work hard for it. Prospecting for any ore is a physical challenge and only the toughest are equal to it. These men and women didn't intend me any harm; it was territorial—they wanted to be the first to stake a claim.

Frank was different: his was a mental game, no risk involved, and it was personal. He wanted to torture me, he enjoyed seeing me suffer, he aimed to ruin me. I had no idea why.

Over the years, I was frequently far away from Littleford and Frank, but even at a great distance he could be obnoxious, because he had a gift, common to tyrants, of insinuating himself into my consciousness, and humming there like a fever. When I was anywhere near him, he was unbearable. I banished vengeful thoughts from my mind and was unfailingly courteous to him, the way you might behave with exaggerated politeness to someone you dislike, because you don't want your contempt to show.

We were born three years apart, to older grateful and therefore indulgent parents. I came second and was the happier for it, because so much less was expected of me. As the firstborn, Frank was adored—he was a pleaser and a prodigy, Mother's favorite. Father consoled himself with me, as both of us were lowly and solitary. Like Dad, I was restless, good with my hands, but slow to speak. I didn't mind the attention that Frank got from Mother; to be overlooked freed me from the responsibilities and high expectations that burdened Frank, who was (Mother said) destined for great things.

In an early family portrait, taken in a Littleford studio, we fitted together as a plausible and matching quartet, parents and children. Mother was small and delicate and smiling; Father, stern, his features echoed in those of the two boys, his beaky face with his interrogating nose, his querying close-set eyes, thin skeptical lips, sharp chin, dense dark hair, thick at the sides, modifying his large sagging ears. Quebecois features, he would have said, but powerful. In a red flannel shirt he'd have looked like a lumberjack; in his expensive suit he could have passed for an aristocrat, a bit foreign, aloof, with an air of concealment—his origins perhaps.

It was this, though he seldom mentioned it: his mother was Native American—and our mother had an Abenaki in her ancestry. So we Belangers were special in Littleford, where everyone but us had an immigrant story. We had no tale of an Atlantic crossing, no Ellis Island stopover, only the simple fact that in hard times the families (Mother was a Bouchard) dropped into New England from the north, after being in Quebec forever, or before recorded time, at least recorded in the family memory.

Dad was mostly silent, watchful, stoical, accepting, somewhat unreadable. His belief was: we have always been here, we will always be here. His out-of-town friends were of the same mind—Ed Pigeon and the others, Picard, Benoit, Tremblay, Parenteau, and Gauthier, his secret friends, though listing them like this makes them seem like members of the Académie française. Settled in Lowell and Nashua, they were almost tribal in their confidences and habits, quite separate but blending in. In their hearts they were woodsmen and fur trappers, and they often conversed in the lingo they learned from their parents, Quebecois French, with its peculiar words and elliptical phrases. *C'est plate!* when something was boring, and the odd repetition in *Tu t'en vas-tu?* for "You going?" There were bluets and plenty of poutine in Quebec, but none in France, so no words for them. As an amateur handyman, Dad called himself a *bizouneux,* and for my elusiveness, I was a *ratoureux,* and Frank the talker, a *placoteux*—words that would have bewildered a Parisian.

That language I absorbed by hearing it constantly, barely being aware of my fluency, and so I excelled in French. This was a relief, because it gave me more time to pursue the sciences—chemistry, biology, and the refinements of these disciplines as they applied to geology, which was my great love.

Without much study I could converse in French and could easily translate the passages Miss Sirois gave us at Littleford High School. Once, looking through an anthology of poems, I found a poem, "Le Chat," and read it with pleasure, because we had a dark cat just like the one in the poem. I told Miss Sirois that I wanted to read more of that poet's work.

"You're not ready for him yet," she said.

He was Baudelaire, his book *Le Fleurs du Mal*—magical title to a sixteen-year-old—*The Flowers of Evil*. I found a copy in the Littleford Library and sat entranced, reading it, thrilled by "Abel et Caïn"—"*Race de Caïn, dans la fange/Rampe et meurs misérablement*"—which was how I secretly felt about Frank: crawl and die in the mud miserably. And I

loved "*N'importe où, pourvu que ce soit hors du monde*"—Anywhere out
of the world. That line, the wicked word *evil*, the poems about death
and flesh thrilled my teenaged imagination.

I longed to leave Littleford, and go anywhere out of the world, to
distance myself from Frank and cease being a Bad Angel brother. To
rehearse my escape I joined the Boy Scouts and went for hikes in the
woods, the Littleford Fells, often camping there at a secluded hillside
spot known as Panther's Cave, or farther in, past a pond (Doleful Pond)
at the Sheepfold. I was practicing my ultimate departure, and a fellow Boy Scout—he of the gashed hand—Melvin Yurick, often accompanied me. Daylong hikes and overnight camps were legitimate: we
weren't fleeing from home, we were earning merit badges.

Yurick lived in the Winthrop Estates in an elegant brick house,
surrounded by a lovely lawn. In the summer I mowed the lawns of
his neighbors and aspired to live in the Winthrop Estates. *Someday,* I
thought, *when I'm married, and have enough money, I'll come home and
buy a house there*—maybe one of those grand houses with columns and
porches, where I once cut the grass. I'd raise a family, away from Gully
Lane, and Frank, and the neighborhood where I grew up.

"I want to get out of here, too," Melvin Yurick said quietly on one
of our hikes.

I smiled, thinking: *You live in the Winthrop Estates—why would you
want to leave?* But I admired his ambition to want more.

That's who I was and where I came from; but the early family photographs of Frank and me are misleading. Family features are not fixed.
You start out looking somewhat alike and then you change; in time,
experience and circumstances and moods begin to work on those
features. In high school, even with his palsied face, Frank and I re-
sembled each other enough to be recognized as brothers, but after I
left home for college, becoming myself—my face reflecting the person
within me—my features softened, my eyebrows growing owlish, my
lips readier to smile, my eyes more welcoming to new scenes; and I'd
become muscular, while Frank had grown fatter, his face more asym-

metric and complacent, a malicious mask for his ruthless ambition. By my late twenties no one would have taken me to be Frank's brother, and that suited me. We made our difference emphatic in the two ways we pronounced our name. I kept to Dad's slushy Quebecois way of saying it, "Bel—onzhay," while Frank's clanged, "Bel—anger." But never mind—in Littleford we were always the Bad Angels.

The focus was mainly on Frank, who'd stayed in town. He said he had a righteous reason. The summer after Frank graduated from high school, Dad died from a heart attack in his office, Belanger Insurance, in Littleford Square. He was forty-nine years old. It came without warning. He smoked a pipe, he was a moderate drinker, and he seemed to be in good health. This was an ominous sign to Frank and me: a warning that we too might be struck down at an early age, and I'm sure it was a factor in both of us living with a particular urgency, the shadow of Dad's death hanging over us. Being an insurance man, he was convinced of the necessity of being heavily insured, and shrewd in devising the most beneficial policy, so his death made Mother wealthy in a manner that she found daunting. What to do with all this money?

That was when Frank announced that he would not leave Littleford. After he graduated from law school, he would remain in town to protect Mother. "I'm staying. I'm looking after Ma. With all this money, she's got a target on her back."

Mother was relieved, because Frank was exceptional. But this notion of his high intelligence was a burden. The assumption of his having to work wonders was so powerful it made Frank a cheat at an early age, and this cheating altered his features, first his eyes—a flintiness, then the exaggerated droop in his face. He knew his lopsided gaze was intimidating. Needing to win, to be best, made him into a bully; having to score high marks meant he often had to bluff his way, fudge his answers, and that pressure turned him into an arguer and an explainer and a blamer, a public school pusher, later a neck-biting lawyer.

This makes him sound repellent, and if this were the whole of him you'd write him off as a monster and avoid him. Yet there was more, not another side of him but a subtler aspect of that same treacherous side. He could seem kind, he had a residue of charm, he knew how to be generous, he had mastered the arts of persuasion. All these plausible qualities made him likable, yet they were insincere and shallow, merely strategies to aid him in his manipulation. And really this charm and apparent generosity in such a man was proof of his darkness. At his most sinister he seemed trustworthy. His skill lay in knowing how to exploit a person's weakness. He would have made a great actor, a master of tonalities and gestures, convincing in every role he chose to play.

That's how he looked—those were the outward manifestations of his thrusting personality. What lay behind all this—what Mother's expectations produced—was a habit of ruthlessness that left him without a conscience. He could hold a dog turd in his hand and look you in the eye and swear that it was an orchid.

If you were not immediately convinced, he would work on you, first by flattering your intelligence, wooing you with praise, and winning your confidence. When he saw you waver, he would emphasize that this object in his hand was something of value, to cherish. He would wear you down with a monotony of insistent description—and might raise his voice, or whisper, or blandly list its attributes—until you were either exhausted from being browbeaten, or actually persuaded. And then he offered his hand and you sniffed the dog turd and remarked on its fragrance.

He had no conscience. This seems like a diabolical trait—and of course it is, shared by mass murderers and villains—but it is also useful to anyone with ambition. It leaves a person who wants to win with an enormous arsenal of weapons and it frees them of any moral considerations. But someone without a conscience is also unknowable—you have no idea of what they will do next, or what they're capable of, because—conscienceless—they are an enigma, capable of anything.

Frank was so full of surprises that it occurred to me early on (and the thought persisted throughout my life) that though he was my brother, and we'd grown up in the same house, I did not know him. But one day he offered a glimpse of his heart. I was in grad school, pursuing my studies as a prospector; and Frank, in his last year of law school, for the first time took an interest in my career. He was swayed by one word.

We were home for Thanksgiving, raking leaves in the driveway, while Mother roasted the turkey and, in Dad's memory, was making his signature dish, a poutine his Quebecois mother had made for him, but one that Mother disparaged as "peasant food," since it was a mass of French fries topped with cheese and brown gravy, hearty but not much to look at.

While we were raking, Frank asked about my classes. I mentioned metallurgy and chemistry, x-ray diffraction and assaying.

He misheard this last word as "essay," and so I explained what it was and that I wanted to buy my own assay kit, which included a small furnace.

"To what end?" he said, skeptical when I mentioned the price.

"Gold," I said.

That was the word. It silenced him, it gave his face a look of hunger and his eyes traced a sort of pattern on my face as though trying to read my expression or penetrate a secret. His fingers twitched on the handle of his rake, clutching motions that matched his hungry face. I had uttered a magic word.

I tried not to smile, because the emotion throbbing in him was one of the oldest in the world. Yet all I had told him was my simple ambition as a student of mines and metallurgy—to look for gold, or platinum, or copper, much as a lawyer might be looking for clients.

In an old historical novel about an early European voyage, I once came across the sentence "Precious metals excited the greed of conquest." There it is in a few words, the history of world exploration and colonization, the politics of plunder, the lust for gold. For the Spanish in the Americas, the Portuguese in Africa and India, the Dutch in the Indies, the English, too, the quest for gold was paramount. DeSoto looked for gold in Tennessee but didn't find it. Cortés massacred the Aztecs for gold, Pizarro killed the Inca king Atahualpa because the Incas, too, were gold seekers, and Atahualpa's throne was made of 183 pounds of gold. In 1595 the Spanish Captain Mendaña sailed the Pacific Ocean from Peru to the Solomon Islands looking for gold; that same year, Sir Walter Raleigh crossed the Atlantic and splashed his way up the Orinoco River in search of El Dorado—the Golden Man, in his fabled City of Gold. Twenty years later, in 1614, Captain John Smith tacked up and down the New England coast, tramping the dunes, for gold. Gold in China, gold in New Guinea, the Gold Rush in California, and fifty years later the gold rush in the Klondike area of the Yukon.

I did not tell Frank any of this; I knew it as a geology student from the history we studied as part of our courses—the quest for precious metal was as old as humankind. A gold bead ornament found in Bulgaria was determined to be sixty-five hundred years old, the boast of a seminaked member of a Neolithic tribe.

"What?" I said, because Frank had not said anything but was still running his tongue over his lips and swallowing, as though in the throes of gold fever.

"Gold," he whispered.

"Dentists need it, you find it in electronics—gold is a great conductor," I said in a matter-of-fact tone, the way you might talk about plastic or rubber. "It's in medicine. It helps treat arthritis. Oh, yeah, and jewelry."

"That's what you're studying?"

"One of the metals," I said, more casually, because I had his attention. "There are other precious metals. Palladium. Iridium. Osmium. Your pen nib is probably osmium. Lots of that stuff in Alaska."

He was swallowing urgently, he did not know what to ask, but he wore a fixed expression of longing—one of the rare instances when I could read his mind.

"Dinner's ready!" Mother called from the porch.

Frank did not move. He was staring at me with greedy eyes, and he looked at me differently after that, as someone who, after a long journey, might return with a sack of gold.

But metallurgy was work for me, a way of making a living and, most of all, getting me away from home—away from Frank.

We were different in many respects—perhaps in all respects; but something that set us apart was our attitude to risk. Frank was risk averse, he dreaded the unknown, he needed a sure thing. This might have sprung from Mother keeping him by her side, praising him, encouraging him, but always suggesting that he'd be happiest at home. And there Frank stayed, making it his mission to please her.

I was formed by Dad, who had a restless Quebecois nature; but as an unselfish parent he lived through me, urging me to get out of the house, join the Boy Scouts, go camping. *God's fresh air!* was his cry. He admired hikers and backwoodsmen, trappers and forest rangers.

There were no women in Dad's fantasies—no girlfriends, no wives. His dreams were of hearty excursions into the wilderness, and I fulfilled them. It seemed he longed for the freedom of the forest, while still understanding that hiking and rock climbing and swimming involved an element of risk. But he trusted me to surmount obstacles and to minimize risks through experiencing the outdoors. A long hike needed to be planned, a camping trip required equipment. Dad insisted that to overcome risks I had to be prepared. And so I became a connoisseur of camping gear—backpacks and tents and sleeping bags and hiking boots. And the revelation to me was that, with this gear, I was completely portable and independent: with shelter and a sleeping bag. I had a mess kit and food; early on I learned to cook. As an outdoorsman—while still in my teens, hiking with Melvin Yurick—I was liberated. Dad's death was a blow but it also inspired me to follow his advice and leave town. And later, after Yurick vanished from Littleford and my life, around the time I bewitched Frank with the word *gold,* I was able to trek for days, even in winter—on cross-country skis—camping in the snow, collecting rock samples.

Meanwhile, Frank was indoors, in his bedroom, readying himself for his final exams in law school.

3

THE BLACK CREEK

IN FRANK'S LAST YEAR OF LAW SCHOOL, MY SECOND YEAR in grad school, we spent a few weeks of spring vacation on Cape Cod, near the town of West Barnstable. Mother was in charge—she'd found the rental. It was another gesture in Dad's memory. As a boy he had spent his summers on a farm in West Barnstable. And that small town, reachable by train from Boston, was still very rural and seldom visited and thus easily affordable. I suspect Mother felt that as our studies were ending I would soon be going away; that she saw this might be the last time for a while we'd all be together as a family, in a place Dad had loved.

One of those weekdays I said I was going for a walk.

"What for?" Frank asked—to me an absurd question but his natural reflex, as a challenge.

"Might find something."

"Like what?"

Fresh air, I thought. But I said, "Arrowheads. Trilobites. Micro fossils."

Our rental house was just off Cranberry Highway, the narrow country road that ran along the miles of coastal wetland known locally as the Great Marshes, where—as I said to Frank—arrowheads and trilobites might be found, sunk in the ancient clay. What I did not say was I simply wanted to get out of the house, go for a hike across the salt marshes, and end up two miles away on the shoreline of Sandy Neck, with its lovely beach and sprawling peninsula of dunes and nesting seabirds.

I could tell from Frank's tone that he resented my going, and his posture told me he was conflicted, his body oddly twisted, his upper half angled to set off with me, his lower half planted firmly on the porch, the thwarted Frank with the divided features, one half resisting the other.

"It doesn't look far, but it's slow going because of the ditches," I said. "You have to jump them."

"As if I don't know how to jump."

He seemed to take what I said as a challenge, though I had meant to discourage him. I wanted to go alone, as I usually did, at my own speed. But my mentioning the obstacles provoked him. Frank never went for hikes, and seldom for long walks—he'd never been the outdoor type—yet he untwisted himself and took a step toward me.

"I'm going," he said, making a megaphone of his hand and jamming it to his mouth as he called out, "Ma, I'm going for a hike with Cal!"

From inside the house came a small strained voice, two rooms away, "Be awfully careful, Frankie."

Even at odd moments like that, in the ordinary routines of the household, I knew she was fretfully cautioning him, while ignoring me. But I thought at those times: *She won't miss me—when the day comes, I'll slip away and be free.*

Heading to the road, and crossing it to the tall grass at the margin of the marsh, Frank walked slightly ahead of me, pumping his arms, almost marching, to stay in front of me, making the hike a sort of competition. But I went at my own pace, because I knew what was coming—mud and ditches and marsh grass—cordgrass and spartina, with sharp edges that would slash our bare arms and, since we were wearing shorts, our legs as well. You couldn't move fast in the marshes; you needed to pick your way across the grass that had been flattened by the outgoing tide, and you had to find the narrowest section of the ditch for jumping.

The ditches had been dug decades ago to drain the marshes, to control the mosquitoes and keep the marshes from being a saltwater swamp. The ditches were deep and symmetrical, six or seven feet wide, many of them running parallel or crisscrossing, and from the air would have looked like an enormous grid, or more likely a maze of black water-filled trenches cut in the green of the salt marsh.

"I can jump this," Frank said, when we came to the edge of the first one.

"It might be easier farther along, where it's a little narrower."

But Frank had positioned himself on the bank and before I had finished speaking, he vaulted the ditch, defying me, staggering a bit on the other side and falling forward, then breathless from the effort, slapping at his muddy knees.

He had made it a contest, so I played along, jumping across and like him staggering and dropping to my knees, muddying them, which seemed to please him.

When he set off again, striding ahead of me, I said, "We're going that way."

I pointed to the dunes in the distance, the lumpy horizon of bone-white sand, like a landscape of heaped sugar—magic and unreal—at the far side of the solid green of the marsh. One of the oddities of Cape Cod weather was its fickleness, blustery wind giving way suddenly to calms, humidity to chill, the sun unexpectedly breaking through fog. We were hiking under gray clouds, but far ahead the sun was shining on the dunes, bleaching them and gilding the boughs of the pitch pines below them. That sight of the sunlit dunes seemed to offer us a dramatic destination, hiking from the gloom of the wet grass into a zone of light and warmth.

As it was late spring there were no other people in sight. We were alone in the marsh, nor was there anyone visible on the dunes. I loved being solitary and was annoyed having to share it with Frank. The only satisfaction I had was that he was struggling to jump across the ditches. After his first successful jump, he found the following ones more difficult. His sandals were muddy and his legs dirtied, like mine. Both of us were wearing shorts, in anticipation of going for a swim at Sandy Neck beach.

All this time he kept in front of me, as though he'd put himself in charge of the hike. We kept on, altering our course to find the best places to jump the ditches and avoiding the lower portions of marsh where there was standing water surrounded by mud. Now and then we startled a sitting gull and it took off squawking. Still, Frank hurried ahead of me—*Good,* I thought, *I don't have to talk to him.* He was muddier than me, the mud black against his skinny, white, law student legs; he had muddy hands from breaking his fall and mud in his hair where he tugged at it. Now I saw that he had stopped walking, that he was standing, leaning forward, his arms hanging down. I could not see his face but his was a posture of perplexity.

I had forgotten the creek. It ran more or less parallel to the dunes, forming the edge of the peninsula, called a neck locally. The creek was deep, and dark, on this gray day, and it flowed with the ebbing tide, draining miles away into Barnstable Harbor.

But to call it a creek was misleading, because it was forty yards across at least, a tidal creek, at high tide as wide as a river, and what probably bothered Frank was that, peering at its current and the boils and eddies of black water, he could not see the bottom.

"What do we do now?" He stared at me, a gob of mud on his chin making him seem vulnerable and uncertain.

"Swim across," I said, bending to loosen the straps on my sandals.

He was conflicted. That is, one eye was fixed on me, but his droopy one looked doubtful, while his muddy chin was thrust forward.

"My watch," I said. It was an Omega, a Christmas present from generous Dad, because I'd admired it on his wrist. I was not sure it was waterproof, but in any case did not want to submerge it.

"It'll get wet," Frank said, sounding hopeful. "Maybe we should go back."

"We've come this far," I said. "I can swim with one hand—backstroke. I'll keep my left arm out of the water."

The Boy Scouts, the summers as a lifeguard, and my love of the water had made me a good swimmer. I was not so sure about Frank.

"Can you make it across?"

"Sure," he said. He stepped out of his sandals and buckled the straps together and hung them around his neck, as I had done.

I walked along the bank of the creek, looking for a notch or a slope where I could lower myself to the water. Kicking along I saw broken clamshells and scuttling crabs and small squirming fish stranded in pockets and puddles in the mudbank.

"See you on the other side," I said, calling behind me, concentrating on entering the water, leaning into the cold creek and floating on my back. I paddled with one arm, holding my other arm—and wristwatch—above me. This awkward posture meant I swam slowly, but as I was on my back I was looking upward at the masses of clouds, gray and white, some like hanks and sinews of smoke, others like burst pillows, a bulging sky above me, the occasional shaft of sun heating my face. And there were warmer currents in the creek, too, where surface water on the marsh drained from the ditches, emptying into the creek.

This was pleasant, floating on my back, propelling myself with one sweeping hand, my face upturned to the busy clouds and the flashes of sun—and more, a marsh hawk drifting slowly, and a small white tern hovering, beating its wings, then dropping like a stone to splash into the creek and seize a surfacing fish.

I was in suspension in every sense. For the interlude of swimming across the creek I was held, outside time, as though in the cupped hand of the natural world, buoyant, weightless, in the bliss of forgetfulness, without a care, not thinking about school, or my future; purified by the water I was floating through, one-handed, in this odd swimming posture, smiling at my golden watch on my upraised arm, its metal catching the sun, its face unreadable, as though time had stopped.

I got to the far side of the creek and found a little dribbling channel, with a fallen chunk of embankment beside it, like a hassock of grass. I dragged myself to it and used it to step ashore and climb to the edge of the bank.

And that was when I remembered Frank. I looked across the black creek and saw him in the middle, his arms lifting and dropping. He was not swimming but submerged and slowly thrashing, as though pushing himself under. His slowness confused me—he looked casual, almost indifferent, making little effort, doing what I had done, but taking his time.

He was swimming like a playful child, with awkward and inefficient strokes, going nowhere. Now I could hear with his splashing, his gasps, spitting water, and while I watched he went under. He rose for a second to spit, then sank lower in the black water and bobbed up again, gagging.

"Are you all right?"

He did not reply at once. He was choking on the water he'd swallowed. Finally, not loud but a strangled, "No."

He slipped under without another sound, his white body seeming to dissolve as he sank beneath the surface. I could see him sinking, not paddling, not flailing, his arms out wide seeming to hug the depths of dark water, a stiffened body, patches of white flesh—white shoulder, white legs, white elbows—as though he'd been dismembered and his body parts thrown into the creek.

All this time I was also glancing at my watch, picking at the buckle of the strap, because I knew I'd have to jump in to rescue Frank but didn't want to get my lovely watch wet and risk ruining it.

But the next time I looked at the creek I saw a set of ripples where Frank had been and only a flutter, like a scrap of rag, of the whiteness of his body.

My whole being stiffened. I leaped from the bank and dived into the creek and swam fast, aware that I was plunging my watch again and again into the water, aiming toward the last glimpse I'd had of Frank, a faint stirring at the surface and to my astonishment, no struggle.

He was just visible in the black shadows of the water, a big white body perfectly still and slipping into darkness. I kicked and canted myself down and dived for him. When I snatched his arm, he turned and gripped my wrist, and I lifted him to the surface. He came alive, he gasped and spat and began to struggle.

As a lifeguard I had learned this to be the most dangerous moment of a rescue, the drowning person clutching the rescuer and clinging with a death grip, until neither of them can swim, endangering both of them and taking them under. So I twisted Frank around, pushing him away from me, and positioned myself to sling my arm across his chest. Then I had him flattened on his back and I was paddling with my free hand.

"Help me," I said. "Kick your legs."

He was weak and still gasping but he did as I suggested, and when he was stabilized and horizontal I stroked with more confidence, all the while reassuring him, the way you might cheer up a child, "We're doing fine—we're almost there—we're going to make it."

At the shallows of the shore I released him. He became an alarmed animal, he scrambled on all fours in the mud and then clawed his way up the embankment. At the top, where the grass was tangled with broken clamshells and tiny dead crabs and sprigs of kelp, he fell on his face and sobbed. He kept on sobbing—the word *keening* came to mind—until he exhausted himself, and he then knelt and got to his feet.

He was chalk white, the blood drained from his face and arms, only a slight redness like a rash at the edges of his ears. His eyes were pink and rabbity from being wide open underwater. He dripped, he was rigid, his T-shirt stuck to his body, his hands and legs bluish where they were not smeared with mud. He was not a man. He was a child, a big blue terrified boy.

"I thought you'd be able to make it," I said. "You can swim."

Frank's lips trembled. He said, "When I got to the middle, I had this weird feeling. That there was a big black hole under me—a bottomless hole—and I was being pulled into it. It scared me, it made me weak. And I was so heavy. The black water was sucking me under."

"You stopped swimming."

"I gave up." He blinked, wet lashes, pink eyes. His lips were livid. "I couldn't move."

It was panic—fear froze him, stiffened him, and this rigidity was sinking him.

I expected him to say, *You saved me,* or *Thanks,* but he looked at me with confusion, a trembling swamp creature—matted dripping hair and mud-smeared body and pink eyes. In a puzzled voice, he said, "What are you looking at?"

I was laughing, wagging my wrist. "My watch—it's still running—waterproof!"

"I lost my sandals," Frank said.

We walked in silence to the margin of the marsh, then into the dunes and along a path to the parking lot where there was a phone booth, a pay phone, next to the boarded-up changing room. Frank stood shivering while I made a collect call.

"Who is this?" Mother said, irked that she was being asked to pay for the call from a stranger.

"Cal," I said.

"Oh?"

"Someone wants to say hello."

As a lifeguard, first at Littleford Pond, then at a municipal swimming pool in Boston, I had saved three people—two young boys and a small girl—yanked them to safety, watched them cry afterward, and got thanked by their parents. None of the rescues were as dramatic as this one of Frank, who was gaping and bewildered and could not explain why he'd panicked in the middle of the creek. I was ashamed I'd hesitated, fearing that the water might kill my watch; but I was glad I was able to haul him out.

He only alluded to it once afterward. I guessed he was ashamed, regarding it as his failure, that he hadn't been able to get across the creek without me. And maybe there was in this silence an element of resentment for what I'd done, because the implication of his near drowning, and my rescue, was that it defined us as brothers—that his life had been in my hands; that I'd plucked him from the black water; that from that day onward he owed his life to me.

The one time he mentioned it, a few years later, we were having a drink, and out of the blue—no prologue, no reminder—he said, "It wasn't that big of a deal, really. You know, I think I could have made it across by myself."

4

LITTLE MISS MUFFAT

ONCE AT OUR HOUSE ON GULLY LANE, SOUNDING FRUS-trated, still in those long-ago years when we were students and still the Bad Angel brothers, Frank cried out, "Women!"

It was a weekend, and I was home trimming some trees that were overhanging the roof and clogging the gutters with dead leaves. I'd just put the ladder away in the garage when Frank drove in and slammed the car door much too hard, making a statement I didn't hear, in a complaining tone, then the shouted word.

"What about them?"

"They're all the same."

Any man who says that is afraid of women, or hates them: even in my early twenties I knew that. Frank pretended to be contemptuous but deep down was fearful and insecure where women were concerned. I didn't correct him. I was curious to know what he'd say next. He hesitated and in profile showed me the drawn-down doubting side of his face.

"You think Julie's different?"

Julie Muffat had been my girlfriend until about a month before this. We'd been together for about a year, long enough for her to begin making plans for after graduation. She'd assumed our romance would continue, but when I mentioned that I was going to travel out west, begin a career as a prospector—alone in the desert with my dirt bike and camping gear—she said, "What about me?"

I didn't have an answer to that, but to reassure her, I said, "I want us to go on being friends."

"Being friends" was not what she wanted to hear. It was too casual, too presumptuous, lacking in passion, and meant to her that our love affair was over. In our year of being together we'd found we were sexually compatible—that is, we knew how to satisfy each other, by taking turns; and I'd found that satisfying her was exciting for me. She said she was aroused by pleasing me. "I have supersensitive lips" was her smiling explanation.

Engrossed in our sexual relationship, we didn't have time for much else—our mutual passion consumed us. I was impatient for it and so was she. It would have been hard for me to think of any interlude when we had a long conversation about books or movies, or idled in a coffee shop, or played cards. Our relationship was primarily sexual, she was as hungry as I was, and we never quarreled. We wanted the same thing, and achieving it exhausted us to the point where we didn't look for more—at least, I didn't.

I was quietly making my own plans—my escape from Littleford, my adventure as a field geologist. I could not imagine going on a camping trip with Julie. The one time I mentioned it as a possibility, hiking the White Mountains—get a big tent, go camping, build a fire, fry some eggs—she laughed.

"Can you see me in a tent?"

That focused my mind: No, I couldn't.

"Like, where would we take a shower?"

"Never thought of that. No hot showers on camping trips."

"So can you blame me?"

"No. I get it."

This was an early indication that we didn't know each other very well. I told myself that splitting up was for the best, that we weren't meant for each other in the long run; that we were able to make each other happy but that it was time to go our separate ways, while remaining friends.

But my "Let's be friends" suggestion enraged Julie.

"After all I've done for you," she said, furiously. And she went on in this vein, as though she'd been working with me, earning points, building up credit; not glorying in our sexual adventures but pondering our future. I did not understand.

This dispute ended without being resolved, and a few days later, she became assertive and invited me to her apartment, as though for a jolly evening—a pizza, a six-pack of beer, and what we called wild monkey sex. After the pizza and beer, I was in her bed, waiting for her to finish taking a shower. With the torrent of water came another sound, an almost animal moan, struggling to breathe, choking, gasping, at times like a tuneless dirge, and at other times like a muffled scream.

When the water stopped, so did the eerie voice.

Julie slipped into bed, looking exhausted. I said, "What was that strange noise?"

"I was crying," she said. "I always cry in the shower. Don't you know that?"

I hadn't, I found it upsetting, and I was ashamed of not asking why or what was wrong. I needed to switch off the light and in the darkness conjure extravagant imagery from our past, to find the right mood to satisfy her.

"I'm trying to make a life—a career," I said in the morning. "It's all too uncertain to involve you. I'm going to Arizona. I'll be in the desert for weeks at a time—no showers, eating beans out of a can. Maybe when I manage to get some traction, we can hook up again."

"'Maybe' is a word I really hate."

There was more, most of it unpleasant, but it showed a side of Julie I hadn't seen before—the sour accusatory side, the rejected side, the surprisingly bitter side, from someone whom I'd known only as an eager lover. And perhaps that was why—because I had only seen her as my one-dimensional and agreeable lover and not someone with other concerns and ambitions.

I couldn't blame her. I had disappointed her hopes and wasted her time. She said I'd taken her for granted—and of course I had. There was her hurt pride, too. She quite rightly hated being rejected—she wanted to reject me. And within a few weeks she did just that. After our conversation about splitting up, I felt awful, I missed her, I wanted her old self back, and I missed our sex life acutely.

When I called her and asked if we could meet, Julie swore at me and banged the phone down. I called back the next day; she accused me of being abusive, and kept me on the phone, struggling to speak and sobbing. She said she was seeing a shrink, and that he told her that our break was too abrupt. His advice as a mental health professional was that she needed a proper farewell.

As before, we ate, we drank, she took a shower, and I heard her sobbing beneath the drone of water.

After that, I could not summon the usual magic, or any imagery, and we slept apart, on our backs, like two castaways on a raft.

Months later, near graduation, I was in the driveway at home tinkering with my dirt bike, the one I planned to use in the Arizona desert. Frank came out of the house carrying a cup of coffee and wandered over to where I was bleeding the master cylinder.

Studying me, he sipped from his cup a few times then said, "Going out?"

"If I can get these brakes fixed. And I might need new plugs. But it's too late to buy them—the stores are closed. I guess I can clean them."

As I prepared to pour new brake fluid into the reservoir, a fiddly job because I needed to keep air out of the line, Frank dragged a lawn chair to the edge of the driveway. He then sat, sticking his legs out, sipping his coffee. From his settled posture I could see that he was planning to sit there for a while, and I guessed he had something on his mind.

"Got a date?"

"Depends on this." I was pouring brake fluid. "And the plugs."

"So, it seems, you just . . ." Frank nodded his head as though to indicate inevitability. But because his face was divided into two distinct planes—one eye finding me, the other one on the bike, mouth half smirk, half frown—the effect of his nodding implied confusion. After a dramatic pause he finished his sentence. "Just make them wait, until you feel like showing up."

Aware that his tone was triumphant, I looked up at him as I finished with the fluid and started to tighten the bleeder bolt, turning my socket wrench slowly and liking the ticking of the ratchet, as though marking time.

Frank's face, the right half, was set in a frown, his gaze having drifted to the side in an impatient, disbelieving way. His half smirk on the other side did not indicate pleasure—it was not an appreciative smile but an expression of defiance.

He attempted a laugh, but this laughter was not mirthful; it was an apelike chatter of skepticism. Real laughter is a revealing sound, showing a moment of recognition—you know a person by their laugh, you understand them better when you see what they find humorous. Powerful people ration their laughter to remain enigmatic. The fact that Frank didn't offer a full-throated laugh meant—I supposed—that he was withholding his feelings. In the best of times he was a sour brooding presence, and so being with him was usually a solemn business.

Frank never told a joke. Jokes are revealing, too. If he made a wisecrack, it always had a note of cruelty in it. So not only did he not emit a genuine tinkle of laughter, he never attempted to make me laugh.

I was summing him up in his silence, as I moved from the brakes to the plugs, using the same socket wrench, enjoying the watch-winding sound of its clicking. And I was thinking: *Soon I will be far away from you, in a happier place, and out of your clammy shadow.*

Remembering what he'd said, *Just make them wait,* he was insinuating, with a grain of truth, that I was a presumptuous brute who took women for granted. I had not wanted to tell him that I didn't have a date; I hadn't wanted to confide anything to him.

"It's not a big deal."

"Nothing's a big deal with you, is it?"

I rocked back on my heels, realizing that just as I had guessed, his tone indicated he was looking for an argument, putting me on the defensive, pressing me in the way he was perhaps practicing to be a successful cross-examiner in a courtroom. He set his cup of coffee on my toolbox.

But I laughed at his ponderous manner, because all this was so trivial—my possible date, the imaginary waiting woman, my delay with the brakes and the gummed-up spark plugs, my greasy fingers.

"I feel you have something on your mind, Frank."

He hesitated for effect, setting his jaw at me, shutting one eye and swiveling the other at me, a piercing gaze he had practiced for a hostile witness.

"Cal, I've just seen one of your victims."

"Victims?" It was an unexpected word. "I don't know what you're talking about."

"Of course you don't. Because she's not a victim to you. She's just another disposable woman."

In his moralizing mode, Frank was plodding, long-winded, point-lessly deliberate. He picked up his coffee cup but didn't drink. He wagged it and then put it back on my toolbox. I could see that he was preparing to needle me, and, feeling that he was in the right, he would take his time doing so. What made this all more annoying was that I had extracted the spark plugs and saw they were fouled. I'd have to clean them and set the gap and screw them back, so that I could fire up my bike and ride away from him.

"Cut the shit, Frank. Tell me whatever it is you want to tell me."

He was unmoved until I got to my feet and picked up his coffee cup from my toolbox with my greasy fingers and set it on the driveway. My smearing his white cup with grease startled him more than if I'd slapped him. And he couldn't pick up the cup without dirtying his fingers.

"Julie Muffat," he said.

"Oh god."

"Your abusive phone calls. Your taking her for granted. Your string-ing her along. Inflicting emotional damage, and then abandoning her."

"Did she tell you this?" I said. "Because if she did, none of it is true. I ended it, but I was doing her a favor. I told her we have no future."

"You destroyed her."

"That's bull. You don't know what you're talking about." I had begun to pace, as he sat in the lawn chair, making it creak as he adjusted his posture. And then I remembered how months before he'd gotten out of his car in a huff and said, *Women!* and *They're all the same,* and I laughed, because he was hopeless where women were concerned and seldom managed to get a date.

My laughter alarmed him more than the grease-smeared coffee cup.

"Julie's a wreck," he said. "I'm talking suicidal ideation."

"You don't know what you're talking about," I said, but if this was true I had a lot to answer for. I had never heard the expression "suicidal ideation" before. "My question is, what makes you think any of this is your business?"

He didn't reply, he sat there staring, as though in condemnation, and then I thought, *He's interfering and trying to worry me because I'm trying to get my bike going, for the hot date he thinks I have, and all he has planned is a second cup of coffee and his law books.*

I turned my back on him and took my gap device out of my toolbox. I flipped it like a coin, and inserted it, setting the gap on each of the plugs. Frank folded his arms as I twisted the plugs back into the piston head and clipped the plug wires on.

"Wish me luck, Frank," I said, climbing onto the bike.

Just as he started to speak I stamped on the starter pedal and the engine roared. I revved it, drowning out whatever he was saying—he was mouthing something, with a furious face. Then I spun my back wheels on the gravel and sped away.

But Frank knew too much of Julie. I was sure he'd spoken to her—and why? He was a manipulator, but where women were concerned, inept. I guessed that Julie must have initiated a meeting, so a day or two later I swung by her house, instead of phoning her. I wanted to see the expression on her face when I asked her.

I surprised her, ringing her doorbell, at eight in the morning, when I knew she'd be getting ready to go to school.

The door opened to her shocked face. "You!"

The screen door separated us, the rusted screen blurring her features and making her seem like a vague memory.

"So you talked to Frank."

She made a knowing noise, a little snort, dismissing what I'd said. Averting her eyes, she plucked at the sleeves of her blouse and smoothed them, as though to show her indifference.

With a shrug, and in a casual tone, she said, "Didn't he tell you the rest?"

"He told me everything you said."

"Didn't he tell you what we did?"

At first I was confused, but when she laughed—a wicked little-girl laugh—I knew. She worked her tongue against her cheek, making an unambiguous bulge, then raised her hand to her mouth in an explicit pumping gesture.

I kicked the door and left, knowing that if I lingered I'd lose my temper and do something I would regret. Frank had portrayed her as my victim. But she had taken revenge on me, and Frank had played along. I didn't confront him; it was better to leave him in the dark.

Knowing about him and Julie Muffat made it easier for me to leave—not a simple departure, but, as soon as I graduated, turning my back on him and home.

5

THE RESCUE

F ROM THE EXPERIENCE OF THAT FIRST SWIFT DEPARTURE
I regarded travel ever after as a joyous form of rejection—
flight from the tedious known to the magical unknown. I had my wish
and was away, so far away, so pressed for time, making a living, that I
got the news from home in pulses—updates without much detail. In
those days before cell phones I'd see a phone booth and think, *I should
call home—I might not find another phone for days.* Because Frank was
usually the subject of the news, the pulses like headlines in his episodic
life, this suited me. I was in Arizona and New Mexico, in and out of
the desert, keeping in touch by pay phones at rural gas stations, or a
booth at a truck stop, feeding the phone with quarters, every headline
two-bits' worth of Frank.

Over the course of a year, Frank passed the bar exams (pulse), got a
job at a Boston law office (pulse), won a case that was mentioned in the
Globe (pulse), and brought home a very attractive young lady (pulse),
who became his fiancée (pulse)—"We're so happy for him."

I had left Littleford on my dirt bike and now was riding it through
the desert arroyos, scooping gravel in piled-up fragments of conglomerate
rock, and loving my freedom. I'd bought an old van in Phoenix, which
I lived in, testing the gravel each evening for gold flakes. I usually found
enough to pay my expenses, and now and then much more, enough to
upgrade my testing equipment.

What had seemed fanciful in Littleford was unremarkable in the desert, where prospectors were numerous. But because mineral exploration is necessarily secretive—there are no boasters among seasoned prospectors—they tended to stay out of view. And I, too, kept a low profile. Frank's behavior had taught me that I had to be secretive; and I liked the desert spaces for affording me freedom to hide. I was sustained in my solitude by thinking of gold seeking as romantic; by believing that I would only succeed in life by taking risks, and maybe suffering a little; by telling myself that what I was doing was not a job but a quest.

I implied to my mother that one of these days I might get lucky. But even as a young man in Littleford I regarded rich people as absurdities, childlike in their love of shiny things and more money than they'd ever need. The conundrum: Why do multimillionaires want more millions? In my heart I was not looking for wealth. The quest mattered more to me than a great strike, because I'd learned in my first year as a prospector that a strike and all that followed—staking a claim, setting up an operation on the site, digging and sluicing—tied me down. What I craved most of all were small regular finds of flakes, and enough money to do as I wished. My great discovery was: freedom is not expensive.

It was helpful when I called home and heard that Frank's news always crowded out my own. I would run out of quarters before I could indulge myself in incautious boasting. The pulses of Frank's updates were sequential—his triumphs as a lawyer, his romance with Whitney, his fiancée, soon to be his wife. Unlike mine, Frank's life seemed to have a plot.

The events in Frank's life were related, had consequences, bore fruit: because he won a big case, he became well known, and as a celebrated lawyer he attracted clients and made money, which impressed Whitney, inspiring her love—one thing building to another, my idea of a plot.

My life so far was plotless and wayward, filled with odd and sudden resumptions, stopping dead, starting all over again, a process of unrelated events that could be summed up by "And then . . . and then . . . and then . . ."—inconsequential, random, and anticlimactic, impossible to explain in a phone call home, and anyway, who cared?

In the beginning, I'd driven by the most direct route to Arizona, noted for its natural beauty and its veins and sprinklings of gold. I bought the van. I made discreet inquiries in Phoenix and found Little Domingo Wash, about an hour northwest of the city. I camped, I sifted, I sluiced; I saw that others had the same idea, so I drove to Vail and from there on back roads to Greaterville, following whispers of gold, finding very little, but loving the landscape, the shimmer of desert, the rosy pastels of rock cliffs, and that was ample compensation. Some days I simply rode my dirt bike through the washes, not bothering to pick up any gravel, just glad to be enclosed by such magnificence—the Santa Rita Foothills and the solitude of the blue slopes, pounding along a narrow game trail in a ravine, gripping my handlebars like a jackhammer.

And then . . . and then . . . and then . . . Still searching, I came to Quartzsite, in the desert west of Phoenix, down Route 95 to the La Paz Valley, the gulches and washes looking unexplored for being so rugged and so remote and almost impassable. In its grandeur, it looked like a foreign country, the foreign country being Mexico, about an hour away, just past Yuma.

All this time I was checking in at home, listening to Mother telling me Frank's news: he was getting married, he had a date for the wedding; the day itself came, the Littleford wedding of the year. But I couldn't make it, because at last I had news of my own, a dramatic event that kept me in Arizona.

Skidding into the declivity of an arroyo, I was greeted by a sight that promised gold: a certain contour seemed to guarantee that gold would be thrust to the surface whenever the rock bed bulged with a freshet of runoff. Distracted by that contour, I skidded, the skid sending me sideways, loosening gravel and small stones that tumbled after me. I brought myself to an ungainly halt at a low cliff and saw a man slumped like a big broken doll.

This corpse—I took it to be a dead man—lay half in shade, its legs protruding in sunlight, wearing lovely well-made boots. It was the boots, so unlikely and obvious here, that got my attention. And of course you think with such a sight that the body cannot possibly be dead, that it will spring to its feet and go on the attack. Something about the newness of the boots seemed to give the body life. It was a man, wearing blue jeans and a leather jacket, lying on his back, his head hidden in the shadow of the outcrop of rock. The other detail, besides the stylish boots, was his belt buckle—silver, cast in the shape of a scorpion.

In those days there were always Mexicans in the desert, border jumpers; but the border was largely unfenced and in most places unmarked. Mexicans came and went but stayed well away from the main roads. As long as they remained inconspicuous, keeping to the side roads and paths, they were not apprehended. There was no police presence in the desert, no border patrol. They came later, when the border was signposted.

In my traveling here I sometimes saw in the distance small groups of men and boys hiking single file through the desert, slipping past the stands of saguaro cactus on their way north. My instinct was to give them a wide berth, because hunger can transform a simple soul into desperate predator.

This was also why I was careful with this corpse—at least he was still as silent as a corpse.

"Hola!" I called out to the shadowy face beneath the protruding rock. He did not reply, but when I repeated it I saw his fingers move in a cramped tickling motion, and I knew he was alive.

I prodded his boot with the toe of my boot—his foot had life in it, it wagged back and forth. I said, "Are you all right?"

His arm was limp and unresponsive. I used it to lift him forward out of the shadow and propped him up. As I did so, he groaned, which I took to be a good sign. I gave him some water from my canteen. This roused him; he reached for the canteen to steady it.

"Thank you." His first words, and in English, which amazed me, because he was so Mexican looking—an old mustached man, jowly, creased features, heavy eyebrows, pushed-back hair, thick fingers; and the silver scorpion belt buckle.

I said, "Can you stand up?"

He struggled but could not get himself upright, so I rode back to my van and brought my tent and some food and water and made camp near him. He tasted some of the soup I heated up. He was dehydrated, so the salt and liquid was beneficial. But I couldn't move him. I covered him with a blanket against the chilly desert night, while I used my sleeping bag.

He was groggy in the morning, still groaning, but when I made coffee in the pot on my camp stove he said, "*Café*," and came awake.

I poured him a cup and peeled a banana for him, which he ate—and something in the way he ate, nibbling the banana, dabbing his lips with his fingers, seemed like delicacy, the manners of a man of refinement. He thanked me again in a courtly way, an odd and unexpected politeness among the wildly tumbled boulders of the canyon.

"My name is Cal."

"Carlos," he said, raising his hand and tapping his fingers in acknowledgment against mine.

"You speak English."

"Enough." He nodded. He was still sipping the coffee. "My house is in Phoenix. My son is there. I am going to see him. I had business over the border, so I came here with a"—he hesitated—"*mal tipo*."

"A coyote?"

"A *cholo*. He took my money. He left me here to die."

"How much money did he get?"

"All." He put his coffee down and weighed an invisible amount with his cupped hands.

"You're going to be okay."

"*Sin valor*," he said, still with his weighing hands. "Money is worthless here in the desert."

"That's true."

He peered at me, and he seemed moved as he said, "You saved me."

My plans changed. Carlos became my burden, my mission, my project. After another day, he was strong enough to ride behind me on my bike. I took him to my van and drove him out of the desert to Phoenix. On the way I asked him what his business was. He shrugged, he made gestures, being noncommittal, and so I changed the subject. But when we got to his house in Phoenix I saw that whatever business he was in was profitable. The house, set inside a high walled compound in an outer suburb, was a hacienda-style mansion—pillars and porticoes, red tiled roofs, statuary on its lawn, a fountain in front, a tough-looking man in a sentry box at the driveway entrance, though the man lost his look of toughness when he saw my passenger.

"Don Carlos!" he said, and the gate slid sideways as he snatched up his phone.

We were greeted by a young man about my age, who cried out when he saw him. They spoke in Spanish but Carlos gestured to me, and the son rushed to me and hugged me, thanking me.

He was Paco, and still with his arm around my shoulder, he called out to some people watching from the porch—servants, I guessed—to tell them what I'd done. They whooped and applauded.

"I was supposed to meet my father somewhere on the interstate," Paco said. "The call never came. I was so worried." He gestured to a woman on the porch and said, "A drink. Then we eat."

The old man whom I now knew as Don Carlos said something rapidly in Spanish.

"He says to me, 'You have a brother now.'"

I was shown to a guesthouse and spent the afternoon sitting by the swimming pool, while father and son conferred. That night, eating with them, tipsy on mezcal, and smiling, I thought: *This is what it means to have a real brother.*

I called home the next day. I got Frank's news, I listened, I said I was fine. But there was no way I could explain what had happened in the desert, or how I had become attached to this Mexican family in Phoenix; that I had my own casita on their property; that I was being treated with great generosity by a family grateful to me for my having rescued the old man, Don Carlos. Saving his life, I had earned their trust.

Confident of their discretion, I told Don Carlos and Paco of my quest for gold in the washes and gulches of the desert.

Paco loved hearing this. He said, "We can help you."

He said he would introduce me to Gustavo. Gustavo knew the likely places to find gold, the places to avoid; Gustavo knew the desert well. But Paco added, "It is hard work—and there is not much gold to be found. If there was more, we would be looking ourselves."

In my week with them—they insisted I stay, though I wanted to return to the ravines—I realized that I'd found my way into a family that was wealthy, and obviously powerful. Don Carlos was the patriarch. I saw no evidence of his wife. Paco—Francisco—had a wife, Sylvina, who appeared at mealtime, not to eat but to supervise the food, directing the servants and attending to the old man. Small children lingered in the doorway to the dining room but they ate separately, an old-fashioned arrangement that left us free to talk.

"I wish I could do what you're doing," Paco said to me. "It's not the gold, but what a wonderful way to live, under the sky. You're free in the desert."

"I found something more precious than gold," I said, and I raised my glass to the old man, who replied with feeling in Spanish.

Paco said, "What he says is true. We can never repay you, but we can help you."

After dinner, we had coffee and mezcal on the porch—a warm Arizona night—and while we sat, Paco's wife came out to say that a man had arrived and was in the next room.

"He is someone I want you to meet," Paco said.

He beckoned a man from the doorway. He was tall, broad shouldered, wearing a leather vest over a red shirt, his black hair slicked back, with a fierce mustache and jeans and cowboy boots of crocodile hide, and carrying a briefcase. An impressive entrance. But what struck me was his humble demeanor—bowing to Don Carlos, deferential to Paco, nodding politely to me, and not taking a seat until Paco indicated that he should sit—next to me.

"This is Gustavo. You can trust him. He doesn't speak English, but I can translate."

Gustavo brought out of his briefcase a large format atlas—*Arizona Atlas*. He needed both hands to hold it, and when he opened it I saw topographical maps of the state on a larger scale than the ones I'd been using. He spread it on the coffee table and smoothed it, speaking in Spanish to Paco.

"He knows what you're looking for," Paco said. "And he knows the desert. He will show you the best places for gold."

For the next hour or so, Gustavo indicated on the pages of the atlas the likeliest locations—gullies, washes, dry creek beds; and Paco, translating, gave me a running commentary on how I could access these places, the roads, the tracks, noting the obstacles, how to remain hidden, where to camp. "You need to be careful."

"What—snakes, scorpions, javelinas, spiders, Gila monsters?"

"They belong there—you need to respect them," he said. "There is only one serious danger in the desert."

"What's that?"

"Other people."

Paco motioned to Gustavo and mumbled a word I couldn't quite catch, though it sounded like *cuete*. Gustavo then took a cloth bundle from the briefcase and handed it to Paco, who untied it, revealing a leather holster. Paco pulled a small flat-sided pistol from it.

"My father wants to give this to you. It's a Colt, .32 caliber. Very smooth, you see. With the safety on you can keep it in your pocket without the holster."

He handed it to me. I had owned a .22 rifle and, as a Boy Scout, had gone shooting at a rifle range with Melvin Yurick to earn a merit badge. But I had never held a pistol. The grips were wood, a small medallion of the Colt horse rearing on the side, the metal bluish and lethal looking.

"You saved my father's life," Paco said. "This pistol might save your life."

With the pistol in my lap, and a drink in my hand, and being attended to by the smiling servants, as Don Carlos and Paco spoke in whispers to Gustavo, I thought: *I'm lucky, I'm happy, I have friends who wish me well.* This was what a family should be, Paco like a true brother. And when I thought of my own family they seemed distant and insubstantial, Frank unfriendly and unreliable—that business with Julie still rankled. I was loved by my mother, but what I felt here with this family, whose name I didn't know, was something I had never experienced before—benevolence.

It was easy for me to call home from here—I had a phone in my casita. Mother answered and as usual she was pleasant, but she became flustered when I asked, "What's new?" She changed the subject to the weather, she did not mention Frank. I knew from experience that no news of Frank was a conspicuous omission; that itself was news.

"And you, Cal?"

I thought: *Camping near Quartzsite I found an old Mexican man who'd been robbed and left to die. I nursed him back to health and took him to Phoenix, where he and his son live in splendor. Grateful to me for saving his father, I was welcomed to the family and told the best places to find gold. I was treated to great meals and given a pistol. I now have friends, protectors, and benefactors. I could not have been more fortunate.*

But something in Mother's silence told me all was not well with Frank, and my good news would be a distraction, possibly hurtful to Frank.

"I'm fine," I said. "No complaints." And Mother seemed grateful that I didn't go into detail.

6

FREE GOLD

RELUCTANT FOR ME TO GO, PACO DELAYED MY DEPARTURE, saying that his father wanted to give me a ceremony of farewell, a *despedida*. This was a whole evening of eating, toasting each other with gulps of mezcal, and grateful speeches. The old man, Don Carlos, had not said much in the week I stayed in their walled compound, but often I saw him eyeing me and nodding, and he touched my shoulder in a fatherly way, murmuring his thanks for having saved him.

"*Padrino*," he said and put his hand on his heart.

"Godfather," Paco said. "Your *compadre*—your *compa*."

I took it to mean he would be my benefactor, and I thanked him, lifting my shirt, to show him the pistol in its holster on my belt.

On this last night after the *despedida*, Don Carlos took a small pouch from his pocket and presented it to me. He urged me to open it. In the pouch was a gold nugget the size of a kidney bean but as rough as a fragment of gravel.

"*Un imán*," he said and queried his son with a frown.

"A magnet," Paco said. "It will attract more gold for you. Keep it for luck."

I thanked him and said, "I'm leaving tomorrow very early—don't get up. I'll be as quiet as I can."

"We'll see you off," Paco said. And then Don Carlos motioned for me to listen. He spoke in Spanish, Paco translating.

"My father wants to tell you something important, and he doesn't trust his English," Paco said, as the old man muttered. "He is grateful that you saved his life—and I am grateful, too, my friend. But you need to know that he was not stranded there in the desert because of disgrace. He was left to die because of his trust. It was his brother, Ramón, who abandoned him there. Ramón is in the same business as us, and we felt there was enough supply and enough outlets for both Ramón's people and us. But Ramón didn't see it that way. He wanted to frighten his brother—Ramón is older and greedier and ungrateful. If it were not for you, my father would have died."

Paco stopped talking, the old man was sighing. Finally the old man stood before me and raised a warning finger.

"He is reciting a proverb," Paco said. "A Mexican saying, *Confiá en tu amigo como harías con tu peor enemigo*."

I shrugged, appealing to him to translate.

"We say, 'Trust your best friend as you would your worst enemy.' But my father says, 'Trust your brother as you would your worst enemy.'"

Then Don Carlos spoke to him, as though reminding him of something he'd forgotten.

"Yes," Paco said. "We want to thank you for something else. All the time you've been here you have been polite. You have not asked any questions. We appreciate that. You have earned my father's trust. But if you need help, know this—you will always be under the protection of la familia Zorrilla."

He waited a beat when he said it, as though to gauge whether I would recognize it, and smiled when I didn't react. How they made a living, how they found the money to build this hacienda, how he'd come to be betrayed and robbed in the desert by his brother, he did not say; but both father and son were grateful that I hadn't asked.

Paco put his finger to his lips. "Our secret, hermano."

"*Un fuerte abrazo,*" the old man said, raising his arms.

They took turns hugging me, and the next morning at six the whole household was up, my breakfast of eggs and beans and ham on the table, a basket of food for me to take on my trip, and after I finished, more hugs, more protestations of gratitude.

It was only when I left, steering my van through the gated archway in the perimeter wall, that I realized that for eight days I had not been outside the perimeter wall. The wall was ten feet high, its top trimmed with spikes, the gate of heavy wood planks sliding on a rail that shut with a thud as soon as I passed through—a fortified compound.

Following Gustavo's advice and using his notations on the topographical map in the *Arizona Atlas* he'd given me, I returned to the Quartzsite area, but this time down a narrow track to the Plomosa Mountains, a spot he'd circled with his pen, Ghost Gulch, beneath an immensity of cracked and steep-sided rock, shown on the map as Black Mesa, an arrow to the southwest, Castle Dome Peak, his scribble in the margin of the map, *Oro*.

Gold had recently been found in the vicinity, he'd said, and that's why prospectors had begun to gather there—I saw tire tracks and diggings of previous searchers. But he emphasized that this was the gateway to the gold fields, that I would need to go farther. In the summer floods and freshets the gold flakes and nuggets migrated deeper into the canyons and down the washes. I'd need to ride my dirt bike five miles into the narrowness of Ghost Gulch, and perhaps continue on foot another mile along the creek bed of tumbled boulders, climbing the cliffs and traversing to where the seasonal water deposited the scraps of gold.

I knew this process in theory from my geology studies in a classroom; Gustavo knew it as a tough man in boots, hiking the hills, crossing this rocky desert from Mexico, observing the movements of prospectors, hearing their whispers.

"Don't hurry," he'd said through Paco. "Don't let anyone see you. Don't run out of water."

It took me a week to pick my way through the gulch and its rocky obstacles, camping on the way in the fissures of its cliffs, to reach the sprawl of rough stones and the heaped ribs of gravel the sudden summer floods had left here—familiar water-shaped forms in a place where there was now no water, an arid inland sea in which I was drifting in the heat.

At my last camp I calculated how much water I'd need to last me until I was able to walk back to where I'd left my dirt bike and resupply myself from my van. Four days, I figured—not much. But I'd work in relays, keeping this spot as my permanent camp and fetching water whenever I needed it.

At first, weary in the September heat, I saw nothing but broken rock. And then, in the stillness, as my eyes became accustomed to the glare and the black shadows in the contours of the gulch, and the desert beyond it, I saw a ground squirrel, flicking its tail, querying my presence there. And in time other creatures—mice, kangaroo rats, lizards and snakes, and one day, slashed by a blade of sunshine, a fox. They were my inspiration: if I was careful and vigilant and kept close to the ground, I could thrive in the shadows here like them. I regarded them as my companions.

Out of touch, on my own, surrounded by fractured rock, and scrub and sand, in a valley as hot and bleak as a crucible, I began to understand who I was and what I wanted. No one interrupted me or asked me questions. I lived without pretension. I was an animal in a purified state of utter solitude. Even if I found no gold I would have the satisfaction that I'd found contentment. There was no shadow of Frank here—he was far away and very small.

The purification was not an illusion. This desert had no smell, it was scorched and simplified. I had the sense that it had been cleansed by the heat and light. So my food tasted better, my senses were sharpened, I felt more alive, and along with those many small creatures—the mice, the lizards, the snakes—I was one large creature moving slowly among the boulders, clawing in the gravel for gold—placer gold—in the old streambeds.

My equipment was primitive but efficient—a dry washer for sifting gravel, and a basic panning kit—pan, rock hammer, hand shovel, whisk broom, tweezers, sniffer bottle. There wasn't enough water available for proper panning, so I concentrated on my dry washer, screening dust and pebbles by gravity separation, looking for gold flakes or nuggets in the hopper.

What mattered most was that I was fully occupied, wholly engaged in my progress through the ravines. I may have called it a search for gold, but that was a pretext for learning how to live as a desert solitaire.

I knew the scientific name for every rock and blade of stone, but living among them, sitting on them, cracking them with my hammer, the names were flat and featureless and robbed my rocky habitat of meaning. I gloried in the colors and shapes, in the sky the plumes of cloud wisp shadowing and tinting the galleries. The rocks were tightly folded and heterogenous. My studies did not help by reminding me they were quartzofeldspathic.

The gneiss and schist glittering before me were hosts of gold. Not much of it maybe, "low tonnage," a serious extractive company might say, but high grade and enough for me. I saw pyrite, and on the surface of the pseudomorph, blebs of metallic gold in the small cavities in its surface we called vugs. In the old dry streambeds I found gold-bearing gravel, gold particles that had been liberated from the pyrite during oxidation: gold from the veins of the pyrite—epithermal veins. Hacking with my hammer I found grains and inclusions of gold in their chunks of galena. The placer deposits were full of gold-rich galena—brittle and blocky and crystalline.

My studies had specific names for what I saw—silicic rocks, basalt, andesite, rhyolite. And sandstone, limestone, and shale in the sedimentary rock. But I preferred to see them as an aspect of my nesting place— slabs of gray or greenish gray, or limey, or maroon phyllites, as ashflow tuffs or tuffaceous sandstone, fine textured and foliated. And I recognized that from here at Plomosa to Castle Dome I was in the presence of gold, floating because of its high specific gravity—free gold.

How did Gustavo and the Zorrilla family know this was gold country? Obviously they sent their own prospectors out in search of gold, or bought it from freelancers, who eluded the big mining operations in the area and the recognized claims. These men burrowed into the rockfalls and scavenged in the gravel and came away with buckets that were sifted for spoonfuls of gold, the blebs and nuggets and flakes and dust.

Instead of science I saw the subtlety of layered rock faces, the glitter or crystal, some of the stone as vital-seeming as flesh, veined like the back of my hand. The beauty of this desert place—its purple and ochre spires, the grandeur of the setting—was appropriate for gold.

I gathered small quantities and kept on the move, resupplying with trips to my van, and remaining hidden. I found more than I expected, and I seldom went a few days without turning up something lovely, even if it was only a scattering of flakes, patterned like glorious fish scales. I'd pick them up by wetting my fingertip and tapping the flakes into my crucible to heat them into a plump gold bead.

Three months of this, and I thought, *I can't imagine ever growing tired of prospecting.* Finding gold was my incentive to continue, and the days when I found nothing were a challenge to go farther and dig deeper. In my ninth week I had penetrated beyond Plomosa to the orangey niches of Castle Dome.

By then I'd traveled so far in the desert I was nearer the direct road to Quartzsite, its provisions and its pay phones. I had called home a few more times, but Mother had deflected my questions. That evasion put me on the alert, since the rarity of a no-news call seemed to me in itself newsworthy.

The next time, when I called from Quartzsite, Mother said, "I think Frank wants a word."

"Fidge," he said. "How you doing?" And without waiting for an answer, he went on, "I want to take you to Mexico—Acapulco. You deserve a vacation."

What I'd been doing I did not regard as work. I thought of it as a quest, every day a new challenge and often the reward of enough dust and flakes to melt into a bead of gold.

But Frank said, "Hey, do yourself a favor," and he spoke with such urgency I found myself agreeing—yes, I was near Mexico now; yes, I could fly from Phoenix; yes, Acapulco might be fun.

He gave me a date—a week away—and said, "I'll have a ticket waiting for you."

When I drove back to my camp, I thought: *Maybe a different Frank.* And certainly a different me: *I have some stories for him.*

As usual with Frank, the reality was more complicated than his seemingly straightforward offer of an Acapulco holiday. Frank met my plane and took me to the hotel, where we shared the same room. It became clear that Frank was there as an attendee at an event at this Mexican resort, sponsored by a large law firm that Frank's Littleford law practice partnered with on the personal injury cases that had become Frank's specialty.

"So what's this, a kind of convention?"

"Not for you—you're here for fun."

I smiled because generous Frank was such a rarity. But here I was in a fancy hotel by the sea. Then I remembered.

"By the way, how's Whitney?" I asked, because he hadn't mentioned her. He first turned away, in profile, losing his smile, showing me the droopy side of his face. Then, as though to confuse me, he looked at me, with his off-center gaze and two distinct expressions, his whole happy-sad face.

"Long story!"

But he said no more. We went to eat at a vast buffet, chafing dishes of fish soup and Mexican stews, platters of crabs' legs and fat shrimp, bowls of salads and fruit, and all the food I'd dreamed of at my camp. The cold beer itself was a novelty, the fresh bread like a delicacy. After my monastic existence in the desert I was overwhelmed, and with the unlimited mezcal and tequila I was drunk most nights. Unused to such feasting, I exhausted myself and turned in early. I swam in the resort pool in the mornings when Frank was at meetings, and some days I dozed in a hammock at the beach.

I had not thought I needed a vacation, and perhaps I really didn't, but the routine of the resort, the eating, the drinking, the mariachi music, the marine sunlight, and Frank's talk of life in Littleford, exhausted me. So the long weekend, Thursday to Monday, was like a necessary cure for its own excesses. I had arrived in good shape, but in the days at the resort I gorged and lazed, and needed to recover from overdoing it. I looked forward to the austere simplicity of my camp in the desert.

At the banquet on the last night, a man sidled up to Frank, and from the way the man grinned and growled, from his teetering posture alone, I knew he was drunk. But I was half drunk, so I smiled back at him.

"That your spouse, Frank?"

"My brother," Frank said, and the man became polite, chastened, and made respectful by *brother,* such a powerful word.

On the way to the airport the next day, sharing a taxi, I said, "This was really generous of you, Frank. I had a great time. I'm not used to such extravagance."

"I thought it would do you good."

That touched me—tenderness from someone who'd been so mean to me at times. I said, "I wish there was a way I could repay you."

He said nothing, half his face was waxen and complacent, the other half reflective. When he was pondering an answer I always seemed to hear a whir, as of wheels spinning in his head, perhaps suggested by his way of humming when he was thinking hard.

"As a matter of fact," he began, and nodded. "That gold you spoke about . . ."

I'd mentioned casually finding placer gold in the old dry streambeds, but had superstitiously understated my success. And though he'd been drinking at the time and had merely shrugged, my statement had registered. He clutched his face, drawing the two different sides together, creating a single expression that might have been despair.

"I could use a few bucks," he said and honked softly. He became tearful. "Whitney dumped me."

By then I'd paid the taxi, we were standing in the sunshine, among tall cabbage palms and an embankment of sprawling nopal cactus in front of the Acapulco Airport. In this tropical setting, with hibiscus and bougainvillea, and elephant-eared monastera vines spilling out of planters, Frank looked grief-stricken, the bright flowers and the abundant sunshine making it worse, the glory of the scene seeming to mock his bleak mood.

I said, "Of course."

"Fidge," he said. He gagged a little. "I'm staring into an abyss."

He hugged me, and steadying him I could feel how thin he was, how insubstantial, the bones beneath his loose clothes. We'd been sharing the same bedroom, yet I had not noticed. Now, touching him, I knew he was fragile, and I was also aware of my strength, from my months of physical labor.

What Frank dreaded most in life, even as a boy, and keenly as a man, was failure. He was physically altered by Whitney leaving him— and what made it humiliating was that he'd only been married a few months. He was smaller and frailer and damaged, and I was ashamed of not having seen it earlier. My offer of money strengthened him a little, at least calmed him and made him seem hopeful.

"How much are we talking about?"

"Any amount," he said in a tremulous voice.

"Five," I said. "Ten?"

"Ten would be incredible. I'll pay you back. Whitney has all my stuff. I've got nothing. I'm living in a tiny apartment in a three-decker in Winterville. Half the time the heating doesn't work. Whitney got the house in Littleford, and the car and the dog, and she's claiming mental cruelty and demanding alimony."

He was still talking, and this was already more than I wanted to know. To interrupt him, I said, "If I get a good price for my gold, I might be able to raise fifteen."

"Oh my god," Frank said, and hugged me again, and I thought: *There goes the spectrometer I was saving for, and the new suspension for my van.* Frank's ribs were like a warm basket under his damp shirt.

"This Acapulco thing has been great," I said. "You've been really generous."

I told him I'd need to sell my gold, and that I'd be in touch.

When I got back to Phoenix I called Paco Zorrilla and asked him if was interested in buying my gold. I'd heard of the rigged scales of some gold dealers, and the fluctuations of the gold price. I knew that the Zorrillas would be fair.

"The magnet worked!" Paco said.

Paco met me at a warehouse outside Phoenix and apologized for not inviting me to the house. But he'd come prepared, with a scale and tweezers and magnifying glasses and glass containers. We worked inside my van, with the curtains drawn.

"This is good," he said, unscrewing the cap of my hoard and poking at the gold, flakes and nuggets, and jiggling the container, making the gold chuckle. He wore an expression of hunger, as though he was about to raise the cup to his mouth and swallow it all. He growled, "*Oro.*"

He shook the gold fragments onto the scale, a small cluster at a time, making notes on a pad, and sliding the gold into a new jar on a chute of folded paper. When he was done weighing it, he tapped at his calculator. "Twenty-two thousand and seven something—call it twenty-three."

I mentally subtracted Frank's fifteen thousand from that and gave myself eight, as I watched Paco unsnapping rubber bands from small stacks of bills. He handed over the money, and we hugged.

Before I left Phoenix to go back to my desert camp, I visited a bank and opened an account and arranged a wire transfer to Frank's account. Because I had cash I was able to do it that very day. Giving him the money he needed somehow squared things. I was energized by giving money away—especially giving it to Frank, who was desperate. It was a good feeling, akin to power, bestowing it on him, something life-enhancing and mood improving. It reminded me of how long ago I'd rescued him in the black creek and given him life.

That act of mercy completed, I drove back to Quartzsite and bought provisions and had the ball joints in my van replaced, then headed into the desert. I camped nearer Castle Dome this time and spent the next five months prospecting, until the intense heat of early summer made the days unbearable. I suspended work, drove to California, and camped by the beach. By then I had enough gold to melt to an ingot, but instead of making a cast bar I made a mold and created a gold egg, the size of a small hen's egg, twenty troy ounces of free gold.

7

TOWER HOUSE

ARRIVING BACK IN LITTLEFORD AFTER MY LONG AB-
sence, having achieved some success in my prospecting,
and pleased with myself, I felt worthy to be welcomed home. In the
glow of this good mood, I was reminded of how substantial a house it
was, as though seeing it for the first time.

Our well-known house, which locals called Tower House, was a Vic-
torian beauty, at the top of a long slope of a grassy embankment on
Gully Lane, near the center of town. It boasted a tower built against it
on the right-hand side, an octagon like an oversize organ pipe rising to
a turret, with a dunce cap roof of blue tiles. The tower room had been
Dad's study, where he sat and smoked his pipe and looked across roof-
tops to the river.

Cedar shingles, weathered silvery gray, covered all sides, with assertive gables and protruding eyebrows over the upper windows of the
façade, a wide porch or veranda across the front, which you approached
by climbing up from the street on fieldstone (metamorphic and igneous) steps. On a late afternoon such as today, the last of the light was
caught in the teasing flaws of the windowpanes of the tower and seemed
to wink in the bubbles and inclusions of the old handmade glass.

People glanced at the house as they passed and said, "Look." It was
admired in town for its classic features and its air of welcome—that big
elegant porch, the asymmetrical façade like Frank's crooked smile. Today I saw that it needed some repairs: gutters to be cleaned, the peeling

white trim to be scraped and painted, the black shutters framing every window to be rehung. The weather vane had to be balanced—a bronze arrow revolving on the peak of the turret slumped a little, and the lightning rods, adorned with glass balls skewed through the middle of the shaft, on the roof ridges, were rusted.

But even with its bruised nobility, it was home, and after my spell in the desert, I was glad to be here.

I'd been summoned home by Mother. I thought it was my gold. People talk of stimulants and intoxicants and drugs, injecting them, smoking and swallowing them, but the greatest stimulant I know is gold. As a geologist, I'm objective, but experience has told me that the very mention of it—the single word—has the effect of transfixing a listener. Gold fever is not just a prospector's term, it is the human condition.

The price of gold is fixed every day, and it fluctuates, but we know to a tenth of a penny what a troy ounce of gold is worth. It sometimes declines sharply in value, but that makes no difference to the average person, who believes it is vastly more valuable than the market decrees. Gold seems like a magic substance that goes on growing, becoming scarcer and more precious. It is warm, it hums—you can touch it, you can fondle it, and display it and cuddle it. You can chunk it in your palm. It is visible wealth.

My success in finding gold was talked about in Littleford—Frank must have discussed it at length with Mother, because she told me how proud she was of me, that it was a satisfaction to her to see that her example to me of hard work had paid off. This was her way of taking credit, but it was innocent and admiring, and I was glad I'd given her some pleasure.

My gold finding gave her an idea. What if she arranged to have my name put on the title deed to her home, Tower House? It would serve two purposes. I was living like a gypsy (so she said), so I'd have a base in my hometown that I could call my own. And it would be a help to her, because I could see to repairs and other expenses.

I said, "Wouldn't it make more sense to put Frank's name on the deed? After all, he's actually living in the house."

Behind on his alimony, Frank had moved from the three-decker in

Winterville and was in his old room here. Even with my loan of the fifteen thousand as a possible down payment, he hadn't found a place to buy.

"I can't do that to him," Mother said. "He wouldn't be able to afford the taxes."

"You want me to pay your taxes?"

"It's your house. They'd be your taxes."

"You're giving me the house?"

"Yes, but I'll go on living in it. When I go to my reward, you can live in it."

I tried to find a problem with this, but it seemed generous and helpful. Mother was bequeathing the house to me in advance. She would live rent-free, as my tenant. And Frank was welcome to stay until he found a place of his own. I would pay all taxes and utilities. Meanwhile, the house would appreciate in value.

"Have you mentioned this to Frank?"

"Yes. He's very excited about it —he's pleased for you."

"That you're giving the house to me and not to him?"

"It's for the best. He'll go on living here until something opens up for him and Whitney leaves him alone. He says he wants to talk to you about it."

He wants to talk to you about it prepared me for one of Frank's long-winded stories. They were attention-seeking, as all monologues seem to be, but more than that—especially in Frank's case—they were a kind of indirection, misleading me, or boring me, to the point where I lost the plot, Frank saying, *So what do you think—good idea, right?* and I'd say *Oh, yes,* out of a dizzying sense that I could not stand to hear another word. And then I'd realize that I'd just agreed to some cockamamie idea that he had masked with his monologue.

"Maybe we should get a lawyer, Ma."

"Frank's a lawyer."

"I mean an impartial one."

"Cal, this is a simple transfer of ownership. It's not necessary to involve anyone else."

She seemed offended that I'd raised this question, as though I doubted Frank's motives, not trusting him to do the right thing. And, of course, knowing Frank, I had trouble trusting him.

"Besides," Mother said, "Frank has power of attorney for all my affairs."

I said okay, and Mother convened what she called "a house meeting" a few days later. I had left my prospecting in suspension when she summoned me. Her sudden message, its urgency, suggested to me there was a crisis I needed to help with. But it seemed it was the house, my name on the deed that was needed, nothing more.

Frank looked haggard, an effect of his humiliating and costly divorce. But instead of talking about that, or Whitney, who had just given birth to a son—news to me—he launched into a long story about the extraction of a wisdom tooth. He pulled a clear plastic pouch from his pocket and showed me the discolored and still somewhat bloodstained tooth: "Go ahead, hold it—look at that root."

I took the pouch; the tooth reminded me of a small water-smoothed fragment of basalt tinted by proximity to red sandstone.

"Not like a normal pronged root—it's called a fused root," Frank said. "Now consider that lower portion left in a person's gum after it's been broken off during an extraction. Imagine the damage. I had a case—great case. Dentist tells the patient, 'Hey, we got the tooth, but the root was attached to the jawbone, but you'll be fine.' Patient goes home and wakes up that night in pain, but what does he get when he calls the dentist the next day?"

"I have no idea, Frank."

"He got a hand job—sorry, Ma, but it was the truth," Frank said. "And then he did the right thing. He called me."

"So what was the problem?" I said, handing him back his tooth.

"Before I could insert myself he opted for more oral surgery. Result—extensive oral nerve damage, chronic pain, a fractured jaw, memory loss, migraines, permanent loss of taste, fear, anxiety and depression." He bounced the tooth in his open palm. "Oh, yes, and our old friend, suicidal ideation."

"I take it this was one of your cases."

"Big case, but it was a referral, so I had to split the payout with about ten senior partners. On the other hand, there was an instructive take-away for me, which is why I'm telling you this story."

"I'm guessing the takeaway was related to your participation."

"Bingo. Ever stand in a running brook and look down and see the stones in the bottom?"

"All the time, Frank."

He leaned at me, turning so that I was presented with the drama of his droopy eye and dragged-down mouth. "I looked into the rushing water and saw clearly the right stone in the bottom—and it represented malpractice, the liability of the dentist. Listen, what if I hadn't seen to the heart of this, and the guy's underlying comorbidities. . . . ?"

Words are sometimes blunt instruments. I stopped listening, my head hurt, my eyes ached as they do when someone is monologuing, directing the unrelenting spiel at my eyeballs. I nodded, I became breathless with impatience, and finally I stood up and backed away and holding my hands up as though fending him off, I said, "I get it, I get it."

"Here's the deal," he said, and he began wagging a finger at me. He droned on that I had to consider his importance to this wisdom tooth personal injury case in relation to the title deed of Mother's house. Yes, I was a big earner at the moment as a gold seeker, but what would happen if the day came when I was not flush? What then—when I could not afford the upkeep, that in the event of my defaulting on the property taxes ("God forbid") someone tripped and fell on the fieldstone steps in front and sued the owner? He'd known many cases where the lien on such a house bankrupted the owner, and the house ended up sold or repossessed by the bank.

My head hurt, my eyes burned. I said, "Please, Frank, what's the answer?"

"I cosign the deed."

"That makes you part owner," I said.

"That makes me your insurance. In case something goes wrong."

"It seems to me a little—what?—presumptuous."

"I owe you, Fidge. You've been really helpful to me. That's why I'm doing this."

"Signing the deed?"

"Yes. I'm doing you a favor."

Mother had been listening, squinting to understand, said, "Frank's doing you a favor."

And she saw this offer of Frank cosigning the deed as something unifying. In the past she'd often spoken of the house as a meeting place for us, after she passed away. She'd said, *I want you to think of the house as somewhere you can gather with your loved ones. Have parties and meals together. Celebrate Christmas. Enjoy your families. It would be a way of remembering me.*

Think of it as a clubhouse, she was saying.

Frank, still toying with his extracted wisdom tooth, said, "Cases like that broken root—if I hadn't had to share, I'd be shitting money—sorry, Ma, but it's the truth. I've got plenty of prospects. I'll be back on my feet soon. I have lots of cases lined up. But at the moment I'm hurting."

"That's why I'm giving the house to Cal," Mother said. "He'll be my landlord."

"Fidge deserves the house," Frank said. "He needs an anchor." He cocked his head at me, fixing me with his good eye. "But will he be able to maintain it in the years ahead?"

"I'm pretty sure I can," I said, though not expecting this question I sounded somewhat uncertain.

Frank said, "Back when Whitney and I owned a house together— before the, um, split"—he gulped and paused to regain his composure. Then he swallowed and started again. "Now and then, one of my friends, or their kids, would ask whether they could stay at the house. 'Could we just crash there for a week?' I'd say, 'I'm glad you used that word 'crash,' because this house is worth five hundred kay. It's as though I have a Rolls-Royce and you're asking to borrow it to go for a long drive. Think of the house that way. Sure, you know how to drive. You can tune the radio, you can find the cup holder, you can tool around in it. But what if you crash it—huh? Do you have five hundred kay–plus to replace it?"

My headache deepened, my eyes blazed, and Frank was still in full flow: the car being totaled was like the house burning down. What then? Or plumbing emergency—what if the flood insurance doesn't cover it? Or, say, a stumble? A back injury—someone falls and becomes a paraplegic?

He went on in this vein until I wanted to scream. Mother was nodding in approval, looking upon Frank with admiration. I was baffled, because he had the lawyer's ability to go on at great length; and rather than explaining simply why he was cosigning the deed, it was as though, through his talk, he was making the whole matter incomprehensible, creating dense fog where, a while ago, there had been sunlight.

"Like I say, I'd be doing you a favor," he said. "With my name on the deed you'd have the confidence that in an emergency, I'd be able to step up."

"I don't envisage an emergency," I said.

"No one envisages an emergency," he said, so gleefully that spittle formed on his lips. "That's why insurance companies exist."

"So I'll insure it."

"What if you fall behind on the payments?"

"I'll borrow."

"Using what for collateral?"

"The house, I guess."

"Then there's a greater risk of losing the house."

Mother was looking anxious. *Losing the clubhouse*, she was thinking.

Frank smiled, and I knew that whenever he gave me his pistachio-nut smile he was about to deliver bad news or a crushing revelation. "What if you get hit by a car?"

"That's simple," I said. "I die and the house goes to my next of kin."

"Your next of kin is me."

"So you'll get it, without ever having to sign anything in advance."

"What if you don't die in the car accident?" He was still smiling his nutty smile, a front tooth snagged on his lower lip. "What if you end up with a spinal injury—cervical, worst kind. Wheelchair—bedridden. Quadriplegia."

The front tooth was yellow and after he'd said this, he smiled more openly, more yellow teeth.

"What will you do then?"

Mother looked at me, and then at Frank, who was gloating.

"Then you'll lose the house," he said.

Mother clucked and said, "I think Frank's right. Cosigning the deed is a good idea."

"Purely a matter of formality," Frank said. "I'd be signing to help you down the line. This is just to ease your mind. You'd be responsible for taxes and utilities, and all the rest of it. Repairs and whatnot. I want no part of that."

"But you'd be half owner," I said.

"In name only," he said. "When the right time comes, I'll take my name off the deed. You'll be sole owner then."

He leaned close to me, facing me with his half-bright, half-grim expression.

"But in the meantime, if you had a problem, I'd be there for you."

One thing I have not mentioned. Frank was peculiar in having very strong body odor that always made family discussions of this sort some-what awkward. It's possible that Mother did not notice, that, being so feeble, her sense of smell was impaired. Yet Frank gave off a powerful smell, sour, like infected meat, hanging like something solid in the air, as though from a hamper of unwashed clothes, or a cage in which a small animal has died, an upper room that has been locked all summer in its pong of sweat and dirt and dead skin.

All the time we were talking I was aware of this corpselike odor, and it made me, in my shallow breathing, eager to end the discussion, even against my better judgment, to agree to his proposal. I craved to run outside and take a deep breath. In his stepping close to me, Frank stirred a cloud of stink around me that was like something physical, his bad breath like a filthy hand against my face.

"Okay, okay," I said and slid out of my chair and backed away.

Frank had a new copy of the title deed in his briefcase. As we both signed it he repeated that this was no more than a formality, but that I would thank him later, if my fortunes faltered. And, in time, he'd cancel his signature.

"I love it when I see my children are on the same page," Mother said. "A mother's dearest wish is to see her children happy."

I said, "I like the thought that I own property here. And I'm glad you'll be able to live here without worrying about maintenance."

"When I get my ducks in a row, I'll get a place of my own," Frank said. "Why are you smiling?"

"Because this is all so unexpected," I said. "Last week I was in a tent in the Arizona desert. Today I'm a property owner in Littleford."

"My landlord," Mother said.

But the other thing, the thought I did not want to share with them, was that, owning this house, I would at last have a place to store my books and mineral samples and the odds and ends I'd accumulated. I'd always agreed with Mother when she called me a gypsy—carefree, no fixed address; and I'd thought I was liberated. But I saw now that owning a house gave me greater freedom to travel, because now I had my own home. The happiest traveler is the one who has a place to return to, with the certainty of being welcomed. I'd once hated the thought of sleeping in my own bedroom. It seemed like an admission of failure. But now Tower House, the grand house on Gully Lane, was mine. Mother was my tenant, and so was Frank, until he was solvent again. I'd gotten the house without using any of my gold, and in the knowledge that I was now a property owner, I had one wish: to go away.

8

NONATTACHMENT

SOMETHING STRANGE AND UNEXPECTED AND WONDER-ful had happened to me as a result of being alone in that desert wilderness. Detached from home, I was transformed—I underwent a profound alteration of mood. From the first I'd been a restless searcher, tapping my rock hammer or threshing with my dry washer, scouring the canyons and ravines for bits and blebs of gold; but alone in the arid majesty of these mountains, their colors changing from hour to hour as the day waned, I came to see myself as very tiny and very lucky, grateful for each minute of solitude in this wilderness, a sense of well-being bordering on rapture.

It was a mental and mystical change, an affinity for the rocks and sand that no longer seemed impenetrable to me, but rather like living flesh that contained marvels. And the long spells in the canyons hardened me. I had never been healthier or stronger.

It helped that I was alone. Had there been another person with me I might not have felt it; or if I was continuously bumping into other searchers, being social as well as secretive, the delicate suggestion of happiness would have been smothered in idle talk. Being alone did not make me feel special; it made me feel almost insignificant, my ego diminished, and so it was easy for me to relate to the mice and the snakes I saw so often. I understood my relationship to them, how tiny and temporary I was, flickering among the stupendous rockfalls and mammoth boulders and stumplike mesas of fissured stone. I was colorless,

I hardly mattered, and when I found a dead mouse, or the bones of a fox or coyote corpse, I was reminded of my conceit as a prospector and my fragility.

What mattered most was very simple: I was part of the natural world—not as hardy and resilient as any of these desert creatures I saw, far more susceptible to heat and thirst, and because of these vulnerabilities I was lucky to be alive. The activity of searching for gold—and later for gemstones—kept me busy and vital. But the search was largely a pretext for living well. I didn't need much money—out here a gallon of water could mean the difference between life and death and was priceless. All material things were an encumbrance. I needed to travel light, to winnow my findings to fill my jar with assorted gold flakes and dust, and my pouch with rough gemstones—amethyst, garnet, turquoise, and jade. But I didn't regard these finds as wealth; they represented the means—when I sold them—for me to return to the cliffsides like gothic spires, the hilltops like cathedral domes.

My being in the bosom of the wilderness granted me silence and self-reflection; my prospecting was a form of meditation. And as the weeks and months passed I became more and more suited to living in the austerity of rocks and stones and cactus, hardier than I'd ever been, but more than that, mentally strong. I saw that my hikes outside Little-ford alone or with Melvin Yurick had been a preparation for this life. I liked the little victories of finding precious metal, but often these finds seemed to me merely a pretext for remaining in the desert, complaining to Mother or to Frank, *I have work to do!* but secretly cherishing my solitude, for what it revealed about myself, the purification of being here, how lucky I was. It was a spiritual awakening in one sense, but with my feet on solid ground, on bedrock, far from Frank's orbit.

After that initiation, grubbing among the rocks of Castle Dome, and a spell of summer idleness on the California coast, I headed to northwest Nevada, as much for the freedom of the glittering hills and the sun-scorched desert as for the prospecting. I turned up gemstones here, rough beauties whose dusty faces I learned to polish—fire opals and black ones, turquoise scored with spiderweb matrix, and veiny variscite, ocherous yellow and arsenical green. They were dull and lumpy when I cut them free, but I buffed them into lustrous jewels. None of them were semiprecious to me.

It was always easy for me to find buyers, especially in Nevada, among the schemers and opportunists who referred to themselves as gemologists and called the gems I found "joolery." They saw I was young, disheveled by the desert, a loner. I allowed them to underpay me, I marveled at their dishonesty; they took me for a fool, but for me it was crookery close-up. Wondering how low they'd go, I understood that their cheating was bottomless, a necessary lesson to me in human nature.

As a result, when Frank was next in touch and asked for another fifteen thousand ("To round it up to thirty, and I'll pay you interest"), I knew exactly who he was. I demanded a written agreement, with a repayment plan over three years, which he provided, 6 percent interest, and what he described as "a balloon payment" at the end.

The rhythm of my year was now driving and digging in the desert, studying the features of rock formations to understand what was inside them, and selling what I collected. I sometimes visited the Zorrillas in Phoenix, and they said they were glad to see me. But I gathered from their evasions and silences that their business was covert, and had I not saved the life of Don Carlos that day in the ravine, and delivered him home, they would not have felt obliged to entertain me. I never referred to the story of Don Carlos being robbed and abandoned by his brother, Ramón, though I often wanted to mention Frank and to tell them I was happier with them than with my own family. I loved being away, especially on holidays like Christmas and Easter. Once you've been away, you stop liking the person you are at home.

I called Mother when I could, and she reported that Frank still inhabited his old bedroom. She sometimes passed the phone to him, but my talks with him were brief. Someone who owes you money is always an anxious conversationalist; there is that weight of an unspoken matter between you, and an unbudgeable obstruction of resentment.

With lots of time in the desert for reflection, and the clarity that solitude offered, it occurred to me that the vacation in Acapulco was not a gift to me. Frank had been dumped by Whitney but he'd already been given the ticket to the company junket—the big-time law firm he'd hooked up with had footed the bill at the resort. I'd gone as his spouse on a nonrefundable airfare ticket. It hadn't cost him anything, but—given the impression he'd been generous—I'd loaned him the money he'd asked for. Nuanced scheming, very Frank.

His fortunes then improved. In a succession of phone calls I heard about his new courtship, an amazing romance when I put all the whispers, the confidences, and the boasts together. Frank had been on a sabbatical in Maine to ease his pain at having failed in his marriage and was looking for comfort in the landscape of spruce forests on the rocky coastline.

He'd remembered a rock hunting trip I'd taken as a geology student, one I'd told him about, my camping on the shore of a bay on one of those elongated coastal peninsulas, and my kayaking to nearby islands where there were the remains of old quarries from which great blocks of granite had been carved. I'd extolled the beauties of Eagle Island in Wheeler Bay, its smooth-sided quarry, its abandoned cabin in a bower of spruce trees.

Impressed by my long-ago praise, he'd gone to that bay for solace and rented a cottage on a hill at the head of the bay, a place I'd mentioned. It was easy for me to fit Frank to the cottage on the drumlin above the glacial grooving formed by the Laurentide Ice Sheet, the bedrock of granite that I'd mapped, the twists and folded layering of the metamorphism of the schist, the sediments and bedding of sea stacks, the angular fragments of volcanic tuff, and the glories of igneous granite varieties, especially those in the jumble of inclusions in the shatter zone of coastal hills, the fractures, the feldspar.

"Big bunch of rocks," Frank had reported. "Filling station up the road sells lobster rolls."

Shatter zone was the expression that came to my mind, because it seemed that Frank, who was a social animal, hating solitude, was having a miserable time in Maine and had no ambition to visit my old haunt on Eagle Island.

But stopping for gas one day at the Huddy station, and buying himself a lobster roll, he saw a pretty woman behind the counter. He had not seen her before. He struck up a conversation, saying, "What a lovely part of the world."

The woman looked at him with widened eyes and bared her teeth and said, "I'd kill to get out of here."

The desperation in her voice thrilled Frank. Here was an attractive woman who was in trouble. Frank saw an opportunity. And her sudden utterance was like a declaration of loss, of distraction and futility, and— Frank being who he was—her weakness made him feel strong. He'd been gloomy for the whole week at the cottage on the shatter zone, and now he brightened.

Relieved to see that shop was empty, no other cars at the gas pumps, he leaned and fixed his good eye on her and said, "How can I help?"

The woman began to speak; she stammered but failed to say a whole word, and then she put her hands to her face and sobbed into her fingers.

Frank was wearing a tweed coat, a folded handkerchief in his breast pocket. He plucked it out, flapped it open, and without a word, handed it to the woman. She thanked him in a whisper, her eyes reddened, her lips trembling.

I could add plausible dialogue to these factual details that I'd learned at the time, more colorful details that I was told later, and all of them had the ring of truth, because I knew Frank so well. He was stimulated by being in the presence of a helpless woman; he was needed, and even in her misery she was attractive, perhaps her pallor and her wounded eyes giving her a greater allure.

"It would take too long to explain." Blowing her nose seemed to restore her, as though she was expelling her gloom into the hankie.

"I have plenty of time," Frank said. "When do you get off work?"

"Five," she said. "Shift change."

"Coffee?" Frank said. "Or something stronger."

"Coffee's good," she said. In a beseeching tone of apology, she added, "Are you sure? Because I have a real sad story."

"I want to hear it."

Frank returned to the gas station at five and parked a little to the side, signaling to the woman when she left the shop. She smiled when she saw him—the first time he'd seen her smile, shy and grateful. And she smiled again but nervously, as she slipped into his car.

"I don't even know your name. I'm Frank."

"I'm Frolic," she said and blinked at him. "My parents were hippies; they came up here to escape New York City. People always laugh when I tell them my name."

With solemnity, as if bestowing an award, Frank said, "Frolic is a very beautiful name."

The woman lifted her hands and looked as though she was going to cry again.

"Where shall we go?" Frank said. "Somewhere quiet."

"I don't want anyone to see me," Frolic said.

They bought coffee at a café in Rockland, and took it to a bench near the harbor, where they sat facing the sea, sipping it from their paper cups. To inspire trust, Frank would have gazed at her with his practiced squint of concern.

"This is nice," Frank said, thinking, *I must not rush her.*

"You don't know what you're getting yourself into."

This stirred him; he liked the thought of a great tangle that would take his mind off his own emptiness and make him feel useful.

"It's like this," she said, twisting her fingers on her lap as she explained. She'd married young to a local man who worked in a factory that made preformed tub and shower units. It was hard work, the pay was poor, but they'd managed. The product was well known.

"Filberts," Frolic said. "Big company. Fiberglass."

The word *fiberglass* was spoken by the woman with a slight lisp, her lazy tongue lolling at her lips—the word, the lisp, thrilled Frank and he too eagerly locked his fingers.

Frolic's husband, Warner, became asthmatic, his condition worsening, and finally he had such trouble breathing he had to resign and apply for workers' compensation. He was given severance, a lump sum for which he'd signed a paper. He wasted away, struggling to breathe, even on oxygen, and after less than a year he died.

"Was there an autopsy?"

Frolic shook her head.

"Pleural abnormalities—very common among workers who use fiberglass. There are studies. Very similar to asbestosis—a lung killer."

"Are you a doctor?"

"I'm an attorney," Frank said. "And I can tell you that you have a case."

The woman moved closer to him on the bench, she rested her head against his shoulder, she was sobbing again, between deep breaths, seeming to purr, a vibration that Frank could feel in his flesh, trembling through his body, like a motor that energized him.

"I want to help," he said.

"But why?" She raised her head, incomprehension and anguish on her face. Tormented, Frolic was tragic and pale and lovely.

Frank became purposeful, taking charge, holding her hand, squeezing it as he questioned her further, details of her husband's illness and their finances. The following day he visited her at home after work and put her medical bills in order. He studied the document her husband had signed, a liability waiver, clearing Filberts in advance of any responsibility. Frank explained to Frolic that the waiver was full of loopholes; Warner had not been advised of the risks of fiberglass and that he might end up fatally ill.

That was the beginning of Frank's five-hour drives to Maine, to create a case, to initiate a lawsuit, and to meet with Filberts's lawyers, who were at first dismissive. But after Frank laid out his case, showing that the waiver was unenforceable, they became attentive.

They knew that a court case and jury trial would attract attention, and probably a class-action lawsuit—obviously other Filberts workers had been affected—and heavy damages would follow. Frank offered them a proposal, naming a large sum. He never disclosed precise numbers to the public and he swore that this amount would remain confidential, so as not to attract other litigants.

Filberts settled. And as Frank had promised that he was taking the case pro bono, the whole chunk of money—millions—went to Frolic, who quit her job at the Huddy gas station. And then Frank began actively wooing her—though, really, he'd been wooing her from the moment she'd lisped the word *fiberglass.*

Frank was never happier than when he went to someone's rescue and came away with a big payday. They had a short courtship and were married in her hometown in Maine. Mother attended. The Filberts settlement remained a secret. Frolic's family organized the reception. She was a country girl, she was surrounded by brothers and sisters—seven or eight of them, an Irish family, her father a weaver, her mother a pastry chef at a local restaurant.

The way Mother described the occasion made Frank seem inconspicuous there, but I suspected that though this might have been true, he enjoyed a sort of celebrity, as the man who'd dried Frolic's tears and made her smile. What pleased him, I guessed, was that Frolic's family felt indebted to him for spiriting this simple widow away to a better life. But no one knew, except the bride and groom, that Frolic had become a multimillionaire.

Mother had used these words about Frolic—*simple, humble, hardworking, decent.* But who is simple? Everyone has depths and unanticipated moods and passions, as Frank was to discover in his life with Frolic.

"Sorry you couldn't make it to the wedding," Frank said to me. He was annoyed, and he went on at length about the beauty of the Maine coast, forgetting that it was I who had suggested he soothe his heart there.

I could have managed to go to the wedding, but I was still buoyant in my mystical mood of nonattachment, and I feared that the flight and the wedding celebration, and seeing Frank, would disturb my serenity. I sent flowers and a polished topaz, set in silver.

People go to weddings to size each other up, and if you're in your twenties and unmarried they make remarks—*You're next* or *Your turn now.* I wasn't ready for that. I knew I'd changed, that I was happier and healthier where I was, and that I didn't want to return to my earlier roles, as a son and a brother, or to be asked questions I couldn't answer.

My slight regret was that in staying away I would be missing Frank's long stories, the ones he saved for big events, with lots of listeners— his own wedding would have been a great occasion for dazzling his guests with his monologues. Or else boring them. His stories were always helpful to me in assessing his mood, yet I wasn't very curious about him now. I was busy living my life, and moving on.

9

DIVERSIFICATION

FEELING CONFIDENT, I WAS STRENGTHENED BY MY SUC-cesses as a prospector, and my horizons broadened. I had the money and the curiosity and the will to roam more widely. I didn't have to explain myself: my work spoke for me. I was an ingot of gold. I was a pouch of gemstones. I was a thick bar of silver. Talk and speculation meant nothing—they were like Frank's long stories, not interesting in themselves but suggesting a state of mind. In my chosen profession all that mattered were results, and mine were unmistakable, glittering for all to see.

Untethered to my family, and single, I could go anywhere I wished. Hardly conscious of it, or planning it, I'd prepared myself to be an explorer and traveler. I'd refined my skills as a prospector, and I'd discovered that I could be self-sufficient, able to camp in the wildest places. I'd learned how to repair my equipment and stay healthy, to prevail and flourish in the harshest conditions.

In the secretive world of prospecting I'd earned a whispered reputation as a gold finder. But finding gold was not what impressed the mining companies that later hired me as a consultant. It was my acceptance of risk, my dependability, my determination, my knowledge of geology, and my youth. It was also my hatred of promises, my belief in results. And it was something else, hard to define or teach: my instinct for finding what I was looking for, which amounted, in terms of rock hunting, almost to an exquisite sense of smell.

From Arizona and Nevada I traveled to Alaska, hired by a firm that bankrolled me to prospect for gold in the Yukon River Basin. The price of gold was at that time high enough for them to commission me to find whatever I could—modest amounts, as it turned out, but of great purity. My youth was an advantage. I was twenty-six and I didn't know what I realized later, that competitive businesses are always on the lookout for young and ambitious workers, eager to learn, able to take orders, even-tempered and undemanding—no family, no mortgage, adaptable, portable, loyal, grateful, who will work for much less money than someone older, to build a résumé and make a reputation.

That was me. I was the young, hardworking risk-taker they wanted. What they did not understand was that I knew my worth; so I allowed them to give me orders, while suppressing my objections to their patronizing me, because I needed this experience. I was successful on the Yukon River, and instead of going back to Littleford for a summer holiday I took a vacation on the Seward Peninsula. There, I heard whispers of jade deposits locally, and after I fulfilled my Yukon River contract, I set out on my own in Seward to prospect for jade and jadeite.

It seems a paradox that I'd gone from the intense heat of the southwestern desert to thirty-below in Alaska. But it is not unusual. A healthy person can acclimatize to any severe conditions—heat or cold. It's a matter of stamina and a mental challenge. Some of the men on Captain Scott's expedition to the South Pole had come from working in the intense heat of India and Arabia and Burma. A person does not merely acquire the ability to endure a certain climate but rather attains a level of health that allows him, or her, to adapt to any extreme temperature. My years in Arizona and Nevada, active in that heat, prepared me for the cold in Alaska, where I had to leave my van idling all night in front of my hut so that I'd be able to drive it in the morning.

The challenge in the North was buying the instruments and equipment for this specialized prospecting. After forming my own small company, I looked for partnership with a big mining company in order to pay my bills and expand. Their confidence in me, and their investment in my modest operation, gave me the freedom to range more widely.

My partnering company had a number of mines in Australia. They offered to send me there to verify a number of gold deposits. I traveled under their auspices and reported on the gold reserves, but at the same time discovered new possibilities. At that time, the innovation of rechargeable batteries meant that rare earths were in greater demand: lithium, for one, dysprosium another for computer guts—an essential in hard drives. The name "rare earth" was misleading: they were not rare in the sense of being hard to find—there was plenty of the stuff in Australia, much more of them than other minerals. But they are called rare because they can't be reproduced or duplicated. There was a finite amount. I made it my business to go out on my own and find these valuable deposits.

I liked Australia for its open spaces. Most of the people lived at the edges, on the coast. I favored the empty outback, the distant bush they called the woop-woop and the never-never. And something else that pleased me: Australian women were hardier than the men. Seeing that I was a Yank (and not a Pom), they teased me, and discovering that I could take the teasing—which seemed to me a form of flirting—I had many friends, and a few lovers. After my celibacy in Arizona, and a few casual encounters with women in Alaska (where the competition was fierce—too many men, not enough single women), my success in Australia heartened me.

I had never believed that I would find a woman to share the hardships of my life. My ideal was not a seductress in a boudoir but rather a woman who would be a teammate, who'd accompany me in the desert or the bush. I thought it was unlikely, but in Australia I met many women who were unfazed by the rigors of prospecting; they were themselves able geologists and knew their hot, red landscape.

They loved the outback, they liked driving long distances, they could drink me under the table, they were capable of overcoming hardship, but they were also women, with reserves of tenderness and understanding. I am generalizing, because I was lucky enough to meet three such

Australian women in my three years there, shuttling from my rental in Perth to various sites in the vast state of Western Australia, looking for gold, and then opals, and finally rare earths.

These women were as strong as me, and more patient. My success in Australia was due to the fact that because I was often prospecting with someone else, we could cover twice as much ground. And with these capable and independent women, I learned in Australia that a love affair was not merely a stewing in sensuality as I had with Julie Muffat in Littleford. Physical attraction was important—essential—but so was a sense of humor; so was respect, and much more.

Rejecting Frank's opportunism with Frolic, winning her a big settlement and then latching on to it, I came to see what a love affair really was—a partnership—and the longest one of mine in Australia was fruitful in every respect. Most of all we were happy, we were strong for being a team, we found the ore we were looking for, and we paid our bills. On weekends or rest days we made love. That was Erill.

She knew what she wanted from me. She had an instinct for being able to please me, she was bawdy and unshockable. She taught me how to please her, she coached me and she was more experienced than me. She was not a coquette, simpering and being shy; she was dominant, with a hunger and ferocity that transformed her, an intensity that would not abate until she was satisfied.

Yes, like that—don't stop.

In those early days I was inexperienced. I didn't know what I wanted—or let's say, only the simplest release. But Erill was able to tantalize me, extending the pleasure, showing me that I could stay in a state of heightened arousal for an hour or more in a condition of near delirium.

This apprenticeship in romance cleared my mind and prepared me for other relationships. I learned a simple, valuable lesson, that sexual compatibility is a wonderful thing—fulfilling, exciting, like a drug— but is not necessarily long-lasting. A real partnership needs much more than a libido to succeed; it needs equality, understanding, intelligence, patience, and most of all, kindness.

That's what I learned from liberated Australian women. And how did they know so much? Because they had to deal with so many alpha males and macho types, they needed to understand them, they'd had to cope with opposition, and they had to work out their future. Such women knew the limitations of their men.

The women geologists were the best, the hardiest traveling companions—well-educated, funny, friendly, adaptable; able campers, instinctive prospectors, and straightforwardly sexual. They knew what they wanted, they knew what I wanted. They were my sexual education. And their greatest gift was that they did not mistake a night of passion as the prologue to a marriage. Such a night was complete in itself, not part of a complex bargain. No power dynamic was involved—it was that welcome thing, sex by mutual agreement.

As an American man I'd been led to think of sex as a favor. These Aussie women set me straight. I'd never seen a shrink, yet this sexual education was something I associated with psychotherapy. I'd gone to Australia with various preconceptions, and secrets, and the usual male hang-ups and embarrassments; but three years of traveling and working and making love had rid me of my anxieties. I became liberated, because they were. They showed me how to be truthful, how to be a better man.

After Australia, my chronology becomes muddled and truncated. I was offered a job in Tanzania, but opted instead for a return to Alaska for a spell. I took a long holiday in Mexico, riding my motorcycle through Baja and then taking the ferry to Mazatlán. In casual conversation there, in a bar with a drunken gringo, I heard, "It's the fault of those feuding Zorrillas," but I just smiled and agreed. I rode south on the Pan-American Highway through Guatemala, El Salvador, and Nicaragua, lingering in Costa Rica, and then finally I ran out of road in Panama.

Instead of returning home, I caught a ship from Colón to Santa Marta in Colombia, bringing my bike, and rode up country to Bogotá, where I knew that the mining company I'd partnered with in Alaska had an emerald concession. I looked them up; they knew my record with the company and were happy to meet me. They said they were expanding an emerald mine here and signed me up as a technical adviser in mineshaft monitoring. The mine was one of many, near the tiny mountain town of Muzo, about two hours north of Bogotá, on steep winding roads, a thrilling ride on my motorcycle.

Emeralds are maddening—even very expensive ones are often full of flaws, prone to cracking, with a lot of color variations and internal imperfections. I was happier digging the harder variscites in Nevada, the colors not so dramatic as emeralds but the stones tough and reliable and lasting. Yet it was the emeralds that led me to Vita.

10

VITA

EMERALD MINING, THE NOISY, DIRTY, DESTRUCTIVE digging for the glowing stone, seemed to attract the wrong kind of people, noisy and dirty themselves—the bullying mining companies, the secretive geologists, the opportunistic *excavadores* who hung around the mines and hacked for the stones, and gangs of violent men intent on intimidation in the hope of thieving the best chunks of host rock or quartz in which the emerald crystals were embedded. And there were the children, almost antlike, scratching in the darkness, deep in the mine. The work itself was tedious, the drudgery in tunnels, the sluicing of mountainsides, the sifting of broken rock, and there were always too many men involved. I disliked the stone for its attraction of ignorant admirers, and for its flaws and inclusions, though the quality of the color outweighed the veins and spots, the clouds and cracks, and it was the deep green that gave it value.

After almost a year in Colombia, I was prepared to leave. It was obvious that the country was unstable, and this instability gave rise to gangs, to vigilantes, and to an aggressive military. In the peasant economy, coffee growing, the drug trade, there was also illegal mining of gold. I missed the routines of law-abiding Australia, I was not prepared for the chaos of Colombia, even though the chaos meant greater profit for me, lack of regulation allowing more money to slosh around. Most of all, I was distressed by the large number of children in the mine.

In the beginning, I'd taken them for very small men, a native race of diligent dwarfs. But I soon saw they were boys in their early and mid teens, scrambling on the hillsides with shovels, or spraying water from hoses, or in tunnels hurrying along the passageways, while I was bent double bumping my head on the crusty ceiling.

"Just one month more, Cal," the mine foreman said. "We need to know whether to extend the tunnel. You know about sediments—you can do the cores, you'll be able to tell whether it's worth digging farther."

This English-speaking foreman, Manolo, was from Spain but had lived in Colombia for years, married to a woman from Bogotá, and seemed unfazed by the corruption, or else he was resigned to it. He'd been fair to me, honored the terms of my contract, and knew that I was determined to go back home. But a great deal of money was riding on the decision to extend the operation, and there was heavy competition for emeralds around Muzo.

I was now past thirty, and I felt I needed (after all my travels) to find a house somewhere in the United States. My inclination was to use the money I'd saved to buy a house and create something resembling a home. Not Mother's house—at this point I still thought of it as Mother's house and considered it mine only as far as a name on the deed—and not with an urge to settle down—far from it. I believed that with the stability of a home, I would be able to range more widely. My abiding belief was that a true traveler was not a wanderer, looking for a place to live, but an efficient person who owned a house, secure in the knowledge of having a place to return to. Tower House, the house on Gully Lane, didn't count. I could not imagine living there as long as Mother was alive.

The money I'd saved was parked in a bank; how much better to spend it, to invest in a house I could live in, to buy chairs I could sit in, pictures I could admire, an office and a desk, where I could make plans.

I told Manolo this. As a Spaniard, living in Colombia, enriched in his exile, he claimed not to understand. It was his way of defying me.

"Okay—one month. Then I'm done," I said.

I'd already given my notice at my rental in town. Sighing, feeling thwarted, I relocated to a hillside nearer the mine where I found a small house to live in, and with regret—because I wanted to hop on my bike and speed to Bogotá and fly home—I began the daily burrowing in the tunnels to test-drill cores, to assess the viability of extending the mine.

I had a scare. In a central gallery, where I was able to stand upright, I lingered to catch my breath, stretching the stiffness out of my arms and the crick out of my neck, when I heard a whisper. It seemed ghostly, a hoarse, skeletal voice, seeming to warn me, cautioning me to step back. I heard it again, now like an angel's wingbeat, and backed away from the gallery into the refuge bay of the tunnel, crouching under the low ceiling heading to the refuge bay, and as I did, the entire carved-out dome of the gallery collapsed before me with a deafening crunch, sending out a choking gust of fine particles. Had I not heard the warning sounds, had I remained, I would have been crushed to death. Was the "voice" a cracking of stone? Perhaps. But it is rare for a mine collapse to convey a warning. In every case I knew, it was sudden and devastating.

This hastened my desire to leave Colombia and this mine. I'd been alone that day. But usually I was in a group, walking hunched over in the dust and airlessness of the tunnels, attended by workers, some with lamps, others carrying drilling equipment, and all along the way I'd passed miners I'd once taken to be undersized workers, whom I now knew to be children, laboring in the darkness of the tunnels, chopping rock, filling wheelbarrows.

One day, exhausted, trudging, a whole hour into the tunnel from the main shaft and still far from the face where the digging was in progress, I came upon a cluster of these small diggers blocking the way.

"*El techo es muy bajo aquí,*" I heard behind me—the ceiling's low here.

I called out "*Cuidado!*" to the diggers blocking the way and took the lantern from one of my men and swung it.

I wasn't angry. I was impressed by the concentration in the young faces in this dismal place, uncomplaining, seeming intent on solving a problem. It was hot and dirty and dark, and yet when I went closer I could see they were using a flashlight to study a document, which I took to be a chart of this section of the mine where—as I saw—the tunnel split in two, a sort of crawl space to the left, branching from the main shaft.

They murmured among themselves and jostled to clear room for us to pass.

Without thinking, I said, "Sorry," in English as I brushed by them.

Then, in the half dark, a piercing voice, "You're interrupting a very important discussion."

An American voice, a woman, seeming to mock me.

I said, "Hello. I'm Cal. I'm headed to the end of the tunnel. Can I help you?"

"I'm Vita. Yes, I'd like to follow you."

"What about your important discussion?"

"*Siento, pero me tengo que ir,*" she said to the children.

I understood that, "Gotta go," and they said goodbye to her.

And so I continued walking, but much happier with this unexpected woman following me. And as we walked through the narrow dripping tunnel, Vita close behind me, breathing beautifully, her shoes crunching gravel, I began to desire her.

Farther on, I slowed down from time to time and called out, "You all right?," and she piped up, "Fine," or "I'm good." And it seemed to me we were walking through this dark wet tunnel as a close couple. It was the ideal I'd had of the greatest romance, meeting someone who'd be a true partner, my equal in all ways, heading into the unknown with me, unafraid.

So far I had not seen her face. She was a shadow, walking just behind me, not trudging as I was, but—being shorter—striding upright.

At the limit of the tunnel, where miners were chipping at the rock, I crouched and unrolled my chart of this sector of the mine and spread it on the stony floor.

"Have a look," I said and stepped away so that she had room to see the whole of it.

But it was a simple ploy. I wanted to see her face. I could tell she was slightly built; her hard hat gave her an air of authority, and she carried a flashlight, but mine was more powerful. When she knelt to examine the chart, I caught her face in profile under the visor of her hat.

Intent on studying the chart, her attention gave her a kind of

radiance—dark wide-open eyes, her pretty lips pressed together in concentration, a lock of black hair drooping from under her hard hat and
brushing her cheek, a slightly receding chin giving her a childlike face,
and for me the most enchanting aspect of her features, a smudge of dust
on her white cheek. She was beautiful.

"So I guess we're right here," she said, tapping the chart with a slender finger.

I said yes, barely glancing at the chart. I could not take my eyes off
her lovely face. Her thick vest and yellow work boots and blue jeans
made her more desirable. She was not stylish and breakable; she was
strong without being tough, with delicate features and wearing miners'
gear. I thought—it was a fanciful lover's wish—*I will always want you
by my side.*

The core drilling went quickly, I was smiling the whole time, eyeing
her as she watched me work. And at the end of the day, as we climbed to
the pithead into daylight, I looked up at the blue sky and saw a flock of
brilliant parrots streaking overhead, yellow and green, a swath of them
soaring into the forested mountainside. The sight of them added to my
sense of exhilaration, which was like an uprush of hope.

"Will you join me for a drink?" I asked.

"I'd love to."

We sat in the late afternoon drinking beer at an outside table of the
company's cantina, and that was when I watched her remove her hard
hat. She shook out her dark hair and tossed her head to arrange it, like
a mare swishing its mane.

I had not been mistaken in the tunnel: she was a beauty.

Seeing me staring at her, she said, "You must be wondering what I
was doing down there."

"Not really. There are some women geologists in this company. I
worked in Australia with lots of them, and they were just as competent
as the men and easier to get along with. They also worked harder than
the guys."

"I like you for not wondering," she said. "That's how life should be—no surprise to see a woman miner, or airline pilot, or brain surgeon."

"Which one are you?"

"Writer," she said. "I'm doing the annual report for this company. They sent me from Miami—the firm I work for got the contract. The idea is that it'll be a big glossy report, with photos of eco-friendly mining operations and diligent miners and glittering emeralds."

"I look forward to it."

She leaned closely and said, "You're an employee?"

"I'm on a contract," I said. "I was scheduled to leave but they begged me to stay an additional month." I lowered my voice saying, "Frankly, I'm sick of this company, this country, and the whole business. I can't wait to leave."

I had not spoken of this to anyone, and I surprised myself by blurting it out—I could hardly believe that I was being so indiscreet. But something in this woman inspired my trust and made me want to be absolutely truthful. That honesty, too, was an aspect of love.

"But don't put that in your report," I said.

With a slight sideways move of her body, and inclining her head, making her long hair twitch at her shoulders, she seemed to be preparing to say something important.

"There won't be a report," she said softly. "At least, I'm not writing it." She sipped her beer, darted her tongue out, and licked froth from her upper lip. "They send children into these mines to work. And they expect me to write a report glorifying it?"

To her beauty and her strength and her easy companionship, I discovered new traits—sympathy, kindness, and a sense of justice.

"I admire you for saying that."

"But it's inconvenient," she said. "You find out something like this— the proof of child labor—and you incur an obligation. What to do about it?"

"You're a writer. Write about it."

"I'm a technical writer. I do annual reports and copy for brochures. Hotels and resorts. Press releases. Human rights horrors don't fit in those things." She sipped her beer. "I can't believe I'm telling you this. I don't even know you."

"I've been candid with you about hating the company. I feel I do know you."

"Really?" She started to laugh, then seeing my expression she said, "God, you're serious."

"Yes," I said.

"Or is that a line? Because if it is, it's a pretty good line."

She said two other things that evening that struck me. One was "So I guess we're alike in one respect—we're both quitting our jobs." And the other, an earnest plea just before we parted: "I like you, too. Please don't turn out to be weird."

I saw her the next day, and the day after that, and every day for another week, before she left for Bogotá, to fly back to Miami. On one of those nights I made a pass at her—kissed her and held on.

"Don't think I'm being *una coqueta*," she said, stepping away. "I know what you want."

"Are you sure?"

"Yes! Because I want it, too."

It sounded bold, her saying that with such assurance, and it was as though it had already happened, that we were lovers. That was all I wanted for the moment; more than a hope, it was a promise, not lust but purer and deeper, something like a betrothal.

"Give me a little time," she said. "I have some unfinished business."

She left for Miami, I completed my contract and was paid my bonus. In my last memo I advised the company against hiring children, using an argument that would persuade them—children were less productive and more careless, so more accident-prone.

On my way back to Littleford I stopped in Miami and spent a long weekend with Vita. She'd finished her business, she said—a boyfriend, as I'd guessed. She introduced me to her parents, Cuban-born father, Ernesto; Italian-American mother, Gala. I took them all out to eat, Saturday lunch, a wonderful meal that inspired the sense of being part of a family. And when I showed Gala a small wad of cotton, and plucked it open to reveal a shimmering emerald, and presented it to her, the woman shrieked, and then began to cry.

The night before I left, Vita and I made love. She was not expert— that reassured me. It was not a night of bliss. It was something better, two people getting acquainted, unembarrassed, looking to the future.

I had not been home for almost four years. Mother was grayer and seemed vague, and more severe. Frank was fatter and better dressed, but unchanged in being his old overcertain self.

A meal at the diner. I told him I'd met someone special.

"Don't do anything yet," he said and snatched at my hand, as though yanking me from a ledge. "We need to discuss this."

11

HOMECOMING

ARRIVING HOME AFTER A LONG ABSENCE ALWAYS MADE me feel like a waif or a wash-ashore, thinking, *Why am I here?* Or maybe that was the effect of the way I was usually greeted, as Fidge, the less popular son. You go home and become a child again, the fidgety kid, reminded of your long-ago lapses. Home is always the past, where you're always small, and known by your high school nickname. At least it was so for me much of the time on Gully Lane.

But I had Vita now. It strengthened me to go home with her. She gave me the confidence to be patient with Mother and to face Frank and Frolic. Odd that I—a traveler, at ease in the world—needed confidence at home, and never when I was alone, in alien landscapes, or among strangers.

We were at the table in the dining room of Tower House and had just finished lunch, Mother in the kitchen making coffee. I'd had my first glimpse of Frolic, who was slim and plain, her brownish hair in braids, with heavy unplucked eyebrows that gave her a judgmental gaze, her pale skin made paler by the dark hair on her arms, and an unmistakable fuzz on her cheeks. In my work I was used to women darkened and roughened by the sun, and Frolic had a pallor that suggested the seclusion of indoors. She did not take her eyes off Vita, looking at her with fascination—the dark Hispanic beauty, her hair now cut short like a boy's, and a boyish figure, too.

Frank, for a reason I could not explain, but perhaps to annoy me, was wearing a baseball hat at the table. Seeing that I was studying his wife, and perhaps self-conscious, Frank said, "Frolic's a fabulous cook, aren't you, Fro?"

This made Frolic laugh, and her laughter, a kind of whinnying that caused her to fling her head back and show her teeth, seemed to relax her and make her more likable.

"If you love chowder, I sure am! My mom taught me to make fruit pies."

"Maybe you can teach me," Vita said.

"I'd like that," Frolic said, still staring at Vita's face.

Vita and I were lovers, that was apparent, and my good fortune was obvious in my new car, an expensive watch—but it was a compass, too—my sense of well-being, and something else.

"I love your earrings," Frolic said, reaching across the table, as though intending to poke one with her finger.

"Cal gave them to me for my birthday."

They were dangly and glittering, and as though to satisfy Frolic, Vita set the gems in motion with her dabbing fingertips.

"Looks like jade," Frank said, turning the bill of his cap backward to look closely.

"*Esmeraldas,*" Vita said in lilting Spanish, tossing her head, making them dance, then seeing confusion across the table, added shyly, "Emeralds."

Just then à buzzing silence-pressure—an upswelling of emotion like grief or joy, a powerful vibration near the point of bursting, that seemed to rattle through Frank and Frolic and shake them into wordlessness.

"From Colombia," Vita said. "Where we first met."

Birthday and *emeralds* and *Colombia:* each revelation was bright and unanswerable.

"Crystals have a soul," I said. "Out of respect, you should take off your hat to look at one."

Just then, Mother walked into the dining room with a tray—a French press beaker of fresh coffee, a small pitcher of cream, and a sugar bowl. She squinted at Vita. Frolic looked tearful with confusion, Frank seemed to be making an assessment of the value of the emeralds, his face flattening, lips twitching as he added numbers, the whir of sums seeming to blink in his eye sockets, but his eyeballs too glazed and bloodshot with effort to be read clearly. He was so obvious a calculator as to be a cartoon of himself, and once again I thought, *Why am I here?*

That was our first visit—and I knew the answer. I pitied Mother for her frailties, her sadness at being without Dad, becoming fussed and feeling inadequate until Frank stepped in to help or meddle—she was in the grip of Frank's domination, weakened by his constant attention. Yet I loved our little town, I was successful enough now to enjoy it thoroughly, and I wanted Vita to love it. She'd been raised in Florida in a one-story suburb of Miami, with Ernesto and Gala, swamp steaming on one side, the sea lapping on the other, between the alligators and the sharks, the strip malls and fast food. She knew nothing of the ancient shade trees and the quiet dignity of the small New England town where I came of age, vowing to return only when I'd made enough money to live well here, and buy a place in the Winthrop Estates.

I had seen enough of the world by now to know that this was where I wished to own a home and raise a family. I didn't want to conduct my business here; I wanted to earn my money elsewhere, and treat Littleford as my refuge.

"I never realized places like this really existed," Vita said, as we left Gully Lane—and Frank and Frolic and Mother, and Tower House—and drove down Main Street, past white frame churches, and the library and the Greek revival town hall, across the river where today a flotilla of swans were gliding—stately and upright and serene.

And what Vita didn't realize, nor did I want to tell her, was that the charming town she was seeing was the result of furious litigation by Frank and his cronies against the fast-food people, and the locals who wanted cheap eats. I didn't want to tell her that Frank's campaign to keep the town free of neon signs and burger joints and pizza parlors had been a success and had kept the soul of the place intact. No pawnshops, no bars, no liquor stores, either—all that sleaze was across the river in Winterville. The Preservation Pact—keeping Littleford fast-food free—was one of Frank's signature achievements early in his career, annoying potential franchisees but winning him many clients. Vita would have admired him for it, unless she knew, as I did, that Frank, having dispatched the fast food and the pizza, had invested heavily in the Littleford Diner just off Main Street, where we routinely had lunch and sparred, when I was home, pretending—as seemed necessary—that we were still the Bad Angel brothers, on the best of terms.

Too much to tell, so I said nothing.

"I feel bad about his face," Vita said, peering at the town, seeming to see Frank.

"He had mumps as a kid," I said. "Got a little palsy but when he realized that it made him special, he sort of played it up. He's actually vain about it."

"Still." She was brooding, looking glum.

"Vita, it's his moneymaker."

As we rode along the bank of the river a wonderful thing happened. As though obeying a signal, the stately floating swans lifted their enormous wings and seemed to step on the river's surface, propelling themselves forward, lifting in a loud beating of wings, like laundry flapping on a line in a high wind, the swans' bodies outstretched, seven or eight beautiful birds in flight, a great slapping of air that as they gained altitude seemed like humming. But it was their beautiful wings, the whisper of their feathers. I was reminded of the flock of parrots I'd seen that afternoon in Muzo, my first drink with Vita.

I turned to Vita to mention that and saw that she was crying.

"I want to live here," she said.

The swans were an omen. They circled and were gone, and we returned to the Riverside Inn and made love, and I thought, *My life is complete.*

I had not said anything about marriage at that visit to Tower House. I'd introduced Vita as my fiancée, I mentioned that we were engaged—a vague word for a future event—another source of baffled wonderment, the ring on Vita's finger, from a stone I'd found in my travels, and kept, for whoever my fiancée turned out to be. This yellow diamond, a sunny one from Australia, was different from a "Cape," from South Africa, but a freakish gem of lively yellow, not highly prized by gemologists who admired purity, but rare in itself, something to crown a woman like no one else, the love of my life.

That was the other hush at the visit—Vita's ring.

"What kind is it?" Frolic had asked.

Frank had needed her to ask the blunt question. Frolic wasn't a fool, nor was she as gauche as she seemed. She was merely taking a hint. She'd been in such situations before. She knew what information Frank wanted to know.

Vita said, "It's a canary."

"That's nitrogen," I said. "It's got fire, like Vita."

"Is it supposed to be some kind of diamond?" Frolic said.

Vita had laughed hard—I supposed laughing on my behalf, helping me get through this meal, the sure sign of a partner and lover.

We promised to get in touch for another meal, and as we hugged Mother on the porch, they seemed relieved to see us go. That was just before we drove down Main Street and the churches and along the river where the swans rose up in their great beating of wings- -an enchantment and an inspiration.

Wishing to have a place of our own, we moved from the Riverside Inn to an apartment, the top floor of one of Littleford's elegant houses, and we looked for a house to buy. I knew what I wanted, I knew the right area from early on, my paper route, my lawn mowing jobs, the houses on the only hill in town—called Winthrop Hill, not really a hill but high ground, where the houses had a view of the surrounding woods, and each house was set on acres of lawn. To own a house in the Winthrop Estates, where I'd mowed lawns and been barked at by dogs, had been one of my dreams—the reason I'd come home with Vita.

A wish of youth fulfilled in adulthood is bliss. And there was another attraction to the Winthrop Estates: it was at the opposite end of town from where Frank lived, on three acres, in style, with a swimming pool and a tennis court, and a studio for Frolic, who dabbled in weaving like her father and made pottery.

After the hard work of prospecting and being a consultant geologist—the travel, the rigors of living in mining camps—it was a pleasure to be in this quiet town, with enough money for a down payment on a prime Littleford house. Of course Vita and I were glimpsed by the real estate agents, observed visiting houses for sale; we were mentioned by prospective sellers at open houses, the lovely woman with me remembered and remarked upon. Littleford was a small town, with a small town's virtues and faults. It was intact and uncorrupted by crass commerce, it had churches and a village green and a sleepy river, and a Civil War memorial; it had no neon signs, no fast food. And it was incapable of keeping secrets.

So we were seen, and one day Frank called and without saying hello or his name, said, "Nest building, Fidge?"

"Who is this?"

"Because if you are"—he kept talking over me, he did not answer my question—"you'll need to take some factors into account, factors that might not seem apparent to you at the moment, in the heat of your romantic haste."

"Frank, don't you have clients to attend to?"

"When I consider how important my brother is to me, all other matters recede into insignificance," he said. It was formal and pompous, the sort of thing he might declare in a courtroom, as he approached the jury.

"I'm not sure what's on your mind."

"Fidge, we have to talk."

"Go ahead."

"Face-to-face," he said. "This is serious. I'll meet you anywhere."

He'd blindsided me with the call and I put him off. He seldom phoned me, and when he did, it was usually preceded by his secretary saying, *I've got Attorney Belanger on the line for you*—always pronouncing the name his way, and in those early days Miss Muntner seldom called him Frank. He always called Meryl, Miss Muntner.

I'd thought when the phone rang the next day that it was one of the realtors offering an appointment to view a property. It was late morning, on a hot August day, the big pinky-pale blossoms of the hydrangeas below our porch going brown, a rosebush needing to be deadheaded, a frantic dragonfly swooping and hovering, beyond where Vita sat in a chaise lounge with a book on her lap but not reading, instead gazing at the gilded dragonfly, which I saw was not a dragonfly at all but a hummingbird darting its beak into the orange blossom of a trumpet vine tangled on an arbor. I'd been about to join her and point this out when I heard the phone.

"Lunch," Frank said.

"I've already eaten."

"Coffee—dessert's on me."

"Maybe some other time."

"Cal," he said in a hot whisper—and calling me Cal and not Fidge meant he was being serious. "We have to meet now. Without delay. Time's of the essence. I'm talking contractual. A drink."

"What about?"

"I'll tell you when I see you. The diner at five. Come alone, it won't take long. It's in your interest. Say yes, Cal."

"Okay. See you at five. One drink."

Persistence was one of Frank's traits, clinging until he got the answer he wanted, it was what he was famous for, not taking no for an answer. I was resolute when I needed to be, but I didn't have the salesman's urgency that motivated Frank, the imperative to win. I could not bear trying to persuade someone to do something they didn't want to do. I took no as a final answer. A no to Frank was a challenge, it didn't mean no, it meant maybe, and maybe was a yes.

Here was the proof, my distrust of Frank, my usual objection to his proposals, and yet hanging up the phone, telling Vita I'd be meeting Frank, walking through town to the diner, keeping my promise to meet him—my yes.

He was early, seated at a booth in the far corner, though he jumped up to greet me with a hug, burying his face in my shoulder and groaning a welcome into my neck. He was in his attorney's uniform—bow tie, red suspenders, pin-striped pants, his suit coat hung on a hook beside the booth.

"What'll you have—I'm paying."

"Beer," I said. "Any kind."

"They've got a fantastic pale ale on draft here—artisanal, very hoppy, new brewery, small batches, craft beer. Or do you want canned panther piss?"

He was still talking as I slid into my bench to face him, smiling, because he was now telling me which beer to order and what kind of glass to drink it in.

"Ballantine for me," I said, when the waiter came over, taking a pad and pen from his apron pocket.

"You don't know what you're missing," Frank said. And to the waiter, "Fitch's Pale Ale, in a chilled pilsner glass."

"Be right back with your order."

"How long has it been, Cal?" Frank asked, with emotion, one eye glistening, the other drooping.

"Two and a half years—more."

"And look at you—picture of health. You're smart, a job that offers travel, fresh air, plenty of exercise. And from what I see, you're not hurting for cash flow."

"Frank," I said, and raised one hand, traffic cop fashion, "please tell me what's on your mind."

He shushed me as the waiter set out two coasters and placed full glasses of beer on them, reminding us of the brands—"Ballantine, Fitch"—and wished us well. Frank picked up his glass, clinked it against mine and sipped. I hated watching him eat or drink with his sloping inefficient mouth and nibbling teeth, and so I looked away and took a swig.

With his glass jammed on the table, Frank holding it with both hands, as though to steady himself, he said, "Tell me about your house hunting."

"We're just looking—nothing definite."

"Market's hot. Gully Lane houses are going for the high six figures. More in the Winthrop Estates. Serious money."

Two of the places we'd been looking: Frank had reliable informants. I said, "We could get a mortgage."

Now he gave me his pistachio-nut smile, as though he'd just scored a point; he sat straighter, raised his glass with both hands, sipped again, and set it down.

"You're smiling. What is it?"

"You said 'we.'"

"Yes. Vita and me."

"That's what we need to discuss."

"I don't follow you."

"Vita," he said.

"There's nothing to discuss."

"You're not a lawyer—you're a rock collector. You have no idea of the implications."

I stared at him, and he probably thought I was defying him, but what I saw was Vita, stretched out on the chaise lounge, smiling into the luminous sky of the summer evening—beautiful woman, new to town, alone, innocent, not knowing that Frank was saying with assurance, "Vita," summoning her for evaluation.

This vision made me love her more and vow to protect her; it made me despise Frank. I had not seen him for almost three years, and after my being home for a week, I was being subjected to him saying, *Here's what you need to do.*

I was guzzling my beer, intent on finishing it and leaving immediately. But chugging beer was something I had not mastered, and I choked, and Frank became solicitous, and my hurrying my beer caused Frank to interrupt himself in his pitch and say, "You all right, Cal? Take a deep breath."

I was winded, gagging, I couldn't speak.

"One story," Frank said, filling the silence. "I had a client, awesome guy, made it big importing carpets from India—traveler, like you. Huge markup on the carpets, warehousing them, selling them out of a catalog, low overhead . . ."

"Is this about carpets?" I managed to say in a stricken voice. "Because if it is . . ."

"His marriage," Frank said. "Met a woman. Very attractive. Whirlwind romance."

"And he gave her a carpet," I said, to annoy him.

"He gave her a diamond. A big rock. They get married, they buy a house. He hardly knows the woman. They move in together and—about six months later—'I don't love you anymore.' She demands that he leave. She gets the house, she needs money to maintain her lifestyle, he's on the hook for alimony and maintenance. At last he does something sensible. He comes to me. I says, 'You're a little late, Larry. You should have come to me before you took the plunge. But, hey, you've got a few options.'"

I was still seeing Vita, a stranger to this town, alone on the porch, serene in contemplating the stars pricking the early evening sky, her hands folded on her book, waiting for me to come back. I was ashamed of being here, listening to Frank. It was like being unfaithful.

"What are you doing?" Frank said, because I had begun to slide out of the booth.

"I'm leaving."

"We have to talk, Cal."

"I don't want to hear it."

"She's from Florida. It's a totally different culture—unregulated, improvisational. She'll be lost here." He raised his voice as he saw me stepping out of the booth. "What do you know about her background? Have you met her family? Have you looked into her finances?"

"Frank, are you crazy?"

"An asset search," he said. "You need to do it."

"No."

"And the house? Joint ownership? Which names on the title deed? What about a prenup? I've got a bulletproof prenup with Frolic. You're making a huge mistake."

I wanted to hit him. I said, "Stop—please, stop," and backed away from him, stumbling, in my hurry to leave.

Frank repeated his argument, hissing so that the nearby booths couldn't hear. "She's an unknown quantity. A stranger! Hire a private investigator! Execute an asset search! Threaten an intimidation audit! Get a prenup! It's a test of love!"

He was sighing, pleading in a low anguished voice, telling me it was for my own good. But I had heard enough—too much, in fact. I should never have agreed to meet him. I knew Frank, I should have guessed that he'd try to interfere.

He was tangled in his suit coat, poking his arm into one sleeve and then blocked by the waiter, who, seeing us on our way out, rushed over with a saucer, the check folded on it. As Frank lingered to pay, I hurried to my car.

Back at the house, I took Vita in my arms and kissed her, and held her.

"What did big brother want?"

"Nothing," I said. "Just wanted to talk."

"The real estate guy called while you were out. He's arranged for us to see a big old house tomorrow."

It was in the Winthrop Estates—not old, but Federal style, redbrick façade, simple windows, colonnaded front porch, a fanlight over the front door, a low stone wall surrounding it, beds of rosebushes, room for a pool at the back. The house was tired, it needed work, which was why the elderly owners were selling—not able to face the cost of repairs. And with the proceeds of the sale, they were planning to relocate to Florida.

"I can tell you all about Florida," Vita was saying to the wife, as the real estate agent and I discussed the cost of renovation.

Within days, we agreed to buy the house, and the deal was done quickly, to my satisfaction. We remained in our rental, supervising the repairs (new roof, many new windows, upgraded kitchen and bathroom fixtures), and within a few months we moved in. When we were settled we planned our wedding, a small affair, Mother, Frank, and Frolic (who announced she was pregnant). Ernesto and Gala flew from Florida— their first visit to New England—we brought them on our honeymoon to Maine, and I showed them the lighthouses and took Ernesto fishing. We chartered a boat and sailed out of Tenants Harbor, into Wheeler Bay as far as Eagle Island, where I'd once done rock hunting. They flew back home from Rockland, while we remained for another week on the granite coast, in each other's arms.

I took an assignment right after that and was away for a month (Canada, copper) while Vita put the new house in order.

On my return, Vita said, "At last, I'm going to do something about those exploited children in Colombia."

"That's great."

"There are abuses like this all over South America—he says we've got the potential for a landmark case."

"He?"

"Frank. He promised to help. Maybe file a lawsuit. He's been advising me—pro bono."

12

THE SOUL OF KINDNESS

I

T'S VERY HARD, WRITING THIS, EXCAVATING OUR BROTHER-hood, for me to be impartial about Frank, whom I found unbearable.

"He's totally on my side," Vita told me. "Frank's a huge asset."

This from the innocent woman who had, not long before, been disparaged by Frank as a gold digger and an opportunist, whom he warned me against marrying, because—he heavily hinted—she'd end up getting my house and most of my money, leaving me in the gutter, bankrupt and alone. His argument was based on lawyers' cynicism and precedent—this had happened to other clients of his, he had proof in documents, binders of credulous men ensnared by greedy bitches.

She's an unknown quantity, he'd said to me. *A stranger.*

I cringed to think that Vita was innocent of hearing these gibes.

Hire a private investigator! Execute an asset search! Threaten an intim-idation audit! Get a prenup! It's a test of love!

She was a stranger to him, but not to me. Frank didn't know what I knew. The Vita that I'd met in the Colombian highlands, a single woman enduring the machismo of a mining camp and overcoming the rigors of the road, was someone I admired. And just as important, she hadn't been daunted in Littleford—the tight little town being a challenge in culture shock. We'd gotten to know each other in sharing the more ordinary problems of the day-to-day—petty nuisances being greater tests of patience than the big drama of hardships. We became partners, cooking, shopping, cleaning, laundry. Loving her, I thought, *This is where the true path begins.*

"Frank's working pro bono," Vita said. "He cares about these exploited kids as much as I do."

When, early on, Vita had asked, *So, tell me about your family,* I'd said, *I don't know where to begin. Maybe it's better that you come to your own conclusions.*

Wishing to be fair, I didn't want to list the grievances I had with Frank. Doing that would, I suspected, make him assume an importance he didn't deserve, and then he'd loom in a forbidding way over our relationship. I didn't say much because I didn't want him to matter. And I didn't want to sound like him, a belittler, a hostile witness, a gossip, a nitpicker, a traitor.

This of course is hypocritical of me, because looking back at what I've written so far, pages saturated with sibling rivalry, I see I have portrayed Frank as a predator and a bully—insincere, hateful, and manipulative—the high-functioning asshole I always disparaged. In a murderous mood I've been building a case against him—a conventional case, prosecuting him as a selfish brute.

But there was more to Frank than bullying and greed and manipulation. There was a darkness in him that did not seem dark. He could be hateful, but hatefulness was not his worst quality, disparagement was not his most serious fault.

From an early age he was a dispenser of favors, and he had a wizard's ability—which is also a huckster's ability—to winkle out secrets, to divine a person's fondest desire. He wanted to be useful, he wished to be indispensable, he needed to be needed.

I have mentioned how he'd had a brief affair with my ex-girlfriend, Julie Muffat, and then berated me for treating her badly. Without looking too deeply into my brother enjoying sex with someone I'd also had sex with—troubling in itself—it was obviously motivated by his seeing that an affair was something she wanted, in order to get even with me. Frank had accommodated her in her vindictiveness, and of course the sex was a bonus for him. Long after that brief sexual episode he remained close to her, helped her in various legal matters, gossiped with her—and all the while he encouraged her to divulge information about me, the shaming secrets of an old love affair. She was willing to tell him, to wound me. But why was he so interested?

Growing up, I'd mention to someone that Frank was my brother, and I'd steel myself in anticipation, thinking they'd respond with abuse, because I'd known him as an adversary. And I'd get a surprise.

Great guy! they'd say. *Know what he did for me?*

They'd mention a favor, often something incidental, but thoughtful, tactical—*He loaned me his car, He helped me get a job, He shoveled my mother's driveway one snowy day when I was at work. God love him,* in the Littleford idiom. *Heart of gold.*

Sometimes the favor would be substantial, involving a sacrifice on Frank's part, an inexplicable altruism. He might respond to a compliment with a bizarre display of generosity, a practice I'd been told about by miners who'd spent time in the Middle East. A naive stranger in those cultures might single out a watch, a ring, a gold stickpin, or whatever—*That's really nice,* the stranger might say—and the pious owner of the admired thing, obeying custom, would respond, *It's yours.*

No matter the value—and it might be a glittering string of emerald worry beads—it was instantly handed over and could not be refused.

Anyone who praised something belonging to Frank was rewarded with it, either that very thing, or else Frank said, *I'll get one for you,* and he kept his promise.

See these cuff links? a Littleford man once said to me. *Your brother gave them to me.*

A shirt, a golf club, a scarf, a penknife, a cut-glass decanter, a necktie—at one time or another, these were items Frank presented because they'd been admired. There must have been many more, but these were ones I had personal knowledge of, Littleford recipients, who praised Frank's generosity.

For a person who desires the thing he or she praises, the praise is the expression of a wish. It is not a simple compliment, it is the candid disclosure of a deep yearning. But Frank was not extravagant. If someone praised his car—he bought a new one every two years—he said, *I can get you a discount on one just like this, or probably better. I know a guy.*

He knew many guys. That was another function of his goodwilll, introducing someone to a person who could help, vouching for both of them, matchmaking.

He got my kid a job, He found a specialist for my father, He put me in touch with a real-estate genius. On meeting someone for the first time he'd study the stranger and wait for an opening, and if the person did not indicate a wish, Frank would say, *I'm here to help—tell me what you want me to do.*

This openhanded offer is often made, but the promise is rarely kept. Frank always followed through, providing aid and comfort, fulfilling the wish; and he never accepted payment. He would often show up later, offering more, to the point where he became a benefactor, unpaid, an angel of mercy.

Frank's satisfaction was being someone who was indispensable. This aim—*I want you to need me*—was something I'd only come across in certain ambitious politicians. *I can fix it,* or *I can help you,* or *Tell me what you want me to do.*

I grumbled about Frank, but the memory of Frank's willingness and generosity was an obstacle to most people listening to my complaints, whose usual reply was *That's not the Frank I know.* For them, Frank was the dispenser of good advice, as well as material things, or introductions, or—because he was a lawyer—a bestower of justice.

"My father scalded his hand in the sink," one man told me. It was Eddie Picard, at a high school reunion, on my first trip home from Arizona, when I was feeling flush. The elder Picard had been Dad's friend. "I went to Frank, because my father said he was a good guy—he'd given camping equipment to my son's Boy Scout troop. I figured he'd know a great doctor. Frank says, 'Tell me how it happened.' I says that we bought a new boiler. The water was scalding hot. 'Maybe it was improperly installed. Maybe a wrong setting. I'll get you a doctor, but you might have a case against the plumbing company.'"

"Then what?"

"Long story short," Picard said, "Frank gets my father a dynamite doctor. He files a suit against the company and the manufacturer of the boiler, proves that thermostat shit the bed, and he gets a judgment—emotional distress, loss of earnings, personal injury, rehab, no trial—they settled. Frank was a godsend. And he didn't charge us a penny."

Of course not, because Frank would have gotten a large cut of the settlement, and maybe a payoff from the doctor, and years of referrals. Picard would not have wanted to hear this.

Camping equipment to the Boy Scout troop, like the scarf, the watch, the cuff links, the golf club, and other trinkets, was Frank's way of chumming the waters.

Back when I was chipping diamonds out of the volcanic tubes of lava in Western Australia, on behalf of Rio Tinto, I got an earnest message from Frank. *Call me.*

"Got a client," he began when I called. "I'm representing him in a personal injury suit against his employer. Big company. They're sandbagging me, but I know I'll be able to drive a bus through them in the end. Listen, this guy lost his sense of smell. Know what that means?" He didn't wait for me to reply. "He could breathe toxic fumes without ever knowing it," Frank said. "He works in a plastics factory."

"Maybe he should get a new job."

I'd heard Frank tell such stories before, and I was irked that I was on this long-distance call, swatting flies in a trailer in Kununurra, Australia, listening to this tale of woe.

"It's not about the case. It's about the guy. He's engaged to be married."

I took a deep breath to keep my composure, and said, "What is it you want, Frank?"

"We won't get a settlement from the company for a while. But in the meantime he wants to surprise his fiancée with a ring."

"I still don't get it."

"A diamond, Cal. Just find me one. It would mean a lot. Not only to keep my client happy, but in the end there's a big payday. I'll settle with you then."

"Industrial diamonds, Frank. That's what I've been digging out of the deep block caves. It's called bort"—and I spelled that word—"It's black, it's brown, and it's not gem quality. Seven bucks a carat. It's used as an abrasive. And in drill bits. He wants to put this on the woman's finger?"

I had mentioned diamonds in letters home, without specifying what kind. I was sure Frank told his client, *I know a guy*. In this case and others, I was the guy. Earlier on, he introduced me to parents whose children wanted to travel. *Cal travels a lot,* he told them—*he can give your kids valuable tips*. I was the guy, I was the favor.

Now I am demonizing him again and making him seem selfish. The truth is more complicated. He wished to be a benefactor, he wanted to please people, he aimed to be a patron, a godfather, a helper. He was a fixer, he was a Samaritan, he was Santa.

For a long while, early on in his legal career, Frank took up photography. He made a study of it, buying himself a plate camera, a boxy Speed Graphic that he used, hunched under a black cloth—*Don't move!*—and got marvelous results, sharp portraits in black and white. And in the two or three years of practicing this hobby he offered people in Littleford—politicians, doctors, company directors, bankers, important citizens—a portrait of themselves, suitable for framing.

Just pose—no charge, he'd say, and he would haul his camera and tripod and black shroud to their house or office and take pictures, lovely ones, rare in detail and definition. He'd discovered that what most people want—especially important people, opinion formers, who had elegant offices with walls for photos—was a flattering portrait of themselves, or their wife or their children, or their dog; or a group portrait, all of them together. Frank developed the plates himself in his darkroom at home, and he retouched them, airbrushing, beautifying the subject—no flaws, no blemishes. He made a fuss of handing them over, showing up at the subject's office with a bottle of champagne and the framed photo, gift wrapped. Then, a little speech, a toast, and the presentation.

Money was always offered but Frank refused it. *This is a memory. You can't put a price on a memory.* Frank's form of indirection lay in saying modestly, *It's just a harmless hobby of mine,* while at the same time offering a thing that people cherished. The recipient had not been conscious of wanting a portrait, but Frank divined that it was the secret desire of most people to own an ideal image of themselves.

He knew that he was giving something of value, that they'd never forget, and as with all such gifts, the receiver was obligated, the more so because no money had changed hands. The photographs didn't cost much—a few dollars' worth of chemicals, but Frank may have been the only person in Littleford who owned such a camera, and the resulting photo was a thing of beauty, singular, and signed by Frank, a sort of icon to hang in the house, leaving them with a feeling of gratitude but also a lingering sense of indebtedness.

The strategy brought him clients, especially well-connected ones, and helped build his reputation. But as he became busier he did fewer and fewer portraits, and finally gave up photography altogether.

What never left him was his impulse to find someone in need, and to offer his services, taking charge. *Here's what you have to do . . .* It was Frank in his role as rescuer—of someone injured, or loveless, or abandoned, an accident victim. He was a suitor to single moms and had a way of wooing them as clients in their quest to receive child support or alimony. There was no immediate profit for him in their cases, but they were small victories, and friendships and visits, that led to referrals, to personal injury suits.

Far from being viewed as a bottom-feeding predator he was praised for being a savior, and in many respects that was exactly what he was. My rescuing him long ago in the creek on Cape Cod was confusing to him, because he made it a principle never to owe anyone. He regarded favors to him as an encumbrance; he didn't want to think that by my saving him from drowning he owed me his life. Though he'd been sinking beneath the black water and looked a goner, he minimized it afterward, claiming that he could have made it to shore on his own.

I laughed when he said that, but we had no witnesses, so he stuck to his story. He needed to be the power figure, the rescuer not the victim. Not owing anything to anyone was one of his boasts. It gave Frank quiet satisfaction to be owed, knowing that at any time he chose he could collect.

Later, he became a regular attender at funerals. He saw one aspect of his role as Littleford's foremost attorney to be designated mourner. He made a point of ostentatiously grieving. He would embrace the ashen-faced spouse and stunned relatives—and leave his card. *If there's anything at all I can do . . .*

He was often summoned afterward by the widow to sort out a will, or deal with probate, or property, and in doing so he became part of the family.

Frank cultivated widows. They were weak and vulnerable, confused as to what their next move should be. They seldom knew the extent of what they were owed—it was Frank's contention that the spouses were notorious for having hidden assets and died before they revealed their whereabouts. Frank delved—asset searches were one of his specialties—he found bank accounts and investments and safe-deposit boxes, and when he was through, he was able to reward the widow with much more than she dreamed of.

And so the widow remained in Frank's debt and, having been enriched, became useful to him. He would extract a fee, often less than he deserved, so that they would stay indebted, and he would become a friend of the family, uncle, godfather.

Frolic had been a widow. I have mentioned how he had chanced upon her clerking at a gas station in Maine, and she had poured out her heart about how her husband had died from a lung disease he'd contracted working in a plastics factory. She uttered the magic word *fiberglass.* Frank had wooed her, slipping into his role as rescuer of a grieving widow, drying her tears and offering to represent her in the lawsuit against her late husband's company.

Frank became Frolic's trusted adviser, and after his success in arriving at a settlement—millions—they'd continued to meet, and become lovers, and ultimately married. But through all this, and even after marrying into her fortune, Frank was regarded as a rescuer.

My brother had his critics (*How do you stand him?*), but he had many more well-wishers. Over the years I was struck, again and again, by the testimonials of people in Littleford he'd helped. I resisted being impressed, because in all matters related to Frank I remained skeptical. He was my brother, I knew him better than anyone, and I had never seen him as a true benefactor, because the dark side of philanthropy was a lust for power.

So when I returned home from my contract in Canada and Vita told me how he'd offered legal counsel in her campaign to draw attention to the exploited children in the Colombian mine, I was on the alert. I'd heard this before. *Frank's a huge asset. Frank's going to help. I don't know what I'd do without him.*

In almost every case I knew of Frank—as attorney pro bono, the designated mourner, *I'm happy to help, I know a guy*, Mr. Fixit, the hand-holder, the godfather—he always gained an advantage with his favors and philanthropy. Though he was known as a good guy to everyone but me, heart of gold, Samaritan, rescuer, lifesaver, Santa, he never failed to collect.

Much worse than his malice, more serious than his bullying, was Frank's kindness. I don't say "apparent kindness," because I could seldom separate the real thing from the pretense. He knew how to be generous and tender, he was able to touch a nerve and evoke a need; to inspire confidences, to be the soul of kindness. That was his most Luciferian trait.

13

PRO BONO

WHEN VITA MENTIONED THAT SHE WANTED TO EXPOSE the child labor in the emerald mines in Colombia, it turned out that Frank knew a guy in Bogotá, a partner in a corresponding law firm. For a fee, which Frank would pay, this man could furnish Vita with background on the mining company, its owners, its profits, its other abuses. The international laws against the exploitation of children were enforceable, but Vita had the testimonies of the child mine workers, as well as a file of photographs—names, ages, statements. Frank said, "This is dynamite!"

Vita wrote her piece, it appeared in a widely circulated magazine, it was noticed by a Boston charity called Rescue/Relief that targeted human trafficking, and her article was used in one of their fundraising campaigns. Her stark account of child labor in an emerald mine—the contrast of ragged little kids and fabulous gemstones—produced a windfall of money from, I imagined, many wealthy, guilty, emerald-wearing donors. Vita was interviewed by the agency and was hired, to write and report.

"Hey—it's Big Charity," Frank said. "Big Charity is a business. Think of the revenue."

Vita's hiring involved a great deal of paperwork—contracts, agreements, copyright of her texts and photographs, fees and retainers; and managing this legal side of things, the go-between, was Frank. He'd put himself in charge of Vita's career.

"Frank hasn't asked for a penny," Vita said. "It's all pro bono."

But nothing with Frank was pro bono. Somehow he always found a way of collecting. Vita would not listen to me on this subject—our first serious argument as a married couple. I wondered how he would collect in this case, and of course I thought, as I sometimes did with Frank, *Maybe I'm wrong*.

The paradox of being helped, in something you can very easily do yourself, is that the help becomes so convenient you lose the ability to act alone, and you become fussed and futile without it—infantilized. This was an imperative with Frank: to insinuate himself so deeply in someone's affairs that he became indispensable. "I don't know what I would have done without him," Frolic told me in confidence, not understanding that she was a multimillionaire and could have done anything. But in this mood she had married him.

Vita lived in Littleford, like Frank, and I was seldom home. It was in the nature of my work as a field geologist, chasing contracts and going where I was needed, that I was often far away. Because of my absences, Vita became dependent on Frank—his advice, his legal expertise, his friends, and she socialized with Frolic, swapped recipes, and shared the experience of child-rearing. Vita became pregnant with Gabe after our move to the big house in Littleford, when Frank had sneered, *Nest building?* I'd denied it, but he'd been right.

As an advocate for exploited children with Rescue/Relief, and as a writer, Vita had found work she loved. I was proud of her commitment and glad she was well-occupied while I was away. I was wary of Frank's advice but he had a habit of spreading himself thin. In the weird fluctuations of his attention as an overpromiser he was constantly saying, *Don't do anything until you hear from me*. Yet Vita was so dependent on his counsel, she didn't mind being kept waiting and hated my saying that it was his way of controlling her.

"It's pro bono, Cal."

"You don't need him."

"Okay," she said. "Wait right here."

We were on the back porch of our house, on a summer afternoon, Gabe gurgling in a bouncy chair. I relished the role of fatherhood, to raise my child with Vita, to spare him the slights I'd felt, to be unsparing in my love, and to do him the greatest favor I could imagine: not burden him with a sibling.

The hydrangeas were in full bloom—pink and blue—set off by beds of rosebushes, intense red buds, blown-open blossoms and a scattering of petals, beauty and perfumed air, a sort of order and aromatherapy I was unused to in my fieldwork in gouged and cracked rockscapes. What I disliked most about the extractive industries was the violence it involved, the tunneling, the splintering of rock faces, or worse, the open-pit mines that looked to me like wounds in the earth that would never heal. In great contrast to that, home was our soft sweet child, and the fragrance of flowers and my lovely and industrious wife.

That day, Vita returned to where I was sitting with a cold beer in my hand. She showed me an inch-thick stack of papers secured by the jaws of a metal clip.

"What have we got here?"

"A contract," she said. "I want you to read it and tell me how to respond to it."

I took the sheaf of papers and began to read the first closely printed page, then—stumped for a reply—I flicked forward a few pages and read, *In the event of a force majeure, the copyright (name of work) shall be subject to arbitration (see addendum C.1).*

"Beats me. What's it about?"

"I'm helping to draft the annual report for the agency. They're using extracts of a piece I wrote and some of my images. I need to be indemnified."

"'Indemnified' sounds like a Frank word."

"Cal, that's why I need him."

Big Charity was corporate, as Frank had said. It wasn't a humble, earnest gathering of do-gooders; it was an imposing edifice of fundraising professionals, a vast business. For the legalese in Vita's contract, and in the day-to-day, Frank was the counselor and interpreter. He emphasized that it was crucial that every paragraph be understood, because a misreading could result in (and here Vita quoted Frank) severe penalties, forfeitures, breaches of covenant, and much more that I was unable to put into plain English. These contracts did not in the least resemble mine—and I was dealing with gold and gemstones and rare earths. The legalese in Vita's contracts seemed to me a form of intimidation.

"Frank's protecting me," she said. "How can you object to that?"

I was usually away, Frank was available, and as Vita said, in helping her, Frank was helping me.

I wondered if I'd made a mistake in having bought a house in my hometown. Yes, it was a mistake. But Vita was happy in Littleford. After her upbringing in the swampy suburbs of South Florida—the buggy summers, the stormy winters, the moldy walls of one-story flat-roofed bungalows, and the whine of air conditioners—New England silences and solidity were a reassurance.

"Florida is no place to raise a kid," she said.

Gabe was now walking and talking, and taking a hint from my father, who had hired an assistant at his agency and spent months helping raise us when we were small, I made a point of staying home in this period. It was also my reaction to the possibility—or near certainty—of Frank's taking over my role and meddling in my marriage.

This meant I had no income for almost a year, but Vita was grateful for my assistance. She spent more time at Rescue/Relief. In her pregnancy she'd become more beautiful, as though she'd drunk a potion restoring her girlhood loveliness. After Gabe was born, she seemed even stronger and more confident than ever, able to take on the world. She insisted that Frank and Frolic be Gabe's godparents, and Mother was delighted, seeing this as a greater bond between her two boys.

I got used to being home, I grew into the routine, I encouraged Vita to spend time at Rescue/Relief. Though it seemed ironic that she was spending a great deal of time away from our child to help children who were far away, I didn't mention this. I was glad to see little Gabe grow, changing from week to week.

The hit on my income began to become a burden. But I reminded myself that some years before, in the aftermath of Frank's divorce from Whitney, I'd loaned him thirty thousand dollars. I waited a few months—I was still on my self-imposed leave of absence—and then I called and asked him to repay it.

"What loan?" he said.

His voice was cold, the tone of a stranger, and I experienced two physical changes in the ensuing silence—my hand went dead, as I tried to grip the receiver, and a stirring in my stomach weakened me, as though it was emptying, the consequences of my dismay.

I struggled to say, "Thirty grand."

Frank snorted, his usual reaction to a joke I attempted. He prided himself on never laughing at jokes, usually saying, *That's not funny*, which left the joker feeling like a fool. I half expected him to say, *Look in the mirror and ask yourself that question*. But he said nothing, until I prodded him again.

"You're kidding," he said. "I would never have borrowed that amount of money."

"But you did—we had an agreement. Payment schedule. Balloon payment at the end. You agreed to pay interest."

Then, in something like mirth, but it was defiance, he said, "Where's the agreement?"

"I don't know. It was so long ago. Socked away somewhere. With all my travel I have no idea where I put things." Not getting a reply, I stammered a little, then said, "It was after your divorce from Whitney. You said, 'I'm staring into an abyss.' You were living in an apartment in Winterville. You said you were broke. You needed a loan. I'd just had a big payday in Arizona. You took me to Acapulco. You asked me for a loan. I came up with fifteen. You later asked me for another fifteen. We signed an agreement. You thanked me."

Conscious that I was gabbling rather pitifully I stopped talking and became aware of a vibration in the hollow of the phone, a buzz of silence.

"Are you there, Frank?"

"The agreement," he said, sharply. "Show me the paper."

Before I could say another word I heard a click, his hanging up. But

I must have muttered something—cursed or sighed—because from the hallway Vita said, "Is anything wrong?"

"No—but I have to run an errand. I won't be long."

I drove to Frank's office, intending to corner him. I wanted to see his face and hear him deny that I had loaned him money. In my hurry, climbing the three flights in Craddock Chambers, the old brick building in Littleford Square, I was breathless when I reached Frank's floor.

Through the glass pane on his office door, lettered in gold, *Frank Belanger Esq., Injury Law,* I could see his secretary, Meryl—Miss Muntner—at her desk, shuffling papers, squaring them and slotting them into folders.

She smiled as I entered. "Hi, Cal."

"I'm looking for Frank." I was still breathing hard, and I was agitated, steeling myself to face him.

"Just left. Seemed to be in a hurry. You know him—vortex of energy." She kept on filing papers as she spoke. "By the way, you have a beautiful son. Frolic shared some snapshots."

"Sweet kid. Getting bigger by the day." I wanted to add, *But I'm not working, and I have no income, and I'm dipping into my savings.* I was still breathless from all the stairs and, hesitating, I saw that Meryl, straightening the papers, was wearing a lovely ring that flashed as she moved her hand.

"That's a nice ruby."

She thrust out her hand, fingers down, as though displaying a badge of rank.

"It was my aunt's. She didn't have any children, so it came to me. She was a world traveler. She bought the stone on one of her trips and had it set here."

"May I see?"

She slipped it off and handed it over, and she watched me as I took it to the window and held it to catch the last shaft of light glancing from the river that enhanced its fluorescence.

"Good color. No inclusions that I can see. Great clarity." I slipped it back on her finger. "Pigeon's blood. That's what they call that red."

"She got it years ago."

"Maybe Burma—Mogok. Famous mine."

She lifted her hand and smiled with renewed pleasure. "I should probably insure it."

"Definitely. It could be two carats. It's a nice claw setting. I'd say six or seven thousand replacement value, to be safe."

"Gosh. That much?" She flashed it again. "Frank said he'd give me a thousand. I almost said yes. He wanted to give it to Frolic. It's her birthstone."

"July?"

"Must be."

Somehow I doubted this, but even so it was worth much more than a thousand. Mogok rubies were scarce. The mine had been emptied. The rubies of India and Thailand and Africa were inferior.

"Heirloom," I said. "Keep it for someone in the family."

"I think of Frank and Frolic as family."

"Listen, Meryl, I can have that ring appraised for you. Don't sell it yet."

"Might just keep it," she said, holding the ring to her face and turning it, so that the glint in the stone flashed in her eyes. "Pigeon's blood. Nice." And shifting her wrist, she said, "Look at the time."

"Sorry to interrupt—it was Frank I wanted to see."

"No, what you said about my ring is real interesting." It was as though in describing the rarity of the stone I had given her money. "The thing is, I can't go home until I file the rest of these documents." She dampened one finger and skidded it over some pages on her desk. "I'll tell Frank you dropped by."

"No need to tell him—in fact, I'd rather you didn't. I'll call him."

I left feeling defeated. But in bed that night, woken by Vita, who'd called out in her sleep, I lay remembering Meryl's desk: the stack of papers, the glimpse I'd had of Frank's letterhead and signature, this clear insight into his filing system and Meryl's staying late to complete the job. Frank was not a hoarder but, unlike me, he was a scrupulous record keeper.

The next time I called Meryl she said, "Frank's in a meeting."

"I want to talk to you, Meryl. Seeing you filing those documents made me think, maybe you could find a document for me. One that Frank and I signed."

"I'll need a date, Cal."

I said, "Do you recall some years ago that big partners' meeting in Mexico—a law firm Frank was associated with?"

"I still have the ashtray Frank brought me as a present," she said. "Hand-painted. I don't smoke anymore, though."

"The document I need was created about a month after that."

"Can't remember the year exactly—four, maybe five years ago? Longer? The files would be in storage. Old files."

"Not thrown away?"

"We don't throw anything away," she said.

"It was an agreement, in the form of a letter, between Frank and me, about a loan. I seem to have mislaid my copy."

"I'll have a look—the Mexico year, a letter agreement."

She was as good as her word, calling me two days later, saying she'd found it, a letter to me from Frank stating that he'd borrowed thirty thousand dollars, that he'd pay me back within three years, that memorable phrase "balloon payment," and the line about 6 percent interest.

It was now almost ten years later and all I'd heard from Frank was *What loan?*

I said, "Meryl, please make two copies. Put one in the mail to me, and when you've done that, you can show the other to Frank."

"Will do," she said. "By the way, I'm in love with my ring. Pigeon's blood! Heirloom. I'm not selling it."

"This is really inconvenient," Frank said, when he called the next day, sounding grouchy. "Meryl showed me the letter, but—listen, let me finish—I can't pay you the interest."

"Just give me my money back, Frank."

"Might take a while. I'm pretty busy."

"When you needed it, I handed it over," I said. I was growing hot with humiliation and anger, remembering how I'd gone to the partners' meeting in Mexico as his spouse—it hadn't cost him anything. The telephone receiver was slick, dampened by my sweaty hand. "I need it now, I'm not working, I'm looking after Gabe, and Vita's not much of an earner. I have no idea when I'll be back on a job. This is important—"

Interrupting me, saying, sourly, "I'll see what I can do," he put down the phone.

Saying it was important was not quite true: I had enough money, and Vita was earning more than I admitted. It was a test, and Frank failed it—first by pretending it had never happened, and then, with the evidence of his signature on the agreement, being grumpy. No thank-you, a refusal to pay the interest he'd promised, only a graceless acknowledgment of how inconvenient it was that after all these years he'd have to repay me the money I'd loaned him. At that moment, still holding the phone, I hated him.

"Before my time—sorry," Vita said, when I mentioned it. She was still being helped by Frank and didn't want to hear anything negative about him.

No one is surprised when a loan to a family member, given in good faith, results in ingratitude. *You have plenty of money—why would you want this loan repaid?* I'd had to exaggerate my need for it, and plead poverty, before I could get Frank's attention. It seemed my generosity was forgotten, my asking for the money back was bad manners, a kind of scheming, very unfair to him. I really had no right.

Meryl's ring was appraised for eight thousand dollars. That was a small victory: it made me her ally and prevented Frank from having it. Although I got my money back—a check in an envelope, no note—I went on feeling frustrated, and it came to me that day I visited his office and saw Meryl filing documents, that what I wanted to do was duct-tape him to his chair and beat him senseless.

14

RISK AND REWARD

I KNEW THEN, AND FOR YEARS AFTERWARD, THAT IT HAD been a mistake to come home and be a Bad Angel brother again. I'd been happy in my solitude and remoteness, and yet my old dream had been to own a big house in the Winthrop Estates, where I'd once mowed lawns and shoveled snow. I'd married Vita, we'd visited, we became homeowners, we now had a child in school. It had worked for a while—worked too well; we were firmly settled in a pretty house, with a rose garden and statuary, and a limestone gazebo, and a lap pool in the backyard. I was now hiring high school kids to mow the lawn and shovel snow.

But the struggle with Frank over the loan had made me miserable. I was too close to him, I was a short drive from Mother, who was living in the house I now owned, I was conspicuous in town, and what was worse, Vita had decided she loved living in Littleford. It was not merely the four seasons, and the quiet dignity of the town, it was her job, her social life—she'd made friends, work friends and the parents of Gabe's schoolmates; she was putting down roots.

No longer anxious about being an exotic outsider with a Hispanic name, she felt she belonged. She was secure. When I met her, Vita was thirty, and her work as a writer had been improvisational, she was underpaid by her company, and what if she faced a crisis in her health or finances? I'd admired her independence, but she was grateful for my friendship, and later my love, and the life we had built together. She had to know that when she entered her house and closed the door she was safe, that she had someone she could count on.

Frank became an aspect of Vita's sense of security, and while I knew that in his attention to Vita he intended to spite me, he and I rarely spoke these days, something to do with the loan I'd asked him to repay, and we seldom met for lunch at the diner. Vita came to depend on him more and more for legal advice, introductions to helpful people, and (because I'd returned to work, and was often away) assistance with household problems (leaky pipes, broken dishwasher). Frank insisted he was glad to help.

"I wish Frank was not so involved in your affairs," I said, on one spell of home leave.

"Then don't go away so much. Stay home."

"And do what?"

"You could be a geology teacher."

"I like my job, darling. It's my living," I said. "I just wish there was someone else who could help you, besides my brother."

She smiled at the absurdity of this. "I like him," she said. "He's a terrific guy, a dynamite lawyer. He's saved me a lot of money. I have this feeling you don't really know him."

"I know enough. And he knows too much about us."

"He's great with Gabe. A real uncle."

"What about his own son?"

"Victor's a slow learner, and kind of a disappointment, being a mama's boy. Frolic's a smothering mother. But Gabe's responsive, he's got a great memory. Frank thinks he could become a really good lawyer."

"Oh my god."

"Don't bring me down, Cal. It hasn't been easy. If you were home more, you'd see I've got it figured out."

"I hate having to apologize for doing my job."

"Why not be grateful that I'm happy, that Gabe has a caring uncle and a caring aunt? That I have a career. Be glad that we have a nice house. And by the way, I spend a lot of time visiting your mom—taking her fruit baskets and little treats."

"I'm grateful," I said.

But I thought, *I don't want Frank to know us. Know your enemy* was supposed to be a wise saying. I didn't want to know him. *Keep your enemies close* was another one, and that seemed much worse.

Frank had access, he knew our habits, he'd inserted himself into our lives. I had always known Frank was a parasite. It took me a while, years of his deception and my inattention, to admit that Frank was dangerous, not to be trusted, my enemy. And, remembering his refusal to repay the loan, I'd wanted to attack him (duct tape, a pummeling), which shocked me.

Ashamed of my violent feelings, I was relieved and much calmer when I was away from home, working. But this also meant that Vita depended on Frank all the more, and his knowing about us, our habits and secrets, left us vulnerable. No—don't keep your enemies close, keep them far away and repel them when they venture near; up close they are dangerous.

An intimate friend can easily become parasitical, a relative is always a risk. The Zorrillas had stayed in touch, their shadowy business now extended to New England, but I knew from them how the old man, Don Carlos, had been stranded by his brother, Ramón, in the desert; how a brother has the potential to be the worst of all enemies. Your brother, more than anyone else, had the knowledge and the means to destroy you. That was why brotherly love was so noble, because it was the ultimate in trust. When Frank had said to me after his divorce, *I'm staring into an abyss,* I was moved. He would not have told that to another living soul. And he was not exaggerating: his eyes confirmed his suffering—one eye deadened, the other dark—he looked lost, defeat was something new to him. When, shortly after, he said he was broke, I did not hesitate to give him a loan.

Later he wanted the abyss to be forgotten and the loan forgiven: ashamed of it, he tried to erase it from his personal history. I was the solitary witness to his failure, and he hated me for it.

Vita claimed I was unappreciative—she was happy, Gabe was flourishing, so I kept silent about it and again thought, *Maybe I'm wrong!* Frank had many friends, most people I knew praised him, he was respected in Littleford, and these days he was making an enormous amount of money. He, too, was happy.

This was my prevailing mood in the years that followed my return to Littleford: gratitude, suspicion, unease, confusion, bewilderment. They were years of my being away for long periods on contracts from mining companies as their consultant geologist. These big companies had blasted and bulldozed open-pit mines and dug miles of tunnels in many countries, but what they wanted most—and what I craved—was an escarpment in some distant place that had never been penetrated, a rock face that had never been hacked, a ravine that was narrow and tight, that could be broken open, to yield the liquefaction of a cascade of glittering gems.

South India had been dug for centuries by miners in search of sapphires and rubies, and yet there were still hillocks and cliffs in Karnataka where, with drilling equipment I'd helped design—that was fabricated in Jamshedpur—I bored test holes and found cores that contained high-quality gemstones. India was distant, and we could not work without having to bribe every official involved in the project, but I found new deposits and I was rewarded with bonuses. I liked the drama of breaking into rocks that had never been touched, and finding a vein, and chopping it free, unlocking the treasure.

Rock is like flesh to a geologist, it is sinewy and muscular and striated; it puckers when it's stressed, it bruises and bleeds. I recaptured some of the thrill I'd felt early in my career in gathering gold from the scree in the ravines of Arizona. Finding gold was only part of the pleasure, and it wasn't the greatest part. My delight lay in being alone in a remote and challenging place, in exploring miles of jagged or undulant landscape and finding evidence on its surface that indicated what lay beneath. What I remembered best of my gold seeking in the Southwest was not the cylinder of gold flakes or the lump of bullion I came away with, but rather the stars twinkling above me as I lay in my sleeping bag in the night air on the bosom of day-warmed rock—layered and striped, blue and purple and pink—eager to rise at dawn and roam between the thighs of these canyons.

A contract to supervise gold digging in Tanzania led to a conversation with a fellow geologist, a Zambian—Johnson Moyo, trained in Colorado—who said to me one day, "Mr. Pascal, what do you think of this?" He showed me a knuckle-sized lump of crystalline stone I knew at once was valuable.

Examining it, I said, "It's a crystal fragment, obviously." I buffed it on my sleeve. "Emerald. But I like the blue in it." I held it up to the Tanzanian sun. "Very few inclusions. If this was cut and polished you could get money for it."

Moyo hugged me and said, "You're an honest man! I have shown this to other *mzungu* geologists and they said it was nothing—but they wanted to know where I found it. You didn't ask. They were trying to take advantage of me, thinking me stupid."

"It's promising ore."

"I have no resources. You have many. We can be partners."

Moyo's father had been a miner in Kalomo, near Victoria Falls, in Northern Rhodesia, and after Zambian independence he was hired by a mining company in Ndola, in the Copperbelt. An intelligent man and a fast learner, he was valued by his employer for his instincts, amethysts in Kalomo, and in the early diggings near Ndola—tipped off by villagers—he'd found emeralds. All this was confidential—he was working in a copper mine. He told his son about the emerald deposit and encouraged him to study geology in Lusaka and then in Colorado. The old man knew the location of the best amethysts in Kalomo, and he had friends outside Ndola, hammer and chisel miners, who'd found emerald crystals in chunks of quartz. These men had dug pits and broken open fat seams of schist that held emerald aggregates, like the one Moyo had shown me.

"I know the zones," Moyo said. "I have the knowledge. But I don't have the money to mount an operation."

I agreed to be his partner, I secured a loan, Moyo registered a claim, and we began a small-scale mine, employing diggers with jackhammers and power drills—Moyo's trusted friends—who carried ore that contained good-quality emeralds out of our shallow tunnel. Instead of living in Ndola, where we would be observed, we found simple houses outside a village in the Kafubu District, where our workers lived, and we kept a low profile.

Moyo insisted on paying our workers well. He said that members of his family would have been happy to work for less but that they would want more of the profits. "Relatives are lazy and greedy. My siblings are parasites."

This was before the days of the gem boom in Zambia, a time when all that anyone cared about was the price of copper. Later the big companies exploited the area and created vast open-pit emerald mines. But our pioneer effort was small, efficient, and barely noticeable, and we were finding a large quantity of gem-quality stones. And because it was a simple overnight trip on the train south from Ndola to Kalomo, we invested some of our profits in an amethyst mine, near the Zambezi, where Moyo's late father had once worked.

As in India, we were forced to bribe local officials, but once they were bribed and on our side it was plain sailing, and instead of transporting the stones to Europe we trucked them to South Africa, where they were cut and sized and polished in Johannesburg. We sold the loose stones to local gem dealers, Moyo and I splitting the profits, and transferring the money from South Africa to banks elsewhere.

This was an enterprise that took more than three years, with trips home every six months or so, Gabe now advancing through the Littleford school system. Vita often said that this Zambian mine was like my having a mistress, abandoning my wife and son in Littleford and fleeing to her.

She had a point. But Vita's own work with Rescue/Relief was also time consuming, and a satisfaction to her. We promised to accommodate each other, Vita once saying, "I understand now—this is your passion. And it seems to be profitable. I think Frank's a little envious."

I didn't scold her for telling Frank about my work, but I never uttered the word *emeralds*. And I made a point of explaining the risks involved in what I was doing. I lived with risk. Risk meant I might die or go broke. Risk produced valuable ore.

"Think of it," I said to Vita, knowing she would tell stay-at-home Frank of my struggles far from Littleford and its comforts. "Never mind the nuisances, the distance and the travel, there are real hardships. There's loneliness. There's the food, which is awful. And as the only white man in the mine I'm conspicuous. I understand why the locals are hostile—they've been treated horribly by foreign miners. The landscape is all torn up by bulldozers, and the weather is either too hot or miserably damp and raw. And there's the financial risk. I keep having to borrow heavily for equipment that gets broken . . ."

And the smell of the village, the gaping latrines, the decaying thatch on the roofs of the mud huts, the scarcity of drinking water, the low shed they called a bar where the fights every weekend turned bloody, and sometimes resulted in death. The women at the bar, screeching, "*Mzungu,* you want jig-jig?," wishing disease on me. The frustrations, the distance, my sense, as the work grew dirtier and the machines broke down, that I was becoming like the worst of them, settling for sour beer and a filthy bed, and why? So that I could claw emeralds from the rock and make money.

I knew that, along with emeralds, I'd signed up for foot rot, tsetse bites, dengue fever, bilharzia, and amebic dysentery; Moyo had regular bouts of malaria. Some of this I told Vita, but wallowing in complaints seemed to invite bad luck. I was not religious but I was superstitious. Complaining, I felt, would bring much worse fortune on my head.

And what were the risks in Frank's life? He was served breakfast each morning by Frolic. He sat in his tidy office all day, attended by Meryl Muntner. He went home to a hot bath and a glass of wine. I knew this to be true, because on my visits home—now every three months, to keep Vita and Gabe happy—I sometimes saw Frank. We resumed our old habit of lunch at the Littleford Diner, maintaining the pretense of brotherhood, Frank asking me about my work, and my telling him as little as possible, in the vaguest terms. Yet he persisted.

"Bet you're finding some real treasure."

"My line of work is very rocky."

"Seriously, any more gold?"

"I leave no stone unturned."

Exasperated, Frank would then enumerate the favors he was doing for Vita. I would listen appreciatively, because he needed attention, and Vita valued their friendship.

"You're lucky to have her," he'd say, as though I didn't know.

"She thinks I take her for granite."

"Enough with the jokes, Cal."

But I had to deflect his questions, without antagonizing him. The news that I was extracting high-quality emeralds from a hidden mine in Zambia would have excited his greed. I wanted Frank to be calm, and Vita to be happy, and for me to be unknowable.

15

THE GEOLOGY OF HOME

ERE'S THE PARADOX OF SERIOUS TRAVEL: YOU GO FAR away to a foreign place and are alienated by culture shock; but after a while, months rather than years, it wears off. Then all is smooth in your life until you return to your hometown and are hit hard, stunned anew. There is no recovering from it. The culture shock of arriving home never leaves you—you long to escape it, to go away again soon. This became the pattern of my working life.

That staggering blow, that longing, was unknown to Frank, who took a few casual vacations yet never left home. Because of that, he didn't know me, nor had he ever experienced the upsetting visits that were routine for me. I saw all this in terms of the fractures in geology, the kind of mineral cleavage that split crystals, or the deformation that separated fine-grained rock, but cleavage all the same. I was separated, yet I kept going home as often as I could, for the love of my wife and son.

What unsettled me was the geology of Littleford itself, the softness, the mushiness of its foundation, the apparent absence of bedrock. Littleford had been built on a riverbank—Boston downstream, at the mouth of the river; mud and pudding stone upstream beneath the town, a scattering of pillow lava showing in the woods and suspended under the town in a thick gray stew of splintery-weathered, sugary-textured gneiss. Glacial drift had deposited a layer of shifted gravel on top of the deep-down bedrock—more properly a conglomerate known as mudstone—the bedrock so deep that Littleford floated above it, on a slush of pebbly sediment.

No mineral had ever been seriously searched for within a radius of a hundred miles of Littleford. Massachusetts was a state without a mine, with no shafts or tunnels, no subterranean life, hardly any mineral glitter except for dull roseate chunks of rhodonite, the state gem—though "gem" conveys the wrong impression. Rhodonite is a pinky purplish crystal that is never cut or polished or faceted. Vita would have been insulted to be given a lump of the stuff, she would have first taken it to be a stale chunk of Christmas candy, and then recognized it as the sort of clutter she'd seen ornamenting the broken gravel glowing in a rubious mass with the sprinkling of fish turds like chocolate jimmies at the bottom of a home aquarium.

As for Cape Cod, where I'd rescued Frank that summer afternoon, and where we sometimes still vacationed, the whole of it was a great soft length of dampness and stunted trees, beyond the bedrock outcrop— no exposed rock, just a terminal moraine, a vast and featureless set of dunes, shoved southeasterly and formed by a glacier, leaving it crooked, a bended arm of shifting sand.

No wonder I got culture shock at home, no wonder I longed for multicolored cliffs and ravines, and the bedrock in the solitude of far-off places. I maintained my silence about the emeralds we were mining in Zambia. Moyo and I valued our ability as pioneering prospectors to work in secrecy. The gem dealers in Jo'burg were persistent in asking, but we refused to reveal the source of the stones.

Had these dealers sent spies they would have found no more than a Zambian village of mud huts, flyblown slit-trench latrines, cassava gardens, and maize fields. And maybe a glimpse of a single *mzungu*—me, in a tin-roof shack—but nothing more. Moyo had admitted me as a partner, but no one else. I owed him my loyalty and discretion, because we both knew that in time the word would get out, and a rush to dig would begin—tunnels, open-pits, blasting, all the resources of the Copperbelt brought in to mine the much more profitable gemstones. We worked urgently, knowing that our days of seclusion were numbered.

Seeking understanding, hoping for a smile, I described to Vita the oddness of my life in the field—far away from Littleford, in an alien culture, the obstacles, the nuisances, the occasional rewards. I'd talked in this way since we'd met. I needed her to know who I was and what I'd seen, but I did not tell her everything: it was important that I distract her from my geology, the jewels, the bargaining, the money.

What I related came under the heading "travelers' tales," which satisfied her and seemed harmless enough. She often asked me to tell her of abuses I'd witnessed—stories of child labor or human trafficking that she could report to her agency. I had no information of this kind. And I'd grown so accustomed to the oddities, I needed to think hard about what I'd seen that might interest her. My African stories produced another unexpected episode in my life with Frank.

As a local boy in porous, gossip-prone Littleford, someone rumored to have done well, I was hailed at the supermarket and the post office and drugstore and greeted with the grateful bonhomie accorded to a prodigal son, because when someone from Littleford left town, they seldom returned.

You could live anywhere, I was told, *and here you are.*

I never mentioned my hometown culture shock; I accepted the praise for my not having turned my back on the town. But not all these people were well-wishers.

Trouble is, some said, *you're never here.*

But Frank, they were quick to add, was always in town, a benefactor, in his prominent office in Littleford Square, loyal to the town, which apparently, as a part-timer, I wasn't.

"One thing about your brother Frank," Sal Ugolino said, "he stayed with us, he's wicked involved in the community, he really cares. He could have been a huge deal in Boston or New York, but did he go? No—he still shoots pool at Joe's."

That was a knock on me. I'd abandoned them by pursuing my business elsewhere, my perverse choice of a mining career. It didn't matter much to these tribal townies that I'd bought a house here and was putting my son through Littleford schools. I had a life elsewhere, and what was worse, an obscure life, something to do with rocks.

"Frank makes us proud," the brothers Alex and Leo Alberti said.

Frank had a way of advertising his concerns for the workingman. It didn't seem to matter that Frank got a third of the payout in personal injury suits—the client got a whopping two-thirds. As a benefactor, Frank was also a self-promoter, and an explainer. He was proof that Littleford produced good citizens and success stories; anyone who became successful elsewhere was seen as disloyal. I didn't object. I smiled at their odd pomposities, as they lectured me, criticizing me by praising Frank.

And who were they? Old high school buddies, former girlfriends, the fixtures in Littleford, the dentist, the chiropractor, the family doctor, the cobbler, the pharmacist. Many I had known since I was a child. They'd married in the town, they still lived and worked there; many were politicians, a number of them were cops.

The mayor, Dante Zangara, made a point of praising Frank to me. He had a small-town politician's habit of being conspicuous, strolling through town on summer days, greeting people, and he always signaled when he saw me.

"What I love about Frank," Dante said, "is he's very humble—a simple guy."

These were qualities Frank utterly lacked—humility, simplicity; but the mayor vouched for him.

What this meant was that Frank hadn't left Littleford, as I had, and that he gave money to Dante's mayoral campaign. Frank donated books to the library. He supported the Little League. I had done none of these things.

"That client he had with black lung," Chicky Malatesta said. "Frank was a godsend. If I ever need a lawyer, I'll call Frank."

"He's beautiful to your mother," Ginny Spatola said.

Philanthropic, caring, generous, social—Frank was everything I was not. And the next subject they were likely to touch upon was how prosperous Frank had become, a hometown boy who had not forsaken his birthplace. The fact that he had the means to leave, and yet stayed, was a reassurance to those who'd dreamed of leaving yet didn't risk it, or couldn't afford it.

I said, "Littleford's a great place to raise kids," which was what they wanted to hear, and I was sincere, hand on heart.

I didn't mention Frank, but they did, because they saw the Bad Angel brothers as a matching pair, and brotherhood as an ideal. They didn't know me well enough to understand how different we were, Frank and I. We had nothing in common, no beliefs, no pleasures, not even the same language. I tried to be specific and scientific, but Frank preferred bluff and hyperbole, loving *in this fashion, at this juncture, in point of fact,* and *prioritize.* And the legal terms he was addicted to, *due process, de facto, prima facie,* and all the ambiguous rest of it, *onus probandi, subrogation,* and *litigation risk.*

I'm crafting a response was Frank's mantra.

He was important in Littleford, a town that had once been a small community on a riverbank but now sprawled, its suburbs overtaking the woods I'd once hiked with Mel Yurick, in pursuit of solitude and merit badges. But the core of Littleford was still tiny and tribal in the way it regarded outsiders or new arrivals, appearing to accept them, yet in fierce whispers that shocked me still regarding them as unwelcome, the waves of Hispanics, Vietnamese, Indians, and a scattering of Africans, none of whom figured in the orbit of Frank and his friends.

All the more reason I was praised for returning. And as though intending to compliment me, the old-timers—high school buddies, friends of the family, shop owners in Littleford Square, the usual politicians—all of them said they thought the world of Frank.

I listened to these people, because in one part of my mind there was always a tug of doubt, a feeling that I'd been unfair to Frank, exaggerated his intrusiveness, overstated his faults, resented his legalistic fussiness (*Define what you mean by presumption*), and this doubt was bolstered by Vita's view of him as a good guy, reliable, more than competent—expert, her adviser and protector, a helpful uncle to Gabe, now in junior high school.

Smacking his lips with certainty, Harry O'Brien, of O'Brien's Plumbing Supplies, where I happened to be buying a showerhead—Harry, from Frank's class at Littleford High—reached and put his hand on my arm to detain me, saying, "Frank was in here the other day—feller's full of stories, God love him."

"That's always been true."

"But they're getting better."

I became attentive, to encourage him.

Harry said, "That old woman he met—can't remember where it was, exactly—she had these kids with her, couple of boys, little girl—amazing."

"What was amazing?"

"She was pimping them out."

"Frank told you that?"

"Yes, all the gory details."

It was not an experience of Frank's, it was mine, in India, on a backstreet of Mumbai, where I'd arrived on my way to Madikeri, in the Western Ghats of Karnataka, the first of our ruby mines.

The woman, the children in tow, had accosted me at a café—"Where you from? Buy me a cup of tea!" I was seated at an outside table, drinking coffee, dazed by the long flight, and was so blindsided by the woman, I said, "Take a seat." They all joined me, laughing, as I called the waiter. They ordered tea, a plate of samosas, and juice. The children ate hungrily, as the woman pestered me with questions. Where was I going? What was I doing? Dodging the questions, I found myself looking at the young girl.

She was about fifteen, birdlike, with prominent teeth, very thin, with large dark eyes, and draped in a green shawl. She wore makeup—mascara, reddened lips, a child dressed as a woman, and strangely skeletal.

"You like her?" the woman said. When I didn't reply, she said, "You can have her."

I felt a surge of desire mingled with disgust, the shame that I was actually attracted. I stood up, gave the waiter some rupees—more than enough—and fled to my hotel. I was glad to leave the next day for Hubli, and the Ghats, and the rubies.

I told Vita the story, as an example of life in India, and also because her agency was concerned with the exploitation of children. This was the sort of trafficking Rescue/Relief investigated.

Harry was still smiling. He said, "Of course, Frank didn't play ball. But I mean, imagine!"

Frank had appropriated my story—obviously Vita had told him. And I had other examples like this. I bumped into one of his golf partners at the post office, a man named Walter Loftus, who greeted me warmly, asked how I was doing, and added, "I see a lot of your brother."

"Golfing?"

"Oh, yeah, up at the club, all over. Great guy, and what a raconteur."

To provoke him, I said, "Amazing tales—that's Frank."

But Loftus frowned and became serious. He said, "Can I share something with you? I get worried sometimes, the chances he takes. Yet he always somehow turns them to his advantage."

"Not sure what you mean, Walter."

"Like the old man he found up in the Fells, stranded there. I would have walked on by, but Frank's not like that. He saw that the man was in distress and needed help. Frank's such a Samaritan. The guy doesn't speak much English but he knows where he lives. Frank takes him home—turns out he's a big man in the Mafia, somehow escaped being whacked. And his family's so grateful they kick a lot of business Frank's way." Loftus sighed in admiration. "I'm sure you know the story."

"I do know the story," I said.

Everyone Frank knew had a story he'd told them that was derived from one I'd told Vita—bribe stories, bad hotel stories, even trivial ones, such as the convenience of raising pigeons to eat. It so happened that in Zambia, Moyo and I kept pigeons in our obscure little village, and Moyo's cook used their little corpses in curry. Frank, it seemed, also had pigeon stories.

These were casual mentions, but I dug deeper, the sort of domestic geology I'd found to be fruitful in knowing Frank. At times I encountered reluctance—"I shouldn't be telling you this"—and had to dig harder.

"It's okay—Frank and I are brothers. We have no secrets."

"It's just that Frank was so upset that it could have ended in tragedy."

"What could?"

"The day he saved you from drowning."

The Frank stories, dozens of them, were not the result of a single visit home, but rather an anthology, the accumulation over a year or two, my being told in admiring tones by Frank's friends in town, his amazing tales, ones I knew properly to be mine. It was as though he'd begun to inhabit my life, making my experiences his own. But why? He was a successful attorney, with a circle of friends, a networker before the word was coined. Why would he feel the need to tell my traveler's tales as his own?

Aspects of the stories were so nebulous as to make them deniable as coming from me, so I resisted confronting him, knowing he'd claim they were his. There was something sad about this, too, because all tales of this kind are boasts, and the notion of a secondhand boast depressed me. As a lawyer with many personal injury victories Frank had plenty to boast about. He didn't need my tales of pimps and bribes and pigeons.

I pitied him for claiming them as his own, since not all the stories were amazing. Many were based on my banal experiences of bumping from place to place, among strangers in distant lands; and I knew that Frank seldom left Littleford. But that mention by a mutual friend (it was Chicky Malatesta) that Frank said he'd rescued me from drowning was the limit.

"Are you trying to start trouble?" Vita said when I told her soon after—this was in the kitchen, Vita studying a cookbook, and surrounded by ingredients.

Vita had a way of turning her back on me in such a conversation, to indicate that she had no interest in pursuing a subject. Now turned away, she busied herself with the dish she planned to make, sorting the ingredients—chicken thighs, carrots, onions, a bottle of burgundy— coq au vin, I guessed.

"It didn't happen. The opposite happened. I saved Frank."

With her finger on the page of the recipe, her head down, Vita spoke to the open cookbook on the counter. "You heard this secondhand."

"From a mutual friend—Chicky."

"Hearsay." She turned the page, preoccupied.

"You're joking."

"It's inadmissible." She tapped the page.

"You sound like him."

Now she turned, holding an onion in one hand and a very large knife in the other, and facing me, said, "Then ask him—put it to him. 'You're stealing my stories.'"

"Twisting the truth," I said. "No point. He'd just deny it."

Now she smiled and looked at me in a pitying and exasperated way. "So why don't you just drop it." She placed the onion on the cutting board and began to slash at it. "Or tell your mother."

16

THE COMPASS

F EW SIGHTS ARE MORE MELANCHOLY IN A MARRIAGE
than that of a man hunched in semidarkness at a plain evening meal alone, like a peasant over a bowl of sludge, while his wife
("I'm not hungry") sits in the next room, laughing on a phone call to a
friend—in my case, the friend being Frank.

To be clear, they were not having an affair. I was scrupulous in my
snooping with that in mind—hyperalert for evasions, contradictions,
unexplained absences, as well as obliquely interrogating Gabe, and
looking at phone records. And an affair, even the most passionate one,
full of urgencies and demands, is never smooth. I found no hint of
messiness or anything covert on Vita's part. Tender toward me, most of
the time, she would have been a total hypocrite to be carrying on with
Frank while whispering endearments in my ear. And an affair—I knew
from my bachelor days in Littleford—is exhausting and complex. What
I remembered of sexual obsession—with Julie, with a few others—was
fatigue and frustration, interrupted by episodes of frenzy: animal hunger, animal fatigue, wasted time, stupidity and sneaking.

It wasn't that way with Vita and Frank—it was a friendship, the
more maddening to me for their interaction being aboveboard and in
the open. None of it was hidden, as far as I could tell, and that was
worse, more hurtful than if they carried on behind my back. An adul-
terous affair is a kind of madness, a drama of selfishness and deception;

but a friendship is serene, humane, generous, and life-affirming. I disliked Frank too much to be part of the friendship, so it was all played out before me, like a dance, Frank and Vita pirouetting prettily while I watched. The kinder and more helpful they were, the more I hated myself for disliking him.

Ask him, Vita had said about the rescue story, and I'd replied that there was no point, that Frank would deny it. But her certainty that I was imagining Frank appropriating my stories made me suspect I might have been hasty. The stories shared similarities, but that was all. As always, I thought, *Maybe I'm wrong.*

At Vita's suggestion I agreed to meet Frank at the diner and ask him about the story Chicky Malatesta had told me, of Frank's saving me from drowning. We had not seen each other recently but when we did meet for lunch, we avoided serious topics. I kept my geology, and especially my successes, to myself; Frank boasted of his wins but didn't elaborate. What he enjoyed was relating long stories about his indigent—but shortly to be wealthy—clients in personal injury cases.

One lengthy tale centered around a tramp who'd stumbled on a crack in a sidewalk in Boston, falling and fracturing his ankle, that allowed Frank to sue the city for the man's physical and emotional damages, in which Frank's favorite, "suicidal ideation," figured once again. The man's case was not the story; what Frank went on about was how the man—ragged, unshaven, limping from his injury—visited his office and complained, "You ain't got no air-conditioning in here, man? Shoot, I'm boiling"—Frank a good mimic, especially of the poor and oppressed. His subject was often the ingratitude of the poor. Another theme was the many ways a winner in a personal injury suit would squander their millions and end up poorer than before.

I was early at the diner this day, but Frank had come earlier than me, eager to watch me enter, studying me as I approached him in his booth, sizing me up. What was I wearing? Had I aged? Was I limping? Maybe I was ill? What was my mood? Did I have something on my mind?

A sleuthing instinct and skeptical nature are part of every personal injury lawyer's character, marshaling details, gathering facts, noting inconsistencies, building a case, while at the same time blandly smiling, giving nothing away. I admired Frank's gift for observation, he could have been a great detective; it made him a winner in lawsuits and so daunting an adversary—being well-prepared—that when he laid out his case in a deposition his opponents frequently folded and were happy to settle, usually on Frank's terms. He was smiling now, the up-and-down smile of his palsied face, and staring at me with his mismatched eyes.

He called out "Fidge" as he slid from his booth and hugged me. I was disarmed for the moment, flustered by the warmth of his greeting. But I also thought: *He sees that I have something on my mind and is squeezing it out of me, leaving me breathless.*

Face-to-face in the booth, we ordered—fish for him, a burger for me—and while we waited for our food, he leaned toward me and seemed to swell, his face reddening, one eye widening, the other squinting. I was about to ask him if he felt all right when he spoke, explosively, as though addressing a jury.

"A guy comes into money, owing to some quackery or humbuggery," he said. "He buys a huge piece of property, because he can't abide the proximity of neighbors. But here's the kicker. The bigger the property, the more neighbors he has. Wait"—because I was about to ask where this was going—"Take me, for example. I've got three, one on each side, one at the back. But the guy with the big estate has a shitload of abutters—twenty neighbors, maybe more, all of them whining."

He said "a guy," but I was sure he meant me, my six acres in the Winthrop Estates. That was Frank's usual method of attack, a hypothetical story as insinuation.

"The guy can't see them, though," I said. "The neighbors."

He rapped the table, he loved this. "That's when they encroach. They're sprawling all over your property line."

"And they stumble on my land and end up suing me?"

He talked over me, saying, "White shoe law firms, ambulance chasers, personal injury hacks—these are the villains, people say. But look at it in three dimensions and you see they're doing a lot of good. Me, I deal with high-stakes, complex commercial and intellectual property in white-collar cases. I get results."

This was a cloud of incomprehensible bluster, and it silenced me, as I supposed it was meant to. The food came, Frank poked at his fish.

"Funny thing happened . . ."

He paused, a smile softening one side of his mouth, looking reflective and somehow grateful. His thoughtful expression calmed me.

"Louis Levesque came to my office, quite by chance." Frank folded his hands and went on. "You may remember that Louis was a close friend of Dad's, and a keen day sailor. Dad called him 'The Bishop.' He had a catboat at a mooring in Marblehead Harbor. Some weekends they'd drink at the French Club in Lowell—all the Canucks together— and then Louis and Dad would head for Marblehead and go sailing. Dad was so proud of his Quebecois roots, and since his ancestors had been mariners, he believed he'd inherited some sailing ability . . ."

I had not known any of this. And as always, listening to Frank, I thought, *Where is this going?* I reminded myself that I meant to ask him about the story he'd told of saving me from drowning.

Between chewing and swallowing bites of his haddock, he extolled Dad's skill on the water, a good ten minutes of background, before he came to the point: one particular day Dad showed up for a sail carrying a compass. Not any old compass but a silver object the shape and size of a pocket watch, stamped *Harrods Ltd, London,* and when the lid was opened, a set of silver bezels—set like collars—was revealed, a mother-of-pearl compass dial in the center. When the collars were tugged upward, the compass danced on the pivot of a gimbal.

Bezel and *pivot* and *gimbal*—Frank loved the sort of lingo that would dazzle a jury. But I could see the compass very clearly, as something Dad might treasure, a vintage mariner's compass.

"And after the sail that day, Louis admired the compass." With a flourish, Frank made a gesture, cupping his hand. "Dad said, 'Take it.'"

Dad insisted that Louis keep it, and though Louis knew he should have refused this valuable thing, he accepted it with both hands, Dad smiling and saying that Louis would put it to good use.

My head hurt, and the image of my saving Frank from drowning in the creek was receding. In a dazed voice I said, "Just like Dad. So generous."

"Here's the kicker," Frank said. "After Louis told me the story and described the compass, he reached into his pocket and pulled it out. 'I'm an old man. I still feel bad about taking it off your father, all those years ago. I asked him to take it back, but you know him—he wouldn't hear of it. So I want you to have it.'"

And Louis had handed it over to Frank—the lovely silver compass that Dad in his youth had given to his friend, now back in the Belanger family.

Frank then went silent and ate his meal, while I watched him. I had finished my hamburger while listening to his story. Absorbed in his eating he seemed uninterested in saying anything to me. At last, he dabbed at his mouth with his napkin and drank his lemonade. This seemed the right time to ask him about the rescue he'd lied about.

"Great story," I said, and as I spoke, Frank shoved his cuff aside and checked his watch, the sign that he was about to go.

Signaling to the waitress for the check, he said, "I have a meeting."

"Wait, there's something I want to ask."

Swirling at the hot edge of my headache was not just the rescue story, but the woman-pimping-the-kids story, and the one about the old man abandoned in the woods.

"Almost forgot," Frank said, as though I hadn't spoken. He slapped his pants pocket and brought out a silver object that might have been an elegant pocket watch. It was the vintage compass he'd described. He pressed it into my hand and closed my fingers over it.

The thing was warm from being in his pocket, the lovely silver compass, the temperature of a body part, snug in my hand.

"You can put it to good use on your travels," Frank said in a kindly voice, Dad's voice, the very thing he'd said to Louis Levesque. "It will show you the way."

With that, he got up and patted me on the shoulder, a gesture of affection, as he passed me, and I sat, still holding the compass. I lifted the lid, then twisted and raised the bezel, so that it became a collar. The dial of the compass danced and spun and finally settled, pointing north toward the cash register. A small ruby, like a drop of blood, winked on the pivot point. I studied the arrow's direction, as though divining its meaning—the mother-of-pearl glittered like a crystal, so it seemed I was scrying—and its slight wobble engaged my attention. I was so moved by Frank's gesture I forgot the questions I'd planned to ask him. When I remembered (the arrow now pointing out the door), I thought, *Doesn't matter.*

The mood had passed, Frank's stories now seemed trivial and forgivable—possibly coincidental, far less important than the spontaneous gift of the silver compass from long ago that had been Dad's.

The warm compass in my hand had energy; it filled my palm, its heft giving it power. It reminded me of my father—his kindness, his generosity, his simple wisdom, true as a compass. When I'd told him I was going to a college in another state, far away, to study geology, he'd said, "Wonderful."

The time I scraped the fender of the car, not badly but a disfiguring ding—he knew I was ashamed, so he didn't mention it and quietly had it repaired. He was proud of me as a Boy Scout, my studying for merit badges, the hikes I took, the overnight camping trips. He encouraged me to be a camper, a solo hiker, a cook, a rock climber, all the skills that made me independent. He did not disapprove of my having a .22-caliber rifle. He, too, had a gun, a small revolver he kept in his office desk. He sometimes took me target shooting. In all his love and attention, he taught me how to leave home.

That was the meaning of the compass point. He derived pleasure from my success. He didn't want it for himself. He didn't boast. Seeing me happy he was content. He inspired confidence, and in this way he'd given me my life.

He'd died relatively young, before I could tell him of my successes, gold hunting, emerald mining. He'd taught me by example how to have a happy marriage. He'd never quarreled with Mother, he never looked for an argument. A man in a car behind him, honking his horn? "Must be in a hurry," Dad would say—he didn't take it personally. He was peaceable, mild, wholly content in his marriage, grateful to be in love with Mother.

The compass still in my hand was something wonderful, like a peace offering, a rare instance of my receiving a gift I loved and needed. I'd take it back to Africa. I saw that the needle was pointing, as though at Dad's instigation, to the north end of town, to Mother's house.

17

MOTHER

STILL WITH THE SILVER COMPASS IN MY HAND, I LINgered in front of Tower House, the mansion Mother had given to me, admiring its superb condition: freshly reshingled, newly painted, buffed and repointed stonework, a massive antique, restored by Vita and me to its former glory, Mother, my grateful tenant. And then I mounted the fieldstone stairs.

Mother must have heard me on the steps, because just as I approached the front door to reach for the bronze knocker—a scowling lion with a ring in its mouth—she called out "Come in, Fidge!"

Seated on the bulgy sofa at the far side of the parlor, among cushions and shawls, she was soft and white-faced and delicate, like one of her own cherished antique dolls. She collected fragile and feathery dolls, giving them names and treating them as her companions. They sat all over the room in chairs and on stools, and one in a wickerwork infant's cradle that mewed when you rocked it. They stared with blue believable eyes out of porcelain faces, wearing gauzy dresses and bonnets, ribbons in their hair, with fixed rosebud smiles.

The dolls spooked me, not in the conventional way—dolls as ghostly, with creepy eyes, making mischief—but as dust-gathering objects, praised as collectibles, like the cushions and the doilies and the souvenir plates. Ever since buying the house in the Winthrop Estates—Vita furnishing it—I had begun to be oppressed by the accumulation of possessions, the burden of clutter. Travel had taught me economy and simplicity. I had never owned a house before, and I liked having a home to return to, but I was not prepared for Vita's weighing it down with objects, pictures filling the walls, rugs overlapping on the floor, knickknacks on the shelves, every surface covered, as though by cramming the house with things she'd bought she was claiming it for herself and was more secure having plumped it with possessions. "Nest" was a cheery way of looking at it, but all I thought of it as was dead weight that saddened me and hemmed me in.

"You've had a touch of sun," Mother was saying, as I reflected on her possessions, reminding me of how Vita had stuffed our house—though she might have used the Florida word *accessorized*.

"Africa," I said, still dazed by the sensory overload of all Mother's things—more it seemed than when I'd last visited—her overflowing knitting basket, the chairs draped with scarves, the clocks and vases, the mechanical canary twittering in a towering birdcage, the frilly lampshades, all those dolls, and a profusion of mirrors multiplying the clutter in glittering reflections.

"I don't know how you do it, Fidge," Mother said. "All that foreign travel."

Aged, elegant Mother was fragile and feathery, too—a wisp of a woman—as usual in a frilly dress. She suited the decor, but I also thought that her acquisitiveness was a form of mourning, the clutter was a comfort. The dolls and cushions and lamps began to appear after Dad died, as though she was trying to fill the space he'd left. I knew that Dad, like me, disliked the accumulation of dusty artifacts. His own study in the topmost room of the tower was severe—a wooden chest, a pine table, two Windsor chairs, a small bookcase, a pedestal ashtray and smoking stand. Dad had been forbidden to smoke anywhere else in the house, because his pipe smoke clung to the curtains and shawls and upholstery.

Dad had deferred to Mother, but it was an easy concession for him to make, because he loved her and was loyal to her. *I feel his presence,* Mother said, which was understandable. They'd bought the house when they'd married, they fixed it up and furnished it and raised us in it. It was the only house they'd ever lived in, and having made it their own, the vibration of their love was strong in it.

Glad to see Mother after being away, I leaned down and kissed her floury cheek and said, "You look great—so does the house."

"It's all yours," she said, "as you know."

I nudged a doll aside on a nearby chair, sat next to it, and said, "Not yet."

"You pay the bills! By the way, there's a few more on the mantelpiece."

"What beautiful earrings." They were gold nuggets suspended on delicate chains—nuggets I'd found on my early prospecting in Arizona. They were the more lovely for being lumpy and irregular, with a rich gold glow, heightened today by the light from the lamp near Mother's head.

"Someone special gave them to me," Mother said in the coy voice of a coquette and set them in motion with a nod.

"You look really well, Mum."

"I've just had my hair done." She lightly clasped her blue hairdo with her fingertips.

She was a little over seventy, not old but brittle, unsteady, afraid of risking a fall. Without makeup her face was so lined it seemed tessellated, but she smoothed it, masking it with face powder and rouge. As an only child, adored by her parents, she'd been raised as a princess, and all that attention had given her confidence. Self-sufficient, a little vain about her appearance, carefully attired, among her well-dressed dolls, her hair stiffened and set—she was the very image of serenity. She hadn't known I was going to drop in, and yet she looked as though she was waiting for me.

Her air of calm was like a reproach to me—Fidge, the fidgety son, who could not sit still. Yet in her stillness there seemed a hesitation, as though she was holding something back.

"But you get out now and then, don't you?"

"Stairs are my bugbear."

"I'll get a ramp built—it'll be easier for you."

"Oh, I'm happy where I am."

Now I noticed a fragrance, a sweetness in the air, her perfume or else the fragrance of the dolls, a ripple of lavender, and with this a soapy aroma, as of newly laundered clothes, with a tang of starch.

Mother still looked tentative, her lips pursed, as though restraining herself from speaking. I recognized that look of hesitancy. She needed to be nudged.

"What's on your mind, Mum?"

"I wish you'd come here with Frank." She blinked, she smiled, she clasped her hands. "I love seeing you two together."

"I usually have lunch with him when I'm back—I just saw him." This did not satisfy her; she looked past me and began to brood. "Doesn't he stop in to see you?" I asked.

She hesitated before answering and finally said, "Poor Frank," in a tone of concern, but the way her hands were clasped, her fingers twisted together, suggested anguish. "He's so busy—doesn't have a minute to himself." She sighed and with more certainty added, "He doesn't get much help on the home front."

She was much too polite to say what she thought, that Frolic was frivolous and undependable, unworthy of the huge settlement Frank had won for her. But of course it was Frank's money now, or at least his to manage. As someone who'd been raised by hippies in rural Maine, Frolic was irrational about money—wealth was unreal. She was either lavish in her spending or else obsessively frugal, reckless in giving large sums away, supporting her now-divorced mother, buying her a pickup truck while she herself was wearing thrift shop clothes, shuffling in old shoes and shaming Frank—who was fussy about food—by lunching on peanut butter and jelly sandwiches. Hers was the severity, bordering on masochism, of the penny-pincher. Nor was she clean, another tightfisted trait, scrimping on personal hygiene—the miser is so often malodorous. Frolic was whiffy.

Yet I sympathized with her, so different from Frank—she was open-hearted and, coming from a hard-up family, a bit lost with all that money and having to live with manipulative Frank.

Instead of disparaging Frolic, I said, "Frank's fine."

Mother winced, her subtle way of questioning that, and she reached up, clasping her head with both hands to steady her hairdo with her fingers, as though fearing her headshake of doubt might loosen it.

"You have no idea," she said.

She regarded Frank as vulnerable, charitable to a fault, overworked—so many people depended on him he rarely had time for Mother. I suspected that this was the way Frank portrayed himself to her, reporting on his woes, to make his excuses plausible.

"He can take care of himself."

In her half-laughing way, she said, "He's not like you, Fidge."

That much was true, but what did she see?

"He's more of a homebody," she said. "He didn't go away to make his fortune, as you did."

"He's done all right, staying in Littleford."

Perhaps detecting a note of rancor in my voice—I was becoming agitated, thinking of her sympathy for Frank—she said, "Frank admires you so much. He envies you your free spirit. He's always praising you. And he's very fond of Vita and Gabe."

"But he's tough," I said, persisting.

"It's a façade. Frank's actually very shy. Always was. But he has a kind heart."

This depiction of Frank was making me cross, yet I didn't want to upset Mother by contradicting her, so I simply said, "Frank is known to be a fierce adversary as a lawyer."

"He defends the little man. He helps people. That's his way."

"He makes a ton of money in these cases, Mum."

"I know about his moneymaking. It's just harmless vanity—making more money than he can ever spend."

Mother's apparent clear-sightedness made Frank seem sympathetic. I had never discussed Frank in these terms before. She was wise and understanding, and subtle in forgiving the complexity of Frank.

"As his mother, I wish he spent more time with you."

I considered this. I said, "We have our ups and downs."

Uttering this mild platitude, I had shameful glimpses of all the times I wanted to hurt him, my duct-taping him and pummeling him fantasy, my shoving him down the steep fieldstone stairs, or frightening him by holding a gun to his face, his gibbering lips, his frantic mismatched eyes.

"That's normal for brothers," Mother said. "Be patient."

"He can be really annoying."

"Forgive him," she said, which sounded as though she knew that what I was saying had merit. "You'll be happier if you overlook his faults—they won't eat at you."

I wanted to give her specific instances of Frank's hostility, but with the compass in my pocket it seemed hypocritical—I'd accepted it, and his giving it to me with such grace I took it to be a sort of peace offering.

"Have a nice cookie," Mother said.

I wanted to laugh at the simplicity of this, and I was also grateful for her changing the subject. She tapped a plate of them that I'd taken to be part of a shrine, because even cookies in this house conformed to Mother's style—the plate was gold-trimmed, scallop-edged, upraised on a porcelain pedestal, the cookies were covered but visible under a glass cake dome. Surrounding the pedestal were fat candles in cups—unlit but aromatic—and dishes of foil-wrapped sweets, arrayed like offerings. Nearby were dainty teacups and saucers, a crystal sugar bowl and silver tongs, like ritual objects. Completing this arrangement was a set of linen napkins, rolled and fastened by gilded napkin rings, all of it giving the impression of an altar, a shrine to cookies.

I lifted the dome and took one.

"Use a plate, Fidge. As Dad used to say, it's more *comme il faut*."

To please her I selected a napkin, too, and sat and nibbled, playing the part of visiting son—grateful because this was the ceremony the altarlike table had been meant for, the ritual of Mother's cookies.

"I love being your tenant," she said. "It's such a load off my mind. I used to worry about all the things that needed fixing. Believe me, I know what a bother it is for you."

"Not a bother, Mum," I said, chewing a cookie. "You gave me the house."

"It was only right. You didn't have a place of your own. And Frank owns so much real estate in town." She looked past me, reflecting, one of her characteristic pauses, before whispering a confidence. "I think Frolic lets her family stay in some of the places Frank owns—he's so generous."

That reminded me of his gesture in the diner, his flourishing the compass, just as I was about to mention the stories he'd appropriated from me and was telling his friends. The one that had enraged me was his saying he'd saved me from drowning. But with the silver compass in my hand I was flummoxed, and then he was gone.

"Frank gave me this," I said.

Holding her hairdo, Mother tipped herself forward to look more closely at the shiny compass in my outstretched hand. She gasped a little, she shouted, "What a hoot!" and she clutched her throat. "I knew this day would come!"

"It was Dad's—he gave it to Louis Levesque," I said. I told her the story of the sail on Louis's boat out of Marblehead, how Dad had presented it, and how Louis had recently given it to Frank.

Mother was still smiling—the sort of smile that suggested she had something in her mouth, unswallowed, that she was savoring with pleasure.

"Louis didn't have a boat—not a sailboat," she said. "He had a snug little canoe, and you always got wet when you went paddling with him."

Catboat, Frank had claimed. But I said, "It's not about the boat."

"And that compass—it wasn't Dad's," she said. "I forgot all about it."

I held the thing in my hand. Now, after her smiles and her laughter, she seemed sad and a little tearful as she glanced at it.

"That's what I was trying to tell you about Frank. He may seem contrary, but he always does the right thing in the end. I knew this day would come."

"Mum, I'm confused," I said, and with all this talk, the compass was heavy and damp in my sweaty palm.

"It wasn't Dad's," she said. "The night you became an Eagle Scout— your big night."

"I was sick," I said. "Tonsillitis."

"Frank took your place—don't you remember? He accepted the medal on your behalf. He gave a lovely speech. And since you got more merit badges than your friend Mel Yurick, you got the compass."

"This one?"

"Yes! Frank was so thrilled, he begged Dad not to say anything about it. 'I'll give it to Fidge eventually,' he said. 'I just want to keep it for a while.'"

Now she peered closely at it.

"It's a nice one," I said.

"We never really got a good look at it. Frank was always so evasive—probably embarrassed. And after a while, with so much happening, we forgot about it. He never mentioned it."

I slipped the compass into my pocket and wiped my damp palm on a napkin. And I felt that strange whittled-down sensation of having been deceived, a light-headedness, and a kind of sudden stupidity.

"But see," Mother said, "he did give it to you after all."

Mother was glad for what she took to be closure, and so I said nothing more. But leaving the house I was unsteady on the fieldstone steps, bewildered by the story Frank had told me, and feeling dumb and clumsy with wonderment. Did Frank believe his own lies? He seemed to believe nothing. His explanation had dissuaded me from asking him about the false stories he'd been telling. Everything he'd said about the compass was untrue. I wanted to know more, but a person who lied like that had no conscience; and a person with no conscience was unknowable.

18

ANOTHER PATH

THAT VISIT HOME WAS PIVOTAL, THOUGH I DIDN'T KNOW it at the time—you seldom do. I was fussed, yet being fussed is not memorable. The great changes in our lives are rarely well-planned capers or dramatic decisions, knee-deep in the Rubicon, plunging forward. They're usually bumbling deviations, barely perceptible at the outset. It's not an apparent choice. You find yourself on a path, you wander aimlessly, and after a while you're awakened to its widening, and its differences. Then it's too late to turn back, or too much trouble, because you'd have to explain too much. It's more comfortable to drift, and you console yourself by claiming this was a good move. Maybe it was. Or maybe it was a mistake. But it all happened simply: way back, you took a turn, possibly a wrong one, and didn't stumble, and kept going, growing, or diminishing, but certainly becoming someone different. That's how it was with me.

My first steps began with silences. It is so much easier and more peaceful to say nothing. I didn't confront Frank in his lie about the compass. I didn't dispute Mother's version. Over family dinner with Vita and Gabe I mentioned I'd seen Frank. Vita volunteered that Frank was helping Rescue/Relief with another lawsuit.

"Pro bono—he's an angel. I have a huge caseload at the moment," she said.

She was helping people, Frank was helping people; I wasn't helping anyone, so I had to change the subject.

Gabe said, "Uncle Frank talked to our civics class about a law career."

"Maybe I should talk to them about rocks."

"The class really liked him," Gabe said, talking over me, in the way Frank often did. "He had some cool stories."

"What about?"

"Like, character. Like winning."

"I sometimes wonder about Frank's character."

Still talking, Gabe said, "Character is the determination to get your own way. That's his definition."

"I'd say character is more like the determination to find your own way. Not conquering, but a kind of quest." While Gabe pondered this, I said, "Vita?"

She was serving a meal she knew I loved. I hadn't prompted her, she was trying to please me: fish baked with black beans and rice, topped with salsa and cilantro.

"Frank's an asset," she said, filling my plate.

"A little complicated maybe? Character issues?"

She sat and began eating, her chewing like a process of reflection, and after she swallowed, she said, "I've moved on."

That was her shorthand in our marriage. It meant *Enough. Change the subject. I'm not listening.*

I couldn't blame her for relying on Frank for legal advice. In his Soul of Kindness role he had a way of making himself saintly and indispensable—the altruist, eager to help, and always getting results. As an altruist herself—Rescue/Relief advocated children's rights, saving lives, keeping families together—Vita felt that she and Frank were engaged in a common pursuit in what I thought of as the Big Charity virtue business. I knew that Vita was sincere—her early campaign, publicizing the exploitation of child labor in the Colombian emerald mines, showed she had compassion and unselfishness. With Gabe in school she was unable to travel as she'd once done but she still exposed abuses and she developed contacts in many countries where children were exploited.

Frank was another story. I knew him to be self-serving, but he was a plausible ally, and as he'd been helpful to Vita and the agency in advising on legal issues I couldn't disparage him without seeming to undermine Vita's efforts. And as she said, she'd moved on.

"I visited my mother the other day," I said, to move on myself. I didn't mention the compass, or Mother suggesting that Frank was weak and rather vain.

Vita said, "I try to see her as much as I can. She never needs anything. She never complains. I see a lot of her in Frank."

I didn't say, *Not the Frank I know,* but instead, "She's a really generous person—she was loved. So she knows how to love. And my father loved her. There aren't many marriages like that. She supported my father in everything he did. He didn't want much, only to be a trusted insurance guy. And he was so proud of us, and her. No matter what my mother cooked—and it might have been baked beans—he always said, 'You serve a wonderful table, Mother.'"

"I'm glad you see that in her," Vita said. "I think it helps that she lived all her married life in the same house. She had stability. My parents were subjected to so much disruption, having to move because of my father's job. Also being Hispanic."

"But your folks were born in Florida and your mother's Italian."

"If you have a Spanish name you're Hispanic, no matter where you're born. Lots of the kids I try to place for adoption are rejected for being Hispanic—and they were born in the States, usually to single mothers."

It was another insight into Vita's world of rejection, vulnerability, exploitation, abuse—her efforts on behalf of the poor and dispossessed. Frank's efforts, too, as she would be quick to point out.

And the next night at dinner, still on this theme, and aware that I was returning to Zambia, she said, "We're getting reports of children being forced to work in mines in the Congo. Place called Katanga."

"I don't know anything about that," I said. "I make sure that no children are working in our mines. Like I told you, we're keeping our location secret, because of the ore we're hauling out. Where do you get your information?"

"Missionaries, medical people in the area."

"The Congo border is pretty near where we are in Zambia. Katanga's on the other side."

"Maybe you can look into it, Cal."

I said I would, I listened, I sympathized. The situation that Vita described was indisputably wicked. I wanted to care and to help eliminate injustices, but I'd seen too much to be indignant. The places where I'd lived and worked were full of barefoot children doing menial jobs—India, South America, and now Zambia, where children working was nothing out of the ordinary. To liberate children and send them to school meant depriving a family of an essential worker. When Vita talked about the children, I saw much more—the family, the village, the clan, a whole culture struggling to survive. Tamper with it, remove one or two crucial elements, and it starves, or fails badly.

I didn't have Vita's assured belief in the charities that were involved in trying to save poor countries. My only solution was: pay people more, treat them better, let them share in your successes, and keep the government out of it all. That was our strategy in Zambia, and the reason our miners were loyal and our emerald mine was productive and still secret.

Yet I admired Vita in her passion to rescue children and her belief that she could change the world. Because all I ever did was creep into the uterine passages of the earth and dig among the rocks, to deliver dusty crystals, and bathe them, and cut them, to let light pierce them, and make them live.

I went away again soon after, drifting into my other unexplained life, my real life of prospecting. I was aware that in leaving home I was separating myself from Vita and her passion and commitment. But I needed to concentrate. Wherever I traveled as a geologist I encountered in those remote places the inclusions and imperfections of rocks, as well as the contradictions and injustices of humans. I beheld the world's nakedness—raw rock, poor people.

Belowground I was at home. The pressures and enjambments that created the faults in rock formations squeezed into being small marvels, in the form of crystals and minerals and metals, fused to the ragged matter of junk rock. I dug and delved in the imperfections of the subterranean world, liberating chunks of loveliness, the sparkle of gems, the glittery crust of minerals, the glow of gold.

Aboveground, I was helpless, unable to resolve the injustices, nor could I—like Frank—pretend convincingly to believe they could be fixed. Vita's idealism and Frank's opportunism evoked in me a wearying sadness and ultimately the tedium of futility. In leaving Littleford I was not rejecting my wife or brother, or treating my travel as evasion. At least that's what I told myself. I was simply going to work.

But the heaviness of home disturbed me, the clutter in Mother's house—a house I owned. And the clutter in the house where Vita and I lived—the melancholy I felt among so many possessions, the acute culture shock whenever I returned home, the disgust I felt among the things I owned, more and more of them as the years passed, the accumulation of these useless possessions, their dead weight oppressing me.

I returned to Africa, and the small village in Kafubu, deep in the Zambian bush, the dusty portal to our magnificent mine, and my simple tin-roofed hut, with a bed and two chairs and a table, the cooking fire outside, blackened pots hung on the bare branches of a dead thorn tree. And each morning, Johnson Moyo would meet me and we would enter the black tunnel of our mine, its passages growing muddier as we descended. Each evening we emerged with our workers, their wheelbarrows piled with chunks of jagged ore, the pick marks chopped into their planes giving them the look of violent stabbings, disinterred body parts from clumsy disembowelings, obscured with the detritus of their burial place. But if you looked closer at the smoother face of the rock, you saw encased in it the greeny-blue gleam of a lozenge of emerald.

Without my being aware of it, this pattern of work became a turning point in my life. I'd drifted down another path, and though I kept returning to Littleford, supporting Vita, helping to raise Gabe, and still seeing Frank for lunch, I'd begun to live an alternative existence that had its analogy in my underground and overground lives, each of them a world apart.

"It's work," I said. The word *work* is indisputable. It was my living, it made my life in Littleford possible, it allowed Vita to succeed in Rescue/Relief, a nonprofit NGO, it paid the bills, it made me look earnest and resourceful in my grubbing among rocks for usable ore.

Going to Zambia in those years I was going off to work, and calling it work meant I didn't have to reflect on whether what I was doing was selfish or else a form of self-preservation. I was diligent in my self-justification, I was supporting my family, in spending those long periods—three months at a time usually—and then a month or more of home leave. It was like being a soldier, as I told Vita.

There was much more to my life, though I didn't disclose it: this life in Africa was possible and sustaining because it was complete. It was more than the extraction of emerald-bearing ore; it was life in the bush—routines, pleasures, friendships, and one of those friendships was with a woman.

In that small Kafubu village, it began in the simplest way. Moyo and I were sitting under a peeling gum tree in the late afternoon after a long day in the mine. We'd pulled our boots off and were drinking beer and listening to birds chirping in the branches above, while the cool air tickled our bare toes.

A woman passed us, keeping her distance. She was slender, clothed in a green wraparound, and barefoot, but walking in an especially stately way because she was balancing a basket on her head, one hand holding it still, her posture perfectly upright on the dusty path, in the gold gleam of sunset.

"She's beautiful," I said.

"What are you saying?"

"That woman."

Moyo swigged his beer and wiped his mouth with the back of his hand. Then he smiled. "She is a servant."

"So what?"

"She has laundry in that *umuseke*. She has just come from the river."

"But she's lovely."

"You are so funny, Cal."

"Don't you think she's pretty?"

"She bends her back in the garden," he said. "She washes clothes in the river."

"Maybe she can work in my garden. Maybe wash my clothes."

That made sense to him, much more than my remarking that she was pretty. He said, "I can inquire."

Her name was Norah, but they called her Katutwa, or Tutwa, because in Bemba, the local language, that was the word for a particular bird called a laughing dove, a brownish bird with a pale head, that roosted in the village trees and sang in a melodious way that seemed like giggling laughter.

Tutwa was a widow, but a young one, her husband having died of malaria a few years after their marriage. The Bemba custom, Moyo said, was the widow would become the second wife of her late husband's brother. But when she was confronted with this, the brother-in-law visiting her soon after the burial, Tutwa refused and laughed so loudly the villagers heard her, and she got the name of the laughing dove.

"Why did she refuse?"

Moyo said, "Because she has been to secondary school. The teachers discourage these people from their traditions."

"Maybe she wants to find her own husband."

"There is no possibility, my friend. She is a widow without children. A woman without children is not fully a woman."

"She looks like a woman to me."

"Because you are a *mzungu*! You don't differentiate." He drank his beer and added, "As we civilized people do."

"All I need is for her to work in my garden and wash my clothes."

"That can be arranged."

Tutwa visited later that week, bowing as she approached us, then kneeling. Moyo offered to translate. But after the initial greetings, I said, "Do you speak English?"

In a soft voice, she said, "Yes. I did my schooling in Ndola District. But after gaining my certificate I was going for nursing. But I married instead."

"What happened to the nursing career?"

"Money was the problem, sah. And when my husband died I had no chance. I refused his brother. So I languish in the village."

Moyo said, "A common story."

"I think I can handle this, Johnson. I won't need you as translator."

"So I will take my leave," he said and saluted me with a tipsy smile and left us.

Tutwa was still kneeling in that submissive pose and seemed more anxious with me alone. In her uneasy posture, crouching, her anxiety, the tension obvious in her dark, widened eyes, lit her face and gave her the watchful beauty of a rabbit on a lawn, alert, tremulous, almost electric, her features shining with fear. I supposed it was her rapidly beating heart that made her more beautiful, her heart pumping madly in apprehension.

"Please don't worry," I said, hoping to calm her.

"When people say don't worry, I worry."

I liked that for its wit. I said, "I live in that hut over there."

"I am knowing that," she said softly.

"I have a garden that needs to be tended. The previous owner planted beans and cassava but it's been neglected. I also need someone to clean the house and do laundry." Then I remembered what Moyo had said. "What's your name?"

"They call me Tutwa."

She inclined her head as though in prayer, and because she was still kneeling, and I was sitting before her, I stood up and walked a few feet away and said, "Please take a seat." I gestured to the chair Moyo had been sitting in.

With obvious reluctance she stood and lowered herself into the camp chair, yet seemed more awkward sitting than she had kneeling before me. Her head was still bowed, and she was whispering what sounded like "Thank you."

"Do you think you can do it—the garden, the laundry, the house cleaning?"

With her head lowered I could see her long lashes. Her hands were clasped, her forearms resting on her knees. Her reply was another whisper. "I can try, sah."

I named a sum of money, turning the dollar amount in my head into Zambian kwachas. She covered her face, and I thought from the movement of her shoulders that she had started to cry. But when she looked up at me, she was smiling, she'd been laughing. She was gleeful.

I was two months into my tour, and so for the next month Tutwa arrived every morning and built a fire and made tea, bringing the cup on a tray to my bedside, then backing out of the room and sweeping the house, before heading to the garden. I waved to her as I set off on foot to the mine, usually meeting Moyo on the way. And when I returned in the evening, Tutwa had made the bed and left a plate of food for me, a grilled fish, or a bowl of stew, and sometimes a sinewy piece of meat I didn't recognize—ostrich, or croc steak.

Except for the hello at those morning cups of tea, we rarely spoke, though I often heard her singing as she swept the parlor, or humming as she hoed the garden. I did not risk more than a friendly hello, or at the end of each week, when I paid her, I'd ask, "Are you happy?" Then she would cover her face shyly and speak through her fingers, "Very happy, sah."

It was June in the village, one of the cooler months, chilly in the Tropic of Capricorn, a season of harvesting, usually overcast, gray and raw, not the stereotype of sunny, lush Africa. I was preparing to head to Ndola, for the plane to Lusaka, to fly to Boston and Littleford, to spend the summer with Vita and Gabe.

Moyo showed up the night before my departure. He was carrying a bottle of clear liquid that I guessed was local gin, an illegally distilled liquor, made from fermented maize—potent, viscous, and sharp, burning its way into your head.

"*Kachasu*, bwana." Moyo uncorked the bottle and poured shots, and we drank and complimented each other on our friendship, and our secret emerald mine and our wealth, until I was near to passing out.

In the morning I was still half drunk—woozy, anyway—in that incoherent and reckless state of semisaturation, a hangover hum in my head that was like the onset of stupidity. I was cold—my uncovered face in the early chill, the mist outside they called *chiperoni* clouding the windows.

The shadow over me was Tutwa. She whispered, "*Chai*," and set the tray down, the cup tinkling in its saucer. I reached and took her by her wrist and drew her toward me. She sat on the edge of the bed, looking away.

"It's warmer in here," I said.

I couldn't see her face. I let go of her wrist. I thought, *I will say nothing else. I won't coerce her, I'll let her choose, I'll accept whatever she decides, and I'll never ask again.* I turned away, burying my sore head in my pillow.

With a bump of the bed frame she was beside me, pressed against me, her cold feet chafing against mine, as though to warm them. She draped her arm over me, a slight soapiness clinging to her skin, her breath heating my neck. I took her hand and was surprised by the hard pads on her fingers—a farm girl's fingers. But when she slid them lower and held me in them, their hardness was welcome. I was enclosed, unambiguously gripped.

But what overwhelmed me, her body on mine, was an enveloping odor, a rich humid tang, a muddy aroma of the earth from the creases of her flesh. It was sharp, almost sweet, the smell I realized of the mine, at the deepest level of the shaft, where among the broken rocks, emeralds mingled with mud.

We parted shyly, hardly speaking, before Moyo showed up to drive me to the airport.

* * *

Back in Littleford, I resumed my other life. I became the person who belonged there, throughout the steamy summer, a ritual meal with Frank at the diner, and a month on Cape Cod at a rental in Barnstable. Vita was content; Gabe—who was now as tall as me—had taken up windsurfing. We spent mornings at the beach, and read on the porch in the afternoons, and lay at night in the heat of the upstairs bedroom.

Vita was often on the phone with Frank, about details in Rescue/ Relief contracts or strategies for saving children. She'd usually hang up saying, "I'm so lucky to have him on my side."

Just after Labor Day, I flew back to Zambia. Alighting from the bush taxi at my house, I saw a wraith seated at the door in the failing light, head down, in a posture of lamentation, someone obviously grieving. It was Tutwa, but so thin I scarcely recognized her. She burst into tears when she saw me, but remained seated, lifting her wrap to cover her face.

"What's wrong?"

"I thought you were not returning," she said in a tearful voice through the cloth.

I led her into the house and switched on the lamp and was shocked to see how skinny she'd become. She seemed to know what I was thinking. She said, "I couldn't eat. But I can eat now."

I was briefly flattered, but quickly saw that I'd subverted her—no different from the colonizer who promotes dependency. And yet—I supposed like some colonizers—I was smitten.

Long before, wandering along another path, I'd been heading to Zambia and in her direction without knowing it—the turning point that hadn't been clear at the time, not a decision, but a way of drifting, that had started with silences, my dislike of Frank, my overlooking his deceptions and his lies, Vita saying, *He's an angel* and *I've moved on,* no one wishing to listen to me—to hear my side of the story. I had turned away, and though I was hurt by Frank and disappointed by Vita's indifference, I'd found a refuge. And I discovered something new and heartening now—I'd been missed. I was needed, I was cherished, it was like being loved. Lame excuses, of course, but I was happy.

19

JUNIOR WIFE

SHE WAS AN OUTCAST, I WAS, TOO—NATURAL ALLIES, lonely, sympathetic, needing consolation. I'd been excluded from Vita and Frank's cozy relationship. Vita had now and then suggested that I was selfish and negligent, Frank said little but his elbows were active. Until then—falling for Tutwa—I'd been resolved to living my monastic life in the bush, my simple hut in the obscure village—simple and obscure because we needed to disguise the fact that we were pioneering the digging of high-grade emeralds, tunneling in an area that would eventually become someone else's vast open-pit mine.

Back in Littleford on my spells of home leave I'd resented hearing how Frank had become essential to Vita's life and work, told that I should be grateful for his assistance—his legal advice, his kindness, his friendship. And he'd become an attentive uncle to Gabe. I had to be thankful for that because I was so distant, my mining in Africa for those long periods made me seem selfish.

I wanted to shout at Vita, *It's my work!* I had idle shameful glimpses of stuffing Frank into a gunny sack and cinching it with zip ties, and clubbing it repeatedly until it was silent and stopped moving. Instead, I went away and became as selfish as I was accused of being, no longer monastic, and not resentful—on the contrary, very happy. It was not travel at all, since I was at home in both places. In Tutwa, I had a lover, a housekeeper, and a cook—wifely roles—in the village adjacent to the mine. Hooking up with a *mzungu* was no disgrace for Tutwa, "the Dove." As a young widow without children, she had no status in the village, she was just her nickname, merely a gatherer of firewood, smacking laundry on rocks in the Kafue River. As a *mzungu,* I had no status either in a village wary of white men. Johnson Moyo was my partner and protector, therefore I was allowed to live in the outskirts of the village and work in the mine. Some village men derived their income from the mine, though they had no idea that the lime-green hexagonal crystals, gleaming in the chunks of black rock, were worth a fortune.

I was a liar and a cheat, unfaithful to Vita, rationalizing my behavior by telling myself that her friendship with Frank was a form of infidelity. I couldn't separate them, or criticize him. That was my lame excuse. I was doing what many industrial miners and geologists on contract did on foreign assignments—and most mining operations are far from urban centers—in the mountains, the desert, the bush, the outback; encampments, improvised villages, where visiting expat workers took local women as lovers, the women vying for their favors.

But for married men—for me—it was cheating. My position was indefensible; yet that, I came to see, was how life's choices often are. It did not lessen my love for Vita, it made me more forgiving and indulgent. I was not guilt-ridden, I was at last supremely content in Africa.

Here was another irony. I was so smitten with Tutwa that I was as passionate about seeing her on my return trip as in finding emeralds. She was my crystal, gemmy and luminous. I was attracted to her because she was lovely and at first aloof. The more I knew about her, the greater my regard. She was kind, she was intelligent; stifled by tradition, she'd never had a chance to shine.

Hers was a life interrupted. Having passed her school certificate, she aimed to study nursing and had secured a place at Ndola Teaching Hospital. But her father died, and as the eldest she needed to support the family, her widowed mother and four siblings. She found work as a menial in an office in Luanshya, a one-hour bus ride away. When her salary proved inadequate, he mother arranged for her to marry a man from the same clan; he lived in a nearby village and worked in a copper mine. Obeying Bemba custom—matrilineal—he moved to her village and took on the responsibility of looking after Tutwa's family. When he died ("fever" she said), the money ended. But there was an issue to resolve.

"My brother-in-law inherited me—it is our way," she told me. "Also he inherited our hut and all my goods. I belonged to him now. But there was a more serious problem, a big badness."

At first she refused to tell me, but finally she explained, covering her face, talking through her fingers.

"I needed to be cleansed—that is the expression. 'Cleansing the widow.'"

"How does that happen?"

"By having sex with the brother."

"What's the point of that?"

"If I am not cleansed, my dead husband's spirit cannot rest."

"So what happened?"

"I refused them. They were very angry—they said I was not honoring my dead husband. Why are you smiling?"

"I'm thinking of my sister-in-law. If my brother died, I'd have to cleanse her and take her as my junior wife."

The notion of sex with Frolic filled me with alarm and gave me some perspective on the Bemba custom, not sexy at all but a burden.

"They called me bad names. I lost everything."

And so Tutwa was forced to gather firewood and do laundry in the river to make a living, and she remained an outcast—was still an outcast, living with the *mzungu*.

The good student, potential candidate for nursing, with a promising career, fluent in English, and still young—twenty-eight—was friendless, reduced to living alone, doing manual labor, rejected because she refused to be inherited and owned. She had nothing, less than nothing, no children, no family anymore, no status.

Maybe her aura of being singular and solitary was what attracted me when I'd seen her on the path with the basket of laundry on her head, dignified, silent, moving noiselessly through the twilight, from the river, the last of the light beautifying her face. As a village woman, she was invisible to Moyo, and it had seemed comical to him that I could be smitten. But I'd recognized her as someone like me, lonely, going through the motions of living and working, unappreciated, misunderstood.

Because the Bemba were matrilineal, Tutwa said, the daughter stayed close to the mother, yet daughters were guided by the mother's brother. Tutwa had failed her mother by refusing to obey her uncle's order to join her brother-in-law—the "cleansing"—and become part of his household, barely a wife, more a possession. This meant she was forced to live on her own, to make a living, such as it was, at the margin of the village.

It was easy for me to help her. She was nominally my housekeeper. But as we were lovers, I rationalized our arrangement by telling myself we were helping each other out. She'd escaped the wrath of the villagers, because she'd ceased to matter to them. What money I gave her she passed to her mother, to live on, and for the education of Tutwa's brothers and sisters. Even so, her generosity didn't restore her standing in the village; she was still seen as obstinate, the widow who'd defied her uncle and refused her brother-in-law: this refusal was tormenting the spirit of her dead husband.

Apart from all this, life was simple for us. Our small house had few furnishings—the table, the two chairs, the bed filling the bedroom, the kitchen outside—stove, sink—the bathroom at the back in a shed (upraised barrel serving as a shower), and the *chimbusu*-slit-trench latrine. Because the house was so bare it was easy to care for and clean, a minimalist's dream, the opposite in every way of our house in the Winthrop Estates, or Mother's Tower House on Gully Lane, repositories of cushions and knickknacks. I was glad for this simplicity—it soothed me— and I delighted on returning home from the mine in the late afternoon and seeing Tutwa on the veranda, sewing, or sifting flour, or feeding chickens, looking as though she belonged.

"Your arm—what did you do?" she asked with concern, one of those days.

"Scraped it on some thorns."

"It will go septic. All cuts go septic here. Let me clean it."

And when she did, heating a basin of water, scrubbing the dirt from the cut, patting it dry and dressing it, I said, "You'll make a wonderful nurse."

"That dream is finished."

"I'd be happy to pay your tuition."

But she shrugged, either didn't believe me, or else was no longer interested. And maybe she had other plans.

She knew I was married. "Your family," she said, meaning my wife. But we didn't discuss that. What was there to discuss? She shrugged and one day said that a man with two wives was not unusual in Bemba society.

I reminded her that she'd rejected her brother-in-law.

"I wanted to choose for myself." She held my head and kissed my ear. "I could be your junior wife."

"But I'm not a Bemba guy."

"I can show you how to be a Bemba guy," she said, and plucked open her wraparound and, naked, buried her face in my lap, murmuring, "My man, my man."

That was my life in Kafubu—unexpectedly complete, the secrecy of our emerald mine, the solitude of my home life with Tutwa. It was so simple and satisfying I avoided thinking about Littleford, and if anyone in Littleford—Vita or Frank, Victor or Gabe—thought about me in Kafubu, they would not have been able to imagine the reality of it. I was not a temporary expat, serving out a contract, or a traveler waiting for the next bus; I was that ideal alien, a contented man, living his life on an African riverbank, and loved.

Kafubu was not the Africa of the travel magazines and safari tourists; it had no big game, hardly any game at all, except for rats and mice and the occasional snake. It had no trees—they'd been cut for fuel; it was low bush, its grass was tussocky, the riverbank bristled with bamboo groves. The land was flat, with musclelike berms and embankments, the soil like fudge; it was so thick it was hard to plow or to break with a hoe and lay in clods in the fields, pierced by shoots of corn or beans. The creeks feeding the river were shallow and dark and buzzed with gnats. The Kafue River was muddy, streaked with scum that lay like green foam in the backwaters, visible stagnation, like froth on fizzy drinks.

The roots of the scrub that grew beside the maize fields were too spindly to hold the soil. Every slope was scarred with erosion, deep as ravines in places, rocks tumbled into them. Without mountains or hills the land was ill-defined; it bulked, shoulders of bare black soil that looked heavy and pitted.

Except for the creases of erosion, and the loose flesh of the muddy creek banks, and the bubbly mudflats by the river, the land was so featureless as to be impossible to photograph. You'd wonder what it was, and you'd never guess it was Africa. A snapshot would show something corpselike, a wasteland, and any visible huts that would be small and sorry.

As the opposite of Littleford, it suited my mood; it was unremarkable, crisscrossed by narrow trampled footpaths. Its plainness I found a relief, but though it was no more than an expanse of low mounds that I regarded as bosomy and bleak, its sunsets were its glory and it was singular for its bird life.

They glided, they nested in the bamboo thickets, they filled the sky, they sang, seasonal swarms of migratory birds from Europe and Siberia filled the riverbanks. Birds gave the place vitality. The year-rounders like the pied crow were fearless and strutted by my house, thieving the food of the pigeons we raised for their meat. Ten different sorts of doves, the sentry stance of the marabou storks that picked through the garbage piles, stabbing with their big beaks; egrets and herons at the river's edge, buzzards and hawks high up in the sky, and at dusk owls and quail were active in the shadows.

I wanted to learn their names. Usually when I asked, Tutwa said, "*Icuni*"—it's a bird. But one day I heard a familiar hiccupping note.

"What's that?"

This time she said, "It is a cuckoo."

And that mocking word reminded me of Frank's intrusion into my marriage, Vita's fondness for him, Gabe's admiration, my sense that no matter how far away I traveled for my work as a geologist, Frank was inescapable, always somehow in my head, or else hovering. That seemed to be the characteristic of a sworn enemy, which is how I thought of Frank. As my rival, envious and greedy, the stay-at-home obsessed with the wanderer—appropriating my stories, befriending my wife, Frank's intention was always to remain at the periphery of my consciousness. In a sinister coincidence, others provided me with reminders of Frank's obsession—Vita, Gabe, and now Tutwa (though how was she to know?). Frank wanted to win; he'd win by displacing me, and in the meantime his intrusion was always on my mind, the word *cuckoo* jerking me to attention for its relation to *cuckold*.

How is a person displaced? By being destroyed, the destroyer taking over your spouse, your child, your household, your life, inserting himself into the space that was left by your destruction.

I woke up at night in my hut outside the little village of Kafubu, Tutwa lightly snoring beside me, her arm flung across my chest, warming me—and Frank was present, darkly glowing, lopsided face, teeth protruding to nibble, Vita just behind him in the shadows, awaiting his advice, unable to see Frank's triumphant expression.

Nights like those provoked me to go home more often, though Vita seemed content with my being away.

"I'm happy with the way things are," she said. "The agency is thriving. Frank's gotten us a lot of funding."

"How does he manage that?"

"It's all about finding someone to write a proposal for a grant."

"Who pays that person?"

"Frank structures the contract so that the guy who writes the proposal gets a cut of the grant."

"Frank's powers of persuasion. He gets the guy to work for no money up front."

"It's a smart move. It motivates the writer to do a good job, because he shares in the outcome. It's how a lot of nonprofits are funded. We'd be underwater without Frank."

"I'm thinking maybe Frank gets a cut." *Big Charity*, Frank called it, reminding me that it was a business; and it was in the nature of big business to be plunderers and scammers.

"If he does, he deserves it. I don't ask."

Vita didn't know, which meant he did get a cut. But I couldn't argue. After all, I was far away when all this happened, and being far away was like not caring. And on any visit in Littleford I was conscious that Tutwa had moved in with me. I was in no position to object to Vita's reliance on Frank.

"Frank is helping to save people's lives—children in Africa, for example. It's pretty ironic that you're right there, oblivious of it all."

"We don't exploit children—we don't hire them. They go to the local schools. They help at home."

"Lots of them work in the mines."

"Where do you get this information?"

"Like I told you, agencies, informed sources, missionaries, local hospitals. There's a lot of literature."

"I don't see it. Mining equipment is sophisticated and very heavy. A kid wouldn't be able to handle it."

"But they do."

Vita with a drink in her hand, in the overfurnished living room of our house in the exclusive Winthrop Estates in Littleford, described with utter certainty the lives of children in rural Africa, and how Frank was helping to save them.

"We're following up reports that children are actively engaged in mining operations. Also child soldiers, underaged prostitutes, farm laborers."

"When you get some more specific information," I said, controlling my temper, "please put me in the picture."

"Ask Frank."

I'd found meeting him these days at the diner hard to bear, this man intruding on my life. But we had a routine. We met whenever I was home. It would have seemed odd if I snubbed him. Many people I'd known associated with those they despised; you mask your hostility, because aggression is exhausting. At the end of one particular home leave, I agreed to have lunch with Frank the day before I left for Africa.

He had a new mannerism for this lunch. Instead of saying my name, he referred to me in the third person, starting with, "So what's he having?" And there were many more questions than usual, which might have accounted for his obliqueness, as though we were talking about someone we both knew but weren't particularly fond of.

"I wonder how he spends his time down there. Any idea?"

Frank began spooning clam chowder into his mouth, bent over his bowl, not making eye contact with me.

"We don't have a lot of downtime," I said. "Work all day, have a few beers, go to bed early. Up at dawn. It's life in the bush."

"One in the bush is worth two in the hand."

It was unusual for Frank to attempt a joke, probably because jokes are so revealing of a person's attitude. I stared at the top of his inclined head and went on eating my lobster roll.

"Must be kind of lonely for him."

"I'm too busy to be lonely." Now I could see he was fishing. "We're running a pretty complicated mining operation."

"What sort of amazing ore is he digging?

"Oh, masses of piled-up fragments of conglomerate rock that, um, looks in a certain light like kitty litter."

Still spooning his soup, Frank spoke out of the side of his mouth. "Guess he doesn't want to tell us about his fabulous finds."

This mannerism of his was so annoying to me I kept quiet and hoped he'd stop.

"I'd personally get a little lonely," he said. "Must be all kinds of temptations for him down there."

I stopped eating—put my lobster roll down, patted my mouth with my napkin, drummed my fingers on the table, saying nothing, staring at his head, the thinning whorl of hair at the back of his scalp. Soon my silence seemed to wake him. He sat back and met my unimpressed gaze.

His lopsided face looked futile and foolish, dabs of chowder on his lips. He'd intended his insinuation to insult and provoke me. He sniffed a little.

"Just saying." He wagged his spoon over his chowder.

"But you're entirely mistaken."

"He's getting shook up." A crooked smile formed on his chowder-flecked mouth.

"You're not me, Frank," I said. "I have a great wife and a son I'm crazy about. I wouldn't jeopardize my marriage by doing anything silly. I don't think Vita would, either. She knows the consequences of that sort of thing."

Frank slurped some more chowder and still chewing and swallowing, as though for drama, he said, "The new lover is anxious to please. She submits. She listens. She has hidden talents. She marvels at the guy's stories—and this is so amazing for his ego. It's his wet dream."

As he spoke I realized he'd been prescient. I had been lonely. I had succumbed to temptation. I hated him for being right and was ashamed and wanted to hit him.

"I guess you know the consequences, too—didn't Whitney dump you?"

This stung him. He said, "She was pressured. I sued the guy. Civil lawsuit. Very big deal."

"What was the charge?"

"Alienation of affection," he said. "I could have won."

"Alienation of affection is a crime?"

"It's actionable. In tort law it's malicious interference in a marriage."

This seemed to me precisely what he was doing in my marriage.

"So what happened?"

"I dropped the case when I met Frolic."

Perhaps he knew he was on shaky ground. He pushed his bowl of chowder aside and began to work on his plate of food—cutting, spearing, chewing—his way of eating meant to impress me with his resolve, his hunger, his superiority, the way he'd devoured his opponents in court, piece by piece, because he responded by launching into a long story.

"Major contract," he said.

He stabbed the lamb chop on his plate and sawed off an edge, then gestured with it by shaking it at me. He gnawed at it while holding it with his fork and chewed as he talked.

"Lots of foreplay, tons of paperwork, thirty pages of clauses and sub-sections. The other party had put a lot of hours into it—and that was a big help." He swallowed and smacked his lips and went on. "Anyway, it comes time to sign the contract, the culmination of the big organ recital. I make them come to my office—my turf. They push the paper across the desk. I pick up my pen"—he shifted the knife in his hand and held it like a pen, as though poised to write—"and I glance at the signature page, then I say, 'I'm not signing.'"

In what might have been an attempt at a smile, Frank's cheek contracted, lifting one corner of his smeared lips upward—disconcerting to me, because only half his mouth was apparently smiling, the other half slack. As his expression had altered he pushed his knife blade into the lamb chop, carved away a fragment of flesh.

Chewing, he said, "They're aghast, naturally," and swallowed.

"'This is what we agreed on,' the other lawyer says.

"'I changed my mind,' I say, and put the pen down, and fold my hands."

Frank placed the knife beside his plate and clasped his hands. He stared at me, but at an angle, always one eye higher than the other.

"They asked me what I wanted, so I said, 'You're confident of a great outcome—right? So instead of an up-front fee you get paid on the back end with the proceeds.'

"'That means I'm working for nothing,' the client says.

"'Bull,' I say. 'You're part of the team. When we get our money, you get yours.'

"'How do I pay my bills?'

"'You make it happen.'"

Frank picked up his knife, he lowered his head, he worked on his lamb chop, sawing at its rawness, the blood seeping onto the blade. He spoke to the meat, as though to something sacrificial.

"They conferred in a corner of my office. I loved the sounds of anguish. I heard, 'We've come all this way,' as a complaining moan. Then silence. They sat down and crossed out the payment schedule. At that point I signed."

Frank looked pleased with himself, but it was not his usual look of satisfaction, more like the strange sourness and perplexity of a fat man who realizes he has eaten too much of something he likes, stuffing himself to nausea. I remembered the story Vita had told me about the man Frank had found to write the application and proposal for the grant to fund Vita's project. As with many of Frank's stories, the message was *Don't mess with me.*

I said, "But you'd given your word. You'd agreed to a contract."

Looking at me in a casual pitying way, he said, "A contract is not worth the paper it's printed on."

"Major contract?"

"Especially those."

Frank lowered his head, cutting, forking, chewing more of his meat, and all I saw was his scalp. In Zambia, I'd heard the story of a cruel chief who punished a hated captive by tying him to a post and ordering one of his men to hammer a nail into his head. I had been shocked, but now I understood, and I imagined subduing Frank and hammering.

"That's funny," Frank said, pushing his plate aside, a bare lamb rib on it, "I'm not hungry anymore." He patted his mouth with his soiled napkin, then took out a quarter and flipped it and smacked it to the back of his hand. "Toss you for the check. Tails! You lose."

But I was still banging a nail into his skull.

After that visit I was glad to board a plane and fly back to Zambia, and my little house, and my sweet companion—junior wife—and my rocks, and the bush. The simple life.

But I was unable to rid myself of Frank. He appeared in my dreams, he gazed at me from the foot of my bed, while Tutwa snored beside me. He was often cutting meat, and the meat was me. A month of this—of digging, of simplicity, of Frank hovering—and I returned to Littleford, on an impulse.

"So soon," Vita said, thrown by my sudden appearance, as though my showing up was inconvenient. She said she was glad to see me, but admitted that she had less time for me than when I'd arrived on schedule.

"You're busy?"

"It's those children I was telling you about," she said. "Thanks to Frank we got the funding. We've done a lot of research. They're in the Congo—like I told you, in Katanga—mining. These kids are being used to dig for minerals."

"What minerals? Where in Katanga?"

"That's for you to find out. You always tell me you're proud of the work I do—that you want to help, like Frank does. Here's your chance, Cal."

20

SHALAPO

FRANK SAW THE WORST IN PEOPLE. HE SEARCHED FOR A crack in a person's character and squinted into it. It was his only interest, his only satisfaction. *At their worst, they're naked—it's who they really are.* I took his cynicism to be his greatest fault. In implying I was tempted in Africa and probably unfaithful to Vita, he put me down as a creep. He yearned for me to be a hypocrite. I denied it with a sneer of indignation and hated him for saying so. Hated him especially because he was right, and because he was right I resolved to correct it, to prove him wrong.

Being face-to-face with Frank disturbed me, like gazing into a mirror, not seamless glass but the dark distorting mirror of family resemblance— versions of familiar features, many of them bordering on mockery. Brother looks at brother in a reflex of anxious discernment and wants to see differences, all of them his sibling's flaws. It was not an antagonistic fantasy of mine that Frank's face was palsied, that one squeezed side was at odds with the other, that his close-set eyes didn't match. Other people mentioned it. He was glad that, as in mug-shot profiles, he was two people. One of them looked at you sideways. The day she first met him Vita had said, *I feel bad about his face*—and I insisted to her that he was proud of his face, it made him special, *It's his moneymaker.*

My work helped me to understand the composition of Frank's character in terms of geology. I saw him—I saw most people, I saw the world—as examples of undifferentiated, uncracked aggregate, an impure mass, a lump of mineral or rock particles. The emeralds we mined were not whole separate gems dug from stone; they were part of the stone, combinations of larger rocks, formed in pegmatite, hosted by metamorphic rock, the sort called protogenic inclusions, and when the emerald itself was released, it contained inclusions—impurities of a kind—that made the emerald's interior a glittering and verdant garden.

I guessed that at the heart of Frank's suspicions was his cynical certainty that most other men shared his weakness, were as mean as he was, as greedy, as insincere; that his low opinion of other people was a reflection of his own character, not strong or moral at all, but driven by instincts bordering on the criminal. One of his core beliefs was that no one told the truth; another was that in most of our behavior we are animals, just as grubby and dim-witted and skittish and predictable. "Fidge, admit it—we're beasts!"

He shocked me once at the diner when a man passing a booth bumped into another man sliding out. The man who was bumped, crouched, his feet apart, knees bent, in an aggressive stance, his head lowered, his neck shortened, his jaw outthrust, his arms slightly lifted, flexing his fingers as though to grapple—threat posture.

"That's pure monkey," Frank said.

Of a man kissing his wife in a parking lot, Frank said, "Dogs do that. He's humping her leg."

A child eating an ice-cream cone, licking her fingers: "Feline grooming. Cat girl. She'd purr if she was stroked."

Of a fat man entering the diner with his wife and children: "The grunting, snorting silverback gorilla, preceding his hairy knuckle-dragging family troop."

I needed this. I needed his bad example to distance me in my own behavior. He was the necessary devil that forced me to examine my own beliefs and defy him. He made me want to see the best in people.

The lesson for me in that last lunch with Frank was that I had to be true. Kissing Vita goodbye, hugging Gabe, guiltily tearful, I flew back to Zambia vowing to end it with Tutwa.

Yet still I saw Frank's face, every peculiar feature of it, the slant of his disapproving mouth, the two sides of his bifurcated face, the sort of happy-sad face you might see on a Greek mask or a stroke victim, one side taut, the other slack, even his eyes on separate planes, two contrasting colors, a peering inquisitive dark eye, a lazy indifferent gray eye, unfriendly and incoherent. All this was exaggerated by Frank's tendency to tilt his head and look sideways when he was speaking to me, to show me the dome of his head, the scratchings of his bald spot, and that, too, was divided, a hairy side, a pale crusted-scalp side. The way he worked his jaw made him seem like an insect, with a pair of independent nibbling mandibles.

And why was his face so detailed in my memory? Because I wanted to hit it—the face you yearn to punch is the face you remember. As always his face followed me to Africa and it ghosted over me while I tried to put my life in order.

Johnson Moyo met me at the Ndola airport saying, "You look like you could use some *kachasu,* bwana."

I didn't, but it was his oblique way of saying that he wanted a stiff drink. He pulled into the forecourt of a roadhouse, where we sat outside on the veranda, our legs up, feet jammed against the rails, sundowner posture, sipping banana gin.

"What a world," I said. "Twenty-four hours ago I was sitting on my porch in my hometown, and here I am, doing the same thing, half a world away."

"That is two worlds," Moyo said. "Myself, I also live in two worlds. My family is one, my business is the other."

I'd expected him to say "the white world" and "the African world," because all the gem dealers in Jo'burg were white, and all our miners were African. As tactfully as I could, I suggested this to him.

"No, my friend. The *mzungu* represents business, but the family is a parasite. You don't know."

"I know a little about families."

"In Africa, if you have money, your family demands a share of it.

Why else do you think progress is so slow here? It is our tradition that the person with an income is expected to look after the whole family."

"You do that?"

"Not at all." He laughed, he swigged. "My family has no idea of my income. And in my case they are far away south, near the Zambezi. If they knew, they would eat my money." He studied me for a moment, sipping and smiling. "Your woman," he said. "Her family has been troubling her while you were away, asking her when you are coming back."

"Why? I don't get it."

"The supply of *kwacha* has dried up." He laughed and made the money sign with his fingers.

"I'll give her some then," I said. "If that's what they want."

"She wants more than money."

I prepared myself for him to say: *She wants you, bwana.*

But he said, "She wants to go away—far away from them."

"How do you know all this?"

"I know these Bemba people. I know their customs. I know their habits—good ones and bad. My people, the Batoka, are quite similar, though we are Tonga speaking."

"What about me, Johnson?"

"I trust you, bwana. That's why we do good business together. We are partners, not brothers. If you were my brother, I would be worried. 'Where is the money, brother?' 'Oh, sorry, I needed it to pay my son's school fees' and what and what."

"You don't trust your family?"

"They have different rules!" He shrugged and lifted his shirt and wiped his sweaty face. "Their customs are incompatible with good business. I love them. I try to help them, but I keep my business secret from them."

"Johnson, why are you telling me this?"

"Because I hate to see this happen. I see that the woman Tutwa is under pressure from her family. When she was fetching firewood, they were despising her. When she moved into the *mzungu*'s house, they saw an opportunity to eat your money. You will go away, and she will suffer."

"How do you know I'll go away?"

"All *azungu* go away—when they are finished with us." He poked my chest with a hard finger. "I put it to you, my friend. Are you residing long in Zambia?"

I had no answer. I could have said: *I came back this time to end it with Tutwa, to be faithful to my wife.* But what he said about Tutwa needing to be free simplified my decision.

"Tutwa wanted to be a nurse."

"Maybe she is still wanting."

"Where would she study?"

"Many places. There is a teaching hospital in Ndola. She could qualify," he said.

"She told me she was accepted there."

"I have heard that."

"You know so much."

"There are no secrets in Africa."

"Johnson, our business is secret."

"Our business does not exist, my friend." He laughed loudly, then became self-conscious in his laughter and looked up and down the veranda to see whether anyone had heard. "We are two men, living humbly outside a small village, who spend their days in a muddy tunnel."

We sat in silence after that, and finally I said, "I'll send Tutwa to nursing school."

"A wise decision, bwana."

"Where will she work?"

"Where all Zambian nursing sisters work—South Africa, or in the UK. She will be far from her family. She will save her money. She will be free."

"Let's go, man. I don't like these roads in the dark."

"And myself, I am not liking."

That night, in bed, after we'd made love, with Tutwa lying beside me, breathing softly, I said, "You should be a nurse."

"It is not possible."

"No. You can do it."

"But the money," she said, her voice trailing off, *Mahnee* . . .

"I'll pay. I'll give you the money."

In the dim light, the lamp in the parlor illuminating the open door-way to the bedroom, I saw Tutwa turn away and clutch her head and bury her face in the pillow, her shoulders shaking, her moans muffled by the pillow.

"Don't cry," I said, panicked and made helpless by the sight of what looked like anguish.

What she said in reply was indistinct, and still she seemed to sob; but then she turned to me and hugged me laughing and said, "I am so happy."

I'd steeled myself to end it with Tutwa, dismissing her, sending her back to her shabby hut outside the village, where she was a pariah, a rule breaker, unwelcome unless she had money for her mother. Moyo's intervention was timely, giving Tutwa an incentive for us to part, so that she could apply for a place at the hospital in Ndola. She'd go, and I'd be able to tell myself that I was virtuous, not the typical expat with a local lover, the women here they called *nyama,* which meant meat and animal and slut.

Tutwa applied, she was diligent in filling out the forms, her school-taught handwriting was beautiful, upright, copperplate, with uniform loops. She sat at the kitchen table writing drafts of the required essay, "Why I Wish to Become a Nursing Sister." I was touched by her exactitude, which was not confidence but rather a kind of desperation, a fear of failure, her frequent vows in her essay, "with the help of Almighty God."

As she rested on her elbows, the lamplight gleamed on her earnest face, a whir of insects gathered around the globe of the lamp, the pale moths fluttering, the black beetles bumping the glass; and some of them squeezed beneath the lip of the rim and, toppling into the flame, burned with crisp snaps.

Motionless, except for when she brushed the nearer insects with the back of her hand, Tutwa seemed to me a gem, not to be compared with anyone I knew, all the finer for having emerged like a crystal from the mud and dust of Kafubu.

Tutwa's concentration in the lamplit room, shadows on every wall, tapping at the white paper, hunched forward, her face bright with thought: I watched with admiration. Her spirit glowed, she who'd suffered rejection because she'd refused to allow herself to be inherited—like a cow, or a chair, or a bucket—by her brother-in-law, or to be "cleansed" through sex with him.

I had not known in my simple lust and loneliness that the pretty young woman in the green wraparound on the path was a whole vital person, intelligent, educated up to high school, with ambitions beyond the village, struggling in the snare of tribal customs. From chopping and splitting and carrying firewood, her hands were toughened; the bumps of her yellow calluses had at first startled me when she tried to caress me, as though she was poking me with a stick. And then I loved her for her hard grip. She could hold a hot pan in her fingers and not feel pain. She was capable and loving; she was kind. In her kindness, guided by her gentle soul, she was anything but a coquette. She could be forthright, she was agreeable, and strong—she could swing an ax and smash a mattock into weeds. All these qualities, some of them contradictory, imbued her with an unsurpassing sensuality—she was whole and human. Her willingness thrilled me. She'd given herself entirely to me, and if I mentioned something sexual that was new to her she smiled and said, "I can learn how" or "You can show me," and was eager to be taught this secret.

Knowing that I was losing her, I nuzzled her, and she whispered, "My man," into my ear, and licked it. Because I hated letting go, there was fury—the frenzy of finality—in our lovemaking, driving us both to exhaustion.

Afterward, she boiled buckets of water and filled the overhead barrel and scrubbed me, and when I was clean she stepped naked into the shower and I watched entranced, and returned the favor, the creamy bubbles of white soap cascading down her body.

I went to work in the dark with Moyo and returned at sunset, our usual routine, to remain inconspicuous. And these days, each evening, I saw Tutwa, the laughing dove, seated before a lamp at the kitchen table, the sauce bottles and condiments, the pickle jar, the toothpicks, in a round tray at the center. She would be writing on foolscap, making draft after draft, or else reading, her fingers tapping at the text, her lips pressed together in concentration.

I was so moved one evening I said, "Don't stop," and studied her, knowing she'd soon be leaving—her application had been accepted, her tuition was paid. I saw her as someone special, earnest—alone—reading the dusty pages, by the light of a lamp that was strafed by moths, intense in her concentration—less a lover than a valiant woman, plotting to escape the entanglements and demands of the village, to venture into the wider world of jostling strangers, to make a life for herself—brave, but also a waif, without the slightest idea of what was in store for her.

She turned to me and prepared to put her papers away.

"Go on," I said. "Finish what you're doing. I'll sit here and have a beer."

I sat in the corner, a little apart, thinking these thoughts, saddened, as though I was watching an orphan I'd briefly sheltered, someone I was sending once again into the world, praying she'd be safe. As always, Frank was watching me.

Tutwa sat back and stretched her arms and yawned. She gathered her papers and straightened them, then slid them into a file folder. She smoothed the yellow ribbon of her bookmark and tucked it between the pages she'd been reading and clapped the book shut. She'd fashioned a homemade cover with brown paper, to protect the book, *Fundamentals of Nursing*. The care in the folds of the paper cover moved me, the way it was carefully taped; her plastic pencil case moved me, her leaky ballpoint, her bruised eraser, these simple schoolgirl tools, kept with such care, all this tore at my heart.

When she was done, she brushed the moths from the lamp and joined me in the shadows, sat on the arm of my chair, stroked my hair with her fingers, her knuckles grazing my cheek, humming softly.

"*Shalapo*," she said.

"What's that?"

"It is goodbye." Still she twirled my hair with her fingers, and then in a shocked voice, "What is this?" and lost all her lightness.

"Never mind," I said. "It's nothing."

But she touched my face tenderly, as though at a wound, and in that same awestruck voice saying, "I have never seen a *mzungu* crying."

21

THE QUEST FOR COBALT

MY QUEST, IN THE TRADITION OF MOST QUESTS, BE-
gan with a solemn chivalrous vow—in this case one I
made to my wife, speaking to her on a bad line from outside Kafubu
village, late night in my small house, dinnertime in Littleford.

"Is there anything wrong?"

"I miss you," I said.

In a fit of atonement—self-justification and born-again fidelity—
back after the long drive from Ndola to my empty house, I sprang to
the phone and called Vita. I had never been so reassuring, so loving, so
certain she was my heart and soul. I was bitterly aware that Tutwa was
an example of my weakness, my sentimental way of consoling myself in
my loneliness, the estrangement for which I dishonestly blamed Frank.

My lame excuse was that, motivated by idealism, I'd taken Tutwa
into my life to help her. But I'd desired her the moment I'd seen her on
the path. I'd given in to the impulse, I was madly attracted, but it was
like clutching a lovely bird with a broken wing: she was lost, I'd taken
advantage of her helplessness.

As every mining company knew, Africans were easy prey. And my relationship with Tutwa was just another example of an outsider's greedy
grab. I had power and she had none. For three months we were lovers, more than lovers—domestic partners—a seemingly romantic but
in reality a fraudulent and self-deceiving arrangement, the fantasizing
folie de grandeur of two people sexed-up and adrift. We had no future

together: I was lying to her as well as my wife, just playing house. I had thought very little about it until Frank mumbled in the diner, *Must be all kinds of temptations down there.*

But I had put things right. Tutwa was at nursing school in Ndola, having swapped her green wraparound for a white hospital uniform, wearing white shoes, a lump sum of money in the bank there—the scholarship I'd awarded her—content in her dorm room, eager to begin studying, no tears at our parting, only a promise from her that she would pray for me to Almighty God.

Now I was home alone, feeling virtuous, relieved to be on the phone to my wife, speaking with gusto about how grateful I was to be married to her, gushing as only an adulterer can gush to the woman he has recently deceived.

In my impetuous flow of endearments, I realized that Vita had not said anything, had not replied to "I miss you." I'd done all the talking. I paused and heard what sounded like a sigh down the crackly line.

"I can't talk now."

"I hadn't realized the time."

"It's not that," she said, and added in a whisper, "Frank's here."

"I love you," I said.

"Thanks." Then the click of her hanging up.

"Thanks" seemed an odd and insufficient reply—why not, *I love you, too*? And *Frank's here* in a whisper was disturbing.

I called her back the next day. I said, "Vita, darling, I want you to know that I think of you all the time. I'm working so that we can have a great life. I understand the sacrifices you make by my being so far away, but it won't always be like this. We've made big progress here with the mine and we'll be winding it up sometime soon. Then I'll be back in your arms."

Blurting this out left me a bit breathless. I stopped, waiting for a reply, but none came. The hum-buzz on the line penetrated my head and somehow chafed my throat.

"Vita, are you there?"

"I was thinking," she said. "With you away so much I've had to make adjustments in my life. It's an issue with Gabe, too, poor kid. I sometimes think I'm a different person. I've had to live without you for such long periods of time."

I wanted to say, *What about the wives of soldiers and fishermen and explorers,* but knowing she'd regard that as self-serving—which it was—I said, "I love you. I want to grow old with you."

"That's tender, Cal. I appreciate it," she said. "But it's a promise."

"Of course."

"It's not an agreement. It's not a contract."

"I'm not sure what you mean."

"It's not enforceable," she said. "It's words. It's just a verbal proposition."

"God, you sound like Frank."

"He was the one who explained it to me," she said. "It was when the agency promised me a bonus. My boss mentioned it. I got really excited until Frank said, 'Did he put it in writing? Was it witnessed?'"

"I'm telling you I love you," I said, my throat aching.

"I know." She sounded unimpressed. "I hear you."

"I can prove it to you."

"I wonder how."

"Those children," I said. "The exploited ones you talked about."

"Thousands of them," she said with feeling, the first note of passion I'd heard from her. "They're kidnapped. They're trafficked. They work in mines." She gasped and then shrieked, "They need to be rescued!"

"I'll look for them—I swear to you. I'll make it my mission, wherever they are."

"I told you, they're in the Congo."

I did not say, *The Congo is bigger than Europe,* but in any case she was still talking.

"Frank says you're nearby—that you can find everything we need to make a case."

"Trust me," I said. "I'll find them for you."

"Good," she said, and as I was trying to assess her tone—Was it loving? Did she trust me?—she hung up.

That was my vow.

* * *

In this self-conscious knightly gesture, I wanted to make an effort, take a risk, to prove to Vita I loved her and was on her side—to please her, to win her over, to expiate my infidelity with Tutwa. But it was not all chivalry. I also needed to get away from the mine, and the village, and my house that held memories of my departed lover.

You live alone for months or years, and the space is all yours, shaped to your being and your routines. But once a person lives in intimacy with you—your lover, your partner, your spouse—that space is altered and deformed, filled with associations, the chair where she sat, the table where she worked, the bowl she used, the bed. More than anything in my case, the floorboard, the bedpost, that caught my eye and became the memory of her saying, *The badness is that I will miss you.*

Tutwa was gone but the residue of her existence was everywhere, her shadow, her echo, a certain odor of earth and soap, the aroma of her food, the crease she'd left in a cushion. And then I found tossed in a closet one of her old sandals, like the emblem of a village laborer, one she'd left behind when I'd bought her the white, crepe-soled nurse's shoes.

She'd been barefoot when we met, so this deformed sandal, which she'd begun wearing when she moved in with me, represented our three months together. I held it and studied it. A sandal, a shoe, any well-used footwear molds itself to the sole of the wearer. It was battered, its strap had been torn and resewn, village stitches, reflecting her life, her struggle, like a martyr's relic, something plain and holy.

Then I realized what moved me more was that the sandal was a macro fossil, with all the geological aspects of a trace fossil, which was a mold, formed when an organism dissolves entirely, leaving a unique hole the exact shape of the live thing that vanished. We sometimes called this "slump bedding," this sandal a contorted mass, scored with flex wrinkles and sole marks, the hollow in the leather left by her toes—toes I had stroked—that any geologist would know as flute cracks.

Clutching the sandal I was clutching the fossil of her foot, and I got sad and nearly wept, knowing I would never see her again—could never see her, or I would lose Vita.

I tried to cheer myself up with the thought, *She left it behind.* It was a relic from her former self, the village outcast who would never go back. I summoned up the image of Tutwa, smiling at the bright lights of Ndola, the city that would swallow her up, as she walked in the stately way she'd learned as a young woman balancing a bundle on her head, her neck straight, her head upright and almost haughty, the posture of a laborer lugging laundry and also that of a noble woman bearing gifts.

In that way, as I'd watched, she walked to the portico of the hospital school in Ndola, wearing the soft white nurse's shoes I'd bought her. The memory of that last liberated sight of her consoled me.

And now I needed to fulfill my vow to Vita, no matter the risks— though I welcomed the risk that would prove my sincerity and win back her love.

Moyo met me as usual at the end of my driveway in the damp predawn darkness. In my absence he'd bought a Land Rover, and though the distance to the mine was not great, he enjoyed its slow clanking and humping progress along what was not a road but a footpath, calling out to our plodding miners.

As I slid in and banged the steel door shut against its steel frame, he said in a mocking tone, "So your bird has flown away."

"Right," I said, but he was still talking.

"You will be allowed conjugal visits, I reckon."

"Maybe," I said, yawning, hating this talk.

"She will agitate on your behalf, my friend. And she herself will also be needing."

"Johnson," I said, "please give it a rest. I've got a lot on my mind."

"What does the bwana have on his mind?"

He leaned against the steering wheel, hugging it, his usual driving posture, an unlit pipe in his mouth, his face close to the windshield, watching for the miners, or early risers on their way to the market in the darkness, indistinct shadows on the path, some of them leading cows or goats, tugging ropes fastened like nooses to their necks.

"Bwana is lonely, missing his bird."

His bud made me laugh. To stop his chatter, I said, "What do you know about mining in the Congo?"

"Myself I have been there, Katanga side. I have seen some digging. Very primitive."

"What are they finding?"

"Hard metals, like here. Some gemstones. And lately I have heard, cobalt. But you know cobalt is rubbish—it has bad effects on health when handled."

"I've heard they hire children in the mines."

"No, my friend. They don't hire." He removed his pipe from his mouth to laugh, as always a gagging and hoicking, as though he was trying to clear his phlegmy throat.

"Hire means wages and insurance. Hire is what we do with our chaps."

"What do they do?"

"They are compelling the children, bwana."

"You know this?"

"I have heard so many rumors."

He blew his horn at a cyclist who'd suddenly appeared on the path, not riding, but in the village way, using his bike to carry a sack of flour or beans that was slung over the crossbar, the man pushing it into the darkness.

"Children?"

"Indeed, children—forced to work. I am hearing from others about them."

The corrugations on the path rattled the loose metal doors of the Land Rover, the noise making it impossible for me to reply. When the path became smooth again, I said, "I don't get it. How can children operate mining equipment?"

"You have never seen children in a mine, my friend?"

"In Colombia. Grubbing in the tunnels."

He laughed. "Yes. No equipment, but the hands."

All this time he was chewing on his pipestem—the unlit pipe an accessory, possibly an affectation. Perhaps he'd once seen a *mzungu* smoking and gesturing and fiddling with a briar pipe. He took it from his mouth and stabbed emphatically at the windshield.

"Their hands only!"

"Where are they?"

The pipe again, pointing. "Just there. Kolwezi side." He jabbed again at the bush, illuminated by the headlights, as though to a spot past the thorn tree boughs. "Congo."

As Vita had said, but another country, of which I had heard rumors, none of them pleasant. I'd seen refugees and migrants at the edge of Zambian settlements, the despised Congolese, fleeing anarchy.

"Johnson, have you driven there?"

"No. I took a plane to Lubumbashi. But I would like to drive. Push across through the *bundu* in this vehicle. Bush bashing!"

As though to demonstrate, he yanked a crank under the dashboard and put the Land Rover into four-wheel drive and swung it off the path, bumping and swaying along the margin of a maize field.

"They say good business."

His pipe was clamped in his teeth as he drove. He seemed to be turning the thought over in his head, examining it as the Land Rover rose and fell, from ditch to ditch. His eyes were lit by the reflection in the windshield.

"The Congo is not like any other country. It is without roads in many places. Without electric. No telephone service. No tap water. And what food? It is not at all like Zambia. We have all the comforts. They have no comforts. They are desperate people."

"I can imagine."

"No, you cannot imagine." Chewing his pipestem, Moyo said through his teeth, "It is primitive, my friend."

"I'd like to see it."

"Maybe it's true—good business. Someday, bwana, our emerald vein will be found by others, with more money and better tools, and we will be finished. We will need a new challenge. Maybe Congo!"

He laughed hard—too hard, a bullying sort of shout, as though commanding attention, taking charge.

After that talk—idle chatter for Moyo, intense for me—it became an ordeal to travel with him to the mine every morning. I wanted to know more, I was impatient to go, but I wanted to conceal my intention to investigate the exploited children. I became silent and moody, which Moyo took to be my pining for Tutwa. He mentioned this in his usual teasing way.

"The bwana is lonely. The bwana needs a holiday."

I seized on that. "Yes, in the Congo."

He laughed, throwing his head back. "The Congo is not a holiday. It is hell. It is one of these countries where you need a friend."

"Do you have a friend there?"

"I have my school chum, Aleke," he said. "The same clan—Mudenda Clan. Our totem is the elephant. But the goodness, bwana—he is not my relative."

22

THE BUSH TRACK TO THE BORDER

VERY EARLY ON A MUDDY MORNING IN JANUARY, THE
month of long rains, Kafubu saturated, the earthen odors
of the yard and the sour night-dampened leaves of the cassava and bananas much sharper in the darkness. It was the village smell, mournful and mildewed, woodsmoke and the muck of the latrine, and the
human smell, too, like the stink of old socks in a place where no one
wore socks. The complaints of chickens, the frantic cries of the first
birds.

I'd woken in the chill and fumbled along the path to meet Moyo, my
shoes heavy from being soaked in the grass before I'd gone ten feet—
the first annoyance of the day; and the second was Moyo's wide-awake
banter. An early riser, he'd been up for hours.

It was his suggestion that we leave before five—we needed the whole
day to get near the border. It wasn't far, but the bush roads were bad,
the rain was constant, and Moyo, who'd taken a plane to Lubumbashi,
had never driven this way before. We planned to bypass that big city,
starting on another route, skirting Ndola and its slums, the back road
fogged with the smoke from cooking fires and people huddled in the
rain, waiting for buses and vans to take them to town. I thought of
Tutwa, probably just waking, readying herself for class.

Before Kitwe we got lost on a side road that ended in a graveyard, the
graves piled with heavy stones. "To keep the hyenas from the corpses,"
Moyo said. Turning back, we were hailed by a man holding a broken

umbrella. He was wearing a flour sack over his shoulders, his sandals
had been fashioned from rubber tires, his trousers were patched. He was
red-eyed, looking ghoulish—I had the macabre impression he had just
sprung out of the graveyard.

Moyo stopped and rolled down his window. He greeted the man in
Bemba, but the man looked at me with his bloodshot eyes, saying, "I
am Simon. I can show you the way."

"We're going to Chingola," I said.

"And the way to Chingola as well," he said.

Reaching behind his seat back, Moyo cranked open the rear door.

This ragged man Simon directed us efficiently from the back seat,
indicating narrow roads, leading us through villages where women were
pounding maize flour in mortars, the thuds of the pestles eerie in the
rain and smoke and soupy air.

"I know where you are coming from," he said, when we arrived back
on the main road.

"Tell us," I said.

"You belong to Satan's world."

Moyo said, "Calm down, my friend. We accept Jesus as our lord and
savior."

"Jesus is not God," Simon said. "Jehovah is God. If you obey him,
maybe you will live forever."

"In heaven," I said,

"Not heaven," Simon said. "But I know you are seeking worldly
pleasures."

Moyo swung the steering wheel and slid the Land Rover bumping
and swaying to the side of the road, where it lay tilted, Simon flung
against the door.

"You have arrived, my friend. Time to get out."

"You are lost," Simon said, tightening his hands on his rolled umbrella, staring with widened red eyes, his mouth gaping, looking hungry.

"Indeed, we are," Moyo said, "and you are not helping at all."

"I have good news for you," Simon said. "If you refuse to worship
idols, you will find the right way."

"In point of fact, we are going to Chingola and then Solwezi."

"The mission is at Kulima—a little beyond it, the Church of the Tabernacle."

"Yes, we are going there, to Solwezi and the border."

"If you declare yourselves to Jehovah, I can direct you there. It is a blessing that you gave me a lift. I have preached my good news there to those people."

"I declare myself to Jehovah," Moyo said.

"Me too," I said.

The man was silent until Moyo gave him his notebook and pen. Tugging his flour sack tighter, he deliberated over a blank page, dabbing at it with the pen, then drew a line representing the main road, and as though sketching whiskers on it, indicated the bypass road, and an X for a certain Indian shop, he said; another X ("flour mill"), a slash for a creek where women would be washing clothes. We must avoid Chingola for its belonging to Satan. An X beyond it marked the turn off to Kulima, a field where cattle would be grazing, and the last X, "a certain veranda—a man will be on that veranda, in a chair. Farther on, the Tabernacle."

"What happens when we get to the Tabernacle?"

"You announce to those people that you have declared yourself to Jehovah."

"He means the road beyond it," I said.

"What is the need? The Tabernacle is the destination. You can tell them the good news." He grunted and bum-hopped out of the seat, slamming the door. He said, "Tell them the world is a sinking ship."

His directions proved to be accurate. After driving on the main road beyond Kitwe, we circumvented Chingola, found the Indian shop and the flour mill, the women slapping laundry on the rocks at the creek side, and the cattle in the field, as Simon had said. The veranda, too, though no one sat in the chair that afternoon.

The road to Kulima and the Tabernacle was laterite, eroded in the rain, bouldery and potholed, some of the holes deep enough to trap the tires. By nightfall we still had not reached the church. Moyo drove off the road and parked under a tree—"We will resume at dawn"—and sent me with a panga in search of dead branches. Reaching for a twiggy branch, I saw a black spider on its gray wheel of a web, and intending to brush it away I spun its web on my hand, the spider itself in my fingers. I flung it aside but didn't see it land and had the impression that it was still clinging to me, but hidden, having skittered up my arm.

"Campfire," Moyo said, mixing maize flour in a tin pot to make *nshima* dough. He cooked dinner with stew from a can he heated in the glowing coals.

While we ate, we heard rustling in the bushes. Thinking an animal was approaching, Moyo seized the panga and jumped to his feet. Two small boys appeared, motioning to their mouths, indicating hunger. Moyo addressed them in several languages, but they didn't understand. We gave them the remains of our meal and while we busied ourselves to bed down for the night—Moyo in the front seat, me in the back—I heard him curse.

"They have pinched my pot!"

A smothering darkness that night, heavy with damp, and buzzing flies and mosquitoes kept me awake. I also sensed that the spider was still somehow crawling up my back, tickling my neck with its hairy legs. We set off at first light, eating bananas, the Land Rover slewing and struggling on the slimy boulders.

Toward noon we came to a settlement—low huts, broken fences—and at its center a wood-framed church, painted yellow, with a square steeple, a bell showing in one of the upper windows. A cross made of two wooden beams had been erected in front, on the road. People walking on the road stopped moving when they saw us, though several dropped to their knees, seeming to venerate our vehicle.

"They take us to be holy," Moyo said. Accelerating past the church toward the road ahead, he added, "We will give them the good news some other time."

From a distance, Solwezi looked to be a good-size town, but low and scattered and colorless, with the improvised and impermanent air of a mining town—more of a camp than a community. Moyo took a sharp right, north on a narrow road, squeezed by thickets of dense bush and overhanging trees. After a few miles we saw groups of people walking toward us, slowly parting to let us pass, some of them begging—

pleading with their hands out—and slapping the side of the Land Rover. The smack of their hands on metal startled me—the anger in the sound, like a reckless punch in my gut. The small boys shrieked, men called out in hoarse operatic hoots, the women ululated in sudden gulps.

"They are fleeing," Moyo said.

"What's it all about?"

"It means we are going in the right direction. They are searching for food in Solwezi—there is a mine nearby—there"—he waved at the bush—"at Kansanshi. We will use their road."

It was a mining road through the bush, pounded into spectacular ruts and hollows by the fat tires of dump trucks loaded with ore, hauling it through the bush. Farther on, we came to an irregular fork, the access road of truck traffic, veering east, and another narrow track heading north.

"This is the way to the Congo."

"How do you know?"

"No lorries," Moyo said. "Just the footprints of hungry people."

Ragged people, as we soon saw, some of them hugging cloth bundles, men with pangas, women with baskets on their heads, babies slung on their backs. They stepped aside and beat on our doors and slapped the windows as we passed.

I saw a skinny arm upraised by my side window, its fist enlarged by a black rock, and then the window exploded, glass splintering against my head and falling into my lap.

Speeding up, Moyo said, "Hungry people are dangerous," and he screamed in fury.

An hour into this back road we entered denser bush, no people, no huts. We stopped and swept the broken glass shards out of the vehicle. The sturdy Land Rover window was not wholly broken but utterly opaque, a web of fine cracks radiating from the point of impact, the dent of a rock, a dimple of glass and dust at the center.

The window's ugliness and its distortion of the landscape prevented me from seeing outside and were a continual reminder of the desperation and anger of the people we were traveling among.

There was something else, something worse, amounting almost to horror: the fact that in his sickeningly viral way Frank was traveling with me the whole time. *Frank's here,* Vita had whispered over the phone. His intrusion in my life had alarmed and saddened me. I had thought I could avoid him and expel him from my mind by setting out, committed to my quest, to prove to Vita how much I loved her, show her what I would do for her, find the exploited children that she had made it her mission to rescue. I was on my way, laboring with Moyo on the bush track to the Congo—dirty, hungry, weary—disgusted by the broken window; and Frank was by my side.

Frank was daring me to fail, mocking my effort. He'd infected my mind. I hated him for making me travel here, to prove to Vita my sincerity and love—to demonstrate to her that I was doing something Frank would never dare to do.

The spider I imagined clinging to the back of my neck, the sinister tickling of its hairy legs—that was Frank. The smashed window was Frank. The bursts of rain, the potholes, the clatter of the metal doors— Frank, obstructive Frank.

As we rounded a hill I saw a steepness on Moyo's side, a deep gully, yellow green at the bottom, a river or creek, but stagnant and slow moving judging from its arsenical color. I looked for people—the flicker of light in the trees I took to be men trying to hide their faces. It was more worrying to seem alone in the bush, not to be able to see the hungry people who were certainly there—or at least I imagined them to be, lurking, waiting to crack the rest of our windows, or fling themselves at us, mobbing our vehicle—all Frank's fault.

Toward noon, now with sun breaking through the tattered clouds, I squinted through the trees—spindly with skinny boughs and tiny leaves—and saw the land more clearly. It was flatter and drier, as though the morning heat had baked the rainfall out of it, leaving pockmarked dust and swarms of insects.

We came to a clearing, and the cold remains of a cooking fire—

half-burned chunks of wood, scattered ash—and a log to sit on, an abandoned campsite, the litter of some tangled rags, a torn T-shirt, a single squashed shoe.

Moyo handed me a can of sardines and a box of crackers, and we sat blinking in the sun that burned through the thin trees. I felt too weary and dirty to speak, and still haunted by Frank, the wisp of him, just behind me, teasing my neck with his sticky spider's claws. To calm myself I took a deep breath, and with it in my throat I began to retch.

"What's that smell?"

"I was thinking the same thing," Moyo said. He pointed. "That latrine."

It was a rectangular ditch at the periphery of the clearing, and the movement in the air just above it, like a skein of woodsmoke, were flies, whirring, gleaming, their blue bodies fattened by the light.

We approached the buzzing hole, but when the breeze lifted and the reek hit us, we drew back. Moyo leaned and looked in, holding his shirt to his face. I stepped behind him and saw a man crammed into the pit, almost filling it, because he was bloated, tightened against his clothes, swollen and stinking, his whole head covered with flies.

"Congo," Moyo said. "We have arrived."

23

ROADBLOCKS

THE GROTESQUE CORPSE WAS NOT LIKE A HUMAN BODY at all but rather a specimen of fine-grained sedimentary rock, or a lump of loamy clay dampened by dew, in a sack made of rags, its stitches on the point of bursting. The flies were so thick, the smell so foul, we couldn't get close enough to know any more. But seeing a dead body in the bush was a cause for alarm—we might be discovered there, we might be blamed. I felt guilty simply by lingering, and turned and walked away.

"We go, my friend," Moyo said. But in the Land Rover, speeding off, as though we were being pursued, I could not rid my mind of the sight of that dark bloated thing filling the flyblown trench, snug in friable dirt. The stink stayed with me, clinging to my shirt, nauseating me.

The next miles—ten or fewer—were lovely, but haunted by the sight and smell of that body; and there was in that unbroken bush, the smooth road, the puffs of cloud in the sky, the sudden birds, startled by our vehicle—in that beauty itself—an unambiguous threat, as though this loveliness, like a false face, masked a greater danger, enticing us into a trap, drawing us deeper into the Congo. I imagined a furious man behind every tree.

"I wish we could turn back."

"Too late, bwana. Easier to push on." Moyo clucked with regret. "This bush road is bad. We will return by the main road, Lubumbashi side."

The road widened, and a layer of smoke floated over it from patches of smoldering humus in the earth—a burned-out village, blackened huts, roofless and hollow, withered leaves on scorched boughs, stones whitened, looking calcified by the heat of the fire.

"They fight here—village feud maybe . . ." And Moyo gunned the engine as he spoke.

This seemed to establish the rhythm of my quest along this back road, a set of hideous clearings, separated by miles of unviolated bush and alluvial soil. I nerved myself for the next clearing, as Moyo drove, sighing and slowing at every pothole, then accelerating after them. He grunted in impatience every time he was forced to slow down. At one bend, where the road descended at an escarpment of fractured schist, we came to a roadblock—a crude one, a heavy tree branch, still with twigs and leaves on it, suspended across a pair of rusted oil drums.

Rolling to a stop, we didn't see anyone at once, but as we scanned the roadside, men sitting under a tree, flecked by shadows, became apparent, as though surfacing in muddy water. They watched us for a while, then got to their feet and stretched, taking their time. The smallest of them, a toothy boy wearing a torn polka-dot shirt, put his face at the broken window.

"*Unafanya nini?*" Moyo said, in the kitchen Swahili he used with non-Zambians.

I said, "*Voulez-vois voir nos passeports?*"

Moyo cackled, hearing me, and poked my shoulder. He said, "You are knowing this language, bwana!"

The boy did not reply, but a man in a baseball cap behind him called out, "*Nous voulons voir votre argent!*"

"Money," I said to Moyo.

"How much?"

"*Combien?*"

We negotiated for a while, and they finally settled for a hundred dollars, five twenties, which they examined closely, handing back the bills that were slightly torn and demanding undamaged ones.

"I don't like to bargain with men who have guns," Moyo said. "Ask them how far to Likasi."

"*À quelle distance est-il a Likasi?*"

The man in the baseball cap shrugged and flapped his hand, as though to indicate, *Over there*. And when he approached the boy and smacked the boy's head, the boy dragged the leafy branch off the oil drums, so that we could pass.

"Thieves," Moyo muttered as we drove on, the road fairly straight but too bumpy to allow us to speed. After a few miles we saw groups of people trudging along in the direction we were going, waving to us, some of them dancing in the road, as though daring us to run them down, calling out for us to pick them up, throwing handfuls of gravel at us as we passed. They were ragged, feral-looking boys, fierce-faced men, and weary plodding women burdened with bundles on their head.

Beyond hills stripped of trees, some of the hills planted with maize, we saw the town of Likasi, ramshackle two-story shop-houses lining the main road, bungalows and huts behind them, a squarish park of pounded earth—no grass—at the center of town, an old bandstand in the park, part of its roof missing. Stalls set up at the edge of the road were piled with used clothes and plastic buckets and rusted tools. Long tables were stacked with bananas in bunches, some on thick stalks. As we slowed at an intersection, a policeman approached us, blowing a shrill whistle, his gloved hand out. He settled for twenty dollars, raising a cautioning hand, saying, "*Attention aux voleurs.*"

Moyo laughed out loud when I said, "He's warning us of thieves."

The storm drains in front of the shops were choked with garbage, and drawing nearer the market tables, and buying bananas through our window, we saw a smeared table of blood and fur, three dead monkeys, gutted, beheaded, with their skinny limbs intact and flung out and partially skinned, looking like hairy crucified children. Another was stacked with fuzzy bats, bared teeth in their tiny mouse-faces.

"Fruit bats. They fly free in Zambia, they are devoured here. And to think," Moyo said, "Zambia is just there"—he pointed south—"A model of civilization."

At the edge of town, the bush thickening, the road contracting to a tunnel through overhanging trees, and dusk coming on, we pulled into a grove of yellow-and-green-striped bamboo and camped—sat in folding chairs, drank beer from our crate in the back, ate the bananas we'd bought in Likasi, and said little. I was too dispirited to speak; I hated this trip, and I resented the vow I'd made. I distracted myself by staring at the stars and in my drunkenness I saw luminous sand grains.

Moyo stamped his boot on the ground and cursed. I heard rustling in the clutter of fallen bamboo leaves behind us, and when I shone my flashlight I saw a mass of rats—mottled, pinkish—leaping among the banana peels and beer cans we'd tossed there.

Another night sprawled and sleepless in the hard seats of the vehicle. We left just as dawn lit the road, slapping at mosquitoes and biting flies, the sun burning through the trees. The bush seemed uninhabited, but each time the road widened, which was every few miles, we saw people crouching in the shadows—behind them the desolation of their tumbledown huts and broken fences.

"Fungurume," Moyo said at a roadblock. "I have been here before. When I came from Lubumbashi. We can find petrol here."

He seemed confident, the roadblock manned by uniformed policemen, who accepted the bribe we offered but said we'd have to follow them. They directed us to a man on a bicycle who led us to a gateway, a house beyond it at the far end of a driveway. It was an old yellowish villa, oblong windows with shutters, stained stucco walls, a veranda at the front, painted green woodwork framing it, a clay tile roof, iron bars covering all windows.

A white man—pale, in khaki shorts and a blue shirt with epaulettes—rose from a chair on the veranda and walked to the rail, beckoning us to mount the stairs. He was about my height, black hair combed back, a hooked nose, sharp chin, his blue shirt neatly pressed. He had a bony face, the sort that showed the skull beneath the skin, the way some grassy mounds of scarp and dip reveal the contour of the rock beneath.

He sized us up—two road-weary unshaven men in dirty clothes—and bared his teeth. "Zambia," he said, glancing at our license plate, and in a heavy accent, "Where are you going?"

"Kolwezi," Moyo said.

"You will need a *laissez-passer*," the man said. "*Une carte d'accès*."

"More money," Moyo said. "Who is in charge here?"

"I am in charge." The man straightened, half defiant, half correct.

"You're Congolese?" I asked.

"I am Greek," the man said. He became severe, as his face tightened over the bones of his face. "We have the concession here at Fungurume."

"How much farther to Kolwezi?" Moyo asked.

"Not far—about two hours. The road is good."

He then walked to a small table set against the rail and made an elaborate business of stamping and signing a sheet of paper, which he tore off a pad.

"One hundred dollars," he said. And with the money in his hand he added, "You will not be disappointed. There is plenty of cobalt."

At last, beyond Fungurume, we were on a well-paved road—it ran west to Kolwezi, east to Lubumbashi—but this smooth main thoroughfare had a disastrous effect on my mood.

Relieved of my anxiety, released from my worry of obstacles—potholes, roadblocks, hostile people—I became hot and angry. As my travel tension eased, I was able to reflect on what we'd just endured. In a tense state of uncertainty I never allowed myself to dwell on anything except the need to arrive—I banish all other thoughts, all past failures and annoyances. In a crisis I have no memory, only an animal imperative to survive. Anger was a luxury I couldn't afford, it reduced my efficiency in risky, unfamiliar circumstances; I needed to keep my wits about me.

But now on this good road, nearing my goal, I could think clearly and could ruminate. I became furious.

Frank was the object of my fury. He'd always been on my mind as an irritant, but now he was active and odious, like the stink of the corpse we'd seen in the ditch, an odor so strong it was like smelly hands throttling me. As we rolled toward Kolwezi I admitted I was exasperated, I was tired, I was hungry, I hated this journey. I had been afraid, and I knew that I would not be here, trying to prove my love for Vita if Frank had not insinuated himself in my life—my marriage—and persuaded Vita that she needed details of the plight of the exploited children. He'd convinced Vita that I had the answers; his efficiency made her doubt me for my delay. Frank had made this quest necessary. My credibility with Vita—her love for me, her trust—rested on my success in finding the children—all Frank's idea. *Frank says you're nearby—that you can find everything we need to make a case.*

I loathed him for it, I held him responsible for the misery and risk I suffered on this journey. I wanted him to suffer like this. Now I was seeing people staggering toward Kolwezi, women with bundles, men pushing wheelbarrows, children dragging sacks—and it infuriated me to think that Frank was sitting in his tidy office in Littleford, with a view of the pretty river, sipping hot coffee in a clean white cup that Meryl Muntner had just brought him. I saw him yawning, tapping his mouth with his fingertips, a characteristic gesture he loved to exaggerate. I saw Vita at her computer, Frank hovering behind her—*Here's what you should do*—and I wanted to snatch the power cord of her laptop and whip it around his neck and throttle him.

"We have arrived, my friend," Moyo said, waking me from my reverie of Frank's eyes bugging out as I tightened the cord.

Kolwezi was not a town, but a vast wasteland, bulldozed, deforested, teeming with people and vehicles, its shabby buildings looking thrown together and temporary, all its roads unpaved and lined with shacks, gaunt people waving for us to stop, offering fruit in baskets, plates of yellow cakes, and strips of stiff dried meat. Some men held trays of black gravel that looked to me like washed and battered ore.

We passed a billboard with an arrow, *Hotel Metropole—AC— Piscine—Bar—Café: 2 Km,* and so we followed the arrow to a fenced compound. We were welcomed by a man in a white skullcap and long loose smock. A dog in the doorway barked hoarsely at us—the man kicked the dog, lifting his feet from under the hem of his smock, and I saw he had dirty white shoes with pointed toes.

"*Bienvenue, mes amis!*"

The pool was green with stagnation, the café was closed, the rooms were small, the air conditioners didn't work. Yet Moyo was reassured by the high chain-link fence topped with razor wire that surrounded the whole of the Hotel Metropole—people clinging to its outside, but an armed sentry at the front entrance. The Land Rover would be safe, Moyo said. I went to my room, took a shower, and slept for twelve hours. Frank was in my dreams, and when I woke in the darkness before dawn, trying to force myself back to sleep, Frank was in the room.

24

SCAVENGERS

THE RAW RAPED LOOK OF THE SCARRED HILLS AND PUD-dled flatland, the mudslides smooth as flesh—one look at Kolwezi gave me landscapes for my nightmares. The mouthlike crater at nearby Kasulo was worse, darker, messier, muddier, torn open and continuously violated by the eager crouching *crueseurs,* as they called the diggers, clawing at the knobs and knees of the scoured earth with dirty fingers. Their faces shone with what looked like lust but was more likely the sweat of effort and fatigue, hacking between the dark thighs of the berms.

"It's a gang bang," I said.

"It's a bloody miracle, man," Moyo said.

He was excited by the filthy bodies scrambling in the puddles, the muscular men, the women in soaked stained gowns, the skinny spidery children with dirty faces, their hands like mitts, enlarged by the clotted mud.

"I've never seen anything like this."

"Because the price of cobalt is vibrant," he said, swallowing as though with hunger, and I knew I'd lost him.

That was our first glimpse at the mining. We poked around separately after that, he with his Zambian friend, Aleke, me with a local guide.

I'd dozed and been wakened that first morning by a hammering on my hotel room door, and thinking it was Moyo I'd opened it and seen a man in a jaunty fedora, an orange leather vest over his T-shirt, laughing loudly at me, ingratiating, yet clownish and pushy.

"*Alors, que voulez-vous, mon amis?*" he shouted, taking off his hat and spinning it on his finger.

"Who are you?"

"*Je m'appelle Jean—je suis là pour vous aider.*"

It was in the nature of a mining boomtown, of which this was a hideous example, for it to be hastily thrown together, flimsy huts and prefab buildings and repurposed shipping containers—a place for opportunists and fortune hunters, not only miners but agents and traders, suppliers of food and booze and heavy equipment, the whole of it frantic and impermanent, a destination of hustlers and whores. Kolwezi was exhausting because of its desperation—there was no idleness here; anyone who hesitated was trampled.

"*Plus tard,*" I said. "*Je suis pressée.*"

I'd expected to be propositioned, but not so soon, before I'd left my room.

I found Moyo on the back veranda, his jackknife in his hand, carving orange shreds from a papaya and chewing them, as he listened to an African man in khaki. The man was handsomely bearded and wearing dark aviator glasses, gesturing at a map that was flattened on the table before them.

"Here is the bwana," Moyo said. "He will back me up. Sit with us, my friend." I drew up a chair and Moyo went on, "Aleke does not believe that we managed to drive here through the bush."

I shook hands with Aleke and said, "It's true—back roads."

"Bush-bashing," Aleke said. "Maybe a good way to ship cobalt ore to Zambia and avoid the red tape and the vultures in Lubumbashi."

"We have pioneered a new route," Moyo said. He slapped my arm. "This *mzungu* is my brother."

Aleke said, "Cobalt is the future. Everyone in the world needs it. Katanga has big reserves. Big possibilities. You see the Chinese here? That is the proof."

"I haven't seen any."

"But you will."

"I'm here to look at the artisanal mining."

"Amateurs! *Crueseurs* they call them—just poor people. But they dig like ants, they find the ore, they wash it, they grind it."

"Better you come with us, bwana. Aleke is Zambian. My old school chum. He is languishing here."

"We have a deep mine," Aleke said. "It is not the messy business of these scavengers in the mud and the water and whatnot."

"I want to see the scavengers."

Aleke raised his dark glasses to show me his amused gaze. "You will need a guide, bwana."

He glanced behind me, and when I turned I saw the man in the fedora and the orange leather vest who'd knocked on my door earlier. He was seated at a far table on the veranda, looking eager. He touched his hat brim in greeting.

"I know that man," Aleke said. "He can help you."

"Jean. He woke me up this morning."

"Yes, he is persistent," Aleke said, and called the man over, speaking to him in Swahili. I recognized a few words—*rafiki* was one, friend; and *twende,* let's go.

"You can take the Land Rover," Moyo said. "I will go to Aleke's mine in his vehicle."

"Before we set out, I want to know what this will cost me. How much for the day?"

Aleke shrugged, the man—Jean—said, "*Plus tard.*"

As a traveler I'd been caught this way before. "No problem" or "later" meant at the end of the day, a demand for a large fee. So I faced Jean and said, "*Combien?*"

"You speak this language," Aleke said. "That is clever. You will manage here."

We settled on a price, and Moyo handed me the keys to the Land Rover, saying, "*Kwaheri,* bwana!"—goodbye in Swahili as a joke.

"*Que veux-tu voir?*" Jean said.

"*Watoto,*" I said. The kids. "*Les enfants. Les crueseurs.*"

* * *

In the Land Rover Jean directed me to Kasulo, on a rutted road, the great muddy dump, like a sea of sinister oatmeal. While we watched, Moyo and Aleke parked near us, Moyo exuberant, seeing the diggers splashing in puddles, in the clawed and scarred land that looked subdued and violated.

Jean explained the process to me, and what had seemed to me a disorderly free-for-all was, in his telling, a cogent system of mining—digging, sorting, washing, and grinding cobalt ore—all by hand, small hands, snatching at stones, sloshing them in shallow puddles, crushing them between larger rocks, filling sacks with the result, the bluish pebbles like gravel, but gravel that had value.

The children were sprawled in the mud, the women were bent double, the men I saw seemed not to be working at all but intent on supervising and shouting at the children.

"They're not digging," I said, of the men, who swaggered among the small boys.

"The children are digging—they work for the men."

"Who are those men?"

"*Ce sont les propriétaires.*"

"Owners of the mine?"

"*Ils poisedent ces enfants.*"

Owners of the children, of course. I smiled, because I did not want him to see how shocked I was. I needed information for Vita, I needed to encourage him. And I had greater admiration for Vita, and a grudging respect at last for Frank, for having sent me on this quest.

What struck me was not just the intimidating size of the men—towering over the small boys—or the hectoring shouts of the men. It was the health of the men, most of them stripped to the waist, glowing faces, muscular arms, some of the men quite fat, giants compared to the small dirty boys, many of whom had obvious skin diseases, reddened mangy arms, faces encrusted with sores.

It was a sea of scavengers, literally so, the boys laboring in pools of water, bobbing like flotsam, and others jabbing with iron rebars in well-like pits, where they hauled out buckets full of cobalt ore.

I was muddy myself, walking in the mire, splashed by passing motorbikes, the riders balancing sacks of ore on the gas tank.

"I want to talk to some of these boys."

"Not a good idea, monsieur."

"*Pourquoi?*"

"Those men won't like it." He clarified by using the word *propriétaires* again.

"I'll take photos then."

Jean looked around, he shook his head, not a no, but a twitch of exasperation. I stepped behind him, concealing my phone, and took a sequence of photos, the wide ravine of the digging grounds, and then individual shots, the skinny arms, the clawing hands, the smeared faces, the diseased cheeks, the big bullying owners walking among them, frowning at the skunky smell of the sweaty diggers, yelling in the heat.

When I was done, Jean laughed at me.

"*Qu'est-ce qui est drôle?*"—What's so funny?

"That," he said, tapping my phone. "There is cobalt inside."

"I know—the battery."

"Probably from here!"

So I was complicit. I counted the children, as many as I could, and made notes—the sort of evaluating observations I collected when I was prospecting or mapping. I was sad, not so much because of the simple fact of the children, but because of their effort, so conscientious, working hard, hurrying, running, splashing, competing. In Zambia I was used to methodical miners chopping at the walls of an emerald mine, filling hoppers with ore, tipping the ore into wheelbarrows, sorting, grading the rocks. But this, children snatching at stones, or hammering the stones into gravel, had the desperate urgency of hunger.

"I want to see the buyers."

"*Négociants,*" Jean said, and signaled to me to follow him.

He led me out of the crater and past a narrow river that was like muddy water rushing through a culvert. When we got to higher ground, we were in a wasteland of trampled earth, no road but rather a mass of crisscrossing footpaths, no discernible pattern, yet fitting the image of rape I'd had when I first saw the place. It also seemed to me that the mined area was the sort of chewed and denuded landscape you'd see after a plague of locusts had descended on it, all of it scoured, its bumps and mounds exposed, all its greenery gone—a great, bald, eaten-away ugliness made worse by the sight of mud-smeared half-naked humans still burrowing into it, like a circle of hell, the damned struggling helplessly in the mud. But that was unfair to locusts: only humans could destroy like this.

"Down there," Jean said.

I saw a row of sheds, some with awnings or screened with chicken wire. They could have been cages, or food stalls, each with a hand-lettered sign giving the menu. The signs showed the price per kilo of the ore, and listed the various grades, with weights, some of the numbers crossed out and new prices added.

The faces at the windows were not African. They were pale, like the men outside the sheds, wearing long smocks and floppy hats, some of them in goggles, solemnly calibrating the scales. They had the look of a kind of cruel priesthood of invaders and violaters, beckoning the men with heavy sacks of ore, the men who had been so fierce among the children now humbled and silent but resentfully watchful in the presence of the *négociants*.

The traders were Chinese, scowling at me in puzzlement when they glanced my way. I raised my phone to take a photo and one of them—a woman—screeched and ran at me and batted my arm, startling the African men. She went on screeching in an accusatory way until I backed off and pocketed my phone, the Africans awed and shyly smiling at this act of aggression against a white man.

"*Chinoise—formidable,*" Jean said. And then with venom, as much to the waiting Africans as to me, "*Parasites! Sanguinivores!*"

He said we were better off riding in the Land Rover, but I insisted on walking: I wanted to remember everything, I wanted to document what I saw, I knew I'd never come back. We wandered over Kasulo, unseen or ignored, and it wearied me to see such activity, the children grabbing and grinding the ore, working beside bigger boys and women, and the men strutting among them, shouting. But even with low spirits, and fatigued in the humid heat, I made notes, I took pictures, I listened. There was too much of it for me to record, and though I understood the order of it—the process of mining and selling—I felt that my photos would depict it as chaos. But I would describe in detail what I saw.

Stamping his boot on the yellowish crumbling earth, Jean said, "All cobalt," with pride, and stamped again. "All money here—*tout l'argent.*"

But I thought, *No, it's hell, where these damned souls are trapped helplessly in mud, struggling to survive.*

With no place to sit I squatted and put my head in my hands, appalled by the scramble, but also knowing that it was one of those defining days—I'd had others—where I was faced with a stark choice.

"So—you want to see more?"

I didn't answer. I thought, *I'm done. I have all I need. I can't stomach any more. I'll take this evidence back to Vita, to fulfill my vow.*

"*Il y a beaucoup plus*"—There's much more.

Jean lived with this, he didn't see the horror or the diseased skin. He was smiling. He kicked the yellow earth again.

"All cobalt!"

I made another vow—that I would leave immediately, from the airport Aleke had mentioned, and fly back to Zambia, liquidate my interest in the Kafubu emerald mine, flee Africa, and find something else, closer to home, that was not hellish.

"You want to drink some beer?"

"I want to find a travel agent."

"Beer first. The *agent de voyage* is nearby. I will show you something special."

In the Land Rover, repeating "*Quelque-chose de très spécial,*" Jean directed me back to Kolwezi, down a backstreet, to a noisy bar. I knew bars like this from Zambia, dirty sheds, with wooden benches, loud music, drunkenness, always fistfights. Moyo had said, *They send such people backward, they push people into the primitive. It is the alcohol.*

"I take my European clients here," Jean said. "They enjoy it."

Tough boys vied to guard my vehicle. Jean chose one, putting him in charge.

Inside—low ceiling, loud music, the room stinking of mud and piss and beer—I saw a Chinese man in a corner conferring with an African, the Chinese man pink-faced, with swollen eyes, drunkenly stabbing his finger at a notebook page, the African eyeing him with contempt. They weren't angry, they were in a circle of hell, doing business. Out the far window, a view of a black canal, probably sewage, but with a thickness of water hyacinths or lotuses floating on it. I remembered the Baudelaire I'd read at school that had thrilled me, not any particular line, but just the title, *Les Fleurs du Mal*.

"*C'est trop bruyant*." It's too noisy.

Jean didn't hear me. He had turned aside. He called to a skinny girl in a red dress—too young to have breasts of any size yet wearing lipstick, her cheeks heavily powdered, her head shaved. She was barefoot, her chipped fingernails painted pink. She approached me, spidery and small, bowing a little, and smiled, not a coquette but a child's appeasing smile, wishing to please, playfully catlike, and a little fearful.

"*La veux-tu?*"

"No, I don't want her. I want to leave."

Moyo was in a jovial mood at the hotel, sitting on the veranda with Aleke. He'd had a good day, he said. He, too, had come to a decision, to become a trader here, partnering with Aleke.

"This opened my eyes," he said. "Never mind gemstones and all that bloody *indaba* with the dealers in Jo'burg. This is the future, my friend."

I contemplated this grim dirty place, the blown-open mine hacked out of the jungle, women and children on their hands and knees, the diseases, the rags, the hunger, the desperation, clawing at rubble in the mud, dragging sacks of cobalt ore to the Chinese buyers who stood impassive, with briefcases of Congolese francs, or dollars. Phones, computers, cars, cameras were powerless without cobalt: yes, this misery was the future.

Moyo said he wanted to sell the Kafubu mine and invest here. I agreed on the spot. He promised to transfer my share of the proceeds.

I paid Jean what we'd agreed upon, though he whined for more. Aleke arranged a ride for me to Lubumbashi where, at the airport, I was quizzed about the absence of an entry stamp to the Congo in my passport. The Congolese question was answered with American money. And I was amazed, comparing this to our bush journey, how simple it was to fly to Ndola. I resisted looking up Tutwa. At Kafubu I saw that my house had been broken into and burgled in my absence—*Good,* I thought, *I am absolved of any regrets about leaving.* And the problem of dealing with furnishings and cans of food and books and cookware had been settled by the theft: all I had left was what I'd taken to the Congo—passport, phone, the computer I'd never used, my wallet, and a duffel bag of clothes.

Some village boys kicking a ball near my house saw me leave early one morning for my flight home. I waved to them. They didn't wave back. It was five hours by taxi to Lusaka, on a good road, the sort of road that allowed me to ponder other things.

Such things as that Africa was unfinished, and broken by corruption, and now I saw, probably unfixable. And I was like all the others, African and foreigners, a plunderer. Time to go.

The familiar flight home was a happy trip for me: I was joyous knowing I'd never do it again—I'd never go back. I wrote my report for Vita on the plane, the narrative of my quest, with all the detail I'd collected. What I wrote was the sort of thing I'd done many times, a report based on my field notes, but instead of writing about specimens of rock I was describing humans.

Back in Littleford, reunited with Vita and Gabe, I printed it all, with photos.

"This is perfect," Vita said. "This is dynamite."

We kissed, I held her. For a thrilling moment I experienced the ecstasy that survivors feel, renewed, reborn, reprieved, saved.

Vita shook herself free of my embrace. She said, "Frank has to see this."

* * *

What remained for me to do after that enlightenment in Africa was the undramatic business of finding cobalt nearer home, to be properly mined. It was a yearlong process of prospecting and travel. Moyo was right—until a new kind of battery was invented, cobalt was the future, in demand, and because of its scarcity, its price was rising. I needed to find a copper source, since cobalt occurs with other minerals and metals. Suspecting that the Southwest was a possibility, I called upon my old friends, the Zorrillas, who were still grateful for my having saved Don Carlos. He was now gone, Paco said. A natural death, in his own bed, a rare event for a cartel boss. His passing, and their memory of me, made them sentimental and willing. They hooked me up with a mine in Yavapai, Arizona, and its trickle of low-grade cobalt, which I mined with the protection of the Zorrillas.

It is in the nature of miners in one region to be keenly aware of mining operations of the same ore elsewhere. And so from Arizona I was led to Nevada, and at last to Idaho, the Northwest, where the right combination of factors, based on facies maps—density, saturation—promised results. I found a partner. We began to dig.

"Just a question of money," we said. But I had it, the emerald wealth I'd kept to myself, in what Moyo called "our gem game." When the mine in Idaho began delivering cobalt, which we boasted was ethically sourced, we were in business.

That was a year or more of plotting and secrecy, with frequent visits home. Using the data I'd collected in Kolwezi, and the horror stories and atrocity photos, Vita had launched a campaign to end the exploitation of children in cobalt mines in Katanga. She was promoted. She became a popular speaker at fundraisers. I didn't say that the quest I'd taken on her behalf, to prove my love, had led to my discovery of the value of the ore; that I'd built a new business on the experience of those desperate scenes. For Vita, and Frank, I was still just a rock hunter. As I had never mentioned emeralds, I never mentioned cobalt.

All this time I'd avoided Frank, although to conceal my hostility I sometimes met him at the diner for lunch in Littleford. He'd become involved, as a pro bono attorney for Vita's agency Rescue/Relief. I knew this role of his, the Soul of Kindness, *How can I help?*—insinuating himself, "*Cherchez le créneau,*" as Dad used to say—look for the niche. I'd given up trying to persuade Vita that he was out for himself, always.

I was happy. Then, one day, out of the blue—I'd just come back from Idaho—Vita said, "It's been ages since you had lunch with Frank. Why don't you two grab a bite?"

I resisted. I'd resented the e-mail from Frank: *Lunch—Be there.*

PART THREE

THE BAD ANGEL BROTHERS

25

FRACTURE AND CLEAVAGE

*B*E THERE WAS THE EXCLAMATION MARK AT THE END OF
fifty-six years of our parallel lives, the uneasy brotherhood
of Frank and me, years that preceded the two lunches. The lunches
themselves, bizarre though they might seem to a stranger, were I think
perfectly understandable to anyone knowing our history—two brothers
who'd spent their whole lives up till then in the push and pull of frater-
nal combat—no shouting, no swearing, only the corrosive stink of distrust. I couldn't stand him. He clearly found me unbearable. But I had
my own satisfactions. I was happy in my work and I was determined to
go on loving my wife. I wanted nothing from Frank. I was well aware,
increasingly so over the years, that his hatred for me was fueled by ob-
sessive envy, that he seemed bent on trying to diminish me.

Frank was malign in a peculiar way—instead of disgustedly rejecting
me—the typical ghosting a hater showed in loathing—he stewed in his
hatred, he refused to leave me alone, he found strategies for clinging,
and he insisted on remaining close to me, in a kind of foul intimacy,
being a brother to go on torturing me. He showed me that the ultimate
in hatred is not rejection; it is the refusal to let go. It was hatred as
haunting.

The two lunches then. In the first, I'd gone at the urging of Vita. I'd
needed to be persuaded, because I was acutely conscious of how over

the years he'd insinuated himself in my family, and I was at last sick enough of this intrusion to risk Vita's wrath in staying away from him. But Vita had said, *You might learn something.* Since this was my peace-making phase, I'd obliged. It was just lunch after all.

What I learned—and was unprepared for—was that it was impossible for me to sit with someone over lunch, and eat, while the other person was not eating, not drinking, using his fork to play with his food. It was disconcerting, seeming to hint at something hidden—but what? He'd ordered the same meal as me, he was snippy with the poor old woman who'd served us, he'd disparaged Dad, he'd resurrected bewildering memories of the past, and he'd told some oblique stories, all the while fiddling with his meal—agitating his chowder with a spoon, pushing his fish around the plate, flipping it over, stabbing it with a fork until it was a mass of broken flakes; poked his peas, eaten nothing, not even sipped his water, and finally forming his mashed potato into a little hut, shingling it with his fish flakes. Then he'd left abruptly, while I sat still hungry, pondering the meaning of his uneaten meal. He'd bullied his food into garbage and left me to pay for it, so since the food was actually mine, was the bullied food a metaphor for me?

I tried to resist the obvious conclusion, not that he hated me but that he wanted to destroy me. It seemed in this odd disrupted meal that by refusing to eat and torturing his food, Frank was enacting a ritual to discourage me from eating, that it was a suggestive way of starving me.

But the second lunch, the cookout, was unambiguous, because Vita was part of it. That sunny afternoon Frank came alone—although we'd invited Frolic and Victor, whom I seldom saw; Frank had brought two hot dogs and two bottles of beer. That was his meal, he ate nothing else, he'd ridiculed my mustard ("high fructose corn syrup"). Bringing his own food was not a gift; it meant he was refusing to accept anything from me—maybe some sort of legal nicety—and if it had a deeper meaning, it was perhaps an expression of hostility.

And for quite a while at the cookout he was off to one side, at the far end of the swimming pool, whispering to Vita and occasionally breaking into triumphant laughter, the sort of hateful, much-too-loud mirth that excluded me from the joke. Meanwhile I was chatting with Gabe and his girlfriend, eyeing Vita and wondering whether they were talking about Vita's promotion, her new career as a spokesperson for the exploited children in Kolwezi. Or maybe they were discussing the progress of the lawsuit Frank had filed against the Chinese conglomerate that was buying cobalt from the muddy urchins. In any case, he stood to gain in damages as well as being hailed as a champion of human rights.

Just before the two lunches, I had cashed out of my ethical cobalt mine in Idaho to be home for a long spell of peacemaking, atoning for my absences. I was still dealing with the business side, the wire transfers to banks, but I was no longer digging. I committed myself to being a loyal husband and father, even though I could not wholly understand Vita's detachment. She's busy, I reasoned; her career has taken off. That explained why I was still often eating dinner alone.

Then Vita smiled at me and said, "Why don't we just admit it?"

"Admit what?"

"That it's over."

This was just after the two bizarre lunches and perhaps explained them. What surprised me most of all was that it wasn't my travel—my prolonged absences—that had provoked her but rather my staying home. We had survived being apart for extended intervals; but these recent months together, this intimacy was much harder for Vita to bear.

"I really can't stand having you around."

She did not soften the blow. It was like a well-aimed hammerhead cracking a rock apart on one of its clean planes, cleaving it in two.

"I don't love you anymore."

After this, the neat slice separating the rock—and I knew from my work that such neat cleavage was often caused by internal weakness between the planes—came a further blow, the fracturing. Fracturing is not neat, it is random, anything can happen—after that smash you're left with chips and chunks.

I moved to the guest bedroom, I ate every meal alone, I went for walks along the river, as I'd done as a child—bored, idle, aimless—skimming stones across the water where Vita and I had once joyously seen the honking swans take flight. I also remembered how, when I was young I'd thought, *I want to be old, I want to go away*. Now I was middle-aged, back on the riverbank, exiled in my hometown. And because I had not cultivated anyone in town, as Frank had—patronizing was perhaps a truer word—I had no social life. Now and then I'd run into high school friends—Chicky Malatesta, Caca Casini, Sal Ugolino, the mayor, Dante Zangara, or the Alberti brothers, Alex and Leo—the wise guys, the mockers, the teasers, who remembered me as one of the Bad Angel brothers; and they'd remind me that I was someone who'd abandoned Littleford, who'd traveled into the wide world to make money, only to return and hide in my big house in the Winthrop Estates. They suspected me of being a snob, for having removed myself from the life of the town, taking no interest in Littleford football, zoning, taxes, or the annual town meeting. I had never been able to disguise my lack of interest in local issues. I had lost the native son's knack for pretending to be a booster. I was taken to be a snob for not caring.

Uneasy in my own home—Vita on the phone, or Vita watching TV, Vita coming and going at odd hours—I felt like a tenant, unwelcome, of no particular social value, temporary, someone to ignore.

Yet I had bought this house, we had built this nest together, and with Vita's suggestions I'd paid for every stick of furniture, every picture, every curtain and rug and lamp. Stemware and flatware and window treatments, as Vita called them. Yet more and more I began to feel like an intruder, an obstacle in Vita's daily life. Her whispering into the phone disturbed me: Was I the subject of those whispers?

Seeing me in the living room one day, Vita approached me with a scowl. It was now late September, the days growing cooler, certain trees beginning to turn, the back-to-school season that I'd always associated with a return to seriousness, a resumption of duties after the idleness of summer days. Vita's head was cocked sideways, scarcely recognizing me—I looked somewhat familiar, I was "what's-his-name." She said nothing to me—her silence like a kind of interrogation—maintaining that stern expression that conveyed squinting peevishness, the unspoken thought: *What is this man doing here?*

Feeling awkward in this accusatory silence, I said, "I don't know what to do."

I hoped this plaintive statement would arouse Vita's sympathy, that she might soften and sit next to me in a gesture of consolation, so we could hold hands, brood a little. She was my wife. Years and years of us together in this nest we'd built together.

Vita remained standing, twitching with impatience. And seated, compact in my misery, I had the sense that I was a dog and Vita my owner, because I lifted my head, with wet imploring spaniel eyes, my mouth half open, muttlike, helplessly panting.

"Here's what you need to do," she said, with a snap in her voice, a tone of decision. "First, you have to move out—we have no future here together. You need to get a place of your own. Your gloom is bringing me down. You'd be better off on your own."

"Maybe we can work it out."

But she was still talking. "And next you need to get a lawyer, the sooner the better."

"You're serious."

With an exasperated laugh, she said, "I think you could say that."

She'd begun backing away from me, as though from a bad smell, and she sighed—an actress's sigh—implying that I was being difficult, detaining her unnecessarily.

"We'll both be happier."

Sometimes, in a productive mine, I scoured a seam, and after a long period of digging, I realized I'd exhausted it. And though I'd invested time and money and energy in sinking a shaft and tunneling, deploying men and equipment, I had to admit I'd come to the end. No amount of digging would yield a profit; it would be pointless effort, wasted motion, an empty hole.

Perhaps reading my thoughts, Vita said, "I want to move on."

She said nothing more. She was quickly out of the room, and her slamming the front door shook the house and me.

* * *

I lingered, clinging to the house for another week, wondering where to go, looking for sympathy from Gabe. He said, "Maybe it's for the best," sounding like Frank. But I also thought that the most annoying thing about clichés is that they sometimes express a truth. Maybe he was right, maybe Vita had been right as well when she said, *We'll both be happier.*

A clean break, a new life, began to seem attractive. I was accustomed to new ventures in distant places. My experience as a field geologist had taught me how to create entire enterprises from scratch, finding fresh opportunities, always moving on.

Vita was rejecting me, but in another sense she was releasing me, so that I'd have another chance. I was still young at fifty-six to move away, to find a place to live that suited me, put Littleford behind me—stay in touch with Gabe in law school—and travel without guilt. I might find another source of cobalt, another challenge, sink another shaft, or turn a hillside into an open pit, be a rock hunter again, which was always romance to me.

A fresh start—the words excited me. My romance with Tutwa—which Vita knew nothing about—that betrayal alone would have justified her dumping me; but it had given me the confidence that I might meet someone to share my life with. I was lost now, but happiness was possible.

Vita had persuaded me that, in divorcing me, she had my best interests at heart. *If we hang on, we'll just make each other miserable, and then we'll be old, and it will be too late,* she said that week, couching it as a kind of favor, moving on as enrichment.

Since she was being rational, not blaming, I saw the whole business from her point of view—I was away for months, she was left on her own, and Gabe, older and independent, didn't need mothering. It was natural that she'd learned to live without me. This was why, when at last I came home and we lived together for extended periods I got in her way, interrupting her in her work rescuing children. I'd become inconvenient. She had ceased to need me or depend on me. *I don't love you anymore* was one way of putting it, but she softened this by saying later, *We can still be friends.*

Start again, I told myself. I'd made my life by leaving home. I'd go away once more, farther than before, severing all ties, making new friends. In this mood, I began to fantasize about other places where I might thrive. I thought of Maine, a shingled house on a ledge by a bay, overlooking Eagle Island, where I'd hammered granite as a young man. Then I saw it all covered with snow, and my focus shifted to a warmer climate, with mining potential. I'd had a taste of village life with Tutwa and found it appealing for its simplicity. This time I'd choose a balmier location in the tropics, a small community of thatched bamboo houses, none of them taller than the coconut palms near them—in the ruby-rich hills of Burma, or the tin mining northwest of Malaysia, a noble steep-sided house on stilts, the villagers glad to be employed in my garden and kitchen. The implication in each of these places, along with the opportunities for prospecting, was that I might also meet a woman with whom I'd share the rest of my life.

Many people dream this way, in futile reverie, knowing it will never happen. How to disentangle myself from this marriage? Where to find the money to fund this dream? But it was different for me: Vita had released me, and I was wealthy—far richer than anyone knew, my secret stashes distributed in numbered accounts around the world. The gold in Tanzania, emeralds in Zambia, all that revenue; the cobalt enterprise in Idaho, for which I'd gotten an enormous payday when I'd sold my shares and cashed out. Vita knew nothing of these ventures.

I was smiling, reflecting on my future, so excited about the possibilities for me, that I saw the divorce Vita demanded not as a dead end, but the beginning of a life of renewal and contentment. Given my savings and investments I would not have to think about work, but only of a sunny place to roost, with a woman by my side.

I engaged the lawyer Vita had said was necessary, not a Littleford attorney, but one from a Boston firm that specialized in divorces. To take the sting out of the suspense until the divorce was final—I was still in the guest room—I went away. It was now October, chilly, the leaves being stripped from trees by rain and wind. I flew to Baja but did not stay in Cabo San Lucas. I rented a car and drove up the coast to Todos Santos, one of those lovely small towns I'd dreamed about—warm, great food, friendly folks, possible romance. And, inquiring casually, I heard there were diggings, too, in Baja—sunshine, music, tacos, as well as gold, copper, and tungsten.

Being in Mexico, near enough to Arizona, reminded me of the Zorrillas. I called on the off chance we might meet. Paco answered, delighted, effusive.

"Amigo! This is a perfect miracle. My youngest daughter, Lupita, is having her quinceañera—and Sylvina said to me just yesterday, 'What about inviting Pascuale?' So can you come? It's in two weeks. We'll have a big fiesta. Church. Dancing. Food—*gran evento!*"

We talked for a while, he gave me his new address, and I said I'd try to come. I knew that giving a present of jewelry was one of the quinceañera customs, and I had some emeralds with me, for luck—a gemstone for Lupita would be appreciated by the Zorrillas.

"I'm pretty sure I can make it, Paco."

A few days later, I was returning from having a drink with a Mexican geologist, when I found a note waiting for me at the front desk of my hotel, *Please call—urgent,* and the first name of my divorce lawyer, Chuck.

"I hope you're sitting down" were his opening words.

I hated his facetiousness and said nothing, hoping he'd register my disapproval by my silence.

Finally I said, "What's the news?"

"Not good, Cal. I've never come across anything as unusual as this with regard to negotiating a settlement in a divorce."

"Unusual in what way?"

"Their asset search and an aggressive audit. Your wife's legal team knows the details of every wire transfer, bank account, and credit card transaction. They have the numbers of safe-deposit boxes and all their locations. You have money in South Africa?"

"Payments for winding up an emerald concession in Zambia, a couple of years ago. My partner banked it there. I had remittance issues."

"Someone did a deep dive."

"What does that mean?"

"That you've been hacked. All your data—user names, passwords, bank accounts."

"How do you know this?"

"We had a meeting with your wife's team yesterday. I got a glimpse of the paperwork. Naturally, they didn't show me much detail, but what I saw really shook me."

"Is the lawyer my brother, Frank?"

"He's on the team. Another guy did most of the talking."

"The cat's-paw."

"I guess you could say that. Hey, I think you should come home, Cal."

"I just want the whole thing over."

"Better hurry. This might be expensive."

It was. Vita demanded money—a lot of it, more than I could lay my hands on. Her threat, conveyed to my lawyer by her lawyer—Frank, I assumed—was that as I had not reported my income in those offshore accounts to the IRS, they could inform the IRS of this. The quinceañera was out of the question. I sent my regrets via FedEx, enclosing an emerald for Lupita, and tried to appease Vita.

Feeling like a white-collar criminal, fearing legal action and a government audit, I emptied my bank accounts and handed the money over. Lacking any income, I floated a loan. Vita got the house, custody of Gabe—his being in law school made him a dependent: I was on the hook for his tuition—and I was now destroyed financially.

My dream of a new life I put on hold. I was as miserable as Frank had described long ago, in his divorce from Whitney, when he'd said,

I'm staring into an abyss—one of his rare confessions of distress. And, as a geologist in chasmic landscapes, I knew something of abysses.

As for the two lunches—the diner, the cookout—I thought: in many years of being brothers I was able to name the exact occasions when I knew that Frank had gone completely cold on me, making no secret of being my enemy. The evidence was unmistakable: not eating the food at the diner, bringing two of his own hot dogs to the cook-out. He was Vita's accomplice in cleaning me out, though he denied it when I called him.

"It was a team effort," he said. "But one of the guys—hey, no names—was a real bulldog, excess-to-requirements type."

He was inviting me to lunch when I poked my phone off, silencing him, and cursed out loud. As though summoned by my shout, Vita appeared at the door to my room.

"I have some errands to run," she said. "When I come back, I don't want to find you here."

I approached her, attempting a last touch, a farewell embrace. She allowed it, she stiffened with a kind of horror, of such rigidity, it was as though she'd turned to stone.

I packed my bags, then tapped some familiar numbers into my phone, and when it was answered, I said, "Mother?"

26

MONOLOGUES

ONE OF THE STARKER EXAMPLES OF ABJECT FAILURE IS A man of fifty-six, broke, divorced, out of work, and living back home with his mother, sleeping in his old bed, hands behind his head, his eyes upturned to the familiar stains on the ceiling. I reflected on the ogre in profile with the long warty nose, the misshapen island, scattered clouds, the pickax near the cabin, the cocked pistol, the bobbing boat, the broken bird's wing that speaks of arrested flight, injury and loneliness and despair—all this and Mother's odors: soap, cologne, hair dye ammonia, meatloaf.

Inattentive in my prospecting, looking hard for a meaning in some thing inconsequential, I had stepped from a sunlit cliff into a steep ravine, and bumped and battered by the long drop, I lay in darkness, pinched by the narrowness of the ravine's bottom and up to my neck in water in the downslope channel. I could not budge. I wondered if I might be insane. *Nervous breakdown* had always seemed to me a hard-to-define condition—what was it exactly? Feeling shattered in this pit? Where I was and how I felt made no sense.

How had I ended up with nothing—less than nothing—debt?

Prospecting is all about risk, borrowing big against a possible strike, failing spectacularly with a dry hole one day, hitting pay dirt the next. I was used to failure, but this was something else, something bottomless, as Frank had once said of his condition, abysmal. I had no experience of absolute ruin.

It was mental—confusion in my brain—and a sadness that made me tearful. But it was physical, too, a dull ache in my shoulders, as though I'd strained my back lugging a box of rocks. And with that the nausea you feel from chronic pain. I felt a slackness, a weakness, an inability to hold a thought for any length of time, enfeebled by a sense of helplessness—action of any kind seeming absurd, what was the point? I'd let myself down, I felt guilty, I felt stupid and sorrowful, I was dying, locked in bewildering immobility. Being home was confinement that amounted to a kind of paralysis, and being in Littleford meant I was reduced to being a Bad Angel brother once again.

I needed someone to lean on, but who? The human voice was an irritant, sound of any kind upset me. I was sick inside, I couldn't eat. I thought: *So this is what it's like, being abandoned.*

Well aware that my condition—motionless in my childhood bed—was related to Vita dumping me, Mother said, "Dad and I had such a wonderful marriage. He was a kind and loving man."

She was standing at the door to my bedroom, holding a glass of milk in one hand, a plate of homemade cookies in the other, a mother's innocent comforts.

"Do you remember the time he surprised me with that beautiful painting?"

A gilt-framed oil of Littleford in colonial times, men in frock coats and tricorn hats, women in bonnets, holding parasols, horse-drawn carriages, a trotting dog, some children chasing a ball, and in the foreground a young man and woman—lovers—strolling together.

Mother set down the glass of milk and the cookies on my bedside table and crept away, smiling at the memory of Dad's present, the painting that still hung over the fireplace.

I tried not to cry, but before I turned aside I saw Mother limping to the top of the stairs, then pausing, trembling a little, nodding at nothing, gripping the banister, poor arthritic woman, bracing herself for the descent. I was ashamed of my idleness, feeling sorry for myself. And this lame old soul had not uttered a word of complaint, while I lay feeling sorry for myself.

With my hands behind my head, I interpreted the stains on the ceiling. They were like water streaks on a cliff face, or the weathered crusty rinds formed by deposits, the blotches I'd seen from manganese oxide, rock coatings accreting on surfaces of exposed scarp. I knew from a college textbook that Leonardo da Vinci, sometime geologist and full-time artistic genius and describer of cliff faces, was one of the first to understand the origin of sedimentary rocks and the former life of fossils. He was also a connoisseur of stains. He urged in his "Treatise on Painting" to pay close attention to the stains on a wall or ceiling as a way of stimulating thought or provoking ideas. All the stains I saw hinted at villainy and my own stupidity: now my ceiling made sense, as an indictment of me, for all the bad decisions I'd made.

My great mistake was the local boy's shallow brag of returning to his hometown, flush with cash, to buy the big house he'd craved as a youngster, mowing lawns. And I'd idealized my days at Littleford High School, hoping that Gabe would graduate there, an improved version of me at that age. I'd introduced Vita to Littleford, planting her in the town as though to prove how better life was here, more solid and orderly, compared to the improvisation of South Florida—hot, flat, sand and mud, hardly a rock to be found. As though I'd rescued her, delivered her to safety, the sort of selfish motivation I'd ascribed to Frank when he'd taken up with Frolic—his lawsuit love affair that made him rich.

I'd gone away—digging—leaving Vita at the mercy of Frank. I had allowed all this to happen. My staying away had contributed to the breakdown of my marriage and given Frank a chance to encourage Vita to doubt me. And here was another irony: I'd thought that taking a leave of absence and coming home would reassure Vita and heal us, yet my constant presence, intended as loving and comforting, had annoyed her. *You again,* she seemed to murmur whenever she saw me in the house. My being home had demoralized her and hastened the end of our marriage.

I was sure that Vita had confided in Frank, that she had solicited his advice. It would have been operatic and bizarre if they'd been lovers, but Frank was sexless and too manipulative to allow himself to be passionate. What he did was worse—out of sheer spite he turned Vita against me, in a calculated and cold-blooded way, became her advocate, demonstrating in one of his legalistic memos that she'd be able to profit mightily by divorcing me.

I could hear his pitch: *Vita, listen, you could end up a very wealthy woman.*

It was my fault. I had allowed it. I had selfishly busied myself elsewhere. I'd even taken a lover in Africa. I'd let it happen—left the door open for Frank. I'd been preoccupied with emeralds and then cobalt, and I let my marriage collapse. Frank had taken advantage of Vita's loneliness, and he'd helped her rise in the Rescue/Relief agency. As always, his most satanic quality was his helpfulness, his availability— discreet, at her service. *How can I help?* and *It's no trouble at all.* In this way (*I'll nip right over*) he'd subverted me, turned her against me in his pretense of generosity, with endless promises. Vita had welcomed these words, because she'd had so few words from me.

Working this out, seeing how I was mostly to blame for the undoing of my marriage, saved my sanity. I'd delivered Vita into Frank's hands. A better man than Frank, a better brother, would not have behaved this way—used her to try to destroy me. But I knew Frank well enough to realize my error in settling in Littleford. I'd lost Vita, I'd lost the house, Gabe was oblique with me, and here I was in my old bedroom. I didn't mind having very little—I'd managed quite well prospecting as a camper on a motorcycle—I'd thrived. What I found hard to bear was having less than nothing, being deep in debt.

Frank, being Frank, was still hovering. "It's for you," Mother said, handing me her phone, and she mouthed the word *Frank* with a smile.

"Lunch?" he said—no greeting.

I couldn't believe that after all that had happened he was insisting on being in my life, that he wouldn't leave me alone.

"Can't do it," I said.

He was talking as I handed the phone back to Mother, who limped away, looking defeated.

I came to see that for him, for most sociopaths, he had no memory—

took no responsibility for anything he'd said or done—had no past, no history, it never happened. Memory is essential to conscience; he had no conscience.

The clatter in the upstairs corridor just then was Mother bobbling and dropping the phone. "Sorry!" she called out in a high and quaking voice of apology.

That was another thing. On my visits home while living with Vita, I always found Mother seated on her favorite chair, among all the bric-a-brac—the shawls, souvenir plates, the ornaments and teacups, the porcelain shepherdesses, the dolls in dresses, the sofa piled with pillows she'd crocheted. She seemed so serene sitting there, often knitting, sometimes sipping fruit juice, unchanged since the last time I'd seen her, months before. White-faced and brittle, in a chiffon dress, wearing small furry slippers, her feet barely touching the shag rug, she was doll-like, resembling one of her own souvenirs, but life-size and twinkling and glad to see me.

Those were brief visits, when I'd brought her chocolates, or the groceries she'd requested.

But living with her, seeing her cook and clean and chop vegetables and peel Brussels sprouts, I realized how frail and uncertain she was, frailer than she admitted. I was ashamed, because she exhausted herself in trying to please me, being an active and nurturing mother again. I saw this too late. I was the reason for her fatigue and her frailty. Her shortness of breath worried me. Mild exertion turned her face pink. She sometimes sat gasping, unable to speak.

Now, in her house day and night, I saw that she survived on pills. I hadn't known this until it became part of my routine to pick up her medicine at Littleford Apothecary—pills for osteoporosis, pills for arthritis, red pills, green pills, blue pills, for ailments I couldn't guess at. Sorting them into her plastic pill organizer with trembling fingers, four or five to a daily slot, she smiled as though savoring treats, and the multicolored pills did have the appearance of Halloween candy.

She was weirdly whitened, not simply pale and old, but calcified, crusted, her skin like tissue, a flakiness at her neck, fissures in her face distorting her features to the point where it was hard for me to read her expression. Was that a smile, or was she wincing in pain? Was she relaxed, or was she weary?

Mother was, I finally saw, exhausted. She had managed well enough alone, but my presence in the house, feeling low in spite of her diligent mothering, wore her out. She was increasingly forgetful, she had little arm strength, and a poor grip, often dropping things that she was bringing to me—the glass of milk I didn't want, the cookies she thought I liked, the runny soft-boiled eggs I'd eaten as a child but now disgusted me. They ended up on the floor, and I mopped them while she stood by lamenting her clumsiness. She was becoming visibly fossilized and seemed to have gone into steady decline since my moving in with her. Those press-and-unscrew caps on the yellow plastic pain pill containers: she was in too much pain to press and unscrew them.

And her deafness meant that she didn't hear water running in the bathtub and sink—flooding was frequent; she didn't notice the buzz of a badly tuned radio she'd forgotten to turn off. She seldom heard with accuracy anything I said.

"Have you thought of having a hearing test, Mum?"

"Silly!" She laughed. "Why would I ever have a urine test?"

"Soup's on!" she'd call out in her cheery way, summoning me to lunch from my bedroom, where, instead of lightening her load, I still selfishly and single-mindedly looked for implications of the ceiling stains.

What she served was almost inedible. She'd once been a good cook, but she'd lost the knack, or skipped crucial steps or ingredients.

Yet I ate it all because she sat with me, proud Mother observing her half-cracked and hopeless son at the meal she'd made specially for him. I choked it down, tears of disgust pricking my eyes, while she watched as I struggled to swallow.

I loved her too much not to eat what she made for me, and she knew how saddened I was by my failed marriage. Her motherly mission was to heal me. But her effort was taking a toll on her health.

She denied that, but I could see she needed help more than I did. Feeling responsible for her feeble condition, I roused myself to get a grip. Still she insisted she was fine, though her dropping things and leaving water running or the stove on continued to the point where I knew such forgetfulness could be hazardous.

"What can I do for you, Mum?"

"Just eat my food and cheer up," she said, naming two things I felt were almost beyond me.

"What else?"

"I hate to ask," she finally said.

She was knitting, studying her stitches, and had said this shyly, as though concealing something important. I said, "Mum—anything— name it."

"It would please me so much if you'd have lunch with Frank."

This rattled me. I said, "I see him all the time."

"Frank said"—she spoke slowly, at the rate she was knitting, a phrase for each twitch of her needles looping the yarn—"that he hasn't, um"— another twitch—"seen you"—one more loop—"for months." Her eyes were cast down at the thing she was knitting, which looked all wrong to me, strangely knotted, lumpy where she'd drawn the stitches too tight, as though she was creating an unusable clumped rag. "That you don't answer your phone."

She seemed so sad, her head bowed over her mangled knitting, I said, "Okay. I'll give him a call. We'll have lunch."

She glanced up and beamed at me, her face filling with color, bright- ening, as with a mood-enhancing pill. She looked younger just then, and drugged and delighted.

It was a cold bright day in December, my face tightened against an icy wind from the river, my hands jammed in my pockets, scraps of dirty snow refrozen after the last brief thaw, a coating of sand on the side- walks with a white rime of salt—I associated winter in Littleford less with snow than with sand and salt, the scattered grit that I kicked and crunched as I made my way to the diner.

Frank was in the booth—I saw the top of his head, the dent in his hair left by the rim of his hat, and I smiled at it for the way it made him look silly. But his arriving early always suggested to me that he had a preconceived plan for ambushing me. As soon as he saw me he slid out of the booth and hugged me. I was so startled by this unexpected show of affection—or pretense of affection—that I couldn't think of anything to say. As I struggled out of my coat I realized his hug had left me breathless.

"You need a heavier coat than that, Fidge. And where's your scarf?"

"I guess I need a new wardrobe. I haven't spent a whole winter here in years."

"This is yours," Frank said, snatching up a scarf from the seat beside him. Instead of handing it to me, he pulled at my hanging coat and stuffed it into the side pocket.

I'd begun to thank him when the waitress appeared, saying, "A beverage to start?"

"Cranberry juice," Frank said. "And my son here will have . . ."

"Tomato juice, please."

"Shall I tell you today's specials?"

"I know what I want," Frank said. "Turkey sandwich with cheddar, and a cup of clam chowder."

"Just chowder for me."

"That all? You look like you've lost weight."

"Lost my appetite," I said.

"You need to look after yourself."

He'd shifted his head so that I did not see his full face, two expressions, but rather gave me the somber angle, with its pleats of distortion, the drawn-down mouth, the doubtful side, crazy clown hair on top.

He was still talking, in a tone of urgent concern, about my health and well-being, how I'd always been the outdoorsman, hiking and camping while he—the nerd—had been in his room studying. He'd envied me for being robust, the strength that had taken me to so many parts of the world, prospecting, pioneering new claims, guiding big companies in their mining. I'd need good health to look after Mother, and of course it was essential for when the time came for me to resume my geology.

"That's what I keep wondering . . ."

He raised his hand, showing me his stern palm, as if stopping traffic, and I was silenced. I needed to prepare for that, Frank said—for starting again, in the same spirit that had inspired me to make my fortune in the first place. Someone of my caliber, who'd gone into the world and made such a success of it, could do it again, would be better at it, because—didn't Chairman Mao say this?—all genuine knowledge originates in direct experience. Not sitting in an office like him, staring out the window and munching a turkey sandwich (our food had been served, I'd finished my chowder), but the real thing, the wide world, breaking rocks, digging up gemstones, balls to the wall.

"I doubt whether . . ."

"State of mind," Frank said, interrupting again, tapping his finger to his dented hair. "It's all mental. I keep telling Victor that he could learn a lot from you, but he can't hold a job, and now he's got a hippie girlfriend with a neck tattoo. It's all negative energy with these losers."

I'd always been the positive one, he said, the adventurer—and look how it had paid off. Travelers were optimists, confident that they'd find something amazing just over the next hill, around the bend, down the road. Conquerors were unfazed, their confidence assured their victories. He admired me for my traveling, for my finding gold. Anyone who'd made a fortune had his head on straight, and even if he lost it all somehow—run of bad luck, whatever—he could do it again.

"You're hardwired to win," Frank was saying, as the waitress came and stacked the plates on her forearm, and—Frank still talking—I made a thumb and finger gesture indicating a cup of coffee. When she brought the coffee—"And that's not all," Frank was saying—I made the scribbling signal, meaning "the check." She brought that, presenting it on a plate, and Frank pinched it and slapped it on the table, covering it with his hand, and still talking.

He'd seen my destiny in high school, how I'd turned away from school sports, while he'd warmed the bench at football games, not good enough to play unless Littleford was crushing the other team and Coach Rizzo put in the third string for the last few minutes of garbage time. But I was—what?—hiking in the Fells with Melvin Yurick, identifying rock formations, hammering at granite, earning merit badges, serving a kind of apprenticeship that would lead me to great achievements in geology, and Yurick to become a billionaire.

"Meantime, I'm in the locker room, the big jocks snapping towels at my ass," he said and paused and looked at his watch.

In that pause, I said, "You just reminded me—you once said that no woman is sexier than a cheerleader. And you specified 'not those NFL hookers, but a high school cheerleader, a Littleford Lioness.'"

"You're thinking of someone else," he said. "I never said that."

I was protesting, half laughing, saying he had, as he placed a pile of bills onto the check and slid out of the booth, one hand lifted to silence me, the *I need a minute* upraised hand.

"Catch you later," he said, shrugging himself into his overcoat and hurrying away. "Give my love to Mum. The scarf's yours."

Another lunch, but with a distinct difference, all that talk. Such a talker prevents his listeners from asking a question. He had smothered me with his monologue.

And something else. All that talk had been sympathetic, morale-boosting, showing concern, encouraging me, praising me, comparing himself unfavorably, humbling himself, remarking on my strengths. Reflecting on this, walking back to Mother's house, the winter wind slashing my face, I was reminded that in his role as the Soul of Kindness, Frank was dangerous.

Christmas came. A dark and tormenting season for anyone estranged. I made excuses and drove to Maine and holed up in a rented cabin, microwaving canned chili and splitting wood for the potbellied stove. I returned when the festivities were over.

I now saw there was magic in what I had lost—my old instinct for finding gold and emeralds and cobalt; my love for Vita; my son, our house, the routine I'd taken to be harmony—all gone. In my misery I replayed Frank's monologue and I became more miserable, realizing that his talk had prevented me from asking about Vita, and all that I'd once had.

Being in the house with failing Mother, who talked but was too deaf to listen, was like being alone. I'd become one of those loners who talked to themselves; I lived in a world of monologues, with no one listening.

27

A FART IN A MITTEN

O NE AFTERNOON AROUND THAT TIME, SUNK IN THE misery of my boyhood routines, I walked into the parlor and did not see Mother, and I panicked. She'd been there ten minutes ago, and now I feared she'd gotten up and fallen and was lying injured behind the sofa, or at the foot of the stairs, or collapsed beside the piano. I was frantic, I looked for her in those places, and then I hurried to the kitchen, calling out, "Ma!"

And I heard a faint voice from the parlor, not a word but a whinny, as though from someone trapped under slumped gravel and suffocating. When I reentered I saw a small flapping hand, Mother's, signaling from beneath some bulky cushions. She'd fallen asleep, and in her pallor and fragility and smallness, she was indistinguishable from the fringed cushions and the draped shawls, her chalky face matching the chalky crockery just behind the sofa. Back from the dead.

"Are you all right?"

She gasped a little. "I was resting my eyes."

I helped her upright; she was a splinter of a person, almost weightless, fragrant with cologne and talcum powder, smacking her lips, catching her breath to finish a sentence.

"Frank said he gave you a nice scarf."

"When did you see him?"

"He called. He's ever so busy. And Frolic's parents are in a bad way.

Her mom has spinal stenosis, and her dad's laid up with diabetic shock. They might have to amputate his leg."

"That's a shame."

"Did you say he'll be lame?"

Invisible in all that clutter, she was so comforted by the cushions and shawls and bric-a-brac she'd been buried in, she had snoozed, like a chick in a nest, curled into a ball.

I continued my boyhood routines, mostly chores, emptying the trash, mopping the kitchen floor, shoveling the snow from the front walk and sprinkling rock salt on the icy stairs, then retreating to my room to avoid Mother's mentions of Frank, and lying in my bed, wondering, *What about the rest of my life?*

I'd somehow become Mother's caregiver, and I was glad to help her and to feel useful. She'd been a doting and unselfish woman who'd rejoiced in mothering, and she was glad to have me back, to mother me again. But everything she said about her happy marriage was a reproach to me, my long absences from Vita and Gabe, my waywardness with Tutwa; and I had paid a high price for trying to hide my profits. I was grateful for a place to stay, but it also seemed that Mother's welfare had become my responsibility. Frank was busy, Vita was more involved with Rescue/Relief, Gabe was studying for the bar, and I'd reverted to Errand Boy.

I put Mother's fatigue down to her intake of medicine, the great number of pills and capsules she swallowed every day, their side effects, the ways in which one pill reacted with another, the cocktail of drugs that left her drugged and listless.

When I mentioned this to her one day, she said, "Read the leaflet. What does it say?"

"May cause drowsiness, or itching, or nausea. Do not operate heavy machinery."

I laughed, then noticed she'd dropped off to sleep.

I made a weekly trip to the square to pick up Mother's prescriptions from Littleford Apothecary, a place hardly changed from when I was a boy and still with a soda fountain. The pharmacist was a bald jovial old man—eightysomething—named Wallace Floyd, who always inquired after Mother—"How's the Queen?" And he remembered that, as a soda jerk, he used to see me sitting alone in a booth with a chocolate frappé.

That was another thing—returning to the town, I was not an adult anymore: I was the boy I'd always been, mower of lawns, runner of errands, drinker of frappés, one of the Bad Angels.

"This here is something new," Floyd said, handing me the bag with the bottle of pills. "Metoprolol. Make sure the Queen doesn't exceed the dosage."

"Thanks, Wally." I read aloud the dosage recommended on the label of the bag. "One capsule, morning and evening, with food."

"There's a good boy."

Back on the street, heading into the square, I saw Chicky Malatesta approaching. He was one of the many locals who vouched for Frank, along with Dante Zangara, the Alberti brothers, Caca Casini, and all the rest of them. I expected him to ignore me, or turn aside, but he put out his hand and said, "Cal! How's it hanging?"

That sort of greeting, vulgar teasing, was a form of affection in Littleford. Any sign of politeness from him I would have taken to be hostile.

"The usual," I said. "I'm getting hind tit."

He laughed, then he said, "You want to go for coffee?"

This surprised me, his spontaneous friendliness. I'd anticipated a rebuff by my being a supposed snob in the town, and here he was inviting me to sit down with him for a cup of coffee. I was touched, glad for some relief from the isolation at Mother's.

"But not to the diner," I said, where we might meet Frank. "Let's go to Verna's."

That was the donut shop across the street from the Apothecary.

Inside, we sat at a table in the back—his idea—and ordered coffee and each of us a donut. Chicky lifted his donut but before he took a bite he looked aside and still held the donut, wagging it a little. A black man and white woman were choosing donuts from the glass display case, pointing and laughing a little.

In a low voice, Chicky said, "Breaks your heart."

"We used to call those jimmies," I said to change the subject, indicating the colored sprinkles adhering to the chocolate frosting of my donut.

"We still call them jimmies," Chicky said and eyed me. "What have you got against the diner?"

"I've been spending too much time there," I said, and hesitated. "With my brother."

Chicky made a face. "Funny you should mention him."

He stirred his coffee, rotating his spoon, as though to convey that he was absorbed in serious reflection. He was Frank's age, three years older than me, a plump version of the swarthy, skinny student he'd been in high school; fat faced, gray hair, the toughened fingers of a workman, but still recognizably that spirited boy, hardly changed in demeanor, because he'd never left Littleford.

"Aren't you and Frank big buddies?"

Chicky shook his head, tapped his spoon against his cup, and looked grim. "What a pisser."

I sipped my coffee. I was wise to the culture of Littleford, and the social strategies of locals; I immediately guessed he was conning me—disparaging Frank as a way to talk about him, perhaps running him down. Then Chicky would go to Frank and ingratiate himself by ratting on me. *Cal called you a pisser.*

I said, "Isn't he your lawyer?"

"Used to be."

To motivate him to fill the dead air I said nothing.

"Until he shafted me," Chicky finally said.

"I was under the impression that Frank had a great reputation for winning for his clients."

"Thinks his shit's ice cream."

"Not a good match?"

"Like his face and my ass," Chicky said. "He wins, the client loses."

"I did not know that," I said, hoping for details, while being noncommittal.

Chicky stared past me, past the display case, past Verna, into Littleford's main street, looking rueful.

"You know I was maintenance at the hospital for twenty-five years— seniority, the whole nine yards. So when I got injured on the job I figured I'd get a good payout, maybe take early retirement."

"What kind of injury?"

"Spinal. Chipped vertebrae. Plus wicked emotional distress."

And then he spread his hands over the table, our coffee, our half-eaten donuts, the scattered flecks of jimmies, bracing himself.

"I goes into the basement, I walks into the boiler room, checks the temperature, and on my way out I trips at the foot of the stairs and I falls on a hazardous waste disposal bag, which some shit-for-brains tossed there, and what's inside? An improperly discarded syringe. So not only do I injure my back but I'm stabbed in my hand by a friggin' needle. I can barely walk, my hand gets infected, and it's wicked serious. I'm put on disability and when Frank sees me limping into the diner he gets happy, and why? Because Frank loves cripples."

"I guess Frank took your case."

"He sued the hospital for liability—the syringe. Plus he made up some bullshit about how I tripped on a stair tread that wasn't up to code, and how it was affecting my sex life."

"I think that's called loss of consortium—neglecting your wife," I said, and then—eager to get him to stop—I said, "How did it end?"

"Long story short, he settled out of court—damages."

"Big money?"

"Not for me. For one thing, I didn't want to settle. I wanted my day in court. But Frank said, 'What if we lose in court? You'd end up with squat.' So I accepted the deal. And that wasn't even the worst part. He shows me an agreement I signed when I was hurting and in a hurry. It gives him fifty percent of the payout, plus his legal fees, which come out to almost a grand an hour. By that time I'd quit my job at the hospital, meaning I've got no income. And the money Frank got for me isn't enough to support me and my wife. I'm basically screwed. All Frank's fault."

Knowing what Frank would have said—probably did say—I said, "But you knew what you were getting into."

"Wicked small print," he said. "I told him, 'I wish this had worked out better for me.' He says, 'Wish in one hand and piss in the other, and see which one fills up faster.'"

I knew that line of Frank's. But still believing that Chicky might be trying to get me to pile on Frank, then report it to him, I took another bite of my donut and stared. Finally I said, "Frank's a funny guy."

"He's a scumbag." Chicky drummed his thick fingers on the table. "Candy ass. Beats his meat." Still drumming. "Banana man. Stronzo."

I slapped crumbs from my hands with an up-and-down chafing of my palms that also signals finality, saying nothing.

Chicky said, "Your father—who I really liked when he was a scout-master for Troop 25—he used to call me 'a fart in a mitten.' But the real fart in a mitten is Frank."

"You said it, not me."

"Take a gander," Chicky said. He rolled up his sleeve, showing me a great gouged portion of his forearm that was scarred and badly healed. "Flesh-eating bacteria. From the syringe. I could have died. Plus my back injury." Tugging his sleeve down, buttoning his cuff, he said, "Bas-tard."

His vehemence only increased my suspicions that he wanted me to say something quotable against Frank, though Chicky's injuries seemed real enough, and there was pain in his voice in his telling his tale.

"I'm unemployed, too," I said. "I moved back home—ditched my job—hoping to save my marriage. But my wife had already made up her mind to leave me. I lost everything."

"Frank must have been her lawyer."

"I guess you'd have to ask him that," I said. "I lost my house and all my savings. She won't speak to me. My son treats me like a stranger. I'm living with my mother—can you imagine that?"

"Yes," Chicky said. "Roberta and I are living with her folks, because of Frank."

"I hate this cold weather. I don't know anyone in Littleford any-more."

He looked pityingly at me. "Why don't you leave?"

"I can't. I want to see my son. I need to look after my mother. And I have no resources—I'm in debt because of my divorce. I'm trapped."

"Cal—it's your asshole brother, Frank. Why don't you admit it?"

"Because it's complicated."

"It's not complicated. It's obvious. He always puts himself in charge. He's the master—everyone else is a slave."

"Have you complained to him?"

"Sure. He said, 'Go look in the mirror and ask yourself that same question, and see what answer you get.' It never ends."

Chicky lapsed into a resentful silence, and I began to look at him differently. He was no longer the wise guy from high school, or the maintenance man at the hospital. He was another of Frank's victims. His indignation made him seem intelligent and wounded; he'd been wronged, but he was helpless to do anything about it.

His saying *It never ends* struck a chord. Frank was one of those lawyers for whom nothing is final. There was always another letter to write, another appeal to file, another lawsuit, another angle, another folder to fill, more briefs to discuss, in the quest for billable hours. Nothing was black or white, he existed in a cloudy wilderness of *maybe* and *we'll see,* because the law was amorphous, its plasticity always open to interpretation, in the slow plod toward resolution. But resolution was not justice, only paper-chewing and pettifogging, the wheels of the lawyers grinding you down until, for your sanity, you surrendered and settled, realizing that you couldn't win, only the lawyer won.

"I'd like to kill him," Chicky said, showing his teeth, raising both hands, flexing his fingers in a strangling gesture.

That startled me, the force of his saying it, as though he was prepared to whip the butter knife from the table here at Verna's and march down the street to Frank's and stab him in the eye. And what was particularly upsetting to me was that Chicky was giving voice to a dark impulse that had lain hidden in my heart, words I had never dared to utter.

"Two in the hat," Chicky said, raising an imaginary pistol to his head. "I think about it all the time. But know what? It would make me feel great—for about five minutes."

"Let's talk about something else," I said.

Chicky was resting his elbows on the table, leaning across with sour yeasty donut breath and a whiff of chocolate. "Want to know what he says about you?"

"Not really." But I did want to know, because now I was convinced that Chicky was genuinely a victim of Frank's manipulation, that he hadn't really wanted me to bad-mouth Frank to rat on me. Still, I resisted. I had nothing to gain by disparaging him, and I had a lot to lose, because Frank was unforgiving.

"That he's the reason you're a success in mining," Chicky said, persisting. "All his advice, all his contacts."

I smiled at the absurdity of this, because the opposite was true—Frank was nothing but a belittler and a begrudger.

"That you blew it," Chicky said.

"How did I do that?"

"Stayed away from Littleford."

"Lots of people stay away for long periods—soldiers, fishermen. Geologists, especially."

"That you didn't do your homework."

That was a Littleford idiom for neglecting the sexual side of a marriage, and it took an enormous effort of will for me not to respond to this.

"He called you his evil twin."

"That's enough, Chicky."

"That he has a better relationship with your son than you do."

I said, "That may be so—and now I have to go. I don't really need to know this."

But I did, it explained so much, it justified the anger I felt, especially Chicky's admission, *I'd like to kill him,* that had so disturbed me. *Two in the hat.* I wanted to linger with Chicky and hear the worst, and bare my heart. I burned to conspire with him, but my instinctive mistrust of him and Littleford made me clutch the bag from the drugstore and rise from the table.

"Sorry, Chicky—this is all fascinating—but I have an errand to run." I swung the bag. "My mother's medicine."

"What is it?"

"Pills," I said and took out the yellow plastic container and read the label. "Metoprolol."

"My mother used to take that," he said. "Your mother has heart trouble?"

"Not as far as I know."

"Then why is she taking beta-blockers?"

I was stumped—this dim, disgruntled man in a donut shop diagnosing Mother's ills and telling me something I didn't know.

"You better hurry on home," he said. "Your mom's going to need that shit, wicked bad."

28

INCLUSIONS

THE DOLDRUMS OF A LITTLEFORD WINTER, UPSTAIRS IN my bedroom, on my back, in the gloom of home, listening to Mother down below, tottering from room to room, humming a tune, but interrupting herself each time she stumbled. I feared she'd fall but I kept away from her to avoid hearing her talk about Frank, urging me to have lunch with him and see him more, his son, Victor, failing at his most recent job and with a girlfriend Frank disapproved of, and the ailments of Frolic's parents—some of this Mother's way of reassuring me how well she was, good food, regular habits, sound sleep, and Frank in constant touch, by phone.

"I can depend on him for everything. Cal, his whole life he's never left Littleford."

She was stating a fact. The implication was that I'd been absent. Mother was a kind and generous person, she was not trying to hurt me by saying that, but it was clear that she credited Frank with deep concern for her, as though his remaining in Littleford had been a sacrifice.

"It was Frank's idea that I take you in," she said.

No, I had gone to Mother's as soon as Vita told me to move out, and Frank had no knowledge of that. But I smiled and said nothing.

"He told me it would be beneficial to us both," she went on. "You could do odd jobs, and I'd cook. Like old times."

She was saying that Frank was the reason I was here, a useful tenant,

Frank helping Mother by having urged her to take me in. I was an in-strument of Frank's generosity.

I said, "Do you see him often?"

"You can't imagine how busy he is," she said, which meant she sel-dom saw him. "He has so many responsibilities." She took my wrist in her skinny hand, and it was as though Frank was gripping me. "Cal, he helps people."

I nodded my hot head. It would have upset her if I'd disagreed or disparaged him. But I suffered overnight, sleepless under my stained ceiling, and in the morning at breakfast—Mother buttering my toast with shaky hands—I said, "I'm thinking of leaving."

"Whatever for?" She was puzzled. A break in routine is always alarm-ing for an older person.

"Make my fortune—pay my debts," I said. "Maybe head out west again."

The Zorrillas were never far from my mind as part of a backup plan. Having saved the old man, I could always depend on them to save me. I'd earned their trust, the old man owed me his life. And perhaps out of pride I hadn't asked much of them. But because I'd made a point of not overplaying my hand, they were always eager to find ways to help me. Maybe this was the time to ask. After all, I'd sent an emerald to them for Lupita's quinceañera celebration.

"How will you manage, Cal?"

Mother saw me as helpless; I'd also been seeing myself as helpless: How could a middle-aged man living with his mother be anything but a loser?

"I'll figure it out," I said. "But what about you?"

"Oh, Frank will be an angel." She'd handed a piece of buttered toast to me, but I hadn't touched it. Now, smiling at the mention of Frank, she took a bite of her toast and I had to look away. It disgusted me to see old people chewing, and I was ashamed of my disgust. She said, "He'll find someone to help me."

Much as it annoyed me to think of Frank replacing me, it also helped me focus on my departure. But I needed money to fly to Arizona—I couldn't ask Mother for a loan. She'd mention it to Frank, who'd sneer. And I had an idea. Long ago, I'd given Mother some earrings made of gold nuggets that I'd sifted out of a creek. I'd only seen her wear them once. She'd probably forgotten them. I could pinch them and pawn them for a plane ticket. Once I was in Phoenix I'd turn up at the Zorrilla house, and Paco would bail me out. Maybe the dirt bike again, prospecting in the gullies and washes, or I could pick up where I left off in Idaho, the ethical cobalt option. I could count on the Zorrillas for seed money. When I was solvent, I'd redeem Mother's earrings from the pawnshop.

It was a plan. I knew from experience that the difference between success and failure in mining was just a matter of money. If an investor was available, the right equipment was found, the scope for prospecting was enlarged, the paperwork for the claim, the infrastructure, the shaft, the pit, the manpower. An underfunded mine didn't stand a chance.

The Zorrillas had made me one of their family; they'd help get me out of this hole. I needed to leave Littleford again, and this time never return.

This prospect excited me. I was reminded of the first time, heading to Arizona to look for gold, leaving home, riding out of Littleford on my dirt bike, the thrill of departure always to me indistinguishable from escape—fleeing to freedom. But when I replayed the moments of this long-ago move, what I now saw clearly was the figure of Frank, formally dressed for his office—bow tie, red suspenders, and white shirt with cuff links—his lopsided face and mismatched eyes, his manipulation and half-truths, the blight he'd cast over my youth, his longing to see me fail.

What I at last understood was that, all those years ago, it was Frank I was fleeing—not the town, which I had affection for, or the school where I'd flourished, or home—a loving father and the sweetest mother imaginable, so fragile, so generous and unsuspicious.

It was Frank I'd fled long ago, it was Frank I was fleeing now. I simply did not want to know him. The sight of him, or any mention of him, spoiled the day for me.

Away then—but my first stop was Mother's jewelry box. While she was knitting in the parlor, I went to her bedroom, and there it was on her dresser, a hefty box that, when I opened it, cranked up a neat stairway of trays, each tray divided into a row of shallow compartments, containing a pouch or a piece of jewelry, a brooch, a bracelet, a ring, a gemstone, earrings, most of them neatly labeled or tagged. I was reminded of how, before she was married, Mother had been a schoolteacher in Littleford—and her jewelry box reflected her teacherly neatness and order. Each label or tag on a piece was impersonally printed, as though for listing in a catalog. I easily found her earrings made from the two good-size nuggets, my airfare to Phoenix.

My knuckles grazed a pendant I'd made from an emerald I'd mined in Zambia. I dangled it in front of the window—a lovely thing, pure until the light struck it and I saw the flaw inside, a complex crystal—mineral, not a bubble or gas, but a single phase inclusion, the sort that either refracted light and gave it beauty, or clouded it so badly it was opaque. We took no chances in Zambia: Moyo and I soaked our emeralds in oil until like this one they glittered like silk.

The inclusion in my life—the flaw in my otherwise gemlike existence—was Frank. Much of the mining I'd done, of gems especially, was the study of flaws—blemishes on the surface, occlusions within. In Colombia, our emeralds were flawed in all sorts of ways—cracked, brittle, spotted, veiled, with feathering and tubing—always rendering them worthless, you might guess. But often such apparent flaws gave them greater radiance, with jungly, fern-featured innards, the two- and three-phase inclusions, like the luminous eyes of panthers and certain parrots, not a pure color but a glow bristling with needles of green light.

That was the paradox, the inclusions in gemstones—pits, nicks, knots, fractures, haze, clouds, cleavage planes—sometimes enhanced their beauty, and just as often made them valueless. Flaws gave them life, or else killed them. And there's a certain inclusion in a stone that always devours the light: that was Frank.

I'd bumped into Chicky, the odd man out, who saw Frank for what he was, a deeply flawed person, a human inclusion. Chicky, too, was an inclusion, of the helpful kind, clarifying Littleford and Frank's predatory lawyering. Frank marred the pretty town, he robbed it of its luster, and when I'd returned, he'd lodged himself in my life.

Had Frank lived elsewhere I would have flourished and would probably still have been married to Vita. But he was a cheat, an infection; he'd corrupted and sickened the town and sabotaged my marriage. It had taken me years to see this, because I'd been happy and hopeful and had plenty of money, and I assumed that Vita and I could work things out. I hadn't understood how determined Frank was to destroy me, and that as someone penetrated with an inclusion he was impossible to get rid of. The flaw is part of the gem; you don't eliminate it without smashing the stone to pieces.

All this was clear, Frank and his flaw, in the flawed pendant I was holding up to the sunlit window.

I had to go at once. I slipped the pendant back into its compartment in the jewelry box, poked the gold nugget earrings into a small velvet pouch and tightened the drawstrings. I closed the lid, the stairlike trays folding back to nest in the box.

Mother, snug in her armchair, swathed in shawls, was fumbling with a yellow plastic container of pills, murmuring with effort. She was too deaf to hear me approach, but when she saw me, she called out, "Cal!"

"Going out," I said. "Are you all right?"

"Heartburn. Too much ketchup on my beans."

As she spoke she still tried to twist the cap of the pills. A poignant sight, Mother in too much pain to be able to twist the cap of her painkillers.

"Push down and twist," I said. "Here, let me do it."

I opened the container and shook out a pill, then brought her a glass of water. Mother poked the pill onto her tongue and held the glass in both hands and hoisted it to her mouth, gaping in anticipation, and then she drank, her eyes widened, gasping as she swallowed, looking starved, the sinews in her neck tortured with the effort. I wanted to turn away, but I forced myself to look, as she seemed to choke. She pinched an embroidered hankie from her blouse and spat a clot of phlegm into it and sighed.

"Got an errand to run. I won't be long. Anything I can get you?"

"Frank said he might stop by."

I doubted that—Frank's promises were intentionally ambiguous. But even the vague possibility of seeing his face or hearing his insincere chatter were good reasons for me to get out of the house.

With the sort of serenity I admired in her, Mother said, "I have everything I need." And softly, as though to herself, "I'm so lucky."

Turning away, I felt tearful, knowing that I was pawning her gold nugget earrings for a ticket to get out of here. I blamed Frank, conspiring with Vita, for my needing to go—bankrupting me in my divorce, having to leave Mother, to make some money to live my life. But I was done with him. He didn't have love affairs or friendships—he was a man of projects and schemes, transactions always tilted in his favor. Now he'd make Mother his project. And he could gloat about how I'd abandoned her. Never mind, I'd be far away, deleting his messages, not answering the phone. Already I'd begun to grind him out of my life, the way we often used grindstones to polish and shape the stones we'd mined. But when I thought of using such a grinder on Frank, what came to mind was a large-diameter grindstone, the size of a manhole cover, jammed against his face and whirring furiously into his flesh until there was nothing left of Frank but shredded meat—hamburger where there'd once been a human.

Littleford was too dignified a town to have a pawnshop, or a bar, or a liquor store or a tattoo parlor. Those were the businesses that flourished in Winterville, on the far side of the river; working-class Winterville, with its saloons and pizza parlors and its rowdy football team that trounced Littleford in the game every Thanksgiving.

I drove through town and crossed the bridge to the Winterville town line, and the first bars and what were known locally as "package stores"—liquor stores. I soon came to a pawnshop, which fitted right in, as a consequence of debt and drunkenness and the sort of reckless improvidence I associated with Winterville—though, to my shame, here I was, fresh from Littleford, debt-ridden and desperate, having thieved Mother's earrings.

Normally I enjoyed browsing in a pawnshop, surveying the bugles, brassware, power tools, air guns, archery sets, military badges, and the bowls of old coins. This one, Premium Pawn, had those items and more—knives, slingshots, silver cutlery, college pennants, boxes of postcards, split-open geodes and trilobites, and trays of real gems in a glass case, a fat man on the other side peering through a jeweler's loupe at the bottom of a souvenir saucer.

"Excuse me."

But absorbed in the saucer he didn't look up. He was balding and bearded and overweight in a food-stained turtleneck jersey; what remained of his side hair was yanked back in a mullet. His goatee was darker than his mullet, and he was weirdly decorated—tattoos on his fingers, one dangly earring, and a wristlet of blue beads. Beside him was a Styrofoam container of coffee and on a paper plate a Danish pastry.

He set down the saucer, plucked the loupe from his eye, and took a bite of the pastry; chewing, he said, "What do you want?"

I hated myself at that moment, I hated Frank, I hated Vita, I hated this man and his junk shop and the crumbs of sugar from his pastry adhering to his beard. It was a testament to my desperation that I stayed there and smiled and placed the gold nugget earrings on the countertop before him.

"I'd like to pawn these—just for a loan. I'll redeem them in a couple of months."

With the pastry in one hand, he licked the fingers of his other hand, and then poked at the nuggets.

"I'll give you a month. After that, I'm selling. I'm not running a charity here. I need turnover."

The Zorrillas would front me the money I needed—I could count on them. But I had to get to Phoenix first. As I was pondering this, the man put down his chewed pastry and dropped the earrings onto a small scale—another indignity: Mother's earrings in his damp hairy hands, tossed with a clink onto the scale, just merchandise in his tattooed fingers.

"Gold nuggets," I said.

Flicking them, he said, "Coupla hundred."

"Gold is fourteen ten and change a troy ounce."

"Raw nuggets. They got impurities. They could have all kinds of other metals in them."

I resisted screaming at him. I said, "If I melted them, you'd see they're pure. But I'm not talking melt value. These earrings are unique."

"Two fifty."

"They're worth six times that."

Using the back of his hairy hand he pushed them off the scale and nudged them across the counter to me.

"I guess you know what you can do with them."

I was not sorry to have them back; I regretted I'd come here and endured this oaf, who now had picked up his pastry and was chewing it defiantly. A dignified exit was not possible: I left, passing a pair of skis, a ukulele, a knitted bobble hat, and a stack of dusty microwave ovens.

My failure to pawn the earrings I regarded as a sort of success; I felt virtuous having them back in my pocket. Pondering other strategies for hustling some money, which did not involve stealing Mother's jewelry, I turned into Gully Lane and saw Frank's car. And not just his car—as I slowed down and considered making a U-turn and driving away, I saw Frank himself, standing on the porch, looking stonily in my direction.

"So this is what you call looking after Ma!" he yelled as I got out of my car.

"What's wrong?"

"She's at the hospital. She was flat on the floor when I got here!"

By then I was mounting the steps. Frank backed away when I got to the porch and showed me the snarly side of his face. He looked as though he was going to spit, his lips pursed in disgust.

"The ambulance just left," he said. "And where's her gold earrings?"

I was astonished, appalled, caught off guard—I couldn't answer. I

quickly calculated that the contents of Mother's jewelry box, neatly labeled and tagged, each item in its compartment in the steps of trays,
had been cataloged by Frank. His was the labeling that had looked so
professional. He'd sent Mother off in the ambulance, gone straight to
her bedroom and her jewelry box, seen the empty compartment, and
checked it against a detailed inventory he undoubtedly had made.

"You took them!"

"I was having them cleaned."

He honked in disbelief, a strangled sound came out of his dragged-
down mouth and rang in his nose. It was intended as mocking laughter,
but it sounded futile and feral.

"Look," I said. I showed him the pouch and pinched it open so that
he could see the gold.

"Give it to me."

"No. I haven't finished cleaning them."

"Who cleans gold!"

"I do—I needed some ammonia. Gold nuggets aren't pure. They
have traces of nickel and copper. Frank, I found these nuggets in Arizona. I had them made into earrings. I gave them to Ma."

"Hand them over."

"I'll put them back in the jewelry box when I'm done."

"I have the jewelry box."

"It's not yours, Frank."

"It's for safekeeping. It's too valuable to be left around."

"Why aren't you at the hospital?"

"Why aren't *you!*"

29

THE REFUGE CHAMBER

A DARK SEALED ROOM OF SURVIVAL GEAR—TUBES AND tanks and lighted instruments—in a mining tunnel we called it a refuge chamber. Safe but severe, useful in the event of a rockfall or other hazard, it came to mind when I entered Mother's room in the ICU in Littleford Hospital. It was sepulchral in its gloom and its paraphernalia, spooky, shadowy, a subterranean burial chamber, shaped like a refuge bay where we sometimes sheltered.

Frank said in a low voice, "This is costing a shit ton of money, like you wouldn't believe."

Droning through his nose, he sounded like one of the moronic machines in the room, the peep-peep of a monitor, the hiss of air in a pleated hose, the glug of a tube in a glowing dial—Mother herself on an upraised bed that was like a platform, her face slack and yellowy, her half-closed eyes angled upward, her flesh like marble, the poor woman wrapped in white sheets as though on a shelf in a deep recess of a pyramid, like a glimpse of the pharaonic: her head immobilized with a cranial clamp that could have been a halo over her marmoreal skull. It was how I imagined a mummy in a tomb.

"She's about as comfortable as we can make her," the nurse said. "Are you family?"

"I'm her son," Frank said.

"I'm so sorry." The nurse touched his arm in consolation.

"I'm her other son," I said, from behind Frank's back.

"This bozo left her in the house alone. He was supposed to be looking after her." Frank leaned toward the nurse, as though making a crucial point to a jury. "I found her on the floor, facedown."

"She must have fallen when she had her stroke," the nurse said.

Frank turned to me and said, "See?"

When the nurse left, Frank smiled at the door, his face wolfish in the pale light flickering from the dials on the chugging and peeping machines, and his tone changed, not scolding any longer but sighing with pleasure as the door sucked shut.

"Nurses are so hot," he said. "The way they fondle sick people. They're not afraid of anything. They've seen it all—blood, bodily fluids, naked flesh"—he chuckled a little. "They're unshockable. I love that."

He was still whispering when we both stepped into the corridor; he looked up the corridor at the departing nurse.

"Whereas, your average doctor—he's got these women to do the dirty work. He shows up, makes an ambiguous pronouncement, always tentative and noncommittal, all the while wearing a goofy hairnet and blue booties."

Jerking his head at the passersby, Frank was alert and talkative, as the medical staff strode purposefully past, nurses, doctors, an orderly pushing a gurney with a cadaverous man on top; then a limping man on crutches, one of his feet encased in a big plastic boot. With the nurse Frank had blamed me for leaving Mother alone, but now he was almost jaunty, engrossed in his narration.

"Cal, you're looking at a fortune here in potential lawsuits—I could score so big with these people," he whispered as they went past, the bruised and the bandaged. "Ankle injury, probably fell, tripped on a sidewalk crack. That's actionable, that's a payday. Broken arm, concussion, knee brace—someone's responsible. Medical malpractice. Maybe workers' comp case I could inflate—they have no idea." He slapped the wall. "Know what I should do? Advertise right here, buy some space right on this wall. Run an ad on the TV in the waiting room, put up my posters. Hospitals are always hurting for cash infusions. They'd gladly let me advertise here for a fee."

He went on in this vein for another few minutes, eagerly imagining his strategies for suing someone on behalf of these poor shufflers and limpers.

To stop him I said, "I'm thinking about Ma."

"You weren't thinking about Ma when you stole her earrings." He said this with gusto, as though I was squirming in the witness box, watched by a jury.

"Correction. Having them cleaned."

"Extraordinary notion—dirty gold. The one metal that doesn't tarnish. And you say you wanted to give it a good scrub. Imagine that."

He was bobbing his head, he was energized, weirdly so, because this was hushed, busy Littleford Hospital, nurses moving swiftly, with urgency, not acknowledging us; patients seated awkwardly on benches, wounded and silent. The doctors loped, clutching clipboards and stethoscopes. And Mother was just behind that door in the refuge chamber, supine, sunken cheeks, hooked up to a purring monitor, tubes inserted in her nose, stuck in her arm, her wrist, one finger pinched in a clamp.

"What's with you?" I said. "This lawsuit talk. Are you all right?"

"Never better," he said. "Funny, but I get such a rush in hospitals. Among all these feeble people. Don't get me wrong—I don't feel superior, not at all, just amazingly lucky."

He did feel superior. Frank often denied the very emotion he felt, stating the obvious. *I get no pleasure from this,* he'd say when he had the upper hand and was pleased with himself. Being in a hospital, among weak and sick and sorrowing people, he felt strong.

"It's not sexual—ill-health is an unsensual downer."

No—he believed the opposite. He could exert his will on these sick people who were too weak to resist, susceptible to any ray of hope. The young woman pushed past in a wheelchair, a pale, almost angelic face, tousled hair, loosely buttoned smock—no ability to refuse him—Frank was aroused by her passivity. Maybe it wasn't sexual, maybe it was the knowledge that he could get her to sign anything he put in front of her.

"I'll be right back," I said.

I couldn't stand listening to his gloating.

I slipped into Mother's room, the refuge chamber, and was grateful for the darkness and the murmur of the machines, reassuring gulps and beeps, screens flickering with jumping lines and twitching dials, a bubbling in a tank somewhere. Mother—plugged in—was silent, unmoving. She scarcely seemed to be breathing; she was a slender shallow oblong under her sheet, a small head, a young girl's profile, a frizz of hair, sunken cheeks, a skinny naked arm stuck with tubes. The activity in the room, the only proof she was alive, were the beeps and the whirring of the machines she was attached to, the dark diminishing transfusion bag, the emptying saline pouch.

"You're welcome to take a seat." It was a soft voice, the nurse entering behind me.

"How's she doing?"

"She's struggling a little. She was in distress when she was admitted. We managed to stabilize her." The nurse was in the shadow of the monitors, though her arm was illuminated when she reached to tap on a dial. "She's very weak. Poor old heart."

"A good heart," I said.

Hesitating a little, the nurse said, "I understand she's been under a lot of stress, coping on her own."

"No," I said. "Very happy. I've been looking after her."

"But doesn't your job keep you overseas most of the time?"

"I quit my job. I've been living with my mother—fixing her meals, doing her laundry, making the bed, monitoring her medicine—all those pills"—I found myself going hoarse as I protested. "The only time I left her on her own was when I had an urgent errand to run"—I looked at my watch, it was ten thirty at night—"earlier today."

"Was that with the gold earrings?"

"Who have you been talking to?"

My tone seemed to startle her, she excused herself, and as she ducked out I followed her, hoping to get her to repeat these slanders in front of Frank, so that I could bust him. He wasn't on the bench, he was nowhere in sight. I found him downstairs in the hospital cafeteria, talking to another nurse, sipping coffee, holding the cup askew to his crooked face, a bubble of coffee seeping from the lower corner of his mouth as he began to speak.

"Here he is, brother Cal," he said, and before I could speak, he licked his lips and said, "Cal, I want you to meet Nurse Nicole. She knew our mutual friend, Chicky Malatesta."

"Pleased to meet you," the nurse said, tugging her green scrubs straight and smoothing her sleeves. "Poor Chicky, he took a real bad fall. But I'm glad it turned out okay for him. Now I have to go. My shift begins pretty soon."

"What are your hours?" Frank asked.

"Eleven until eight A.M. I'm on nights this month."

Frank took a sip of coffee and with damp defiant lips said, "Graveyard shift."

Nurse Nicole looked flustered, excused herself, and left us.

As she hurried away, Frank said, "Even in plain hospital scrubs, a magnificent body—maybe enhanced by plain hospital scrubs, which resemble peejays."

He lost his smile when he saw me glaring at him. I said, "What did you tell Ma's nurse about me?"

"Nothing." He twisted his face into a haughty form of indignation, and with stiff offended legs he strutted away from me—so fast, so determined, that I next found him in Mother's room, his face yellow from the glow of the monitor he was studying.

"You said that I neglected Ma," I said, picking up where I'd left off, and hissing to keep my voice low. "That I was always away, traveling for my business. That I boosted her gold earrings. Jesus, Frank, you know very well none of that is true."

"Keep it down, Cal," he said in a scolding tone. "You probably don't know this—most people don't—but Ma can hear every word. Even comatose people, ones in vegetative states, they show no outward manifestation of cognition . . ."

"Wait a minute," I said.

Frank lifted his hand and lowered it to signal that I must not interrupt and went on in the same dismal drawl.

"One example, of many, true story. Bedridden man, seemingly at death's door, is visited by his supposedly grieving relatives. He hears them discussing the disposition of his estate, and they're sort of conspiring, as he lies there silent and motionless. Then—surprise, surprise—he recovers, wakes from his coma, and is restored to health. And he disinherits all these low-life relatives who had no idea he'd heard them. How do I know this? Because I'm the counsel who fought them off in court. The man was able to recount what had been said by the grifters in his hospital room—huge case, landmark judgment . . ."

"Now you're doing the shouting," I said, to annoy him, and looked to see whether Mother had moved. But she was motionless, the breathing sound came from a machine with a bellowslike gasp, as the monitors blinked and beeped.

"And of course the relatives who lost out on the inheritance banged on my door and countersued."

"So what did you do?"

"What I always do. I bit them on the neck, except one persistent cousin."

"What did you do to him?"

"I mugged him with a rusty razor."

"Like you did with Chicky Malatesta."

"Supposition! You don't know what you're talking about."

"You scammed him. He told me the whole story."

"Hearsay! He was lucky to get a penny. I dramatized his falling-down tale of woe."

"Let's take this outside," I said, because if what he'd said was true, about Mother being able to hear us, she would be upset by our quarrel.

In the corridor, Frank said, "Chicky could have ended up with nothing. But I fought for him. I know he wasn't happy with the payout. Some people . . ."

"He thinks you're a cheat."

"Ha, you should hear what Chicky says about you!" Frank looked delighted. "That you think you're better than people in Littleford. That you're secretive about your business. That you have money stashed in foreign banks. That you were unfaithful to Vita and a bad father to Gabe."

"Please stop." I knew Frank was repeating things he believed about me, or blamed me for, things that he whispered to people in town.

But I trusted Chicky: Frank was every bit the cheat that Chicky had described.

Then I remembered what the nurse had said, and I began to object, lowering my voice when nurses of patients passed us in the corridor, the air thick with a soapy smell mingled with body odor and disinfectant and floor wax. But before I could resume and remind him of how he'd slandered me, he saw a doctor walk importantly past, in a gown and blue booties.

"I'm a doctor," Frank said. "I'm a JD—*Juris doctor*. I could be a judge or a magistrate, whacking a gavel on a big bench, but no, I decided to help people—defend them, get them a fair trial and a payday. I don't have a team of handmaidens in pajamas doing my work for me, like these guys."

He kept this up, talking over me whenever I said something, and I thought, *I hate this. He's unbearable.*

What stopped Frank was the door to Mother's room opening, the nurse putting her head out and saying, "I think you need to be here."

The room was unchanged, Mother still motionless among the sighing, wheezing machines and the beeping monitor, the shadowy atmosphere of a refuge bay in a mining tunnel. The lines on one monitor were flattening, the beep-beep slowing, the bag of saline drip down two-thirds, the pouch of blood almost empty.

"I put her on morphine," the nurse said, reaching and lightly tapping a tube. "She's weakening. I could increase the dose if you approve."

"If you do that, she'll be out of it," Frank said, slipping his phone out of his pocket. "I need her to listen."

I said, "She might be in pain."

"I have to do this."

He poked numbers into his phone and when it was answered he said, "Frolic, I want you to say goodbye to Ma," and held the phone to Mother's bluish ear, Mother herself motionless, her mouth half open, Frank hovering with his phone jammed against Mother's head. And when Frolic was done there were more calls: he got his son, Victor, on the phone ("but keep that girlfriend of yours away") and had his dog woof into the phone; he dialed Vita—a new home number I didn't have, and Vita said a prayer of farewell. Frank asked for Gabe and spoke warmly to him, holding the phone away from me.

"She can hear you," Frank kept saying, as Gabe said goodbye to his grandmother, while I sat silently, detached from this leave-taking by phone, too tearful to speak, devastated by this deathwatch.

I hated to listen. I resisted, thinking, *I never want to see Frank again. The house is mine. I'll sell it and go away. I will be free of him. I need to concentrate on Mother's suffering, to cling to her, and give her strength to breathe.*

Frank shut down his phone and beckoned to the nurse. "Go ahead, increase the morphine now."

"You know, it'll depress her breathing."

"Maybe that's not a bad thing."

The nurse hesitated. "She might not have long."

As the nurse fiddled with the knob of the morphine drip, I heard Mother gasp—a sorrowful deflation, not a single gasp but a series of agonized breaths, her struggling to suck air into her half-open mouth, laboring and losing the breath, suffocating in the still air of the shadowy room, as though she was underwater.

It pained me to look, I hated to listen, I glanced at the monitor and saw the line on the screen—no longer jumping and jagged, no peaks and troughs, but squeezed and finally flattening to a vibrant horizontal stripe.

Only then did I turn to look and saw Mother's chin fall, her mouth gaping open in defeat. I wanted to run, but in a reflex of concern I remembered Mother's piety.

"Let's say a prayer."

"A lot of good that'll do."

I loathed Frank too much to reply to that—and now I knew I was free of him. Walking out of the room, I said, "I'm going back to my house."

Calling after me, Frank said, "*Our* house!"

30

IPSISSIMA VERBA, YOU ASSHOLE!

WAKING IN THE MIDDLE OF THE NIGHT, SORROWING for Mother, infuriated by Frank, I brooded over "our house" for the next five days. Frank was in meetings, Miss Muntner said, though she gave me a date and time for the church service, and added, "Frank hopes you can make it," a typical Frank gibe, unnecessary and insulting, as though I'd stay away from Mother's funeral.

No wake was held, the obituary in the *Littleford Standard* listed Frank's accomplishments, and the funeral itself was small and sad, Mother having achieved the lonely outpost of old age, and all her friends had predeceased her. The few nonfamily members at the church were Frank's friends or clients. Frank and Frolic and Victor sat at the front, behind them Vita and Gabe, and I sat alone in the third pew. A homily by a new pastor, who mispronounced our name, then the convoy to Elmhurst, and the prayers over the casket, which rested on two beams above the freshly dug grave at the family plot. Apart from the ritual condolences offered by strangers, no one in the family spoke to me, though Vita nodded, acknowledging me. Lingering by the casket in the bewilderment of my grieving—was anyone listening to my murmuring farewell to Mother?—I found myself a few feet from Frank, who stood on the opposite side of the casket. The other mourners had left, silently creeping to their cars.

I turned to Frank's misshapen face. I could never read his expression, since there were always two of them, the calm one contradicting the pirate sneer that was his boast. Then I remembered his smile at the hospital, and that memory provoked me to speak.

"What do you mean 'our house'?"

He looked away, stood motionless in his dark funeral suit, black tie, as a surge of sunshine from behind a cloud flashed on his head, making him balder. He was now facing the cemetery path, down which the mourners had gone.

Without looking back at me, staring across the gravestones, he said, "We'll have to talk about it."

A typical Frank response, the provisional *I'll get back to you later.*

"It's my house," I said.

"Cal—headline—my name's also on the title deed."

"Sure, but it was just sort of an insurance thing, in case I couldn't finance it or needed money for repairs. But none of that happened. You said you'd take it off."

"My name," Frank said, and now he turned to face me, with what might have been a smile, "is on the deed. I suggest you have a look. We both have copies."

"I know that. But the understanding was that it was strictly a formality. That's what you said."

"*Ipsissima verba,*" he said, and now he was certainly smiling. I could tell by the tightening of his scalp, a twitch of his ears. "What were my precise words? *Ipsissima verba,* you asshole."

I stepped back, surprised, not because he seemed adamant— snapping at me across Mother's casket—but because he had not spoken to me in this way before. I had always known such words were in his head, but he had never uttered them. Perhaps because Mother was no longer alive to hear him, he felt licensed to curse me.

"I forget your exact words. Only that you said you'd remove your name."

"Show me a piece of paper." Frank gestured with his hands, fingers clutching paper. "Show me where I put it in writing."

He snorted a little in satisfaction, then tapped his knuckles on Mother's casket, rapping as though signaling to her with a familiar knock, and paused as he turned toward me with his distinct chuckle of satisfaction, and he began to walk away. After a few steps he turned again.

"Funeral lunch—noon," he said, tapping his watch. "My house. Be there."

My inability to speak transformed me into a mute furious monkey, stiffened in rage and on the point of vaulting over Mother's casket and clawing and biting Frank's face, tearing at it with my teeth.

I was too stunned to respond, or to say anything. I lingered by Mother's casket, murmuring to her, and trudged to my car. Instead of going to Frank's and seeing him again with all the others, I drove to the Littleford Diner and sat in a booth at the back and considered my options. But I had no options. Frank's name was on the title deed; he'd put it there long ago when Mother had urged him to cosign the deed, for my sake. Mother had heard him promise that he'd remove his name, but now she was dead, and there were no other witnesses.

"Where's your partner in crime today?" the waitress said, putting down a glass of water and laughing, but she did not wait for a reply.

I did not go directly home, I drove to the far side of town and parked facing the river. I watched the twigs and leaves, borne by the current, float past me; some of this flotsam spun in eddies nearer the embankment. It was this river, flowing to the sea, seven miles away, that inspired me to leave Littleford. I was that twig, I was that leaf, I had thought, and I saw how the river could carry me away, to the ocean and the world beyond it.

In my car that winter day, the dark river rippling past, Mother gone, my marriage over, I was ashamed to think I was out of money, foiled in my scheming to pawn Mother's earrings. I had no means to leave now, I was trapped in the house, Frank stubbornly clinging to the title deed. Then a plastic bag floated by, filling and swelling until it was snagged by the twiggy fingers of a broken bough mired in the far mudbank. Snared and struggling, it emptied and shrank and became a rag, strung out on the current like a foul pennant. I watched for a while; it tightened, hooked for good, twisting, going nowhere.

I drove home in low spirits. When I got there the porch lights were on. I could not remember having left them on. The parlor lights, too,

were blazing. And the front door was unlocked. I heard the aque-
ous voices of the TV, and I was sure I had not left that on—I seldom
watched, though Mother sometimes did, offering me a spooky intima-
tion that I was experiencing a fugue state, that Mother might be inside,
her death a bad dream, and all had returned to normal, Mother on the
sofa, wrapped in a shawl, dozing in front of the TV set.

A hooded figure on the sofa, where Mother habitually sat, was facing
the TV. I shut the parlor door with a bang, the hood rotated to reveal
a gaunt face.

"Uncle."

It was Victor—Frank's son, whom I seldom saw and hardly knew—
wearing a Littleford High School hoodie, his big sneakers on Mother's
embroidered footstool, a video game on a screen in his hand.

"How did you get in?"

"Dad gave me the key."

"But why?"

"I'm living here from now on."

"Vic, I don't understand."

"I won't bother you," he said in a mild mollifying voice. "I'll stay in
Dad's half of the house."

Victor, who hardly figured in my life except as an occasional name,
was a tall pale boy, five years older than Gabe. Frank seldom mentioned
him but had urged him to go to law school; the boy had quit after a year
and gotten a job in a restaurant in Winterville and had shown promise
as a chef. But a cook was a failure in Frank's terms, and for years Frank
did not mention him. In my absence, Frank had become a mentor to
Gabe, who'd taken his advice and graduated from law school and was
now attached to a Boston law firm, while studying to take the bar exams.

I felt sorry for Victor—lost, cheated, damaged—another of Frank's
victims. But even so I was taken aback by his sitting in the parlor of my
house, playing a video game, with the TV on. I found his sprawling on
the sacred space of Mother's sofa offensive, a sleepy oaf in a grubby high
school hoodie, his dirty sneakers on the footstool Mother had embroidered with flowers.

"Dad said it was okay."

"There's some dispute about your father's name on the deed."

"I don't know anything about that."

"Are you still at the restaurant?"

"That's the thing. I got laid off. I lost my apartment. It's sort of why I'm here."

"You could be home with your father."

"They object to Amala."

"What does that mean?"

"Amala, my girlfriend. They don't approve."

"Where's Amala?"

"She's, like, upstairs. She had a headache. She's in bed," he said. Then, clarifying, "In Dad's half of the house."

It was not late, hardly seven, but I told Victor I was going to bed, and at the top of the stairs I heard music from the spare bedroom—Frank's old room. I closed the door to my room, and lay on my bed, and studied the stains on the ceiling—no longer ambiguous hinting shapes, but specific and stern, landscape features and weapons, and forbidding figures of interrogation.

Next morning, after a bad night, I was eating my oatmeal when Amala appeared and introduced herself, saying, "Now Victor's feeling sick. I think I gave him my germs."

She was small, and slim and waiflike, barefoot, wearing blue jeans and a T-shirt, her lovely hair falling straight to her shoulders, a tattoo on the back of her hand, and another on her neck, and probably more of them under the T-shirt. She'd been carrying a cloth bag, which she put down to open the door of the refrigerator. As she did her jeans tightened on her bum as she leaned over to study the shelves.

"I'm going to eat you," she said. "Then I'm going to eat you and you."

She took out a container of yogurt and a peach.

"Want anything, Mr. . . . um."

"You can call me Cal. What kind of name is Amala?"

"It's, like, Tibetan," she said. "I used to be Polly but I changed it.

Hey, I could fix you something. I bought some stuff while Vic was at the funeral. I wasn't welcome there. Frank and Frolic don't approve of me. Gee, I'm really sorry about your mother. I met her a few times. She was a real sweet lady. She showed me how to knit."

Amala put her yogurt and the peach on the table and picked up her cloth bag. She pulled out a length of knitting and some balls of yarn.

"Scarf," she said. "Your mom's design. She calls that a basket weave stitch. She gave me all this yarn. She said she couldn't see too good and was giving up knitting, but she was one great teacher."

"She was a teacher before she got married," I said. And as I watched Amala carefully folding the unfinished scarf, I recognized Mother in it, the symmetrical stitches, the colors she loved, lavender and pale yellow. Amala was sweet and small like Mother, too, and as kind. *I could fix you something* was something Mother often said.

Amala tucked her bag away and then sat with me and talked about Mother until I grew so sad I couldn't listen anymore.

"Gotta go," I said. "Big day ahead."

It was not a big day, it was a sad and confusing and empty day, in which I wanted to hide myself, to escape Victor and Amala. It was unexpected, I was crowded, it was not only Frank's presumption and this intrusion, it was my thwarted mood. I couldn't grieve. I needed silence and privacy and solitude, to sit and think of Mother, to reflect on her passing and to ponder my future. I slipped out of the house and drove back to the riverbank and parked.

I was an orphan now, living in a house that was only half mine, which I was sharing with my destitute nephew and his girlfriend. I had no money. I had no other place to go and no clear idea of what to do next. I missed Mother's goodness, the calming effect she'd had on Frank and me, and I was shocked when I remembered Frank at the cemetery, shouting from the far side of Mother's casket, *Ipsissima verba, you asshole!* and his gesture, motioning with his fingers, and snarling, *Show me a piece of paper.*

His being part owner of the house meant that I could not sell it without his agreement, nor could I prove that he'd promised to take his name off the deed. The kind, susceptible witness who'd said, *Do it for me,* was dead. The house had represented freedom to me—money—my selling and moving on, or staying for a while, to plan for my future. But I was encumbered. I couldn't do anything without consulting Frank. He'd stuck Victor and Amala in the house to remind me of his part-ownership, and so I'd lost my privacy.

The plastic bag that had snagged yesterday was now wrapped around the branch and was part of the bough.

I went back to the house, aware that I was not alone, that Victor and Amala were somewhere in it. Over the following weeks I heard their music, the sound of their TV, the pings and bells of Victor's video game, and now and then I saw Amala on the sofa, the very spot where Mother had sat, a shawl over her shoulders, knitting a scarf. She'd look up and smile—Mother's sweet smile—and hold up her knitting to show me her progress, and I remembered how she'd explained her name, *It's, like, Tibetan.* Victor seldom left the guest room, and I often heard him quarreling with Amala, his bullying snarls, her submissive whispers, after which the hostilities ceased with muffled sex (thumps, groans, the boing of bedsprings). Whenever they went out, I had the house to myself and could think clearly, but it was never for long: no sooner had I settled down, ruminating, than the front door rattled and they were back.

I couldn't blame them. They were pawns in Frank's chess game against me. And they were childlike in the way hopeless, aimless youths sometimes are, innocent of any strategy to counter life's reverses, lost, bereft of ideas, uneducated, always improvising and failing. Amala, who said she made her own dresses, began wearing a shapeless smock of her own design.

"This is for you," she said, one morning at breakfast, handing me the scarf she'd made—Mother's stitches, Mother's colors. When I resisted, out of politeness, Amala said, "Please take it. It'll look great on you. Plus, I love giving stuff away. Who said 'You have to start giving first of all and expect absolutely nothing'?"

"Can't guess."

"Dalai Lama."

* * *

In the days that followed, Victor showed he was skillful but slow, re-placing the rails on the back porch, repointing the stonework, paint-ing the downstairs bathroom, cleaning the gutters, using a ladder and power tools I'd never seen before.

"You're good at this," I said.

"Dad's idea."

"Did he buy these things—the ladder, the tools, all that lumber and paint?"

"You both did, I suppose."

And soon Victor gave me the invoices for them, and a bill for half the expenses. The amount was modest at first, but soon there was a snowblower, a new microwave oven, a carpet for the hall, the sofa reup-holstered, a flat-screen TV—thousands.

I said, "Please tell your dad not to buy any more stuff for the house. I can't afford it."

"He said he'd loan you the money."

"I don't want a loan. I don't want a new TV. Tell him that."

It was Frank's way of pressuring me, putting me in debt to him. And because this conversation with Victor took place in one of our end-of-the-day encounters in the parlor, I saw how the room was being transformed. In atmosphere and furnishings, the room had matched Mother's delicacy and grace in its frills and pillows and porcelain; but now it was becoming Frank's room—the big TV, the plain carpet, the chrome floor lamp, a leather footstool, a beefy armchair, a huge oak desk by the front window that Victor told me was a law office item, "a partners desk."

I said, "I suppose your father talks about me a lot."

"Not really. Just stuff about how he's given you tons of help."

I would not allow myself to be provoked. I said, "He's an odd guy."

"He can be a total asshole sometimes."

"Victor, let me tell you—to me, he's just a piece of furniture." I rapped on the partners desk, to make my point.

"He talks about Gabe a lot."

"How he got Gabe into law school?"

"That, and Gabe's issues."

"What issues?"

"Like, juvenile detention and stuff."

"Gabe was never in juvenile detention." I found my neck growing hot as I rebutted this false assertion.

While we were talking Amala crept into the room and had crouched at Victor's feet, still knitting, but not speaking.

"Kind of rebelling against you," Victor said, talking over me. "Petty theft, drugs, and stuff. And Dad had this story about how Gabe sort of liked it in the detention facility. The food especially. Like when Gabe got out and Dad asked him about it he talked about the great meals. 'Chicken! Burgers!'"—Victor did a convincing imitation of Gabe's gusto regarding prison food—"'Ice cream with chocolate syrup! Pizza!' I mean, stuff he didn't get at home."

"Your father told you this?"

"Yeah."

Amala said, "I heard about that. And the ankle monitor he had to wear."

"Listen to me," I said, trying to control my anger. "Your father is lying. Gabe was never in detention. He was never a thief or a druggie. He never wore an ankle monitor. Got it?"

"When you were away," Victor said with confidence. "Like, you were away most of the time, right? Gabe was compensating, like kids do. Like I did a whole bunch of the time."

"Were you in juvenile detention?"

"Kinda."

"Did you wear an ankle monitor?"

"Sorta."

Amala's face crumpled, and she reddened and covered her mouth with her hank of knitting, as though she was going to cry.

"Amala, it's okay—don't worry about Vic."

"I worry that he might lose compassion for his father," she said.

I went upstairs to my room and punched the wall.

After Frank refused to take my calls, letters began to arrive, Victor picking them up at Frank's office and slipping them under my bedroom door. The first ones were about nonpayment for the snowblower and the new TV and the desk; Frank suggested "a payment plan" and a loan. Then the letters became more detailed and reverted to what he called "discoveries and dispositions" related to my divorce, bank accounts I had not reported to the IRS, profits I had not disclosed, the letters growing lengthier, with numbered paragraphs and subsections and italicized clauses, some of them four or five pages long—too long for me to read without becoming enraged. Nor did I have any wish to reply, though I had replied to the earlier ones, saying in effect, please, no more. But this stimulated him to enter bewildering legalistic depths and send more accusatory letters.

On one of his infrequent visits to Tower House, Gabe asked how I was doing. I said, "I think I need a lawyer," and explained my plight— the title deed, the purchases for the house, the letters.

"There's a dynamite lawyer in my firm that can handle this for you. One of the senior partners. A woman. Lilith Milgrim."

"Yes," I said, hugging him. "I need to put this in her hands, so that I can get on with my life."

31

HOLIDAYS

I'D LIKE TO TALK TO GABE BELANGER," I SAID INTO THE phone.

"Mr. Belanger's in a meeting—can I take a message?"

"I'll call back," I said, hating my crestfallen voice.

What broke my heart was my new dependence on Gabe, not in any sentimental way of seeking affection or sympathy from him, conferring in that tender manner of a father and son sharing a common interest. No—I was a helpless old client, in the hands of a young gunslinging lawyer who had just passed the bar, and being referred by him to the senior partner, Miss Milgrim. Gabe was busy. Gabe's specialty was copyright law, intellectual property and infringement, and much else that I didn't understand. All I knew was that Frank had wooed him and made him into a lawyer. In doing so, Frank had co-opted and corrupted him, like a wily old crook making a clever lad into a pickpocket.

I had lost Gabe. I'd hoped he'd leave Littleford—strike out on his own, blaze a trail as I had done—be a traveler, a free spirit, madly singing in the mountains. But he sat in a law office in Boston, pushing paper around a partners desk, and I only saw him when I was there myself, meeting my lawyer, the stony-faced Miss Milgrim, because Frank's letters kept coming.

There is no drama in the silent business of sending or receiving a letter. It is a mute and almost motionless activity. It would be pointless to describe Frank's letters here, except to say there were many, sometimes two a day, hand-delivered by Victor, who apart from household chores had little else to do. I had to sign for them, to record my receipt in a logbook. I avoided reading them. They were couched in the sort of wordy hostility that is routine in the legal profession, a tone that is both adversarial and unhurried, since the meter was always running and no end was ever in sight.

Lilith Milgrim was about sixty, crowlike and forbidding in her black pantsuit, a tight hairdo, curled close to her head, like a chic swimming cap. She did not gesture, she spoke in a monotone, she was immobile at her desk; her manner that of someone playing a game of cards with strangers, she gave nothing away. Like many lawyers, she always spoke as though the room was bugged and an adversary happened to be listening.

Yet in that same dull voice she reassured me. When I told her I was worried, she said, "Let me do the worrying—after all, that's why you're paying me."

Even so, I glanced at Frank's letters, tried not to look too closely at them, and passed them on, and fretted. They stunned me with their veiled threats: I could not think clearly after looking at one. This seemed to me the definition of an existential crisis: I was trapped, possessed by such uncertainty I was prevented from moving on. Mentally tortured, of course, but it was also physical—I was paralyzed by anxiety.

I had lived an active life as a rock hunter in the rich world of field geology. I regarded paper as a nuisance, and contracts baffled me—I seldom read more than a few pages before I skipped to the signature page and signed with a flourish, agreeing to everything. I'd been savvy in choosing my partners and lucky to deal with honorable people, who like me loved the thrill of the chase for veins of ore more than a big payday, though we seldom failed to make a profit.

Before I moved in with Mother, desperate for a place to stay, I'd hardly spent two nights in succession there. I was her caregiver for months. Then she died. And now I lived in the house with no notion of when I'd be able to leave. I wanted to be elsewhere, but I was broke, and I was encumbered by Frank's name on the title deed. He refused to admit he'd promised to remove it (*Show me the paper*), and I could not move, or work, or resume my life until the house was all mine. I wanted to sell it and begin prospecting again—Idaho cobalt beckoned and so, too, the gilded ravines of the Southwest.

The letters of Frank that I passed on to Miss Milgrim were always prefaced by a headline, and the page was set out like a manifesto. *De jure* was one of Frank's favorite tags. I was acting *mala fide,* he said. He asked *cui bono?* And explained that all he was doing was *se defendendo.* I was, he said, uttering *suggestio falsi,* when I knew very well we had a *consensus ad idem* agreement where the ownership of the house was concerned. Would I agree to a competency hearing?

"He gave me his word!" I shouted to Miss Milgrim.

Barely moving her lips, like a ventriloquist throwing her voice, she said, "But that's *nuncupative.*"

Meaning just words, no paper, yet—long pause—the title deed might be voidable under the terms of adverse possession. And Miss Milgrim ("and my team") would work toward crafting a solution to reach a settlement of real property, the house returned to me wholly and without encumbrance, unquote.

The back-and-forth, unresolved, maddened me. I simply hated Frank.

On a day of no letters, Victor said, "Dad has some kind of melanoma thing going on at the back of his neck. He's in for a biopsy."

Cancer, I thought. *That's a start.* But it was benign, and his letters resumed.

As the go-between, Victor was part of the process of my being entangled in letters. I had never envisioned being paralyzed by paper, and yet here I was, trapped. Frank was energized, the situation pepped him up, because I was important to him. Frank was happiest when people were dependent on him, his perverse need to be needed, dependent for his happiness—his power and self-esteem—on weak people seeking his help. He clearly enjoyed the fact that for my peace of mind I wanted his name off the title deed. He was thrilled knowing that he would not grant my wish, and so he would have me in his web. I was living in his house, with his unemployed son and his son's dreamy girlfriend, and I had no means to leave. I was his captive.

And there were the tax returns. On another visit to Miss Milgrim I asked, "Why does Frank want to see ten years of my tax returns?"

"He seems to think you haven't reported all your income."

"Why is this even his business?"

"If Frank reports you as delinquent in disclosing your income, he stands to collect a reward from the IRS—a percentage of the unreported amount, which of course you'd be obliged to pay, with penalties and fees."

"God, how do I stop him?"

Miss Milgrim relished silences, and though she remained poker-faced and seldom gestured, today she tapped her finger on Frank's most recent letter, as though to indicate that she was thinking. I longed for a straight answer.

She finally said, "He may be hinting in his furtherances that he would desist and relinquish ownership if he received some sort of payment from you."

"I have no money."

"A portion of the house equity, assuming it could be found."

"I can't afford that. I have nothing else. My divorce cleaned me out. And Frank keeps buying things for the house—appliances, gadgets, upgrades—and sending me bills for them, which obviously I can't pay. You've seen those letters."

Miss Milgrim's head remained still, her expression unreadable, her only movement her finger tapping the letter before her on her desk, perhaps keeping time to some tune in her head.

"I understand your position," she said. "But I'm behind in my replies to him. He keeps asking for documents. My team is working on it." She flattened her hand on the letter with conviction. "Leave it to us—we'll find a solution."

What Miss Milgrim was not saying, the truth of the situation, was that Frank was torturing me. It gave him pleasure to send long letters to me—entangling letters were one of his specialties, a form of litigation. It was a relief to me that I had Miss Milgrim to respond to him, otherwise I would have replied with the obscenities I mumbled in my room on sleepless nights.

Through Victor, Frank invited me to a fancy dress party at his house. "Might be fun," Victor said. "You need a costume, maybe a mask." This was intended to show Victor what a good sport his father was. But I knew that a party would prevent me from getting to him. He'd be protected by the mob of partygoers. For my refusing this pretense of generosity he could whisper about me for being a truly bad angel.

It occurred to me that we might meet for a hatchet-burying lunch at the diner. I almost suggested it but soon realized that if I saw him I'd attack him, throw myself on him, claw his face and kick at him, as I'd wanted to do at the cemetery after Mother's funeral, the "show me the paper" day.

The holidays came and went, rituals I'd missed when I was abroad, when I'd lamented my absence, regretting that I was missing something important. But now I knew I hadn't missed anything except the forced jollity of a tedious meal. Vita invited me to her birthday dinner, to support her in her pretense of our amicable divorce. But I was the past, hardly known, unwanted. I didn't want to be there, though I badly wished to see Gabe in a casual setting. I remembered times, just home after a long absence, when Gabe had been glad to see me, and we'd sat on the porch and he'd told me what he'd been reading, and it was often a travel book, and he'd speculated about countries he might visit, and it might be one in Africa or Asia, where Vita's agency had uplifting projects. But he was a lawyer now.

These days I had the choice of being with Victor and Amala in the house I only half owned, or else trying to smile at a celebration with my ex-wife and lawyer son, and many guests. Gritting my teeth, I went to the house I used to own, to have dinner with the woman who'd once been my wife, in a room that seemed fraudulently festive to me. The guests were not Littleford people, but rather Vita's coworkers and friends in Big Charity. I winced when they praised the house and its artifacts, the life I had lost.

More holidays, more invitations. I remembered how for years, whenever I'd set out in my car on my way to a Thanksgiving lunch or a Christmas dinner, I'd see a man on a bicycle spinning forward at the roadside, pumping his legs, a real cyclist in a helmet and gloves and snappy shorts; and I'd wished I was that man, doing exactly what he wanted to do. I always assumed that he was pedaling away from some grim holiday gathering.

Vita persisted. She tried to be positive. "Cal, let's move on."

I relented and I suffered, hiding in plain sight among other guests in my former house. Vita made a point of not introducing me, and I suspected that a bearded man being attentive to her ("Shall I carve?") might be her new feller. I brought a bottle of wine. Gabe said he was glad I'd come, then he sat in the den in front of the TV set with others, watching sports. I knew the layout of the house well enough to slip out by a side door, unnoticed.

On my next visit to Miss Milgrim, bringing a folder of Frank's letters, she repeated, "You might consider settling," but I resisted.

"No money," I said.

She said evenly, "I imagine he'd like a resolution as much as you would."

"I doubt that, I really do. He's enjoying this. Resolving this would mean the creep would have to stop torturing me."

Miss Milgrim pressed her lips together, keeping her opinion to herself in a lawyerly way. She did not welcome words like *creep* and *torture*.

"I think he wants to destroy me."

She tidied the letters I'd brought her, tapping them square with her fingertips.

"As I suggested once before, you might consider offering your brother a sum of money, to induce him to take his name off the deed."

Your brother seemed absurd and offensive. I said, "How much are we talking about?"

She hesitated, then blinked, her eyes like digits in a calculator. "It could be in the five figures."

"Ten thousand?"

She looked doubtful but, still blinking, said nothing.

"No," I said. "I want to fight and win. No money. He has to keep his promise."

"Maybe in terms of fifty thousand," Miss Milgrim said, as though she hadn't heard me.

"I don't know how I'd find anywhere near that amount," I said.

"Maybe consider a work-around."

"I'm not familiar with that expression."

"An alternative," she said and sat back in her chair. "You could raise a mortgage on your portion of the house. Maybe convert your half to a condominium and sublet it. Maybe consider renting some rooms."

These suggestions, one after the other, made me think she'd been quietly elaborating these options on my behalf, devising ways for me to make some money. But when I came to the reason for it—to pay Frank money he was not entitled to—I said no.

Eager to see Gabe again, I accepted Vita's next invitation to dinner and, predictably, on my way there I passed a pair of cyclists in biking gear, looking like they were having the time of their life, pedaling like mad and grinning into the headwind. I longed to do something similar, but remembered Gabe.

He met me at the door, Vita waving at a distance in the parlor full of people, but after a hug and some pleasantries, Gabe withdrew with the fruitcake I'd bought at Verna's. None of the guests seemed familiar, though looking closely I recognized the bearded man I'd seen there before, the one dogging Vita. He was dogging her again, and—more ominously—I saw that he was wearing an apron, the ultimate symbol of domesticity, the uniform of submission and belonging.

I sat and stared at the flaming logs in the fireplace, the mantelpiece holding an antique clock I'd bought long ago.

A man in a tight green turban approached to warm his hands at the fire. He said, "Hello there, I'm Dilbag."

"Hi, Dilbag."

"Just moved here. I'm with Rescue."

"Welcome to Littleford."

"You lived here long?"

"I was fucking born here, Dilbag."

In my misery, swearing, I said this with a sharpness that antagonized him, as though I was pulling rank. He excused himself and walked into the crowd, where I saw Gabe. I beckoned to him.

"Mom said it won't be much longer," he said. "We're eating Cuban—turkey with yellow rice and plantains. Buffet style."

"Nice," I said, but the mention of food reminded me I had no appetite. "Gabe, this Miss Milgrim, is she going to get it done for me?"

"She's really professional, Dad. She's got a great team."

"How many on the team?"

"Three or four, I guess. I know she's trying to resolve this."

His casual tone annoyed me. I said, "Listen, Frank is torturing me."

Looking slightly affronted, Gabe took a step back, becoming wary.

"Frank broke his word," I said. "Can't you be disbarred for that? Maybe sanctioned? Lose your license to practice? Listen, he promised to take his name off the title deed. I have no money—I can't do anything until I own the house outright." Gabe looked unmoved, I recognized the unreadable Milgrim mask. "It's been months since Grandma passed. Gabe, I'm dying here."

"Gran was such a special person," he said.

In a strangled and insulted voice, I said, "She witnessed Frank's promise—she urged me to let him sign, she heard him say he'd cancel it. This situation is offensive to my mother's memory."

"Maybe you and Miss Milgrim can work it out with him," he said, unconcerned.

"Gabe, he's threatening to report me to the IRS."

Gabe squirmed and looked around, as though hoping to be rescued. "I don't know anything about that."

Gasping, I said, "That's why I'm telling you."

"I think it's better that I don't know."

"You need to know that all this is unethical. It's torture. It's abuse. Look what he's doing to me!"

Now Gabe smiled, and the smile told me I'd lost him entirely. "I can't help. It would represent a conflict. I'm working on a big copyright case with him."

I saw them together, the old villain and the corrupted lad, conferring in a shadowy room, face-to-face, a pile of incriminating documents stacked between them.

"What case?"

He smiled again, the signature Frank pistachio-nut smile, crooked and unconvincing. "Confidential, I'm afraid. Let's eat."

We lined up and shuffled along the buffet, another jovial crowd from Big Charity, and we sat to eat in various parts of the living room that Vita called the Great Room, in chairs, on the floor, some standing and nibbling. We talked about the turkey, how moist it was, and the rice, how yellow it was, the plantains, how excellent Vita's Cuban-born father Ernesto's recipe was—"The secret's in the slicing"—and all this time I was dying.

Gabe found me at the fireplace once more, staring at the crackling logs, tearful with regret and confusion, seeing Frank howling in the flames, his body bursting and sizzling like a sausage.

"You up for dessert?"

I turned my mournful face upon him.

"When these people finish, we're all going to Frank's for dessert, like we did last year."

"I don't remember that."

"You were in Idaho then. You didn't come home."

Vita had crept up behind me. "You'd be welcome, Cal. Frank and Frolic are very hospitable. They asked me to invite you."

In a small voice, I said, "I have other plans."

My room, my bed, the menacing stains on my ceiling.

32

BILLABLE HOURS

I T WAS NOT SELF-PITY I FELT BUT ANGER AT FRANK, RE-sentment against Mother for coaxing me to agree to Frank co-signing the deed, rage at the idea of my son working with him. I never said, "Poor me." I was big enough to survive this, but I hated my life on hold, now four months of this in the house with Victor and his banana remarks—"You look bummed, Uncle"—and Amala, who in her placid disposition and her knitting of scarves seemed like a sweet incarnation of Mother, except for the squiggly Sanskrit tattoo on her hand, as she explained, "My mantra, 'om mani padme hum'—the jewel in the lotus."

Gabe called one evening, full of life for a change, eager to talk, and I was hopeful we'd turned a corner. But after the chitchat all he said was, "You should really listen to Miss Milgrim, Dad," and he hung up.

When Miss Milgrim had suggested I pay Frank off, I'd thought, *Never*. He didn't deserve anything, and the melancholy fact was that even if I'd agreed to her suggestion I had no money to pay him with. But when I called Miss Milgrim again—from my car, I had just finished grocery shopping—she became more explicit.

"You might consider settling."

"I'm sure he'd want a lot of money. And, as you know, I have a cash-flow issue."

She repeated, "Maybe a work-around," and again mentioned floating a loan, renting the spare room, converting the garage into an efficiency apartment, and I sighed because I didn't trust myself to reply, fearing I might scream.

After a pause, Miss Milgrim said something that I was to remember for a long time afterward—not just the words, but the circumstances of my hearing it, the way you do when, staring at ordinariness, you hear unexpected words. I was in the parking lot of the Stop and Shop in West Littleford, where I'd worked bagging groceries as a high school student, wearing an apron and wishing I was elsewhere. In Miss Milgrim's pause, I noticed that I was parked next to a chutelike enclosure made of iron pipes where shoppers pushed their carts when they were done with them—I'd rounded up shopping carts, too, another after-school chore. These carts—designed to be slid one into another, basket fitting basket, saving space—were shoved sideways, higgledy-piggledy, butting up against the pipes and crowding the chute. Some of the shoppers had left trash in the carts, plastic bags, scraps of paper, discarded wrappers. As I watched, a shouting boy shoved a cart like a battering ram into the mass of other carts, smashing them with a clang.

The noise jarred me, and I was still rattled when at the same time I realized that Miss Milgrim had resumed speaking.

"Because you might find it cheaper to settle."

"Cheaper than what?"

"Than to go on paying my bills."

Simultaneously, I saw the jumbled shopping carts, the disorder matching the derangement in my head—items designed to nest neatly were banged together and entangled, cluttered with trash.

"That reminds me," she said. "Have we sent you a new invoice?"

"Not yet."

I drove home and saw that more furniture had arrived, and in the garage a crate of office equipment. In the following days, a pickleball set, a visit from pest control—a man with a cylinder like a jet pack strapped to his back and a wand in his hand, squirting poison into the baseboard cracks where later carpenter ants tottered, with sawdust in their jaws, or cockroaches lay upside down in death.

Victor supervised, saying, "Dad's paying me for this," when he passed me my share of the bills. Was this what Miss Milgrim meant by *Might find it cheaper*?

In the mail soon after this, I received the invoice from Miss Milgrim, for the sum of $63,243.

I blinked at the sum. The invoice was closely itemized, even to the recent phone call, thirty minutes at the Stop and Shop parking lot, assessed at just over five hundred dollars. And I learned that three other attorneys, "the team," whose names I was seeing for the first time, were also part of this invoice, covering the work dealing with Frank's demands, fielding Frank's letters, summarizing them, and drafting replies for Miss Milgrim to sign.

I called Gabe and mentioned the amount of the invoice.

"That sounds about right, at this juncture," he said, with a certainty resembling Frank's. "Lilith Milgrim gets eleven hundred an hour. And there's the team. Billable hours."

Later that day, a call from Miss Milgrim, who I guessed had been alerted by Gabe. When I heard her voice I groaned, imagining a meter furiously spinning, displaying higher and higher numbers.

"We'll have to keep this short," I said. "I'll need some time to sort out your bill."

"As I said, you might consider settling."

I didn't say, *Where would I get the money?* I said, "It's a little late for that. In the meantime, I can't afford your services anymore."

"I'll instruct Frank that you'll be dealing with him directly."

I now had to read Frank's letters, which were officious and verbose and full of Latin legalese, repeating his demands and questioning why I had not paid for the various services and the new furniture and the improvements to the house. And the real estate taxes were coming due. In one letter he informed me that he'd created a maintenance committee and had appointed himself chairman, responsible for carrying out "detailed inspections of the premises." He called these inspections "fortnightly appraisals" in his memos. Appended to the memos were lists of requests—for duplicate keys, space in the basement for his personal items, outlines of repairs he wished to make, listed as "essential upgrades," repainting the house, installing solar panels, regilding the weather vane, and more.

His letters were more frequent now, all of them demanding replies. I now understood why Miss Milgrim's bill had been so high. I pawned my watch and wedding ring in Winterville, and paid a small proportion of her bill, and begged for more time.

One morning the doorbell rang, the man from pest control again, the same jet pack, gas mask, and wand of poison. In spite of the nuisance of his reappearing, I marveled at the efficiency of his squirting poison at the baseboard, and the cockroaches I saw later, lying on their backs, rocking slightly, feebly flexing their legs. Studying them I imagined Frank on his back, his arms and legs upraised, twitching in his death throes.

"Mind if I come in?" he said, lifting his mask.

"I didn't order this."

"Your landlord did," and he showed me the work order with Frank's name on it. "I've already done the exterior. I'm supposed to squirt the closets."

"Not necessary."

"Suit yourself." He handed me a piece of paper. "That's your invoice."

More billable hours. I gave the invoice to Victor to pass on to Frank, as I'd done with the other bills, saying that I had no intention of paying it, or funding any of the other proposals.

Frank's reply was immediate, a lengthy memo explaining that as co-owner of the house and concerned for its upkeep he envisioned "major structural repairs," which he listed in an appendix to this memo. Without Miss Milgrim to deal with his letters I saw that he had an inexhaustible appetite for tying me up with demands, immersing me in invoices. It was something like being buried at the bottom of umpteen sedimentary sequences, layer upon layer, holding me down.

I was now in serious debt, owing Miss Milgrim, owing Frank, barely able to meet my day-to-day expenses. I had not allowed the "fortnightly appraisals" and inspections to go forward, because I didn't want to see Frank in the flesh. It was bad enough to have Victor upstairs, and these days his whispered quarrels with Amala did not end in muffled thumps and squawks of pleasure and the twang and boing of bedsprings, but only in silences.

Frank's intentions could not have been clearer. He wanted the house, he wanted me destroyed. These thoughts woke me in the night and coursed through my brain, heating it, causing it to throb, keeping me agitated, staring at the ceiling, seeing Frank's face in the stains, hearing his chuckle of satisfaction as he turned aside, the catch of his laughter dying away to a decaying breath, and his insolent shrug.

I stopped appealing to Gabe for help, yet he was on my mind, because I'd left the house to him in my will, as my only asset. In the event of my death he'd be faced with Frank, claiming half ownership, and subjecting Gabe to the same onslaught of letters and demands I'd endured—was still enduring.

After a sleepless night, I got up in the morning, ill with fatigue, my mind clouded. I spent the day trying to devise ways to pay Miss Milgrim and to fend off Frank's demands, the thousands I owed him for the improvements. The papers were a blur in my glazed eyes and my stupor of weariness. I took to my bed but my anxiety made me wakeful. The ceiling stains became violent images, whirling furies, winged demons, figures locked in combat.

I considered inviting Victor and Amala out for a pizza and, before we left the house, opening a tap on the gas stove, and leaving a candle—one of Amala's Ayurvedic candles—burning in the parlor, and letting the house explode. I saw it alight, a great rush of flames, the old highly combustible and well-insured wooden house burning, the pleasure I'd feel at this simple solution. But in this case, I'd risk incinerating the neighbors' houses, their children, their cats and dogs.

I was cornered, I saw no way out, I had no means to leave Littleford, and in a manifestation of paranoia I sensed the house shrinking around me, becoming smaller, imprisoning me in plaster. The human-shaped stains on the ceiling were still embattled, thrashing, two of them, and then one toppled, his limbs upraised—Frank, twitching like a dying cockroach, and I saw that the victorious figure was me, standing over him, as he died.

The thought did not disturb me, the notion of murdering him gave me joy. Kill him.

33

AN ACT OF PURIFICATION

WHEN IT CAME TO ME IN TWO STARK WORDS—*KILL him*—that day became the happiest I could remember, and my memory seemed to extend as far back as my boyhood, better than those blissful moments I knew as a child. Maybe the intention had been in my mind, unspoken, all that time. I laughed out loud when I uttered it. It was the simplest solution on earth, like swatting a fly or squirting bug spray on a roach, or bringing a hammer down on the skull of a sworn enemy. Like shutting a door forever.

I was happy the whole day. I couldn't stop smiling, and after a while I was glowing with satisfaction, serene, restored to health, imagining Frank dead at my feet.

He had haunted me as a threat, but he had never loomed large as a physical presence. He was smaller than me, potbellied, pinheaded, and pale. His size was exaggerated somewhat by his strong body odor—people who smell seem bulkier than they are—but scuttling and insectile, bug-eyed and obvious one moment, and gone the next, but always somehow present, even when I couldn't see him, like an infestation in the timbers of a house, an inescapable stink.

In my anger and despair I had not seen his behavior as fully human. He reacted the way a rat or a roach might, the creature surprised as it nibbled in the murk and then flashing away before I could stamp on it. In the Zambian mine we'd had biting flies that fastened to any bare skin—neck, wrist, ankle: Frank was like that, predictable and persistent, he was vermin, feeding on my blood. Frank always maintained that in our passion and essence we are animals, just as predictable and vicious. I was now persuaded of that, of Frank's belief, despising him as he despised other people, for being animals.

He was not a person, he was a problem, he was a pest, the virus he'd always been, sickening me—cruel, without a single redeeming feature. He had no humanity. Not evil—*evil* is a spooky peasant word, implying dark magic, damnation, the baffling superstition of organized religion, wickedness as power. I was so thrilled by the title *Flowers of Evil* when I was in high school and read the jet-black poems. But later I saw evil was just simpleminded horror cooked up to scare you, and that Frank was dangerous in a different way.

Lacking in sympathy, Frank was easier to explain. Something was missing in him that normal people possessed—that I had myself. He wanted to destroy that thing in me, happiness perhaps, or at least contentment. I saw that from early on he had wanted to displace me. In my attempt to dismiss these thoughts, I had run away. I supposed at the back of my mind I knew I'd have to defend myself and that ultimately I'd have to dispose of him before he killed me. If I didn't, he'd pounce; yet now he'd succeeded in cornering me.

Had he been an obnoxious stranger, one of those awful men I sometimes saw jostling on city streets, looking for trouble—or someone more passive, dangerous when roused—I would not have cared. But he was my brother, with his pestering letters and threats, pressing me for answers, always with the implied threat of jail, or a lawsuit, or my eviction from the house that was rightfully mine. Brotherhood made him my worst enemy.

Gnawing at me, in the solitude and helplessness he'd imposed on me, never letting up, he'd had the persistence of a hungry animal. In the previous months, during which he was hounding me—one of the coldest springs in years—a family of raccoons climbed each night to the roof of the house, just above my bedroom, and clawed at the cedar shingles, attempting to get inside for warmth. They tore the shingles away from the insulation and tar paper and chewed the battens. Although they were unable to break through to the attic, they damaged the roof and exposed the seams between the planks and allowed snowmelt and rain to leak through and stain the ceiling again, sketching more wicked imagery.

Again I saw Frank's face in those stains, an evolving face, merciless and more determined to destroy me. I saw Frank in those raccoons. I heard him clawing at the roof above my head, the scrape of splintered shingles, the crunch of teeth against wood, the slushy grind of chewing. Frank, whom I had not seen for months in the flesh, was now a menacing noise.

He was the ache in my brain, too; a cramp in my muscles, a griping in my guts, he was not human. He was a sinister sound that wouldn't go away, a sickness infecting my body, weakening me and keeping me awake. He was flat and dark, shadowy, disembodied most of the time. I imagined him two-dimensional, like a tick fastened to my flesh, wishing to be engorged, fattened on my blood.

I had moved into the smallest of the upstairs bedrooms to avoid the worst of the roof noises, the chewing and the leaks. Yet there were stains on this ceiling, too, a new version of plunder and persecution, fiendish faces, claw marks; and still I couldn't sleep.

"You could stay with me, at my apartment," Gabe had said, when I hinted at my distress, but I spared him the details.

Gabe's offer sounded tentative; he knew Frank was the problem, and he was working on a case with Frank, so there was a conflict. I knew it would be inconvenient for him to come home to me every night, after a day conferring with Frank. And anyway I was a grown man; I could figure this out. There had to be a good answer.

My never seeing Frank, my only sense of him as a chewing animal— his repeated demands, the letters I'd stopped opening, the bills I could not pay—all this kept me from regarding him as a whole person, or a person at all. He was an obstacle, he was a rock to be removed, slag to be flung aside.

Inspired by the stains (stains I regarded as prophetic, omens to be seized and understood), I saw Frank as an infection. In my mind I simplified him and made him small. He was teeth and claws, he was a greedy appetite, he was a yellow stain, he was a bad smell. He was not a person. I needed, for my sanity, to be rid of him, so that I could go on living.

And then that day like a liberating whisper—as though remembering something I'd forgotten, a fabulous secret revealed again—it came to me, *Kill him*, words vivid in their simplicity. The sky was clear, my room bathed in sunlight.

I didn't at first consider how I'd go about it, I only knew murder was the perfect answer, and it kept me smiling as something programmed and deliberate, not an act of passion. I wasn't angry, I didn't feel vindictive, I felt righteous. With this intention in my mind I experienced a sense of exaltation and power that made me confident and quieted me. I was suffused with a refined sort of joy, the intense peace of veneration, as though I was beholding something beautiful and incandescent, the holy glow of the empty space I'd be creating, the hollow on earth that had once been occupied by Frank.

I would be deleting him from the world, ridding myself of him and all his buzzing conjectures—his threat, his nuisance, his smell. Though the precise definition did not come to me, only the vision, I saw in its radiance that my killing him was an act of purification.

The thought of being punished for it never entered my mind—far from it, what I expected from this calculated act was a reward: everything would improve afterward. I had a further justification. Long ago, when we were still students, we'd set off across the Great Marsh on the Cape, and attempting to swim across the wide black creek, Frank had struggled and sank. I had saved his life. Ever after, his life had belonged to me. And because of that, if I wished, I could end it. The world would be better off, and so sweetened that, soothed anew by its fragrance, no one would miss him.

* * *

"Dad!" Gabe said the next time I saw him. I'd driven to his apartment, not to tell him what I was planning, but to share my mood.

"Give me a hug," I said.

"No—wait—stand back," he said, admiring me. "You look great!"

"I'm fine."

"I was worried about you," he said, and hugged me. "It's wonderful to see you." He held me by the shoulders. "To what do we owe this transformation?"

"A new serenity of mind."

"I'd love to know your secret."

"If I tell you, it won't be a secret."

"So Frank's not a problem for you?"

"You're fishing," I said. I knew that he was asking on Frank's behalf and that whatever he found out from me he'd tell Frank, his patron now.

"Because Frank knows how to be provocative."

Being cautious, so as not to be quoted, I remembered my conversation months before with Chicky, how Chicky had asked similar leading questions; and although he'd disparaged Frank, I had not said anything that would incriminate me.

I found myself telling Gabe, as I had told Chicky, "You said it, not me," to remind him that I could quote him to Frank.

In this exchange I guessed that Gabe now knew he'd said too much to me, that he knew Frank well enough to realize that Frank was both untrustworthy and untrusting. If I ratted on Gabe to Frank—though I never would do such a thing—Frank would bring it up to him, and Gabe would deny it. But Frank wouldn't believe him, Frank didn't believe anyone because, being a habitual liar, Frank believed that no one told the truth. Liars are chronic doubters and deniers.

"Whatever it is that's put you in a good mood," Gabe said, "hey, I'm not asking, but it seems to be working."

His saying that concentrated my mind, gave me the resolve to imagine myself in the half-light of Frank's office on a late afternoon, standing before him with a pistol as he sat in his leather chair, his hands raised, palms facing me as though to protect himself in my firing at him, too terrified to speak, gibbering perhaps, looking utterly helpless as—absurdly—he used his hands to stop my bullets.

This back-and-forth with Gabe caused the wronged and resentful face of Chicky Malatesta to appear to me. I realized that in him I had a brother, someone with the same hatred, and like a true brother, someone I could unburden myself to, perhaps the only one I knew. He was a man who'd said to me with grim conviction, *I'd like to kill him,* all the while flexing his fingers in strangulatory gestures.

Although he'd doubted himself (*It would make me feel great—for about five minutes*), I had no such hesitation. I knew that Chicky and I were equal and like-minded; we were damaged and indignant, and we knew we had a punishment for Frank, to prevent further damage to us, and to save anyone else Frank might wish to victimize.

I'd said nothing to Chicky at the time; I'd been overcautious, fearing that he might report anything I might say to Frank. I had suspected that he was trying to provoke me. But on reflection I saw how wounded he was—he'd been hurt physically and financially. I could now reveal myself. It would ease my pain to have a fellow conspirator, a brother in the best sense.

"Chicky Malatesta," I said, after this reverie.

Gabe smiled, looking startled at the name.

"How do I get in touch with him?"

"He's in the database. He was one of Frank's clients a while back."

"How do you know that?"

"Frank needed some muscle. He brought me in when Chicky got obstreperous about the billing."

To ask why or to inquire further would have raised Gabe's suspicions, so all I said was "He's a good mechanic. I can use someone who can fix things."

Checking his phone, Gabe said, "Like a lot of guys in your generation, Chicky isn't on e-mail. Frank wrote him letters and scanned them to me, so we'd have a paper trail, in case he acted. He was, like, uttering threats."

"I always knew him as a friendly guy," I said. "I haven't seen him for a long time."

Gabe was still consulting his phone, not reacting to what I said, swiping with his forefinger, looking down with the sort of preoccupied insolence that Frank practiced to seem enigmatic. Finally, he said, "Here it is—West Littleford, near the Winterville line—last I heard he was living with his relatives."

He gave me Chicky's address, and a parting hug.

It was the Italian section of town, a district of squarish, shingled three-decker houses, set close together, their narrow yards fronting the street, the melancholy uniformity of the earnest working poor. There was little to distinguish one house from another, except in the colors of the paint on shingles. I was abashed to think that I lived in the same town and never came here. Like Frank, I lived in the nice part of Littleford.

I found the house easily and saw that it was in need of painting, conspicuous on the street for being in bad repair, some shingles missing, broken windows duct-taped, an old sofa with burst cushions on the porch. Chicky had not exaggerated his being cheated by Frank and suffering a loss of income. He'd told me he was living with his in-laws, and it had sounded grim; this weather-beaten house was the proof. The names *Bocca/Malatesta* were inked in block letters on a label by the door.

Knocking, I heard a dog roused inside, a sudden and insistent yapping, and then a curtain tugged aside on a small glass pane in the door, and a pale mournful-looking woman pushing her tangled hair away from her eyes.

"I'm looking for Chicky." I spoke loudly, because the door remained shut.

The woman opened the door, releasing odors of scorched tomatoes and fresh basil and dog fur. "He's gone."

"When are you expecting him?"

"You didn't hear?" She looked at me with imploring eyes and whispered, "He passed."

The dog yapped just behind her, and a man inside the house called out in a complaining but incoherent shout.

"I'm so sorry to hear it. Can we talk?"

"On the piazza," she said, slipping out and indicating the ragged sofa pushed against the porch rail.

She moved slowly, bent over, wheezing in sadness, her hands folded under her chin, as though in prayer.

"I'm Cal."

"Roberta," she said. "His wife."

"When did it happen?"

"It was sudden, but the doctor said we should have expected it, being as it was related to his case."

"I saw him in . . ." I tried to remember. It was at the donut shop, before Mother died. He'd recognized her medicine in the pill container—heart medicine. "It was about five months ago."

"He passed last month. Just before his birthday. He would have been fifty-nine. That's not old!"

She began to cry, her face contorting, her lips trembling. She was in poor health herself, heavy and slow, her sorrowing like an illness, making her short of breath, asthmatic in sadness.

"We were in high school together. He was in my brother Frank's class—Frank Belanger."

"That bastard's your brother?" Roused by anger, Roberta twisted her face at me and seemed healthier, stronger in her ferocity.

"Yes. That bastard is my brother."

"He screwed Chicky so bad."

"I know. Chicky told me."

"He lost his job. The settlement was so cheesy we had to sell our house. This is my parents' place. They're on disability." Her voice trailed off, she rocked a little, also like a kind of mourning. "He's your brother! He should be in jail."

Her face fixed on mine, her eyes astir, glaucous in grief; she crossed her arms, holding herself, needing to be comforted.

"He should be dead," I said.

"Yes—God forgive me," she said. "But I don't believe in God no more, because Chicky should be alive. There's no justice. Good people always get screwed. It's not fair. Bad people like your brother—they get all the breaks and go on living."

She began to cry again, lavishly, gagging a little, her face freakish, ugly in her misery, tears smearing her cheeks and gleaming on her chin.

"Bad people also die," I said.

34

JUSTIFIABLE FRATRICIDE

FRANK HAD NO IDEA WHAT I WAS CAPABLE OF DOING. NO one knows the limits of what another person can do, especially an angry, humiliated person, furious at finding themselves trapped.

By trapped, I mean, seeing some faceless hated thing swelling in the only possible exit, blocking it; and escape—survival—requiring the removal of that thing, by force if necessary. The impersonal thing being a dumb dense obstacle in shadow, to be flung into oblivion, or crushed.

Outwardly I was a busy householder, spending my days in domestic chores, vacuuming dirt from the carpets, knifing sausages apart, banging nails into stair treads, boiling eggs in a pot, seething stews, watching Amala crazy-legged, eyes shut, beatific in her lotus posture in the room facing the back garden, practicing yoga breathing or chanting. Inwardly, I was committing murder.

The simplest way was what my father would have called *envoûtement*, killing him with a curse, by casting a spell. I needed a witch for that, but I had a gun.

Like a flash of light illuminating the bright needles in a soulful crystal, I saw it clearly, the confrontation, swift and conclusive, and—like that (I was chopping a banana)—the deed done. With the pistol the Zorrillas had given me long ago, a souvenir from my beginnings, the .32-caliber Colt semiautomatic, flat-sided, hammerless, small enough to conceal. I could carry it in my pants' pocket. The magazine held eight rounds, more than enough to punch the life out of Frank.

On the pretext of a deal favoring him—settling the house business for good—I would call ahead to Miss Muntner to arrange a convenient time to see Frank. She would say, as she always did when I called, *He's in a meeting, can I take a message?* And I'd say, *I'm prepared to agree to whatever terms Frank proposes. I need to get on with my life. Please tell him I concede.*

Because the words *yes* and *no* were not in Frank's vocabulary, time would pass, Frank deliberating, not saying anything definite. But I knew that it was part of his manipulative nature to enjoy his adversaries coming to his office, cap in hand, being kept in his waiting room for an hour or more, suffering in silence, the unexplained delay such a humiliation that they often crept away without seeing him, defeated by his stubborn intransigence.

He would keep me waiting—that would please him—and the prospect of my having to wait would induce him to agree to see me. I was humbled, a petitioner, in a weak position, pleading for a resolution. He could get me to sign anything: I was desperate, I was small, he loomed over me, he'd won. But if we settled he would not be able to go on torturing me. He valued delay, preferring the power to torture over the finality of resolution. Frank loved unfinished business.

Still, he'd agree to the charade. A day and time would be fixed. He'd instruct Miss Muntner to tell me to wait. I'd be happy to wait, it would anger me and fill me with resolve, tense in the chair, a tightly wound spring, contracting further with each passing minute, my hand in my pocket, my loaded pistol in my damp hand.

Just before closing time, around five, Miss Muntner would say, *Frank will see you now.*

And as this was the end of the workday, she'd excuse herself and leave, knowing that Frank was about to engage me in a long and evasive discussion. Being a tormentor he was someone who hated conclusions. The torturer never wants his victim to die, he needs him to go on feeling pain.

As I entered his office he'd remain seated behind his big desk, probably would rock back in his swivel chair as a sign of defiance.

Have a seat, Fidge.

I'll stand, thanks.

My reply would bewilder him. He'd expected me as a supplicant, prepared to agree to anything, even to his suggestion to sit down. In his confusion, his lopsided face would register a smirk of doubt, because I hadn't sat when he told me to.

Frank, I've got something for you.

I'm waiting, he'd say, uncertain, now suspecting a trick.

Then, in one movement, I'd pull the gun out and aim it at his mismatched eyes. He'd jump to his feet, backing away, whining and pleading, holding his hands in front of his face, in a futile gesture of protection, just as I'd once imagined him doing.

I'd allow him to gibber, I'd savor his fear, I'd smile as he begged for mercy. His clownish, bug-eyed look of terror would stay in my memory as a continual satisfaction, a souvenir of my triumph.

Bang, into his face, blasting through the meat of his hands, snapping off his fingers. Then, *bang,* a body shot burst through his chest, and when he fell, a coup de grâce, exploding his scheming head.

Very messy, though, and loud.

I was in my car, shopping for frozen peas and canned salmon and a pot of cream, when I saw a subtler way of disposing of him. His parking garage was in the basement of his building on Main Street, his car always parked in his designated stall. I would sneak into the garage and crawl under his car with bolt cutters and weaken his brake lines, not sever them but cut them so that they would only snap when, at high speed, he stamped on the brake pedal. Oh, yes, and I'd monkey with his airbags—they were tricky to remove but easy to deactivate.

And when he braked, a car stopping in front of him, or his taking a sharp curve (I imagined him at the turn into Gully Lane), or careering down a hill and wanting to stop (leaving Vita's at the hill descending from the archway to the Winthrop Estates) his lines would snap, his brakes would fail, and Frank who never used seat belts would find himself thrust into the windshield, and if not killed instantly then so badly injured he'd spend the rest of his life as a quadriplegic, perhaps with brain damage, drooling and incoherent, dangerous only to himself.

The thought of Frank in a wheelchair, incontinent, wearing a diaper, infantilized, or living out his life in a vegetative state, was actually more satisfying to me than seeing him bleeding to death on his office floor.

No drama or looming shadows accompanied my fratricidal imaginings. I saw the whole procedure bathed in sunshine. This was not a crime of passion but rather a carefully planned execution, like frying a serial killer in Old Sparky. Frank was a danger to me and to the community; he was in my way, and I needed to remove him for good, to destroy him before he destroyed me. And it would cheer me up if he suffered in the process. It was justifiable fratricide. I was entitled to kill him, and blameless; nothing could stop me, and the only hesitation I felt was that I was faced with so many possible methods—such a rich variety of ways to dispose of him. I wanted the best way, but each time I imagined a magnificent murder I thought of how I might improve on it.

At dinner, "salmon pea wiggle" (Mother's family recipe), I sat eating, and visualizing a peacemaking feast, attended by Frolic and Victor, Vita and Gabe, Amala watching from a window, because Frank would object to her being at the table. I liked the thought of her watching, her elbow on the sill, her chin propped on her hand, her lovely hair backlit by the sun.

Frank would preside, monopolizing the attention, offering advice, thanking me for seeing the wisdom of my caving in to his wishes—I had promised to bring a check, the large five-figure sum that Miss Milgrim had suggested. It was a complete climb-down on my part, I'd agreed to his every demand, I had surrendered, and it was obvious that I was ruined.

After Frank's sermonizing, and the others' fawning admiration—perhaps Vita's bearded boyfriend would be there—it would be my turn, my concession speech.

"I'm here to acknowledge that we've reached the end of the road, one we started on long ago, as children, the so-called Bad Angel brothers in Littleford . . ."

In this somber vein I would speak about finality, how—after this wonderful meal—we would go no further, our protracted negotiations were on the point of concluding for good.

"All that remains is one last act—the toast."

Handing Frank a wineglass, I'd make the toast, praising his tenacity, listing his many accomplishments, speak of his ingenuity—and anyone who knew Frank well would discern a measure of ambiguity. Astute listeners like these family members would understand that, as I listed his achievements, I was also enumerating his scams and transgressions.

"Drink to my health," I'd say. "I'll drink to yours."

He'd say something sarcastic, not witty, playing to the table, Frolic and Vita and the two boys, and Vita's boyfriend, and Amala squinting at the window. Then, following my example, he'd drain his glass.

Potassium cyanide is so fast acting that within a minute he'd be dazed and staggering, then collapsed on the floor, frothing at the mouth, his legs thrashing, his nerves like hot wires fizzling and fusing, his synapses burned away. And while the others knelt over him, fretting and trying to coax him back to life, I'd slip out and be gone, on a plane that very night to Arizona, unfindable, in the care and protection of the Zorrillas.

Patting the cream of the salmon pea wiggle from my lips with a napkin, I thought, *Yes, what about the Zorrillas?*

Forever in my debt for saving Don Carlos, the Zorrillas could be recruited to help kill Frank. They'd been in touch from time to time, notably with cobalt suggestions and the quinceañera invitation, but I had asked very little of them. Now I considered a carefully plotted scheme, a classic cartel hit, first a phone call from me to Paco, and then his putting me in touch with one of his *sicarios*. Their drug business must now extend to New England, and they needed enforcers to guarantee their control of the market.

El Alacrán will help you . . .

I'd meet the man they called the Scorpion; I'd show him where Frank lived, where he worked, his office, his usual haunts, the diner, the Littleford Golf Club where he met clients. I'd provide photos of his car and of the man himself, not in profile, but the whole complicated face, the sagging eye, the drawn-down mouth, the palsied cheek, and the other sporty frat-boy side.

The Scorpion, with some of his men, would ambush Frank and take him to a secluded area, the Fells, upriver, a warehouse, a back alley, and they would deal with him in the brutal manner of a meaningful cartel killing, never a simple hit but a set of specific mutilations—cut out his tongue, because he talked too much and lied, hack off his hands, because he stole, castrate him because he meddled with my wife, and last a decapitation, the cartel expression of supreme power, his head swinging from a lamppost in Littleford Square.

It pleased me to imagine Frank's mutilated corpse, discovered and photographed, a horror to all. But reflecting on this savagery, I decided that I wanted it to be personal. I needed him to see me making him suffer and striking the last blow. I didn't want to outsource it.

At my desk one day, I conceived a better idea. Using his letterhead (I had plenty of examples in my desk drawer), I would create a copy of his stationery and write his remorseful suicide note. Addressing it to his wife and son, and to the world at large, I would list all his regrets, all his lies and deceptions, the many instances when he'd cheated on me, as well as the ruses he'd employed to scam his clients. A long confessional letter. *I am a hollow man,* I'd write in his voice. *I don't deserve to live.*

And with my pistol in my pocket, I'd visit him in his office, holding him hostage as he pleaded for his life. I would demand he sign a letter indicating that he wished to remove his name from the title deed.

"Oh, and this, too . . ."

Concealing the first page of the suicide note I'd have him sign and date the last page, no text above his name.

"At this juncture, we're square," he'd say. "You have what you want. Put the gun down, Cal."

"I don't have what I want yet."

And approaching him I would contrive to shoot him in such a way that it looked self-inflicted. Or perhaps make him drink poison. Or push him out the window—anything that could pass for a convincing suicide, leaving the remorseful note behind.

Plotting it in my mind, enjoyable though it was to contemplate, I envisaged resistance—the staged suicide becoming a struggle, Frank flopping around the room and frustrating me so badly I saw myself bludgeoning him to death with the oversized gavel he kept on his desk, souvenir of a big courtroom win. But I loved the detail in a confessional letter, and I spent many evenings lying on my bed, my face upturned to the Frank-like stains on the ceiling, elaborating versions of it in my head.

I was cracking the top of a soft-boiled egg one morning, planning to take a drive, when I thought, *Something simpler.* A trip together, the pretext being a way of finding harmony (and offering him money). He was proud of his vacation home on the South Shore. The deed would be done there. No letter, no confession, no signatures, no evidence: this would be a sudden and unexplained disappearance, a knock on his head, or a pill in his drink, the Zorrillas' cyanide. When he was unconscious, I'd hedge my bet by suffocating him, since shooting always created blood spatter. A plastic bag over his head would do the trick. Imagining him sucking at it, and finally expiring, gave me hours of pleasure.

When he was dead, I'd stuff his corpse into a barrel and roll him into a trash compactor at the town's transfer station. Disposing of his body would be easy. The hard part would be getting him to agree to the pretext, the little trip out of town to discuss peace and harmony and cash. The trouble was that he didn't want a resolution. He'd refuse to get into a car with me. He didn't trust me.

A news report on TV of a melee at a bowling alley in Winterville gave me an idea. What about a brawl? A fight with Frank in a public place would satisfy my need to hurt him before killing him. I could invite him to lunch at the Littleford Diner and start a fight with him there, witnessed by sixty people in booths, who'd swear it was a fair fight.

After sitting down with him in the diner, I'd object loudly to something he said, toss a cup of hot coffee in his face, and we'd go at it. He was weak, not a fighter with heft. While pretending to be seriously injured I'd batter him senseless before a shocked roomful of people. Hey, a fight between brothers that got out of hand—where's the headline? I'd find a way to break his neck. But what if he didn't die, and recovered, and sued me?

Strolling on the footpath by the river on many afternoons, I thought of other ways. As a miner I knew enough about explosives to blow him up in his car. Or take him sailing, no serious violence, just tip him over the side into the ocean, screaming abuse at him, and linger near him until he sank. Or corner him at knifepoint. Colombians I'd worked with regarded a stabbing as the truest way of killing an enemy, since it was done at close quarters. A shooting implied distance, but a knifing was intimate, the blade an extension of your arm. Stick him in the eye, stick him in the heart.

My Zambian partner, Johnson Moyo, told me that in West Africa one year, scouting a source of diamonds, he'd heard the story of a rebel leader in Liberia, also called Johnson (this coincidence of names was the reason for the tale). He'd captured his enemy, the country's president, Major Doe. Doe had been responsible for the massacre of six hundred people hiding in a church, many of them women and children. This Johnson sat Major Doe before him in shackles and had his men strip him naked. Johnson interrogated Doe, and for every unsatisfactory answer, Doe was beaten with clubs. Johnson sat before him, drinking beer, upraised at a table, like a judge at a bench.

"Cut off his ears," he said to his men. And this was done, one ear at a time. And while Doe bled and begged for his life, Johnson shouted at him, ordered Doe's fingers and toes cut off, unshackled him and forced him to stand on his mutilated feet. Doe implored them to put him out of his misery, and Johnson finally granted this wish, stabbing him in the face, later putting his body on display in the town,

Given time, and a little assistance, I was capable of that.

35

CORNERED

FRANK WAS A SNOB. SNOBS ARE FULL OF BULLYING OPIN-
ions, but snobs are not strong. They're insecure and unreliable, they're usually liars. Snobs will agree to anything, no matter how
implausible, as long as it gives them an advantage, something extravagant to boast about; and because they can be tempted that way, they're
easily manipulated. Snobs are less substantial than they appear. And
yet, with their crass ambition, pathetic as they are, they can still succeed
in their wish to hurt your feelings, they can inflict pain, they can cause
unhappiness. The snob thrives best among the minor differences of a
small town and is always an annoyance, and often harmful, and sometimes a cancer.

It was not Frank's snobbery that pained me. I knew that his insults
and affected air of superiority were examples of his weakness. But in
his lies and legal strategies he had cornered me with debt, he was an
obstacle to my living my life. But his boasts showed that he was hollow
and gave me an advantage. I could tempt him away from his office; I'd
bait him with a possible boast, then I'd abduct him and take him away.
Where to take him and how to kill him were questions I'd soon answer.
My imagination convinced me that I was capable of anything. In spite
of his obnoxious snobbery, and his reputation for collecting huge contingency fees, Frank was important in Littleford, respected for being
feared, known to be dangerous.

It seemed that only Chicky Malatesta had stood up to him, but

Chicky was dead. There was, however, a Littleford man who was feared and respected more than Frank, my Littleford High School friend Melvin Yurick. I'd known him well. I'd been a restless student in school, preferring to go for hikes in the nearby woods to staying in my room and doing the homework that came easy to me, a natural Eagle Scout and a geek. One of my satisfactions in school was that Yurick, a fellow geek, fellow Boy Scout, was as uninterested in sports as I was, and as dedicated to losing himself in the woods.

Frank mocked Yurick—though not to his face—for his high intelligence, his seriousness, and his solitary nature, all of which set him apart. Our teachers admired Yurick's studiousness; he was a role model for always having the right answer, and that caused him to be a greater target of ridicule to the other students. His intelligence was also a sign of strength, and his ability to succeed on his own made him singular. We bonded over our being geeks and loners. We often hiked together, usually in silence, except when Yurick identified a bird ("That's a phoebe—they love insects"), or a spot of nature ("This is a fiddlehead fern—you can eat them"). My love was for the physical sciences, Yurick was a math whiz and could solve algebraic equations in his head.

There we were, two Littleford misfits, tramping through the Fells, wishing we were older and far away from Littleford. I have mentioned the story that Frank appropriated, how Yurick cut his hand one day, sliced it with a hunting knife he was using to lop twigs off a branch, slashing the meat of his thumb. I bandaged it and helped him home. His father gave me twenty dollars as a graduation present.

After high school I didn't see him. Yurick went to college and so did I. But he stayed away from Littleford. For years I never heard his name. He was a friend from long ago, one of those pals you grow up with, who disappear.

But Yurick reemerged in another dimension. I began seeing his name in news stories, when I was looking in the financial pages, studying copper prices or bauxite futures, or—as when I'd returned from the Congo—I was researching cobalt prices. Yurick was often a headline in business news, the hedge fund, Yurick Venture Capital, Yurick Industries, the trading conglomerate Yurick Global, the news division, Yurick Digital Media.

Yurick had such clout, I imagined partnering with him to look at mineral prospects—his funding my travel and research, his investing in a mine I'd run. I wrote to him several times, with proposals—*Remember me, Melvin?* He always replied in a friendly but offhand way—brief, brisk, showing no interest. *We must get together sometime,* he wrote with studied vagueness, a tactic for deflecting me, being nice but noncommittal.

I once showed one of these letters to Frank, who pretended to be unimpressed, an obvious concealment that proved he was dazzled and envious. He later asked me—trying to be casual—if I could give him Yurick's address or phone number. But knowing how predatory Frank could be—and anyway I hated him—I told him in an equally casual way that I'd lost his contact details. *Maybe just write him in care of his company. I'm sure he'd remember you.*

That was my tease. For Frank, for everyone I knew, Melvin Yurick was unapproachable, far too remote and grand to respond. And he would have remembered the high school taunts, his solitude in Littleford. We'd been friends long ago, but he was too severe, too ambitious, to be sentimental about a small town that had been indifferent to him, yet he was generous in funding local projects, philanthropy from afar. He lived in the big world now, of Yurick Global and Yurick Digital, he owned many houses, including a mansion in New York City—and, oh, yes, he was now a multibillionaire.

Frank had sometimes asked about him. I always replied, "*Mel? I hear from him now and then. Great guy. He talks about investing in mining and maybe using my expertise.*"

A dishonest boast, but credible enough to impress Frank, who knew Yurick and I had been friends.

I now owed Frank more money, for house repairs, appliances, taxes, and his legal fees, than I would ever be able to pay back. I owed thousands to Miss Milgrim, having paid just a fraction of her huge fee for dealing with Frank's demands. *I'm underwater,* people say of their debt. It's an accurate image: I was sinking and suffocating.

I was still living in the small room at the top of the house, as far from Victor and Amala as I could get, avoiding them whenever possible, and mildly shocked when I saw Amala, who often had a new tattoo—neck blotch, wrist blotch, blotches on fingers and toes—and hairdos that ranged from tightly braided ("cornrows" she explained) and dreadlocks to—most recently—a mohawk. She had put on weight, she wore billowy Buddhist dresses and black lipstick. Rejected by Frank, and in an uneasy relationship with Victor, she refused to be unhappy, making a hobby of her body and knitting. But I found a great deal to admire in Amala's strategies to remain serene. She burned aromatic candles, she practiced yoga breathing, she chanted.

Except for passing messages from Frank to me, Victor was unemployed. I got a letter or a memo almost every day, usually tucked under my door and poked into my room. I had stopped reading them. There were so many of them, like bills headed OVERDUE, they had no meaning except punishment. I let the envelopes accumulate, I stacked them on a shelf at first, and when the pile became unsteady I crammed them into a drawer. I didn't want Frank's words in my head.

A new plan formed in my mind. After my pondering the stages of justifiable fratricide, I began to put it into action.

My first move was to remind Frank of Melvin Yurick, my old friend, now immensely wealthy and philanthropic and influential, someone a lawyer on the make would want to meet. In the archives of the *Littleford Standard* I found a photograph of Melvin and me in our Boy Scout uniforms, aged twelve or thirteen, standing together at a town event, hoisting a flag on the town green, Melvin tugging what he knew to be a halyard, while I saluted. I photocopied it and gave it to Victor to pass on to Frank, using it as an excuse to distract him from dunning me with invoices. I wrote on the back of the photo that Yurick had a regional office in Boston. I said I was in talks with him on various projects that would help me settle matters with Frank, moneywise.

Frank did not respond to this message or the photo. This meant he was dazzled, but stumped for a reply. Frank's silences were more meaningful and eloquent than when he actually spoke. It was felt by Frank's clients and adversaries that he was adept at concealing his motives or strategies. But I knew better: it was never concealment. Experience had shown me that most of the time he had no idea what his true motive was.

I wonder what Frank's thinking, someone would say. *I wish I knew.*

What they had not considered was that Frank himself did not know what he was thinking. Liars, cheats, trimmers, and crooks are habitual improvisors.

Maybe he was waiting for a sign. Being unscrupulous, he had no settled beliefs, except a compulsion for self-advancement. He had no conscience, he was not guided by any ethical code. He was purely an opportunist, waiting for a chance to pounce, but he could never tell you what it was he really wanted, because he wanted everything. Someone who wants everything has no direction, and is easily distracted, and never satisfied.

A visit for lunch by Melvin Yurick would be my distraction. But another element was needed.

I called Paco Zorrilla.

"*Hermano!*" he cried out. "Nice to hear your voice." Before I could ask him a question he said, "I'll call you back on a better line," and did so a few minutes later, because (I assumed) he was not sure his phone was secure. On this new call, he said, "What can I do for you, *amigo?*"

I said, "I have money worries, but I'll be fine."

"We send you money! How much you need?"

"Too much—don't send me money," I said. "Send me some product."

"What product?"

"Mexican valium. Rohypnol."

"Roofies," he said. "How many?"

"It's not business. I only need a handful."

"That's easy. Give me an address—I'll have someone drop them off. But listen, *amigo*. If you have a problem, I want you to stay in touch. We can help you."

"I'll need your help," I said. "Give me a good number and I'll keep you posted. I'll need to hide at some point."

"We help you disappear. We make magic."

I gave him my address and hung up and had my first doubts. *We help you disappear* had done it. Until hearing that I'd been certain of what I wanted to do—kill Frank. But now I had another option: I could turn my back on him and the whole business, simply vanish, leaving my debts and entanglements behind.

For a day or two, awaiting the delivery of the roofies, I debated calling Paco Zorrilla again and asking him to arrange my disappearance. But just as I was to call, and vanish, Victor pushed another letter from Frank under my door.

In this, he claimed that he'd gotten more copies of my tax returns— implying that Vita had found them—and he said that as I had not reported my true worldwide income for the past ten years, he was passing the returns to the IRS, along with the bank statements he'd discovered in his asset search, noting the discrepancies, "and all that that implies. Draw your own conclusion."

If what he said was true, and he ratted me out, he would get a reward, and I would face a heavy fine and jail time. Having been confined for months in Tower House, I had an inkling of the torments of the sort of captivity that might be enforced by a plague or pandemic.

Was I in arrears? as he said. I had no way of knowing. I'd had to list all my foreign bank accounts when I split up with Vita. Frank had used these accounts in his asset search. Maybe he'd held back some of his findings to have something to punish me with later.

The fact that, after more than thirty years of mining successfully in the U.S. and around the world, I was deep in debt, living in Littleford and without a clear path forward, testified to my careless bookkeeping.

I'd always reasoned that if I kept working and turning a profit I'd be fine. But my divorce, my lack of work, and my dispute with Frank over ownership of the house had knocked me sideways. I owed money I didn't have and, worse than that, it was possible that Frank might make good on his threats, in which case I'd end up in jail, disgraced, ruined.

Something else bothered me, an apparently slight thing, but full of significance. It was Amala. Often Victor was invited to have dinner with Frank and Frolic, and out of loyalty, or because he was browbeaten by Frank—reminded that he was living free in the house—he went to these dinners alone, leaving Amala behind.

One of those evenings, scheming to kill Frank, I passed by the kitchen and saw Amala sitting at the dining table. I said hello and lingered in the doorway.

She looked up. "Hi, Cal."

She was smiling; I saw a peacefulness in her eyes. And she'd changed her appearance. In the past she varied her hairdos, cornrows, dreadlocks, shaved the side of her head, braided what was on top and mounded the braids and gave them a tail that flopped down her back, as though she was wearing the corpse of a hairy animal on her head.

Now her whole head was shaved. On the nape of her exposed neck she had a new tattoo, a possibly spiritual image, but to me the sort of ink that makes a person unemployable except as a garage mechanic. She had a small dull-colored nose ring, pierced through her septum. She was heavier than when I'd last seen her and dressed in a simple smock. I'd interrupted her drinking a cup of green tea and poring over the dense text of a book.

Most of her adornment was new. I'd regarded her as a shy simple soul, but she'd transformed herself, become a conspicuous presence, big and bald.

"New look," I said.

"I'm studying to become an *ani*."

"Right," I said. "Where's Vic?"

"His dad's house. They've got stuff to discuss."

Idle, unemployed, feckless people become ingenious in making excuses. No one is more creative in procrastinating than a truly lazy person.

326 *The Bad Angel Brothers*

"An ani is a bird," I said.

"It's a nun."

"Right," I said. A *nun*? "Anything I can do for you?"

"I'm good," she said. "I'm almost finished with this sutra. We could hang out."

"I've got some unfinished business."

Shaved as though for a delousing, her baldness—her piercings and tattoos—should have made Amala seem sadder, lost and left behind, another of Frank's prisoners. Yet she was serene, her whole head glowing, sitting in a relaxed and peaceful posture, her legs drawn up under her, while I mounted the stairs to my room in a heightened, indignant state of homicidal rage.

PART FOUR
THE LAST LUNCH

36

SCARRED FOR LIFE

LWAYS OBLIQUE, CAUTIOUS IN THEIR DEALINGS, HYPER-
alert to the intrusions of authority and their hated rivals,
and circling them like watchful wolves—their own instinctive caution
easily spooked—the Zorrillas did not deliver the roofies to my house.
As far as I could tell, they did not approach the house. I knew they'd
keep their word, but I didn't know how they'd get the drug to me. That
made me hyperalert, too, my nerves quickened by suspense, in my impatience to murder Frank.

Then one afternoon (rainy, bleak, the mud season in Littleford), I
was walking to Littleford Square for a cup of coffee at Verna's. I had
just turned into Main Street out of Gully Lane, when a man in a black
hoodie drew abreast of me. I let out an involuntary squawk of fright
as he pressed an envelope into my hand and said in a gnawing nasal
accent, "From your friends."

I was ashamed of my unmanly outburst, but before I could recover
he was down the road. He must have been watching the house from a
distance. Now, walking fast, he was dissolved by the cold flinty rain.
But I had the roofies, and in that same envelope some money, a brick of
Benjamins I hadn't asked for.

Good news, I e-mailed Frank. *My old friend Mel Yurick is coming to
town. He wants to meet you. I see an opportunity.*

The other weakness of snobs—how predictable, how punctual, how
easily flattered and fooled.

It's a private visit. He doesn't want to be seen in public. He's coming to the house for lunch. But Victor and Amala need to be somewhere else.

A person does exactly what you want them to and you think, *This is pathetic.* You despise them for agreeing so readily to walk into your trap; their willingness to be dead meat is the proof they deserve to die. I named a day. I told Victor and Amala they had to be out of the house that afternoon.

Victor said, "It's okay, Cal. My dad already told me. We'll catch a movie."

Months had passed with no progress, but this was a solution. Frank knew that my old friend Melvin Yurick was worth billions, a man who had fulfilled Frank's boyhood ambition—*I want to be so rich I can shit money.* Though Yurick was a Littleford man, he was never seen in the flesh. His philanthropy was evident all over the town, yet there was a sort of contempt in his giving money, while never showing up. This frustrated people like Frank, who thought—as schemers do with the very wealthy—*What can he do for me?*

On the appointed day of the lunch, I made sure Victor and Amala had left for their movie; then I set out drinks and a teapot and waited for Frank.

I had not seen him since Mother's funeral, months ago. In the intervening time he'd become a monster in my mind, beady-eyed, the whopper jaw, the piratical snarl, a calculating pest, bombarding me with messages and bills and invoices, demands I could not possibly meet, threats that paralyzed me. The burden he'd imposed on me made him seem hideous and huge, stinking with aggression.

And so when he appeared on the porch—he didn't knock, he swung the door open and swept in (after all, he claimed this as his house)—I was startled to see a smiling man in a well-cut pin-striped suit, red suspenders, stylish horn-rimmed glasses, yellow tie, and a face that was far less grotesque than the one in my memory. He was polished again, with a black briefcase, confident, almost handsome—his fine clothes over-coming the crookedness of his palsied face. He made me feel ferretlike and shabby and conspiratorial.

He put down his briefcase and approached me, as though to offer a hug, then paused, and stepped back, and beheld me, sighing.

"Fidge—aren't you going to put on a tie?"

"It's a casual visit. Just a simple lunch."

"Melvin Yurick," he said in a blaming way, but smiled, straighten-ing the knot in his tie, as though concluding that his looking smart, in contrast to my scruffiness, would be to his advantage in impressing Yurick.

He sat in Mother's wing chair and opened his briefcase and brought out a folder, opening it to a stack of newspaper clippings, mentions of Yurick in the *Littleford Standard*, his success in the Science Fair, his American Legion medal, his Eagle Scout ceremony, as well as features related to his local philanthropy, and items about his parents' big birth-days and anniversaries. Frank fingered them, shuffling them proudly, showing me how he'd laminated them in plastic.

"Mementos, for the man who has everything, except these over-looked rarities." He said this as he rose in his seat, as though expecting to see a limo arriving.

"It's still early," I said. "You want tea? How about an aperitif?"

"Soft drink," Frank said, and glancing at the side table, "Ma's teapot. Wedgwood. That thing's worth something."

Rising again slightly, elevating himself to peer out the window again, a slant of light fell on his face, and I saw that what I'd taken to be a shadow or a food smear on his upper lip was a pencil mustache. That, and his red suspenders and his low zippered boots, made him look dan-dified. I told myself that his trying so hard to impress Yurick revealed his insecurity—or was I justifying my grubby clothes in thinking this?

Frank was dressed as though for a job interview. But, thrown by his stylishness, I found myself—against my will—revising my opinion of him. I needed him nasty, looking like a villain. His silkiness, his way of seeming unpindownable, I decided was sinister, his elegant clothes making him look manipulative. But rather than hate him for it I pitied

him. His effort in dressing up to meet Mel Yurick made him pathetic
and obvious and needy.

It pleased me that his mustache was a mistake, his lopsided face
twisted its pencil line like a cocked eyebrow and exaggerated the crookedness of his mouth.

"Soft drink, right," I said and went to the ornate bar cart Mother
called "the drinks trolley." I had ground the roofies to powder and
mounded it covertly in a tiny dish. With my back turned I spooned
some of this white dust into Frank's drink and stirred it.

"Cheers," I said, lifting my glass.

"Cheers." He raised his glass but did not drink.

Wagging his glass, Frank began to walk around the room, reminisc-
ing, tapping a photograph framed on the wall, a certain lamp, a souvenir dish.

"They were a handsome couple," he said of the photograph, Mother
and Dad at a Littleford fete in summertime, Mother in a white dress,
Dad in a panama hat. "Dad was always a little too dressy, but that was
to impress his clients." He fingered the fringes of the lampshade and
poked the lamp. "This is actually a Japanese bell, mounted with an
electric socket. There's no clapper inside. You're meant to strike it with
a kind of ritual hammer."

I did not remind him that I'd found the lamp in an antique shop and
given it to Mother for Christmas, with this explanation.

Frank raised his glass to his lips, but distracted by the souvenir dish
on the mantelpiece, he did not drink.

"Niagara Falls—their honeymoon." He tapped the rim of his glass
against it. "They took a boat ride on *The Maid of the Mist*. Jesus, is
Yurick always this late?"

"He hasn't been here since we were in high school," I said. "But don't
worry, he'll show."

Frank went to the window, using the back of his hand and his glass
to nudge the curtains aside, looking for a limo.

"We were very close in high school," I said. "He hasn't forgotten that
I was his friend. I never mocked him, like the others."

Frank was one of the others, but he made no reply. He set his glass down on a side table.

"On second thought, I think I'll have a whiskey."

"Right," I said, back at the bar cart. "It's a good idea to fortify yourself. But those clippings you brought will please him." I stirred a spoonful of roofie powder into his whiskey and poured a glass of whiskey for myself. "Let's do shots, Frank."

I clinked his glass with mine. Now he was forced to match me, swallow for swallow. He tilted his head back and opened his mouth and took a swig, some drops running out of the corner of his slanted mouth and glistening on his thin mustache, his lips quivering as he pursed them to swallow more.

"One more?"

"I'm good." He lapped at his mustache. "Mel Yurick—great guy, but a klutz. I wonder if he remembers the time we were out hiking in the Fells. It was a cold day, so when we got to the Sheepfold we decided to start a fire. Yurick pulls out a hunting knife and begins hacking a branch and slices his hand." Frank stopped and took a long noisy breath. "He's bleeding like a stuck pig, so I untied my neckerchief and wrapped it . . ." Frank sighed, he glanced at his watch. He said, "Blood," still looking at his watch. He grunted, "Rescued him."

He sagged a little, seeming to deflate, pondering his watch, his head twitching, as though struggling to read the dial. He chewed a little, a gummy utterance, then sat heavily in the wing chair, dropping his shot glass onto the carpet.

For fifteen or twenty minutes, fascinated, I stared at him, saying nothing, awaiting the full effects of the roofie, smiling at how he'd again appropriated my story. Then he swayed, and before I could stop him he pitched forward into the bar cart, snatching it clumsily, tipping it, his full face hitting the bottles and glasses, falling on his twisted arms that became tangled and crushed in broken glass. He lay motionless, blinking, squirts of blood starting from points on his face.

"Feel funny," he mumbled with a mouth full of saliva. I was unprepared for this and became frantic. I pulled him away from the mess.

Seeing how bloody he was, I ran to the kitchen and returned with a roll of paper towels and wiped the blood from his face and hands, picking shards of glass from his cuts—none of them deep, but there were many of them. The deepest one was next to his nose, an inch-long slice that revealed raw meat. I saw that this cut on his face was still seeping blood, and a bruise on his forehead was swollen and darkening where he'd knocked it against the cart. While I plucked the bits of glass from his hands, I lifted his right arm. His hand swung like a rag—he'd broken his wrist in the fall.

I found bandages in the bathroom cabinet but there was no point applying them until his bleeding stopped; so I put a cushion under his head and sat with him and blotted the blood. The mingled smells of whiskey and wine and vodka from the smashed bottles stank like a witches' brew on the soaked carpet, stinging my eyes, and now I had Frank's blood on my hands and my shirtsleeves.

Fearing that he might have wounds I couldn't see, I got a pair of scissors from Amala's knitting basket and sliced his sleeves, cutting away the whole suit coat from his body. Except for his broken wrist, now puffy, none of the wounds were very serious—there was no possibility of his bleeding to death. Within fifteen minutes or so, I'd stanched the blood and was able to apply gauze pads and bandages. I pressed a dressing to the deep cut next to his nose and held it in place with surgical tape that I crisscrossed over his face, securing the pad to his nose.

Unexpected, inconvenient, not part of my plan, but I'd attended to him on impulse—he had fallen because I'd given him roofies, he was lacerated by broken glass, he was bleeding. His wounds were messy and needed attention. He'd been helpless, he seemed to be unconscious. And so I'd acted. I went to the bathroom and washed the blood from my hands—and there was blood on my chin, too, where I'd touched it with my sticky fingers.

I looked at my face in the mirror, a smeared image of incompetence, and yelled, "You fuckup!"

When I returned to Frank, who was stretched out on the carpet among the broken bottles and glasses and the overturned drinks trolley,

I knelt down next to him. His eyes were shut, but he was smiling, as though possessed by a cheerful dream.

I had resolved to kill him. My plan had been to steer him while he was semiconscious through the side door, to the driveway, where my car was parked, to tip him into the back seat, where he'd lie like a big grotesque doll, too misshapen to be human. The streetlamps flashing through the car as I passed them would illuminate this heavy, inconvenient bundle, something to be disposed of.

In my weeklong wait for the roofies, I'd rehearsed this, and made the necessary phone calls to prepare the way, how I'd drive north in the night as though through a dark tunnel, to the Maine coast I'd known long ago as a rock hunter, a place that became Frank's inspiration for a holiday, the place where he'd met Frolic.

Frank was mine, I'd rejoice in his being comatose in the car. He had kept me captive—a greater punishment for a free spirit and a traveler than any I could think of. I had once thrived by going away, liberated myself through travel; but since my divorce and Mother's passing Frank had found a way to subject me to the stupefaction and slow death of captivity. As his prisoner I was dying and my loss of vitality seemed to delight him and give him energy. But he was my prisoner now. I longed for him to wake up, so that I could remind him of that.

Pushed flat on the seat, a blanket thrown over him, no one at a tollbooth would see him. Through New Hampshire to the Maine state line, and onward to the coast road, tunneling through the late winter murk of Route One, to Thomaston, and a side road to the waiting skiff at Wheeler Bay, a world of granite lapped by cold water.

Unconscious—gaping mouth, green tongue, his shirt and tie stained by slobber—Frank would be unable to resist being dragged into the skiff, where he'd lie corpselike, twisted in the stern, as I shoved the boat into the moonlit rockweed that floated on the surface of the chuckling shore—a chilly night, but with little wind to stir up a chop.

Visible to the south, Eagle Island was small and humpbacked, thick with spruce trees, a cabin tucked at the corner of a granite ledge, above a pocket beach—my destination. I'd row across a moony sheet of water to a ramp of sand and gravel, between the bulge of two smooth-hewn boulders, like a pair of staring eyes, the sign that the island had once been a quarry.

Frank would begin to revive in the cold smack of sea air, would feel for the gunwale to steady himself as I stepped out of the skiff and pulled it above the tidemark.

"Where are we?"

"Eagle Island."

"Fidge, what are we doing here?"

No memory of Littleford and the failed meeting with Mel Yurick, cold and frightened, hugging the blanket against his shoulders, as he lifted his legs out of the skiff, and staggered as he tried to stand.

"You're my prisoner, Frank. You're going to do what I tell you to do."

"I'm freezing. I can't see."

"Never mind. You won't be here long."

"What do you mean?"

"I mean I'm going to kill you."

He'd clutch his face and whimper, then turn and begin to run, but after five steps he'd trip against a fallen log and be on his knees when I stood over him, aiming my pistol into his eyes, dramatizing the threat by shining my flashlight on the muzzle, my finger on the trigger.

"Get up"—slashing my beam of light across the cabin—"We're going there."

"Don't hurt me, please."

Stumbling ahead of me, grunting in fear, he'd press himself against the door, until I unlatched it, thrusting himself inside when it swung open. As I lit a lantern and raised it to fill the cabin with light, he'd flee to a corner, whining, "What's this all about, Fidge?"

"It's about the money you say I owe you. Your name on the title deed of the house that is really all mine. Your threats to report me to the IRS."

"I didn't mean it—please, I'll take my name off the deed. I'll do whatever you want."

"Yes, of course you will."

"Then can I go?"

"No. Like I said, I'm going to kill you."

Howling, throwing himself at me, but too weak and dazed from the roofies, he'd fall, upsetting a chair, and lie on the rough planks of the floor, pillowing his head on his arm.

To frighten him further I'd lift the lantern to my face, to create a play of wicked shadows, like kids do at summer camp. "It doesn't matter whether you sign. When you're dead, the house will be all mine."

"I'll do anything, Fidge. You can't kill me."

"Yes, I can, but I want you to suffer first. You kept me captive out of pure spite. Now you're my prisoner."

He'd roll over and become doglike, scrambling on all fours past me and finally getting to his feet, staggering out of the cabin into the distortion of milky moonlight on the clumps of yew bushes, collapsing against them, moaning for help.

After a contemptuous glance from the doorway, I'd go inside and start a fire in the potbellied stove, soon warming my hands; then the door would open and Frank would appear, holding his arms high in surrender.

"Anything, Fidge. Name it."

"Admit that you tried to cheat me. That you broke your word."

"Yes, yes. I'll make it up to you"—edging toward the warmth of the crackling stove, his arms still raised, his sleeves muddy from where he'd fallen, flecks of pine needles coating his face, his knees smudged, his bald scalp scratched, his side hair wild.

"There's nothing you can do. You can't make it right. You've done too much damage. You corrupted my son. You turned my wife against me. You bankrupted me."

Feeling for his wallet, snatching at his pockets—"Money, Fidge. I'll give you money."

"Admit it—you're a phony and a scammer."

"I tried my best . . ."

"A phony and a scammer."

"I'm a phony"—an eager voice, almost a screech—"I'm a scammer."

"Say, 'I deserve to die.'"

His face crumpled, clawing at his eyes with his fingers, he'd begin to cry, as I raised my pistol.

That was my plan, the way I imagined it. I'd bury him at the back of the island and bide my time until one morning, before dawn, I'd row ashore and flee, with the money from the Zorrillas. Frank's body, covered with granite slabs, would never be found. The perfect crime.

But I was still in Tower House on Gully Lane, Frank twisted on the floor that was littered with broken glass, a white pad stained with leaked blood taped to his face, one hand bandaged like a mitten, the other slack and dark and claw-fingered from his broken wrist. I'd scissored his whole coat and half his shirt away, and so he lay half naked in a mass of rags. Emitting bubbly snores, his tongue thick in his half-open mouth, he'd been asleep over an hour. His smile had softened, he was wounded, but he didn't look defeated.

Appalled by the mess, I made an attempt to clean it up, but there was so much of it—stains and spikes of glass and the splintered cart—I smacked my broom at it all in frustration. Agitated by the disorder, hating the delay, watching him sleep, I kicked Frank's arm—not hard, just a prod—then dropped to my knees again and peered at his slumbering face. It was less palsied for being relaxed in sleep. I saw smugness on his lips—saw the bandages I'd carefully taped, the lacerations I'd blotted, having picked out fragments of piercing glass, all my efforts at easing his pain, my impulse at ministering to him—irrational, given that I intended to murder him. His clattering ill-timed fall had delayed my proposed trip north, the planning I'd done, frustrating me in my scheme to kill him.

Maddened by these botched plans, and hunched over him like a monkey, I couldn't control myself. I grabbed his pale head and held it to scream at, which I did, howling into his face. Then, intending to nip it maliciously, to leave a mark, I clamped his cheek in my jaws. I could not let go, I bit hard into his flesh, breaking the skin, my teeth almost meeting in his muscle, tearing at him so fiercely I was whinnying with the effort, horrifying myself with his blood, a taste that gagged me, and only then did I let go of his bleeding head.

On my feet, but unsteady, ashamed, I wiped my lips, but the salty sourness of Frank's blood remained on my tongue. The raw wound I'd made, this mouth-shaped declivity on his cheek—crimped, hickey-blue teeth marks—the bite of my fury on his face, was the Mark of the Beast.

My cannibal rage had exhausted me. Sitting across from him, watching him sleep, listening to the flutter-blast of his breath, I now saw him as helpless and sad and soft, and for the first time in ages—perhaps the first time ever—this soulless calculating crook with the hideous wound on his lopsided face seemed human and breakable.

Oh, just shoot, I thought, and pointed my pistol at him, when the front door scraped open—Amala.

She clapped her hands to her face, her eyes bugged out above her black fingernails, the silver rings, the stipple of tattoos on her knuckles giving it drama.

"Cal, what the fuck happened?" she murmured slowly through her hands.

I thought a moment, then said, "Frank fell down."

She backed away. "What are you doing with that gun?"

Instead of answering, I said, "Aren't you supposed to be at a movie?"

"Vic told me to go home. He said he hates me meditating. He called me a Buddhist freak. He can't stand me anymore." She began to cry, and she stroked her baldness with sorrowing fingers as she sat on the floor, holding her head. "And now this, oh god. Cal, are you flipping out?"

Again I pondered. "No."

"You've got blood on your lip."

I dabbed at it—Frank's blood. "I'm okay."

"Are you trying to, like, kill him?"

I felt prodded by her to reflect on why I was holding the gun. I can't shoot him while he's sleeping, and if I do kill him here in the house, he doesn't go away. What do I do with him? He's heavier than ever, more obnoxious, a bad smell like this spilled booze and sour crusted blood.

"Don't you think he deserves it? After the way he treated you?"

"Hurting him wouldn't make me feel better," Amala said. "I'd feel a whole lot worse."

I remembered Chicky saying that saying that if he killed him, it would make him "feel great—for about five minutes."

"I had a plan," I said. "Justifiable fratricide. Make him dead."

Thinking hard, she swagged her mouth sideways, her face emphatic and memorable and masklike from her Tibetan tattoos and her nose ring, her ghoulish mascara smeared with tears. But she was not shocked, she was holding her breath, considering what I said.

"Frank." She looked pityingly at him. "As far as I'm concerned, the way he treated people, all that bad karma, he's pretty much dead already."

This tearful bald tattooed girl stating the simple truth. Yes, in every important respect he was dead, had been dead for years. My hatred for him he'd taken for fear, giving him an illusion of power, and that hatred had weakened me. But now he lay snoring like a whipped dog, a bubble of snot swelling in one nostril.

My pistol was in my hand, aimed at his inert body. I knew I could shoot him when he woke, when he faced the horror of his death—a bullet in his heart. Then what?

The music in my head stopped and gave way to a hum like a rock drill opening a seam. Stumped by the delay, I sensed the blur of drama draining from my plan, Amala, an inconvenient witness—staring at me—making me hesitate. I saw that by murdering Frank, he'd belong to me, he'd follow me, I'd have to explain him, his death would always be part of my life, a bigger burden to me than if I left him alive.

"Who put all those bandages on him?"

"I did."

"You missed the one on his cheek."

That wound shocked me. The bite mark on his face had become a puffy and livid mouth, scored with teeth punctures. The strange thing was that this puckered snarl seemed to address the lopsidedness of his features, giving them balance, a kind of alignment his face had never known before. It was now a cadaverous version of a face much like mine. But the bite mark would be visible to anyone who looked at him, a barbaric scar he'd forever have to explain.

Amala said, "When do you think he'll wake up?"

"I don't know. I gave him roofies."

"Roaches," she said, knowingly. "Mind erasers."

"Maybe a few hours."

"More like a ton of hours." She seemed more composed now that she realized I was listening to her.

"He makes me sick." I waved my pistol over his body and pointed it at him.

Suddenly, Amala lost it, her affronted face tightened, looking bruised with righteous anger, and she flung herself onto me and clawed at me, whimpering. Though much shorter than me, she clung to my shirt and pushed me away from where Frank lay, rage reddening her wet face, saying, "I won't let you. I'll call the cops." She gasped and took a breath. "That's killing a sentient being!"

I held her, hugging her, so that I could pin her flailing arms to her sides. "He was horrible to you."

"He's a horrible person. I'm not."

"What do you want me to do?"

"Cal." Amala gagged on my name, breathless from her shouting, then said in a small, sane whisper, "You could just walk away, genius."

Years ago, deep in the emerald mine in Colombia, I'd heard an ominous creaking from a gallery—a small audible lurch of cracking stone, but cautioning, also like a warning whisper, an angel's wingbeat, that made me back away into a refuge chamber—and just as I did, there came a great crash, the whole stone ceiling of the gallery collapsing before me. Dusting myself off, I had walked into the sunlight at the mouth of the tunnel, reprieved, exhilarated.

I put my pistol down, my arm becoming light, almost buoyant, and felt a surge of health and hope.

"I want to be gone before Vic gets back," Amala said, lifting the top of her smock and pressing it at the look of relief on her face.

I gave Amala my car at the airport and flew that night to Phoenix and Paco Zorrilla, who welcomed me like a true brother. I was free—a wise fugitive, a happy wanderer.